LEFT HANGING

Caught Dead In Wyoming
Book 2

Patricia McLinn

From the deadly tip of the rodeo queen's tiara to toxic "agricultural byproducts" ground into the arena dust, TV reporter Elizabeth "E.M." Danniher receives a murderous introduction to the world of rodeo.

Caught Dead In Wyoming Series

Sign Off

Left Hanging

Shoot First

Last Ditch

Dear Readers: If you encounter typos or errors in this book, please send them to me at: Patricia@PatriciaMcLinn.com. Even with many layers of editing, mistakes can slip through, alas. But, together, we can eradicate the nasty nuisances.
Thank you! – Patricia McLinn

Cover Design: ArtbyKarri.com
Cover Art: Debra Dixon
Photo Credits:
Landscape (manipulated) © Kevin Eaves | Dreamstime.com
Hat (manipulated) © Olivier Le Queinec | Dreamstime.com

DAY ONE
THURSDAY

Chapter One

DEATH IN THE Bull Ring.

KWMT-TV anchor Thurston Fine's intoned words swelled across the newsroom, emanating from TVs hung from the ceiling like clusters of Chinese lanterns, so every staffer could see a screen. His televised expression remained solemn, despite the indignity of wearing a haphazard beard of pink and yellow Post-it notes.

More on the tragic demise of long-time rodeo contractor Keith Landry after we come back.

Actually, Fine didn't wear the beard. His televised image did. As a number of his colleagues—professional to the core—watched the five o'clock news and lobbed wads of sticky notes at the image. Only the best throws stuck.

"Oh, good one, Elizabeth!" a co-worker congratulated me. "Right in the eye. A buzzer-beater, too."

The giddy mood of cynicism that overtakes a newsroom when a big story combines with management ineptitude had infected the half-dozen staffers on hand. It's harmless, if tasteless.

Adrenaline churned up by a big story has to go somewhere. It certainly wasn't going into our coverage. We were the outsiders, the ones well beyond Thurston Fine's circle of trust. As a newcomer and the possessor of a one-time vaunted career, I was the farthest outside that circle, and that suited me—if you'll excuse the expression—fine.

"Thank you, thank you." I took a bow for my final shot before Thurston's face gave way to an ad for the Sherman, Wyoming Fourth of July Rodeo scheduled to start the end of next week. As if everybody in KWMT's viewing area didn't already know every detail. Especially after today's unnatural death of one the rodeo's main figures.

"So, tell us, Elizabeth Margaret Danniher," said sports anchor Michael Paycik into the fist he presented as a mock microphone, "did you feel the pressure to get that shot off before time ran out?"

I leaned over and spoke to his fist from an inch away, glancing up to make eye contact with a non-existent camera. "I take 'em one at a time, Mike."

"How does the thrill of hitting Thurston Fine in the eye with the sticky-note version of a spitball," he intoned in a plummy voice unlike his natural on-air delivery, "measure against years of spitting in the eyes of scumdom's major-leaguers?"

"I'll tell you, Mike—and I wouldn't lie to you—Thurston Fine ranks right up there."

"That sure as hell is true," Mike Paycik grumbled, dropping his assumed voice.

He nursed a grudge, because our anchor had decreed that coverage—done by guess-who—of stock contractor Keith Landry's death would be allotted *all* of the five o'clock evening news as well as the entire 10 p.m. newscast. Except weather. He'd left the weatherman a few seconds to report that the sky had not fallen. That's right. No national news, no international news, no features, no sports, and certainly no consumer news, which meant my scheduled contribution was staying in the can.

"Editorial comment creeping into your reporting, Paycik," I said.

"Your comments haven't been exactly unbiased, either. Especially not when Fine passed down his edict. God, who'd ever think I'd miss Haeburn."

Les Haeburn, who passed for a news director at KWMT, had gone on vacation earlier this week and left Fine in charge. It wasn't clear if Haeburn hadn't said when he was returning, or if no one had been interested enough to ask.

"That's where I benefit from having an older and wiser head, experiencing many years in this business while you were still in leading strings—"

"In what? Is that a synonym for playing pro football?"

I waved off that irrelevance. "—while you were playing pro football and otherwise frittering away your time. I don't miss Haeburn even in this extremity."

Commercials ended and, too soon for my taste, the face of Thurston Fine reappeared.

Keith Landry and his partner built their business up from their roots in Enid, Oklahoma, and had been stock contractor for the Sherman Fourth of July Rodeo in previous years. Glorious, successful years for our community's greatest event.

The screen cut to a choppy montage of Cottonwood County notables riding in convertibles in parades.

"What do you know?" came from the back of the room. "Fine got in a shot of himself doing the parade wave."

The montage continued with western-clad young men in various rodeo events, rodeo clowns playing tag with lumbering bulls, and a string of girls with big smiles, big cowboy hats, and increasingly outdated hairstyles. Going backward in time was a disorienting finish to the over-long, under-relevant package.

But last year, under new and inexperienced committee chair Linda Caswell— Back live, Fine's voice and face registered grave disapproval.

Mike growled, "Wrong again, Fine."

—the rodeo signed with a new company. In an effort to save money.

"It had to save money after losing sponsorships because the former committee chair and Fine's great buddy was disgraced," Mike inserted.

"Details, details," I murmured.

But when that new, cheap rodeo producer turned out to be a chimera—

"A what?" chorused his newsroom audience. He'd pronounced it like *shimmering*, confusing those in his audience who knew its Greek mythology origins, along with everyone else.

—Keith Landry returned to Sherman in its hour of need and rescued this rodeo that he continued to love, even after it had thrown him over for another

contractor.

"And was paid a big fat bonus for his trouble, which Fine would know if he'd listened to my reports," Mike said.

Photos on the screen showed a middle-aged man, his belt dropped low by the bulge above it. His hair was going gray under the inevitable cowboy hat. In all but one photo, he'd posed wearing sunglasses, smiling broadly and with at least one arm slung across the shoulders of a companion. The exception was a candid that caught puffiness under his small eyes and his mouth in an arch of displeasure.

Then, tragically, the white knight of the Sherman Rodeo—a groan filled the newsroom—*lost his life before he could enjoy the fruits of his rescue efforts by seeing next weekend's spectacular rodeo.*

"Yeah, boy, I bet he'd've been happy to be stomped to death by bulls if only it had happened after the rodeo. Don't even know why the bulls were there anyway." Mike added in a mutter low enough that only I heard, "We should be on this story."

Yes, the long, successful, storied association between Keith Landry and the Sherman Fourth of July Rodeo came to a tragic end today in the Sherman rodeo grounds' bull ring. Fine shifted to a ghoulishly chipper tone to add, *More on that when we come back, including exclusive video from KWMT.*

"Twice! Twice the jerk called it a bull ring, like Keith Landry was a matador. God, I told him in the pre-rodeo meeting that it wasn't a bull ring. I told him three times." Paycik's dour mood was beginning to worry me.

"That isn't even where Landry was found. He was in a bull pen, not the arena," said a cameraman named Jenks. Since he and Fine had been first on the scene—literally—he should know.

They'd arrived at the rodeo grounds for an early morning interview, then discovered Keith Landry would not be granting any more interviews. Unless he answered questions from St. Peter.

"I bet you never saw a case like this in your big-city reporting, did you, Elizabeth."

"You'd win that bet, Jenks."

After a career-long, steady climb on the TV news ladder, I'd had the ladder and my job yanked out from under me. Call it a final, surprise clause in my divorce decree from my network exec ex. To complete my contract, I'd been ordered to work in a market struggling to attain the status of small.

When I arrived in Sherman this past spring, my coworkers were wary. The attitude of some had undergone KWMT's version of global warming since Mike Paycik, a camerawoman named Diana Stendahl, and I put together a special about a murder case a few weeks ago. News Director Les Haeburn and Fine, however, remained rock solid on their polar caps. The other holdouts were primarily Fine's pets. Until today, that had included Jenks.

"We should be out there reporting this," Mike grumbled. "It should be my story, anyway." He was the only full-time sports reporter, in addition to being sports anchor.

"You'll have to take that up with our fearless leader," I said.

He grumbled a suggestion, the fulfillment of which would have required far more flexibility on Fine's part than he'd shown any evidence of possessing.

Diana Stendahl, the KWMT shooter I most often worked with, peered around the doorway that separated the battered and cramped newsroom from a hallway. I waved her in. She said, "This is something, huh? I can't ever remember a death where a bull was the weapon."

"Is it still a weapon when it's an accident?" debated Audrey Adams over my shoulder. She was one of KWMT's utility infielders—officially an assignment editor, but frequently used as a producer/director. At the lower pay level, of course.

"Sure," I declared airily. "If someone's accidentally shot, the gun's still a weapon."

"Is it weapon or *weapons* when it's a bunch of bulls that did the killing?"

Such debates can go on for days in a newsroom not otherwise kept busy. I've seen editors come to blows over a comma versus a semicolon—and that was for on-air copy when no listener could tell the difference.

Everyone had something to add.

"Weapon if you can pin it on one bull."

"Weapons. It's the cumulative effect."

"Weapon, since the herd of bulls did the killing, and you view herd as a collective noun."

"It's the *Murder on the Orient Express* of rodeo. You know they each went through and stabbed him, not knowing who really did the deed."

"Shh! Fine's back on. Don't want to miss this."

Before we show the next piece of video, I want to warn our audience that it is not for the squeamish. Parents should consider before exposing children to this sight. Mr. Landry's remains—

"Not much remaining," muttered Jenks.

He'd told Fine not to use this. Not only had Fine insisted—at suppertime, no less—but he'd screamed at Jenks, demanded a new shooter, and sent Jenks back to KWMT, where the convert to the not-so-Fine camp entertained us with footage of the tantrum. It was captured because one of Fine's rules is to never stop rolling until he says so. He'd been too busy having a fit to say so.

That was not the only footage Jenks shared. He'd also shown us what had happened when he and Fine encountered the body.

It started with Fine's fussy instructions over exactly what B-roll to shoot. From the arena, Jenks and Fine had moved around the end chute used by bull riders to mount bovine tornadoes and started down an aisle beside a holding pen, with close-ups of bulls' massive bodies, intimidating horns, and occasionally malevolent expressions.

"What's that?" Jenks' sharp question was caught by audio, as he'd zoomed in on a lump that trailed partially out of the pen.

Fine's peevish voice demanded Jenks stay focused on what he wanted—*texture*, he kept saying. His foot came into the frame. Then everything happened fast.

Jenks snapped, "Stop. Don't step on it. I think . . . I think it's somebody." The camera bobbled.

"That's ridic—"

The sound of Fine screaming. I would describe the high-pitched sound as being like a little girl, except I know a number of little girls who would never scream like that.

The camera kept running as Jenks used one hand to fumble out his cell phone for 911.

The camera caught two early-arriving rodeo workers coming at a run, attracted by the noise. Oh, yes, and a shot of Thurston vomiting—adding, I'm sure, to the forensic team's pleasure.

—are visible. As well as blood and agricultural byproducts. And—

"Agricultural byproducts?"

"Maybe he wasn't trampled. Maybe he was smothered in agricultural byproducts."

"If bullshit killed, we'd all have died the day Haeburn arrived."

Jenks had kept a copy of his footage, handing the original to the sheriff's department. "Thought about what Diana did with the Redus murder case," he said now. "If I'd known Fine would air it, I'd have skipped making a copy."

An unnatural quiet settled over the newsroom as the humans inside the wise-mouthed journalists looked on the televised version of violent death. A swath of green resolved itself into the remnants of a shirt. The shot panned up, toward a recognizable shoulder, jerked sharply to the side before reaching an ear, veering away.

"Holy shit," breathed someone behind me.

"Was that his . . . face?"

"Yeah. Fine wanted me to pan all the way, but . . ." Jenks swallowed. "There wasn't much there."

The camera's focus shifted back to a distorted torso in green.

"Jesus."

"Grim," came a murmur.

The cut to commercial left a momentary silence in the newsroom.

"We shouldn't have aired that."

"Once it was shot, we had to air it."

"That's crap. Journalism requires judgment, and leaving out things is part of judgment."

The newscast ended with a surfeit of platitudes from Fine about tragedy and an exhortation that the rodeo must go on.

The now-subdued newsroom quickly emptied, until it was only Mike, Diana, and me.

I spoke the thought that had been tugging at me for a while: "Why are we sitting around?"

"Because Haeburn's an idiot." Mike was definitely bitter. "We thought it would be better after the Redus case, but first chance he gets, Haeburn goes and puts Fine in charge."

"My question is: Why are we paying attention to them?"

His sour expression lifted slowly, then his grin came in a flash. "*All* right. Let's go."

"The Newsmobile's out front, equipment's loaded," Diana said.

"You are a gem."

"I know."

Now that it was almost July, and I was a veteran of my first month of Wyoming's summer, I snagged a jacket from the back of my chair. Bright sun made it plenty warm now, but just wait.

"How do we approach this?" Mike asked eagerly.

I eyed him. "Gee, Jimmy, what do you think we should do?"

"Jimmy? What . . . oh, Jimmy Olsen, huh? Nice, Danniher. Just because I want to learn from one of the best in the business—"

"First time you call me Lois Lane or Clark Kent, this friendship is over." He slanted me a look I didn't meet. "We do what Fine won't—report the hell out of the story. Accidents happen, but they still have who, what, when, where, how, and why. We find people who knew Landry, and we ask. What was his last day like? Why on earth would he have been in that bull pen?"

"Where do we start?"

"With inconsistencies." I spun back to him. "What was that you said before? Something about the bulls, and not knowing why they were where they were. We start there. And let's grab Jenks."

Chapter Two

"I'VE BEEN working since early morning," Jenks objected.

"A couple more hours," I bargained. "You were there at the beginning. Besides, with you along, we have two teams. We can cover lots more territory." Diana had gone ahead, checking equipment in the station's aging four-wheel-drive she drove.

"One hour, and ask your questions while we drive out," Jenks countered.

I batted innocent eyelashes at him. "Questions? Whatever do you mean?"

"C'mon, Scarlett." Mike grabbed my arm. "I'll drive Jenks' vehicle, while you use the thumbscrews on him. Diana can come separately. We'll get a ride back with her later."

Before Jenks could object, we put that program into action, conveying the first part of it to Diana by gestures as we headed for Jenks' KWMT four-wheel-drive.

I slewed around in the seat to face him. "Tell us what wasn't on camera."

"Not much. I started shooting right off and didn't quit."

"Were there other people around?"

When most people try to remember something, they stare up and to the side or close both eyes. Jenks did something I've seen other shooters do—he dropped his head, squinted with one eye, while opening the other wide, as if seeing everything in his memory through a camera lens.

"Couple of cowboys were heading toward where they park their trucks. Walking away, so I didn't see faces. I noticed them because they were an odd couple—one younger and spiffed up, the other older, dustier, a bit of a limp. The committee chair and a man were going into the rodeo office. Think it was Oren Street, Landry's partner.

"There was something else when I started shooting Thurston. Something . . ." He shook his head. "Can't say for sure. It was way over to my left, and a bit behind. Got a feeling it was a woman."

"Behind you? That was in Thurston's line of sight . . ."

That hope fizzled before it was full-born. Jenks spoke its epitaph, "Thurston doesn't see anything but the camera."

"Why was he meeting Landry this morning?"

"Fine's planning a special on the rodeo's history, and he'd promised Landry he'd use the interview as the news peg."

"I haven't heard about a special," Mike said. "Haeburn never said—"

"Doesn't know. Nobody else, either. Thurston's been pulling archival tape. That's why he had the historical stuff ready to go. He's tried to line up an editor without telling them what it's for. Plans to be his own producer."

A three-way exchange of glances brought us to a silent accord on Fine's delusions concerning his abilities.

"Why didn't anyone find Landry before you and Thurston?"

"A couple guys sleep on the grounds overnight, but they're way back where the stock's usually kept," Jenks said. "Nobody's around the arena."

That reminded me: "Paycik, what's your point about the bulls being where they were?"

"They put the stock they'll use in pens near the arena before each night's events, so they can get individual animals positioned quickly during competition. Afterward, they put the herd back in bigger enclosures away from the arena. Those are valuable animals, and most contractors don't want to risk them getting banged up in close quarters." We considered how *banged up* Keith Landry had gotten in close quarters. "At least that's how they run the nightly rodeo. I'll check if Landry's operation did something different."

"Why would Landry's bulls be there at all? Shouldn't it have been the nightly rodeo's stock in those pens?" I asked. If those regular rodeos, held every night from May to September, were community theater, then the Fourth of July event was Broadway. "His bulls won't be used until next weekend for the Fourth of July Rodeo."

"Good question. I was relying on Thurston's reporting that they were Landry's."

"At least some had Landry's brand," Jenks offered. "But like you said, it doesn't make sense why they were there."

"We'll track that down. You'll be with me, Jenks, and you—" Mike glanced at me "—and Diana work together, okay?"

I nodded back as he turned off the highway, slowing to a crawl to avoid spewing more dust. Outside the rodeo grounds' gates, a handful of people held signs. They shook the signs when they saw the station insignia, which made them harder to read, though I gathered they accused the rodeo of cruelty to animals.

I'd seen one or two lackluster protestors outside the rodeo earlier, including a girl noticeable for a swath of short-cut blue amid otherwise long dark hair. Now, their ranks had swollen. I wondered if it was news of a death or the larger platform of the Fourth of July Rodeo that had attracted them.

None of their signs mentioned the bulls' unfriendly behavior toward Keith Landry.

"One more thing," Jenks said, drawing my attention from the protestors. Then he gave us a gift. Not of useful information, but of a mental picture worth savoring.

"Something not on camera. That young deputy you folks know— the one brought in to headquarters because of his work on the Redus case—he made Fine take his shoe off and turn it over as evidence, because Fine had stepped in remains."

Jenks smiled slightly as he added, "Fine was hopping mad about wearing a sock and one of those evidence booties. Especially after he stepped in, uh, agricultural byproduct."

✦　✦　✦　✦

ON OUR RIGHT, we passed a pen encircled by yellow police tape, with a warren of similar pens beyond. The designated pen was separated from the arena by a structure that looked like a wooden goalpost cut off above its squared-off crossbar. It resembled the entry gate at a lot of ranches I'd seen.

The road through the rodeo grounds curved to the left, then back, swinging around a large fenced rectangle segmented into four smaller rectangles with a horse or two in each. Past this fenced area, the road curved sharply to the right, heading us toward the rodeo office.

Fine—who had procured another pair of shoes, I noted with disappointment—had set up at the rodeo office, a boxy structure embellished only by a covered porch on two sides. He'd have had better light and the banner for the Fourth of July Rodeo in the shot if he'd moved forty-five degrees.

He was too involved with the camera to notice a KWMT vehicle go past as he talked. The interviewee, not the interviewer is supposed to talk. That's a core rule. Yet, I doubted the stocky man I recognized from incessant ads for the upcoming Fourth of July event as the rodeo grounds owner would get much chance to talk. I'd done my best to ignore the ads, and now that I tried to recall his name, I dredged up only "Newt."

More figures stood in the office's shaded entry, but our passing angle as the road made a sharp left away from the arena didn't allow me to identify them. As we drove on, I saw a man on a bench around the corner from Fine. His back rested against the building with a cowboy hat pulled low. He wore a shirt the same bright green as Landry had worn in Jenks' video.

"Guy on the bench is Landry's partner," Jenks said. "Must be handy in his business being able to sleep any place, any time."

"Looks like Fine's grabbing anyone who smacks of officialdom," Mike said.

"Good. Leaves us the interesting people. While you guys find out about the bulls, Diana and I'll see what we get by working the human interest angle."

Mike parked next to Diana, already removing her equipment. As a result of wheeling and dealing after the report she, Mike, and I put together on the Redus murder, she now had a camera from this century, though not this decade.

"How'd you get here before us?" Paycik demanded as we piled out. "We left the station before you."

"Shortcuts."

"What shortcuts? I've lived here most my life."

"You haven't ferried kids to school, sports, and other events while working full-time and running a ranch. You find faster ways or die trying."

Mike had no answer for that.

We divided, with the guys driving to the distant pens to, as Mike said, score information on "the instruments of death."

Diana and I struck out on foot for a flock of pickup trucks, which formed the third point, along with the office and arena, of a lopsided triangle. The sun was strong and hot, but now and then a breeze passing through predicted the cool of evening.

Right off, we caught two young, local competitors arriving for the evening's regular events. They had little to say, having never met the deceased and with no plans to compete in the Fourth of July event. "Entry's too rich for my blood," one said.

I popped off one last question after Diana turned off the camera, and they relaxed enough to stop looking as if their mamas had starched their skin. "If you heard something went wrong at the rodeo, who would you look at first?"

"Them crazy animal people," the one in the black cowboy hat said.

The other one in the black cowboy hat nodded.

Next, we cornered a rodeo worker. He had a bit more to say, but little of it was understandable, since his mouth held a shortage of teeth and an abundance of chewing tobacco. I cut it short with thanks and a big smile. Mistake. He returned the smile.

Diana contained her chuckle until we were out of earshot, which didn't take long, because another pickup was arriving, and the noise blocked anything except a near-shout. "Don't like chaw?"

I shuddered. "The spitting's bad enough, but I swear the smell is worse. At least we don't have to drink it."

"Drink it?"

"An Amazon tribe serves a fermented drink that starts when the women chew on a root and spit into containers. God knows what happens after that. But if you don't drink, it's considered very rude, and it's not a good idea to be very rude to those people."

"Have you ever—?"

"Did I mention it's not a good idea to be rude to those people?"

"Gross."

"Yep," as the natives in Wyoming say.

But my heart wasn't in grossing out Diana, because I'd spotted three more possible interview subjects—all in black cowboy hats. That made it six for six so far. What? No good guys at the rodeo?

One of the three appeared to be about the age of the two local cowboys, but had an air of confidence they'd lacked.

Another appeared closer to my age, but without the benefit of skin care or sunscreen. Likely without the benefit of a clothes washer, either. Possibly without the benefit of soap, I feared.

The third was the leader. It was even clearer in the others' body language than it was in his, which meant he was what those Amazon tribesmen called an Honored Leader, to distinguish him from an elected official or some thug who grabbed power by might. No, they're not always synonymous. This guy was not only an Honored Leader, he was quite attractive.

"Good evening, we're with KWMT. We'd like to talk to you about your reaction to the death this morning of Keith Landry."

The youngest turned and headed the opposite direction, glancing over his shoulder. Interesting.

I'd addressed the leader, but he never made eye contact, and now he melted away as if I couldn't possibly have meant him.

Only the scruffy one stood his ground. I was right about the lack of clothes washer or soap. Ah, the glamorous life of a reporter.

"Would you care to share your reaction?" I asked.

"Sure thing." He shifted a wad I hoped was gum deeper into his cheek, squared to the camera, and spoke as if reading a statement written by someone else. Possibly phonetically in a language he didn't understand.

"Keith Landry was a fine man and a credit to the rodeo community. For many years he has been known far and wide for helping those less fortunate than himself. He will be sorely missed. And this here's a tragic affair."

He turned to me. "Want another take? I know you TV folks like them sound bites to be right. I could do it again."

"Absolutely no need, Mr. . . I'm sorry, what is your name?" I pulled out my pad to draw attention from the still-running camera.

"Evan Watt."

"Thank you. Had you known Keith Landry long?"

"Just on twenty years," he said with self-importance. "Met him right here in Sherman, first year he was contractor."

"Had you talked to him lately?"

"Sure thing. Talked to him last night."

"Did you? What time was that?"

"'Bout ten. I was on the road, headed here—wanted to know if he needed anything right off when I got in, but he said he thought he had things covered, and to report first thing this morning. But by the time I got here, he was gone." He shook his head.

"So, you're an employee of Keith Landry Productions?"

His eyes shifted to the side. "Not to say a regular employee."

I waited, letting the gravity of silence pull words out of him that might get us closer to whatever it was his eye-shift indicated he didn't want to share.

"See, that was the thing about Keith. He'd give cowboys on the circuit a leg up. Give 'em a chance to work to put together a stake to get back in and have a chance to win. You know?"

I nodded, as if I did know.

"I'm not too proud to say I'm one as got helped. Why, even NRF champions have been known to take a helping hand from Keith Landry." This time his eyes shifted toward the direction Mr. Tall-and-Good-looking had gone. "It's not like I'm stove up—"

"Crippled," came Diana's murmur. Nice to have your cameraperson double as an interpreter.

"—and can't rodeo no more. I was going good to start the season. But seems like the weather gets warmer, and my luck gets colder. Thought I'd get the winner's take for sure last weekend, but just missed. If that damned bronc had had a bit of go in 'im . . . But that's the draw, when a kid that's still got milk teeth gets a rank one and walks away with the money."

He spit as punctuation. I didn't look, and I held my breath, holding onto my gum fantasy.

"I came in last night to help with the run-up to next week's rodeo, so I'd have enough jingle in my pocket to pay my entry fee and take my ride. But that's why this don't make sense," he added earnestly. "Don't make no sense. Why would anybody do such a thing to him? He'd let a guy work in a pinch, and look at how he came through with this here rodeo. If it hadn't a been for Keith, there wouldn't've been a July Fourth rodeo this year in Sherman, that's for sure."

"Why do you think he was on the rodeo grounds last night?"

"Can't say." The eyes shifted faster and farther to the side, and stayed shifted. Now, why had that made him uncomfortable?

"Looking after his livestock, perhaps?" I suggested just to keep this going.

"Not him. Didn't have much to do with them critters."

"Will you still compete next weekend?"

He mumbled, "Don't know about that, with Keith gone."

"There'll still be work. I understand his partner has said the rodeo will go on," I said, although I hadn't heard any such thing.

"'Spose I can talk to Oren."

"Have you known Oren Street long?"

"Same as Keith. Funny how fast time goes. Oren's girl was born right about this time of year. But that was the second year they ran the rodeo." He shuffled his feet. "Better get goin' . . ."

"Of course. What time was it you arrived here?"

"This morning, right behind Zane."

I didn't understand that last reference. Maybe Diana or Mike would. I thanked him. As he walked off, I noticed a slight limp.

I made a mental note to ask Jenks to confirm if he was the scruffy cowboy he'd seen this morning.

"You catch that stuff about *why would anybody do this to him?*" Diana asked as we headed toward the arena.

"Oh, yeah." I noted Fine and his new favorite cameraman had left. "Interesting, wasn't it, when everybody's talking accident and—There's another one of them. Let's go."

Chapter Three

THE GOOD-LOOKING cowboy had melted only as far as the enclosures used to send off roping event competitors, giving him a view down the arena . . . and if he'd turned his head, a view of us talking with Evan Watt.

I had his profile, and a nice profile it was under the brim of his hat. He didn't turn, but I had the sense he was aware of our approach. With one hand behind my back, I indicated to Diana to circle around to his far side, while I slowed my pace. Before I was close enough to hail him comfortably, he turned away from me, took one step before seeing Diana, then halted. That gave me time to close in and hit him with questions.

"You stuck around close enough to hear what I asked Evan Watt," I said. "What do you think of what's happened?"

"Nothing to think. Don't know anything."

"Are you a competitor? Will you enter the Fourth of July Rodeo?"

Diana looked at me over her camera, which was meant to convey something, but I didn't try to figure out what because I was focused on him.

"'Xpect so, ma'am."

"Not just in the nightly rodeos?" I pressed that point to be sure he would have been acquainted with Landry. A noise came from behind the camera. I ignored it.

"No, ma'am," he said in that Western way that made me feel I was 143 years old, decrepit, and had never been very bright.

"What's your name?"

"Grayson Zane."

My eyebrows might have hiked of their own accord. Diana cleared her throat again, but I was focused on the subject. "Grayson Zane?"

"Yes, ma'am."

I resisted the temptation to ask the history of that name—Zane Grey, Grayson Zane. There had to be a story. Not because I didn't want to know, but because the faintest note of resignation sounded in his voice. He expected me to ask, so I didn't.

"You've heard about the death of Keith Landry, Grayson Zane?"

"Yes, ma'am."

"Did you know him?"

"Yes, ma'am."

Time to move him off yes and no answers. "What is your reaction to this . . . to his death?" I'd started to say *to this tragedy*, but imagined him parroting back, *It's a tragedy.*

"Real surprised like, ma'am." I caught a glint in his eyes under his hat brim. Not a dumb cowboy. Equally, not a cooperative one.

Diana cleared her throat. Following the tip of her head, I saw Mike and Jenks headed in our general direction from beyond the rodeo office.

I returned my attention to the *ma'amer*. "Why surprised? Isn't rodeo a dangerous sport?"

"For cowboys some. It's us taking the risks. Men like Landry take the sure thing. And if there's not a sure thing to be taken, they rig it so there is." The edge to that sliced right through his laconic drawl.

"You mean contractors?"

He had the drawl back in place as he said, "Yeah. Contractors. Can't say I ever heard of a stock contractor killed this way before."

"Trampled by his own bulls? No, I would imagine that isn't a frequent . . ."

I let my imaginings die a natural death because he wasn't paying attention. He was looking over my shoulder toward the rodeo office. A flicker of something showed for the first time in the strong lines of his face. It made him a lot more interesting. I turned to see what he was looking at.

Standing on the office's narrow wooden porch were a woman I didn't know and a man I did.

The woman was tall, rawboned. Those attributes added to her air of strength. Even at this distance I had the impression the strength was also one of character.

The same description applied to the man next to her, Thomas David Burrell. From encounters this spring I had reason to know that the impression of his strengths was accurate.

Turning back to ask Zane about his reaction, I was left with only his back, now at a distance of several yards, as he strode away. It was a pleasant view, but I didn't let it distract me.

I could chase after him. Chasing after people to ask questions is one of my finer professional skills. But in this instance, I didn't think exhibiting that professional skill would gain me much.

On top of his general lack of cooperation, that flicker of reaction had been too short, and not well enough defined, for me to have an inkling of what I might be messing with. No sense in making an enemy out of him if I might need him cooperative down the road. All I knew was that the sight of those two people had an effect on him: Awkwardness mixed in with some strong, unidentifiable emotion.

I knew exactly how that felt, since the last time I'd spent any time face to face with Tom Burrell, we'd not only been face to face, but mouth to mouth.

I turned and headed toward the arena, wondering if Zane's unidentifiable emotion had been unidentifiable only to an outside observer, or if we had in common that it was unidentifiable to the person experiencing it, too.

"Where're you going?" Diana asked.

"Let's see if we can find that third cowboy."

"Don't you want to check with Mike and Jenks?"

"Looks like they'll be occupied a while." They had intersected with Burrell and his companion. All appeared pleased by that.

Continuing in the other direction, I started looking for a familiar face among kids in black cowboy hats as we wandered through knots of arriving competitors. Diana easily kept pace, despite toting the camera. I needed to start lifting weights again.

I felt a pang for the fully-equipped workout room in the Manhattan apartment I'd shared with my then-husband. What did it say when you missed the treadmill, but not the marriage's rut?

Diana saved me from my own questions with one of hers. "Do you know who that was?"

She knew I knew Tom Burrell. She must mean the woman he was with. "Who?"

"The guy you were just interviewing."

"You heard him the same as I did. Grayson Zane. Why? Do you have reason to think he was lying?"

"I have reason to know he wasn't. Do you know who Grayson Zane is?"

I had a feeling *cowboy* wasn't the right answer. Nor *cowboy in a black hat*. "No."

"He is one of the top rodeo cowboys in the country. Way he's been going this season, possibly *the* top rodeo cowboy in the country. Although it's a long way to December and the NRFs."

The scruffy cowboy, Evan Watt, mentioned those letters, too.

"But Grayson Zane's been there before. He was all-around rookie champion. Then he had a couple real bad years. Got hurt, started to rise up the ranks, got hurt again. That second time it looked like he'd stay down."

I eyed her. "You play in the Fantasy Rodeo League or something?"

"Or something. I have two kids crazy for rodeo. Anyway, he came into town four, five years ago looking more beat up and low down than Evan Watt. But he must have had enough left for his entry, because he won an event here that Fourth of July. Started winning a few more. Had a steady climb ever since. Been to the NRFs the past three years and has taken home a bundle."

"What is—are the . . .?"

"National Rodeo Finals. Rodeo's World Series, Super Bowl—"

My phone ringing interrupted. "Where are you guys? Jenks is leaving."

"Mike wants to know where we are," I told Diana.

"Tell him west end of the arena, near the boxes for the timed events. But I'm not staying, either. I've got to pick up the kids."

"Uh-oh." Two vehicles and both leaving. "Did you hear that?" But Mike didn't appear to be listening to me.

He came back on. "It's okay. Tom'll drive me to the station to get my vehicle. I might miss the start of events. Meet where we sat last time." More talking in the background on his end. "Unless you want a ride to the station, too."

I could go with them to the station and skip tonight's rodeo. We'd get no footage anyway, with both photographers gone. So, all I could gather would be background. Plus, it wasn't like I'd never seen a rodeo. I had. Once.

On the other hand, accepting the ride would mean being confined in a truck with Burrell and Paycik. Most likely *between* Burrell and Paycik.

There's no such thing as too much background.

"I'll meet you in the same spot," I said.

So, there I was, alone behind the scenes of a rodeo, sidestepping black-hatted cowboys, the horses they guided, and stinky piles of agricultural byproducts.

I was about to head to the grandstand, when I spotted Cowboy Number Three.

He stood against a fence, running rope through one gloved hand, with his other hand gathering it into a neat coil. He'd nearly finished, then he unfurled it and began again. From the way he started when I spoke, it had not been my approach that prompted the do-over.

"Excuse me. I'm E.M. Danniher from KWMT. I have a few questions about your reaction to the death of Keith Landry."

At my first words he jumped like he'd been poked with a bull horn—the kind with a point, not the kind that makes noise.

His head snapped up, and the glare he sent me indicated his answer would be, "Hell, no, I'm not talking."

But he had no chance to say it.

"What are you doing? What *are* you doing?" demanded a female voice.

In another half a second, a female form interposed itself between me and Cowboy Number Three.

She was the same age as Cowboy Number Three, wearing a glittering western shirt of a chartreuse so bright it made my teeth ache, a stripe of glittering rhinestones down the outside of each leg of her tight black jeans, and a pink cowboy hat with—I wouldn't kid about this—a tiara attached around the front of the crown.

It required another look to take in the girl inside the outfit. She wore heavy makeup and her long hair teased and sprayed into the stiff bigness of another era. Beneath it all was the attractiveness of a young, healthy, fit female.

"I have a few questions for . . ." I left it for either to fill in the name of Cowboy Number Three. No such luck.

"Can you not see he's getting ready to *compete?*" Brain surgery, rescuing a toddler from a raging flood, or pilots taking off to save the planet from a plunging asteroid—none rivaled the importance she gave that word.

"He's not competing yet."

"You can*not* be serious! You do not interrupt a man's preparations."

"Heather," Cowboy Number Three said from behind her, one hand cupping her shoulder in a familiar way. "It's o—"

"No, it is not. It is not the least little bit okay."

He shrugged and went into the competitors' area, where I was not allowed.

At this point, though, I was at least as interested in her as in him. Talk about an over-the-top reaction.

"I'm E.M. Danniher with—"

"I don't care who you think you are, asking questions all over the place when it's none of your business. It is not acceptable to break a competitor's concentration. You might not be from around here . . ." Dramatic pause for a scathing look at my decidedly unsparkly attire, as well as unforgivable lack of cowboy hat, much less tiara. ". . . but it's only good manners no matter where you come from not to barge right in like that."

"And your name is?"

"Honey," came a new voice, practically dripping that substance. "You go get ready."

"But Mom—"

"Now." Ah, this honey could carry a sting. Quickly soothed. "Go on, now. You don't want to have to rush for your ride."

Ms. Tiara did what she was told.

With the hierarchy clear, Cowboy Number Three at the bottom, then Heather/Honey, then Mom, I turned to greet the top of the pyramid, prepared to spread honey of my own if it got me what I wanted.

No need.

"You're Elizabeth Danniher with the TV station, aren't you?" Her smile was gracious and warm, with a touch of wryness. She didn't look around for a camera, but I had the feeling she'd already determined there wasn't one.

"I am." I held out my hand. "And you are?"

"Vicky Upton, Heather's mom." She gave a good handshake in return. Firm, not rough. Well-tended hands. Well-tended everything. But perhaps the most well-cared for was the iron determination in the eyes and jaw. "I do apologize if Heather was overzealous. She's keyed up, what with getting ready and all. It's not the big event like it will be next week, but they are having her do the rodeo queen's ride tonight, and it's her first time. Plus, she always has been protective of Cas."

Her smile invited me to be indulgent with young love. I was more interested that Cowboy Number Three had at least one name.

"In fact, they're protective of each other," she added. "They've been sweethearts practically from the cradle, and he's a fine boy, from a fine family."

"Yes, I hear it's a fine family. The . . ." I dangled it for her to fill in a name.

She slid right by. "One of the county's first, and such a history with the rodeo. Cas' aunt, of course, owns Cottonwood Drive."

That was supposed to mean something to me. I wondered if the unknown aunt owned a road. "And what is Cas' last name?"

Her eyes widened, which might have been what allowed me to see the wheels turning behind them, as she considered evading, then quickly realized it wouldn't take me long to find out by other means. But why hesitate at all?

"Newton."

"Thank you." I wrote the name in my notebook—not to remember it, but to see her reaction.

Caution slid over the honey. "Why'd you want to talk to Cas?"

"We're reporting on Keith Landry being found dead here." Her mouth twisted, likely a response to the circumstances of that death. "I understand Cas was here this morning."

Okay, so I'd pushed the truth. I didn't understand that at all. I guessed it, wondered it, hypothesized it. But sometimes pushing works.

She pushed back. "Oh, no, surely not."

I gave a you've-got-your-story-I've-got-mine shrug. "I won't know until I talk to him." That line led directly to an impasse, so I shifted focus. "Your daughter is the rodeo queen?"

That explained the tiara, I supposed.

Her smile broadened into the genuine article. "Yes. We've worked so hard for this, and now she's Queen of the Sherman Fourth of July Rodeo. She's an even better roper than I was, or am. But the most important part of being rodeo queen is the scholarship. Biggest one for any rodeo queen in the state of Wyoming. It'll make a difference when she goes off to college next year." Pride gave her a glow, though it was too fierce to be entirely attractive. "And now she's rodeo queen."

Before I needed to produce a suitably impressed response, she looked up as if hearing the voice of God. But only if the voice of God came through the PA system of the Sherman, Wyoming Rodeo Grounds and He concerned Himself with the tie-down-roping competition beginning.

"Got to go cheer on Cas," she said with a big smile. "It was nice to meet you in person."

"Nice meeting you," I parroted.

I'd started away when "Oh, Ms. Danniher" brought me back around to face her. She gave a little grimace, as if in sympathy. Yet I thought I caught a whiff of malice. "You have to watch where you walk around here, what with all the horses coming and going."

I hadn't, and there was no question about the whiff I caught now.

Chapter Four

I'VE WORKED IN Boston, where the brave muster true belief every year, while the rest pray to be proven wrong by the Red Sox.

I've worked in Washington, where the Redskins beat is second only to the White House. That's when the Redskins are losing. When they're winning, the President has to wait his turn.

And I've worked in Chicago, where the biggest gusts come from bellows of delight or sighs of despair according to the fortunes of the Cubs, White Sox, Blackhawks, Bears, and Bulls.

But I have never encountered a community whose identity is wrapped as tightly around a sporting event as Sherman and its rodeo. The Fourth of July Rodeo is religion, patriotism, and sex, rolled into four days of cowboys and beasts.

You'd never get that, though, from looking at the Sherman Rodeo Grounds. The grandstand has concrete block foundations, and the arena has sturdy structures. Other than that, there's a general air of impermanence, like an open, dusty campground whose character changes depending on its current inhabitants.

The nightly rodeos are local workaday events. On weekends and other special occasions, the vehicles flowing into the Sherman Rodeo Grounds show more out-of-state plates, the competitors' outfits flash added bling, and the concession stand flourishes.

Actually, I base that observation on experiencing two rodeos: the preview for locals back in May and this Thursday night regular rodeo. Not much of a sample, but Mike grunted agreement with my assessment. A grunt achieved from the distance he'd established after initially sitting right beside me. We were the only two in the grandstand's upper reaches, with a gap of a good ten rows before the spectators below us.

I held myself in dignified isolation and watched the action in the arena. The structure of rodeo competition is uncomplicated.

A man gets on the back of an animal—bull or horse—which takes exception to a passenger. The man tries to hold on for at least eight seconds. If the trip lasts that long, style points figure in. But first you have to last that long.

That's bronc riding (saddle or bareback) and bull riding. These are called roughstock events.

In the other events, man and horse are allies. That's tie-down roping, team roping, and steer-wrestling. Plus barrel racing for "girls." Mostly one man and one horse work together, but in team roping there are a pair of man-horse combos all going against one cow, which hardly seems fair.

In these events, time comes first, style earns no points, though infractions can earn time penalties or even disqualification. Not surprisingly, these are called timed events.

Apparently, the nuances beyond that rudimentary understanding are infinite to the initiated.

I've toyed with working rodeo into a consumer affairs report.

One pitfall I'd been warned about in doing consumer stories is the dearth of good video, and yes, we still call it video. Even though most stations on the planet shed video decades ago.

It's hard to capture the drama of a senior citizen being scammed by a telemarketer last month. Rodeo, though, has built-in drama. Man vs. beast. Man and beast in union. Man vs. the clock. Man vs. himself. It also has color and emotion and action. Triumph and dejection. Great video. Now, if I found a barrel racer or roper with a consumer problem . . .

"Particularly that one," I said aloud, as I spotted Cowboy Number Three, now identified as Cas Newton. He was among the final riders waiting to compete in tie-down roping.

I reached across the distance Mike had put between us.

Getting his attention wasn't easy, since whatever attention wasn't focused on the arena was on the hot dog rapidly disappearing into his mouth. I saw a potential career for him in hot dog-eating contests if this TV thing didn't work out.

I tugged on the hot dog wrapper.

"Hey, it almost fell," he protested.

"Know anything about the one on the far right, beside the light pole?" I asked. "I'd say the one in the black hat, but they're all wearing black hats."

Mike gave me the eye, silently demanding to be told why I was interested before he forked over information.

"I won't shout it," I said.

"I'm eating, and you smell like horse—"

"It's my shoe, not me. Besides, I wiped it and wiped it and wiped it on the dirt. I hardly smell it at all now."

"That's because you're used to it."

"C'mon, weren't you raised around this stuff?"

"That's why I know not to step in it. Especially not in shoes like that with all that tread and grooves for it to get stuck in."

"You want to know why I want to know?"

"You want to know what I know?" he shot back.

"I can find out what you know by other means. You can't find out why I want to know from any other source."

"You couldn't find out what I know right now, though."

I raised my brows. No one out-stubborned a Danniher.

He heaved a sigh, put the final bite in his mouth, and scooted closer. After chewing, he said, "I know I've said I wanted to learn by sitting at the feet of someone who's built one of the great TV news careers, but I didn't think they'd smell like this."

"It's an appropriate smell for where my career has landed."

"Elizabeth—" Paycik started, all serious.

"You want to hear this or not?"

"Yeah."

So, I told him about young Cas' disappearing act, my next encounter with him, his Rodeo Queen watchdog, and her watchdog mother.

"Oh, yeah, you don't want to mess with Heather Upton if you

don't want her mama on you like prickly pear."

"Voice of experience with our Miss Rodeo Queen?"

"Give me a break. She's a baby. Besides . . ." On the final word his tone shifted from serious, and he waggled his eyebrows. ". . . I'm looking for a woman with experience and ambition."

"It's not ambition you're after. At least it shouldn't be what you're after, because it'll clash with yours. What you want in a mentor is plenty of experience. Besides—"

"Mentor isn't—"

"—if you're talking ambition, I'd say our Ms. Rodeo Queen and her mama have enough to go into the export business and never run out. Is there a Mr. Upton?"

Paycik had taken a drink from a cup that dwarfed even his hand, and swallowed before answering. "Died a long time ago. As long as I can remember, Vicky's been a widow. Never heard her connected with any man. Focus always on Heather."

"She talked about the girl getting a college scholarship."

"A few of them. Not a full ride. She's no scholar and not at a level to get a rodeo scholarship."

"Rodeo scholarship? You're kidding."

He looked at me with surprise that appeared to match mine. "You didn't know there are rodeo scholarships? There's college competition, and top schools offer scholarships, though fewer for women. But Heather's picking up smaller, local scholarships. No individual one's enough money, but put together several, and they'll help. And Sherman Rodeo Queen pays out all four years, as long as the queen stays in college."

I thought of another possible aspect of a mother's ambitions for her daughter, returning us to the original topic. "Any idea of Mama's feelings about the boyfriend, Cas?"

"Never heard anything negative. He seems to be a good kid. His father's not everybody's favorite, bit of a blowhard if you ask me. Tried to exert pressure when I was looking at colleges to get me to go to UM, University of Montana—"

"That one I might have figured out on my own, given enough

time."

"—his alma mater. His disappointment was not subtle."

"Used to getting his way?"

"Oh, yeah. Cas' grandfather came from nothing. Newt—"

Newt. As in eye of a toad. As in the name my memory had dredged up in connection with the rodeo grounds' owner.

"—is acknowledged for working hard to build on what his daddy created. When he married a Caswell, that put him up there on the top rail."

"That would do it, naturally."

"You have no idea who the Caswells are, do you?"

"Nope. Though I got the sense from Vicky Upton that they're a force to be reckoned with."

"One of the first families, one of the first white families." He considered that qualifier and added another. "One of the first respectable white families in the county. Their ranch passed from father to son and kept getting bigger. Until Walter Caswell had two daughters."

"Cas' father married one of the daughters?"

He nodded. "The older one. Inez. She died a few years back. And when their father died, too, the younger sister took over the family business. That's Linda—Linda Caswell, chair of the rodeo committee. I would have introduced you earlier, if you and Diana hadn't gone chasing after cowboys."

"Oh?" Most likely the woman with Burrell. But jumping to conclusions was a quick way to get a broken neck. "Why would I want an introduction?"

"Family's been part of the July Fourth rodeo from its start. As I said, she's rodeo committee chair. That's what she and Tom Burrell were talking about—what'll happen to the rodeo now."

"What *will* happen to the rodeo now?"

"Don't know yet. Still talking with Landry's partner, Oren Street. If they don't hold the rodeo, it'll still cost a lot of money with no chance of revenue. If they do, they could look heartless."

I made a sound acknowledging it wasn't an easy position.

"Linda will make a good decision. She's smart, and she looks out for the county. One of those people who never holds an elected position, but has a lot to say about who is elected."

Not my favorite type. I've known my share of kingmakers. The man I'd married had come to view himself as one. With me as his primary pawn.

For years, the changes in Wes had been slow, subtle, and ignorable. Until we were promoted to Washington.

When we arrived, we bought a suburban house within walking distance of a top elementary school, with the expectation that we'd soon send our kids there. When we left Washington for New York, we got an apartment in a high rise. Sure, it had an extra bedroom. Which immediately became Wes' office.

What happened between those real estate purchases was that Wes found his soul mates in a certain class of Washington insider. The ones you never saw on talk shows, rarely saw interviewed, but always saw at the most important private parties. The ones who consider themselves kingmakers.

Some women marry a husband hoping he'll change. I divorced mine wishing he hadn't.

"And to think I could have met this paragon," I said.

Mike cut me a look. "You'll like her."

I dialed back the sarcasm. "Guess I won't know until I meet her. Hey, do you know anything about a connection between her and Grayson Zane?"

"Not really. She's chair, and he's competing here for the first time in a while. Why?"

"I thought he had a reaction to seeing her."

He snorted. "Linda's a great person, but Grayson has every variety of Belt-Buckle Bunny chasing him."

"Belt whats?"

"Belt-Buckle Bunnies. Rodeo groupies. Especially chasing guys with the biggest belt buckles."

"Is *biggest belt buckles* a euphemism for something else?"

"No. Nice mind you have, Danniher. The bigger the rodeo, the bigger the belt buckle the champion gets for winning. Top cowboys have serious hardware around their waists."

Or considerably below their waists, considering where their belts hit. Whether Mike wanted to acknowledge it or not, with the chaps, tight jeans, and gaudy belt buckles, rodeo attire highlighted relevant portions of male anatomy. An image of what he would look like in that attire flickered behind my eyelids.

"Hey, look," he said, entirely too casually.

Glad of the distraction, I looked where he pointed off to the side of the grandstand.

From this angle, the design of the pens made more sense than they did at ground-level. They were like a series of tic-tac-toe boxes put together into a grid. Then someone erased the cross-marks on every third row to create corridors allowing access to the boxes. A series of gates let workers direct animals from the boxes into one end of an assigned chute. Each chute's other end opened into the arena, released in a clang of metal and a surge of adrenaline for all concerned.

Working amid one set of pens was a man in a bright green shirt. He was wiry and short, with bandy legs and arms, like a pipe-cleaner figure molded to sit atop a toy horse and never freed from that position. Only this pipe-cleaner figure had muscles. I saw the evidence as he slung a full bale of hay over the chest-high fence, then clambered over it to break up the bale. The bulls inside the enclosure appeared to appreciate the results, munching away.

"Uh-huh," I said neutrally.

"That's Oren Street. Keith Landry's partner in the stock contracting business."

"You and Jenks talked to him, right?"

"He clammed up on me," Mike said with self-disgust. "I must have come on too strong. But we should talk to him more, right? Isn't that one of the bases we need to cover on a story like this?"

I homed in on the rock sticking out of that stream of words. "We?"

"Well, you. I'm afraid he won't say much to me, not now. Like you've said, it takes a while to re-set with a subject you've rubbed the wrong way. Should have followed what you said about starting with questions people won't mind, before asking tough ones."

I'd said that? I had no memory of it. If he was going to quote me back, I hope I hadn't said anything else. Ever. "Fine. I'll go talk to him."

He heaved a sigh. "Wish you'd been there earlier. I need pointers on working a subject."

"Quit buttering me up. I already said I'd go."

"Speaking of butter . . . How about getting popcorn? You'll go right past the concession stand. For both of us," he added hurriedly, possibly in response to my dirty look.

"What *did* you get out of him?"

"The truck hauling the portable fence panels to make their pens was delayed, apparently because of coming here early for the Fourth of July Rodeo. They used the competition staging pens as a place to hold their livestock until the truck got here, which was not long after Landry was found."

"That's it?"

"That's it."

"What did you ask that made him clam up?"

"Do we have to go into—"

"Yes. I need to know what's broken in order to make repairs."

"I asked if it was true he'd been shouting at Landry yesterday about yanking around the schedule. And that Landry shouted back that he'd do what he wanted."

"Where'd you hear that?"

"One of the regular contractor's guys. He also said Landry smelled like a distillery."

"And Oren Street said?"

"That people should mind their own business instead of talking about fussing that happened all the time, and was between partners besides." Mike had caught an inflection and cadence that was not his own, giving a hint of the man he'd interviewed.

"Ask anything else?"

"I asked if it was true he got the business now and could run it as he wanted. Well, it's true," he said, defensively.

"Exactly how did he clam up on you?"

"Said he had too much to do to answer darned fool questions, what with reconfiguring the back pens."

"Why'd they have to do that? That's not near the scene."

"The back pens *were* the scene. What you're thinking of is the stock pens farther out. The back pens are the area where the bulls are kept until each is put into a chute to await its rider." He pointed to where Street was now.

"I thought you called them competition staging pens?"

"Same thing."

"You're saying the back pens aren't in back?"

"They're in back of the arena," he said. "They're just not the farthest back."

I snorted. "How'd they reconfigure them so fast?"

"They're portable. Made up of panels that connect together." He switched his attention to the arena. "Contractors travel with their own, set them up how they want. In this case, under orders from law enforcement, they've left the ones near where Landry's body was found, but shifted the rest for use tonight. One chute isn't being used, either. Can't get a bull there without going through the area Alvaro designated off-limits. Your boy's up next. Last to go. He's got a good time to beat."

I watched Cas Newton ride, rope, and tie his calf in the best time and with no penalties to win the event.

Then I started toward the dead man's partner.

"Don't forget the popcorn," Paycik called.

I made no promises.

Oren Street completed another hay fling as I reached him.

"Mr. Street? Mr. Oren Street?" I stuck out my hand.

In programmed response, he rubbed his hand against the side of his jeans, which probably didn't improve its cleanliness any considering their state, and stuck his out, too.

Only with my hand wrapped around his did I add, "I'm E.M. Danniher from KWMT-TV, here in Sherman." His hand gave a slight jerk as if he meant to withdraw it, but I held on. "I'm sorry about the death of your partner."

He mumbled thanks.

Still grasping his hand, I kept on. "I was hoping to ask you a few questions, strictly on background." I stretched the fingers of my free hand wide to show its emptiness. "It would help in getting a handle on what this tragedy means."

"What kind of questions?"

I took that as an invitation. "How long were you and Keith Landry partners?"

He eased, having expected a classic attack question. Say, *How much do you benefit from his death?* I released his hand.

"More than twenty years."

"Sounds like a successful partnership."

"It kept going along," he said neutrally.

"To keep it going along for twenty years, you must have worked closely with him, know what he—No?"

He'd started shaking his head at *worked closely.*

"He handled his side and I handled my side, and we didn't meet much in the middle."

"Except at the bank?" I gave a small smile.

"Except there," he acknowledged, not smiling.

"What was his side and what was yours? They never overlapped?"

"Hardly ever." At last he seemed to relax. "He got the contracts, set our schedule. I get the right livestock to the right place at the right time. Once in a while he'd get us overbooked and we'd be stretched thin as a wire. He'd stamp and holler, I'd go figure a way to do the impossible, and he'd deposit a check fatter than I'd even consider asking for.

"He wasn't an easy man, but his ways let me provide for my wife and baby girl better than I'd ever hoped when we started. When I got married after a stint of rodeoing, then we had our baby, I never thought—" He broke off with a jaw-cracking yawn, took a red bandanna from a back pocket, wiped it over his face, then gave his mouth a good rub, as if chastising that orifice for letting out the yawn. "Sorry, ma'am. I've been short on sleep, and getting shorter all the time."

Working for a stronger bond of empathy, I recalled Jenks' comment, and said, "At such an exhausting time, it's good you're able to sleep anywhere. I saw you on what must be the most uncomfortable bench this side of the rack. By the rodeo office."

"Yeah. Caught a few winks there before that TV man interviewed me."

I'm surprised he didn't catch a few more winks during the interview, considering the interviewer. I nodded, encouraging him to go on. He did.

"Get my sleep when I can. Tending livestock on the move like we do's a round-the-clock operation. Most people don't realize these animals need the right conditions to do their best, just like the cowboys or . . . or an Olympic athlete."

He put more spirit into those words than anything else he'd said. And he wasn't done. "First you got to find the right ones, whether it's buying 'em or breeding 'em. Next you pick through the ones you *think*'ll make it to find ones that really will. And after you sort all that out and have your stock for rodeoing, then you got to feed them right, keep them toned up, make sure their days and nights go as smooth as possible so they're rank in the arena. Travel will wear out your best stock if you're not real careful."

Perhaps my eyebrows rose a bit.

"They got their delicate ways," he insisted. "Folks mostly expect it of horses, but it's cattle, too. Between them being herd animals anyhow and being close together, why, when one gets out of sorts, the rest of 'em follow along like . . . like . . . "

"Sheep?"

I'd only been in Wyoming since April, but I already knew how many of the people I'd met would respond—even a century after the cattle-sheep wars—to the heresy of likening one species to the other, but Street said, "I was thinking like teenage girls."

"That works," I acknowledged. "With such delicate psyches, your animals—livestock—must be extremely upset after trampling Keith Landry."

His animation evaporated. "They don't know what they done. It's not like they got human feelings," he said with a dollop of disdain. Which didn't say much for his opinion of teenage girls.

"You said they were unsettled," I reminded him.

"Sure. Because their routine's been disrupted."

Poor babies. Though, their routine certainly had not been disrupted as completely as Landry's. Or, for that matter, Street's. Rather than raise that, I asked, "What will happen to the business?"

He shook his head in the manner of one at a loss to comment on the strangeness of the world.

He was still shaking it when I got tired of that variation on *no comment*, and added, "Do you get the whole business now?"

That didn't stop the head-shaking, but he also spoke. "Yeah. Never figured it would be this way. Never figured he'd go first. Suppose most people say that in this sort of situation," he said with unexpected acumen. "But in my case it surely is true. Keith was the businessman. All I know is livestock. Mind you, he wouldn't have stayed in rodeo without me buying and breeding and tending my livestock. But I couldn't do the business like he did. He loved the game of it and the winning, especially when he could *beat* the other side. Meeting people, making sales, writing contracts and all. He was a wonder at it, and that's the truth. We'll do fine this year. I suppose we'll get by the next. After that? It'll be like a snake that keeps moving after its head's been cut off because it don't know it's dead."

I saw no indication that he saw any significance in his likening Landry—and their business—to a snake as he concluded, somberly, "I surely don't know what I'll do without him."

Chapter Five

I RETURNED TO our isolated spot in the bleacher seats with two boxes of popcorn and reported the conversation to Mike while watching the end of team-roping, which Cas Newton and another kid won. Now steer wrestling was starting.

"That's all?" Mike asked when I'd finished.

"Wanted to keep the door open, keep him as a potential source of information. I have a question for you, too. What was Landry like?"

"Didn't really know him. He's been contractor here for years, but we didn't cross paths. He bid this year, too, but got underbid by a new contractor. The committee signed the new one end of last year."

"Last year? But Linda Caswell just took over as chair—"

"Yup, Fine got that wrong. Linda wasn't chair when they signed the new, low-bid contractor. It was Fine's ol' buddy Judge Ambrose Claustel in charge then. When Claustel—" He bent a look of significance on me. "—stepped down, Linda Caswell was named.

"Then this new contractor notified them he'd gone bankrupt and wouldn't fulfill the contract. That put Linda and the committee in a real bind. With only a few weeks until the rodeo, they either had to cancel after paying out a lot of money they'd never recoup, or they had to find somebody fast and hope to come out ahead. Landry was the somebody available."

"What about the bankrupt contractor? I remember you reported on the company—"

"More like reported on not being able to find it. One letter saying he was bankrupt and poof! He was gone. Linda gave me her file, but what little contact information it had led nowhere. Claustel must have had the full file, and it went when he did. I tried contractor and rodeo associations, called long-time contractors, and no leads on this Sweet Meadows. Haeburn ordered me to stop spending time, on air or off, on it. I tried digging into bankruptcies on my own, but good lord, do you know how many bankruptcies there are? I didn't even know the state." He huffed out a breath. "I don't know why I had such an itch to find out. It just felt . . ." He looked away. " . . . wrong."

"Gut instinct can be the best reporter tool around. Maybe set Jenny on the bankruptcy search. She's good with a computer."

Good with the insides and the outsides. The newsroom aide/sometimes production assistant had gotten my home computer set up fast, as well as running down information for me on the Internet.

"I will." He sounded significantly cheered.

By this time, steer wrestling had ended. Bull riding came last. It's often the most dramatic, certainly potentially most dangerous. Mike had told me to watch every one of the eight seconds—and well past. After the ride can be the most dangerous for the competitor, not to mention the rodeo clowns, whose job it was to distract the bull from his intention of goring or trampling the competitor. I think I'd skip a want ad with job duties of *Draw attention of angry bull, keep it while everyone else flees to safety.*

Mike leaned forward, focusing on the action in the arena. But I wasn't watching the bull riding.

I'd turned to reach for my jacket on the seat beside me. A flash of something caught my eye. Something visible in the open space beneath the empty bleacher seat behind me. Something blue.

Twisting around and down until I was almost lying crossways on the bleacher seat allowed me to see between the floor and seat of the row behind me. What I saw was the blue-haired girl from the animal rights protest.

Inside the rodeo grounds. The heart of enemy territory. What could she be up to?

She shifted, and I realized she was not alone. Then I realized what she was up to. What many young people get up to under bleachers.

She and her companion were upright and not quite doing the deed, but even in the murky light I was pretty sure there were hands inside clothes, and a definite rhythm going.

I leaned more and made out a black cowboy hat in the faint light.

Great. That narrowed it to every male in the place and a few of the females.

A cramp scratched at my side. I shifted . . . and realized that what little light reached the amorous pair sifted through the open sections between the bleacher seats and foot wells. Considering their position and mine, I figured my legs were shadowing them.

Adjusting my center of gravity, I lifted my legs, balancing on the seat, along with the support of both hands on the foot well behind my seat.

"Hey," Mike protested. I could tell from his voice he was still looking toward the arena. "Put your feet down. I don't want that shoe closer to my nose."

I ignored him. The light was definitely better. I saw the crown of the black cowboy hat clearly. But the darned thing kept the wearer's face shadowed.

"What are you doing?" Mike demanded, now speaking from over my shoulder.

Like the first domino tipping, that started a rapid sequence.

I reached back with one hand to wave sharply in the universal sign to "Shut up while I'm teetering on this bleacher seat!"

The scratch of the cramp in my side turned into a claw. And I was no longer teetering.

With only one hand to balance on and writhing with the cramp, my head dropped, my forehead whacked the foot well, accompanied by an involuntary sound of pain.

Ms. Blue Hair and her companion looked up. For a fraction of a second, the light shone on her companion's face, his tilted-back head removing the protective shadow of the brim.

My feet dropped back to my footwell. By the time I scrambled around to look again—a process made speedier because I no longer cared about noise, but hampered by the full-blown cramp, a sore forehead, and Mike demanding to know if I was having a fit—Ms. Blue Hair and friend were gone.

✧ ✧ ✧ ✧

MIKE DID NOT seem overly impressed with my tale of how Cas Newton and Ms. Blue Hair were consorting, as well as cavorting, with the enemy. He shrugged and mumbled something about teenage hormones as we applauded the bull riding winner and headed down the grandstand steps. He clearly hadn't had much experience with PMS to so lightly dismiss hormones.

I thought back to my encounter with Heather Upton and her mother. Not a pair to take interference with their ambitions lightly, in my estimation. And those ambitions appeared to include Cas.

"What does this have to do with Keith Landry's death?" Mike asked when I tried to explain all this.

"Fair question," I admitted as we joined other spectators weaving around parked vehicles in search of their own. "But if Blue Hair has a mishap, I say we look right at Heather and her mama."

He rolled his eyes, but had no time for more because his phone rang. One glance at Caller ID, and he answered quickly.

"Hi, Aunt Gee. Yes, I'm coming Sunday. I don't know. That hasn't been decided yet." His eyes cut toward me. "Uh-huh . . . uh-huh . . . Oh . . . uh-huh. Okay. Yes, ma'am. I will. Thank you."

He ended the call as we reached his four-wheel drive. The vehicle's outside blended unpretentiously with those around it. Inside, it offered the luxuries befitting his status as a former pro football player, without slipping into flashy. It was a lot like Paycik.

His Aunt Gee—Gisella—was the long-time dispatcher for and acknowledged queen of the county sheriff's department's unit in the town of O'Hara Hill. She'd provided invaluable help in the Foster Redus investigation. I'd worried she might be in danger of losing her job. But since the sheriff was being recalled by voters, going after Aunt Gee appeared unlikely.

While being more circumspect, she'd also provided a mild tidbit or two in the weeks since. So, I was strongly tempted to whack Mike upside the head and demand to know what his aunt had said. On the other hand, she might have been calling on a family matter that was none of my business.

"Mind a detour, instead of going right to the station?" he asked.

"To?"

"The sheriff's department. I have this sudden hunch Deputy Alvaro might have something interesting to tell us."

Chapter Six

"OH, GOD."

"Now, is that nice, Deputy Alvaro?"

"I should have known. If you're . . ." He looked around, saw other deputies in earshot. Instead of finishing, he sighed. "In here."

"Is this an interrogation room?" I asked as the door closed us in.

"No. Observation room. You think I want anybody to hear this? Listen, what happened this spring, that was only because of extraordinary circumstances. You can't think I'll tell you things all the time. And Mike, you've got to tell your aunt to watch her step."

Mike was unmoved. "You were promoted to working here in Sherman based on what happened this spring. Besides, if you want to keep things quiet, don't put hints over the radio. Aunt Gee says she's already had calls from two scanner regulars asking about tomorrow morning's news conference. If you think she was happy to hear about it that way, you are wrong."

"All it said was—oh, hell." He dropped his butt onto the table. "This has been one hell of a day. I don't suppose you two would go away and come back in the morning?"

Mike and I shook our heads.

"C'mon, Richard," I said. "We can't get anything on the air until tomorrow, but we need background now to start working."

"Fine probably won't let anybody else come to the news conference," Mike added gloomily.

"Fine?" Alvaro appeared heartened by that prospect.

"Les Haeburn is out of town, and Thurston Fine's running the show. As in the nutjob's running the insane asylum."

Alvaro blew out his breath. "Tell me about it. Acting sheriff's out of town, too. The number two guy's wife went into labor last night. I added his overnight to my dayshift from yesterday, then right into today's dayshift. And the wife *still* hasn't had the kid, so in this case, *I'm* the nutjob running the insane asylum. At least on Keith Landry's death."

"It wasn't an accidental death?"

Mike's head whipped around to me at that question. He needed to work on his poker face. Alvaro regarded me steadily for a moment before he went to the door and opened it.

Really? He meant to throw us out?

"Lloyd, come in here, will you?"

Or have his colleague throw us out? After we'd kept his role in the Redus case strictly confidential and—

"What's this about, Richard?" Mike asked.

"I want somebody else to know what I've told you. No, don't get huffy. I trust you. I guess I have to after . . . But I need to be sure the people here know what I've told you."

The deputy we'd seen earlier appeared in the doorway. Alvaro waved him in. "Deputy Sampson, this is Ms. Danniher and Mike Paycik from KWMT."

I received a hello. Mike got a big grin, an extended hand, and "Mike Paycik? I saw you play ball. You were really something. Course we all hoped you'd play pro at Denver after UW instead of going off to Chicago."

Mike returned the handshake and a few practiced words of humble appreciation cut short by Alvaro saying, "Sit." He gestured to chairs for Mike and me on the far side of the table. He and Deputy Sampson took the ones opposite us.

"To be clear, I'm giving you a preview of the morning's news conference, and you won't use this material until after the news conference. Agreed?"

He spoke with authority. He'd picked up a lot of confidence since we'd met the young deputy only weeks ago. I was impressed. That wouldn't have stopped me from refusing his restrictions if there'd been a way to get the news on before the morning conference. But since there wasn't . . . "Agreed."

"I caught the call this morning, proceeded to the rodeo grounds, where I found the deceased, Keith Landry. After a preliminary investigation, including initial collection of evidence and statements, I was not entirely satisfied with the scene. After consulting with local officials, and in consultation with sheriff's department colleagues, it was determined that the investigation will continue in consultation with other investigatory professionals."

It took a moment after absorbing all that consulting to realize he thought he'd finished. "What does that mean?" I asked.

He turned mulish. "Just what I said."

"Why weren't you satisfied?" Mike asked.

Alvaro shook his head.

"Why call in other people? What are you going to have them look at?" Mike pursued.

Alvaro shook his head again.

"It wasn't an accident, was it?" I asked.

He started to shake his head a third time, then caught himself. "I've given you my statement."

"You're not sure it's Keith Landry, yet you gave his name—"

"What?" My barb rattled him. "We're sure. We wouldn't have released the name if—"

"How do you know? Did next of kin identify him?"

"No. No next of kin to—"

"You assumed—"

"I did not. We had ID and his phone."

"Pieces of it, just like him," mumbled Deputy Sampson. He looked up, apparently startled by a belated realization that he'd spoken aloud.

"I've given you my statement," Alvaro said.

"Deputy Alvaro, may I speak to you alone?" I asked.

"I don't see what purpose—"

"It's a follow-up on the Redus case. If you'd prefer—"

"Okay. Lloyd, you can accompany Mr. Paycik out. Leave the front doors unlocked. Ms. Danniher will be there in a moment."

I kicked Mike under the table. He flinched, but said nothing. At the door, he looked back and rolled his eyes without either deputy seeing. Message received.

"Richard—may I call you Richard?"

"It depends," he said warily, not as authoritative as before.

"You are a smart, dedicated and honest law enforcement officer. I respect you for that. And we worked well together on the Redus case." His lips parted. No doubt to repeat what extraordinary circumstances that had been. "That's why I want to give you a little advice for dealing with the media."

"I don't need—"

"Oh, yes, you do. If you think that statement will fly at a news conference, you desperately need my advice. I don't know if even Thurston Fine would be satisfied with that example of doublespeak, and I guarantee Needham Bender of the *Independence* would make you feel as if a buzz saw had just had its way with you."

"It's early in the investigation, and—"

"And you want to keep everything to yourself. That's the instinct of every law enforcement type on this planet. It never works. Never. Even in the most repressive countries, there's always leakage. Where there's a free press and emphasis on individual freedoms—sound like anyplace you know?—it's just asking for aggravation. And suspicion. How many people will think you're trying to protect something other than the investigation? Your own mishandling of it, maybe? Or a big shot who's involved?"

He winced and didn't argue. Progress.

"With the recent history of top law enforcement officials in Cottonwood County, people will be suspicious. There's no getting around that. You have to be even more open and aboveboard than usual. Lay it all out on the table. At least as much as you possibly can. You need to think through what's absolutely essential to keep away from the public. But there'll also be aspects you would rather keep quiet that will get out despite your best efforts. You're far better off being open with the media about those aspects than trying to pretend the public doesn't already know."

"The public doesn't know—"

"Everything a civilian saw, heard, or told you will be out to the public by morning, if it's not already."

"We instructed them not to talk about their statements or the situation."

"Richard." I shook my head again. "I've only been in this county a few months, and you've lived here all your life, and I already know that half the county knew Keith Landry had been found dead in the bull pen before you reached the rodeo grounds. If you think anybody you've talked to today won't share the juicy details, you are not half as smart as I think you are."

He opened his mouth to stonewall me. I saw the realization and the weariness hit him, and he slumped. "Oh, crap."

"Exactly." I gave him half a minute before asking, "What bothered you about the scene?"

He heaved a sigh. "You know what shape the deceased was found in?"

"I heard." No point in reminding him I'd also seen, along with every TV viewer of Jenks' video on tonight's news.

"It was real hard to tell exactly what happened. The new deputy coroner didn't tell me anything I couldn't see with my own eyes, either. Seemed awfully nervous."

I could imagine. A young deputy and a new deputy coroner handling the death of a well-known figure. "Why wasn't the coroner there?"

A shutter came down. "Don't know."

Something started ticking at the back of my brain, but the immediate concern was to keep him talking, keep him occupied.

"The coroner wasn't there, and it was you and this new deputy coroner, acting nervous and not telling you anything. Your instincts were telling you something wasn't right. Where did that—" I almost said *feeling*. That would have been a mistake. Less experienced law enforcement types seldom acknowledge having feelings. "—instinct focus."

"The body didn't seem . . . right."

"How not right?"

"For one thing, there wasn't as much blood as I'd've expected. But that's off the record," he said hurriedly.

I raised innocent hands. Also empty hands, reminding him I had no video. And unless it's on video, it didn't happen as far as TV news goes.

"I don't know that it wasn't an accident, Elizabeth. I just didn't want to take a chance of fu—screwing it up when I was in charge."

It was rather sweet the way he reddened after catching himself and softening his language. He'd probably blanch if he heard half of what was said in a newsroom every day.

"A very sensible reaction. What did you do?"

"That's not something the public knows. There's no reason to tell you."

"Will it hurt your investigation if I know?"

He considered. "I wouldn't want it reported."

"Here's how we'll work it. If you tell me something off the record, I won't report it unless I get it from another source." I preferred two other sources, one to say it, one to confirm it, but the population of Cottonwood County was small enough to keep the potential pool of sources a tad shallow. I left myself wiggle room.

"So what I'm about to tell you is off the record?"

"Off the record."

"I called my sister Sandra."

Not what I was expecting, but I stumbled along. "Is she in law enforcement?"

"No. She works for a doctor in Montana."

I started to get impatient, then took another look—the guy was sleep-deprived and stressed. If I sighed too hard it might knock him over. "Why did you call Sandra, Richard?"

"To see when we could get Keith Landry in to see the doctor."

Maybe he was past sleep-deprived. "Get him in for what?"

"An autopsy. A forensic autopsy, I mean. The hospital can do the other kind, but I didn't want any chance of this being—The guy she works for is closest. But if he was backed up, I'd've gone to somebody else."

"You aren't satisfied the bulls were enough to cause death?"

"I don't know. I just don't know."

He sounded weary. I decided to wrap this up. "Landry's body has gone to a forensic pathologist in Montana."

"Will go. About ten. After more preliminary work. The deputy coroner will go with, and Deputy Sampson." A thin smile twisted his mouth. "His first autopsy. I warned Sandra."

"And the forensic pathologist's name is . . ." He told me. "When do you expect to have the report?"

"Couple months before all the toxicology is back."

That didn't mean I would wait a couple months to try to find out early results. It wasn't a huge haul, but it was nice to have the information. Especially since it was a bonus.

My main reason for this conversation had been to give Mike time to pump Deputy Lloyd Sampson. I hoped I'd done that.

✧   ✧   ✧   ✧

I HAD.

As I discovered when I found Mike waiting for me in the parking area for the sheriff's department office.

The office, along with the jail, the Sherman Police Department, and other municipal offices occupied a modern addition behind the 1899 courthouse that showed its dignified front to a square on the main road through town.

"You didn't have to kick me," Mike said, starting his vehicle. "I'd already caught on to what you were up to. Next time, give me a look. I don't have shins of steel."

"Wimp. What did Deputy Sampson have to say?"

Alas, he qualified as only half a source: Willing, but not able to give much detail.

"They're piecing together Landry's last day or so," Mike said. "He got into town Tuesday. They checked the motel he was staying at, didn't find anything interesting in his room or belongings, except enough empty liquor bottles to have supplied a bar for a week. They've sealed it in case they want to go back over it."

Good job, Richard.

"Yesterday morning, Landry had a long meeting with the rodeo committee. Shouting was heard by passersby. Committee members say it was business as usual. Later, he was heard shouting on his phone, something about he'd do what the hell he wanted to do.

"Had lunch at the Haber House Hotel with Stan Newton. On his way back, he stopped outside the rodeo grounds, was seen talking with or shouting at those protestors by the gate, depending on who you listen to.

"In the afternoon, he was heard shouting on his phone again, apparently at three or more people. Early evening, Oren Street arrived with the livestock, and like I said before, there was more shouting. Enough that the rodeo secretary told them to get away from the office so she could hear herself think.

"Had dinner at the Haber House Hotel alone. Tried to pick up the waitress. Wasn't taking no for an answer. Lloyd says she reported he got *handy*. The manager asked him to leave. Landry started—"

"Shouting."

He quirked a grin. "Right. Finally left. And that's the last report of anybody seeing him. Notice anything about these reports?"

"The only time he wasn't shouting was at lunch with Stan Newton."

"You got it. The waitress was the same one he tried to pick up later, and she says it was because he spent lunch leering at your favorite rodeo queen."

"Heather Upton? What was she doing there?"

"She and Cas Newton had lunch with his daddy and Landry."

"That's an odd group, isn't it?"

"Not necessarily. Cas wants to rodeo at a higher level. Landry could be a good connection, since he knows lot of folks running rodeos. Same for Heather. He could get her invited as a special guest with an honorarium at other rodeos."

"Has Richard talked to the Newtons and Heather?"

"Not yet." He looked at his notebook, flipping a few pages. "The one other thing Lloyd said was that Landry's phone was found deeper into the pen than any of them would have expected."

"And the significance of that?"

"One of those inconsistencies you like to follow."

"It has to be *follow-able* to follow it. Do they know who he called? Who called him? Who he was shouting at?"

He frowned. "You heard Jenks. The phone was smashed."

"They should be able to get stuff off the chip." Dex had taught me that. He'd taught me a lot and answered a load of questions in the years since I'd met the FBI lab scientist. "Melting's about the only way to wipe it out. After they do the paperwork to line up an expert, they should be able to pull the phone records."

"Did you know Richard Alvaro's second-to-the-oldest brother works for the phone company?"

"Of course he does."

"They'll get the phone records fast-tracked and won't need an outside expert. Did you get anything from Richard, or were you whiling away the time while I worked?"

"Time spent developing a source is never whiled away."

"So you got nothing."

"Lesson Number Two for the evening, my friend, always give it a try, because sometimes you get a little something."

I recounted the conversation with Alvaro.

"Whoa. That changes things." Mike sent me a look. "Doesn't it?"

"Not for sure. Not unless, or until, Richard's *not quite right* turns out to have more behind it than a feeling."

"But you asked him right off about it not being an accidental death. You were already thinking it was murder."

"No. Richard was trying to shut the door. I lobbed in a little tear gas to make him keep it open. A question's just a question, not a conclusion. A conclusion's built on facts. Sometimes you ask a question that's a hundred yards ahead of where the facts have brought you, just to get the response."

"So, what have the facts built?"

"Keith Landry is dead."

"Gee, thanks. Fine had gotten that far."

"Ah, but Fine doesn't know the second half of my so-far conclusion. There are a lot of questions to be asked."

We pulled into the station lot where my car sat in solitude. "You need a different car, Elizabeth. You should have four-wheel drive and something heavier. You'll definitely need it come winter."

"Uh-huh."

I was aware of him turning to me. "You're not paying attention."

I'd heard. And if I decided to stick around long enough to worry about winter in Wyoming, I would consider a different vehicle. But that was not a discussion I wanted to have with Mike Paycik. Especially now. It wasn't even a conversation I wanted to have with myself. Besides, my thoughts were on a different track. "You heard Richard say the acting sheriff's out of town?"

"Yeah."

I faced him. "Turns out the coroner called to the scene was that new deputy coroner. And Richard clammed up tight when I asked why they didn't call the coroner. Do you think there's something weird going on?"

"What do you mean?"

"I'd like to know who else is out of town."

We looked at each other a long moment, then he pulled out his phone. He started by asking Aunt Gee about the whereabouts of Sherman's mayor. The Cottonwood County Commission chairman. A number of names I didn't recognize. After thanking her and hanging up, he looked at me. "They're all out of town. That can*not* be a coincidence."

"No coincidence," I agreed.

"They're all out of cell reach, too. Definitely weird. It's like they've gone into a bunker or something."

"I suspect it's *or something*. Because when it comes to weird, remember who else is out of town and not reachable."

"Oh, my God. Les Haeburn."

Chapter Seven

ON IMPULSE, I stopped at the Sherman Supermarket on the way home. It was open every other Thursday until midnight, and this was one of its late Thursdays. I'd like to say the impulse was to pursue background material on a now-suspicious death. But I didn't think of that until after I was in the cookie aisle.

Better late than never.

The shopper checking out ahead of me was sent on her way with a "Bye now," and checker Penny Czylinski started on the line of cans I'd picked up to mask two bags of cookies. "Well, hi there—"

I said as fast as I could, "I was at the rodeo."

No pause, no hesitation, no delay—it was as if Penny had been waiting for me to say exactly that. "Real proud to have Grayson Zane. Used to be he'd come most years, then not, what with what happened five years back. It's all good to be saying what a top cowboy he is and how proud we are and all—" As she just had. I did *not* point that out. "—But it wasn't right what he did. You can't give the heart orders, but you can *do* right. Still, that was a few years back and—"

"Did Grayson Zane do something?"

It was hopeless. Penny's flow was a river at flood stage. Something might bob to the surface, you might grab for it, but if it sank, it was gone forever.

"This year our rodeo queen is Heather Upton, like her mama was years back. Some say it helped her get the title. It's not for me to agree or disagree, what with my cousin's girl being a finalist, and as good a rider as you'll find, not to mention smart and pretty and kind-natured.

But fair's fair, and I tell the ones talking against her that Heather can rope like nobody's business. Anything she sets her rope to, she pulls in for sure."

"So, the rodeo—" I tried.

"Now if you want to know about the rodeo, the one you should talk to is Linda Caswell. Knows that rodeo inside out, right back to the start. That's a sad story. Sad, sad story."

"The rodeo?"

She frowned, and I saw a flash of my bleak future if she banned me from the supermarket. Starved of food and information.

"The Caswells. There wouldn't a been a rodeo without them. They've always been important in this county, but had no luck in love. Walter, Linda's daddy, was the worst. Girl he was crazy for ran off and married somebody else. Walter took it as hard as a man can. Was thirty years before he realized that if he didn't do something, the Caswell name would end with him.

"Married a young thing from next county over. Sweet, but anybody looking at her—Well, that milk's long spilt. She had a daughter right quick, Inez, that was." Cas' mother if I had the genealogy straight. "Two years later, Linda. The girls must've been high school age when their mama was pregnant again."

A head shake, though it didn't slow her hands. I'd have to donate the cans to a food pantry or build an annex on the tiny, dismal house I rented. "Worn down, she was. She had a baby boy, but he died at four days. She followed not 24 hours later.

"When Walter got over his grieving, it was like he saw those two girls for the first time. He could have remarried, tried again for a boy, but he didn't. He set about making them the best cattlewomen, best horsewomen, best ranchers around. Linda took to it like a flower getting its first drink of water. Not that old Walter gave her much credit.

"Inez—that's the one he held up as so smart and all. But she wouldn't have anything to do with it. She'd been neglected too long. Or she had too much of her father in her and got her prideful back up. Some say she took up with Newt to get her father's goat. It sure did that. Walter and his oldest didn't talk for years. Linda refused to break off with her sister, but wouldn't go against their father, either. She walked a tightrope between them, even though she's a woman who's got a good head on her shoulders most times."

Penny wiped her counter, having already disposed of my order and taken my money. Nobody was behind me, so I stayed put.

"Inez got sick. When it was nearly too late, the both of them, her and her father, finally put aside their fighting. She had a rough time, real rough, but she was a fighter that one, and she beat it. Walter and his grandson were thicker than thieves, Linda was happy as all get-out, and even Newt seemed to have mellowed.

"Then the cancer came back. Inez fought. But this time—" Penny shook her head. "It was long, and it was hard. It seemed as if any one of the others might go with her from their hearts breaking. In the end it was Walter. Six months later."

I took the opening. "The man who died today at the rodeo—?"

"Keith Landry's not from Cottonwood County, but he's been coming a lot of years."

I heard the creak of a cart behind me. I wanted to order the intruder to go buy more. But I didn't dare break eye contact with Penny. Maybe she hadn't heard—

She had. "Bye now, Elizabeth. Well, hi there."

✧   ✧   ✧   ✧

WHEN I GOT IN the car, a note sat on the passenger seat. Had it been there at the station, and I hadn't noticed? Or had someone spotted my car here and left the note?

Either way, what did it say that I'd left my car unlocked. I couldn't remember the last time I'd done that.

I'd like to talk to you. TDB

Thomas David Burrell wanted to talk.

So, what was I supposed to do with that information at this hour of the night?

The only reasonable thing a grown-up, professional journalist could do. Go home and eat cookies.

DAY TWO

FRIDAY

Chapter Eight

EVEN AS I reached for the phone that had jolted me awake after too little sleep, I knew it was my mother.

She had a knack.

In college, if I'd been out late the night before, perhaps had more than a modest amount of alcoholic beverage, Catherine Danniher invariably called first thing. Last night's overindulgence had not been alcohol. Instead, a serious sugar buzz from the cookies had left me tired, but too restless to sleep for three hours. That, and considering how the situation might change depending on what Richard Alvaro's sister's employer discovered.

"Elizabeth, it's your mother." As if I didn't know.

"And father," Dad added.

"Hi."

"We want to talk to you about that wonderful job offer in St. Louis."

I stretched, hoping against hope this would be quick enough that I could go back to sleep. "It's for a talk show. I'm a reporter. Not a good fit."

"Don't be hasty, Elizabeth Margaret. Before you make a decision—"

"I decided. I told Mel to tell them no thank you. It's done."

"The position is still open."

I sat up. "How do you know that, Mom?"

"We saw Mel at your second cousin Sally's son Kiernan's wedding. The subject came up." Dad made an inarticulate sound. I envisioned her glaring at him. "It's fortunate—"

"Who brought up the subject?"

She gave her signature sound of exasperation—a muffled tongue click accompanied by a huffing out of her breath. "That's unimportant. What matters—"

"It's important to me, if my agent is talking about my business without my consent."

"Very well. I asked. Why you have to get every last detail when all—"

"It's my profession, Mom."

"That's precisely the point," she said in triumph. "It doesn't need to be your profession any longer. Before, with Wes pushing you every step, that was one thing. But on your own, the way you are now, you can take something slower, more relaxed. You've been strained for so long, trying to keep up with that career Wes put you in. This will suit you better. Not to mention it will give you more time to have a normal social life. You'd be closer to home in St. Louis. You could come home for weekends—"

So much for normal social life.

"—and truly be a part of the family."

"Now, Cat, that's not fair. Maggie Liz is part of the family." The childhood nickname inverting and shortening my first and middle name always warmed me.

"Of course she is," she shot back, as if she hadn't just said otherwise. "But how *can* she be, way out there by herself in that shack she's living in?"

It was early, but if I'd heard her right, my mother had contradicted her contradiction. Which, by my counting, still had me not being part of my family. In that case, why had she called me at dawn?

I might be foolhardy at times, but I'm not an idiot. I didn't ask. "Sorry, Mom, Dad—I have to get ready for work. Talk to you later."

I hung up before they could do the time-zone math.

I made good on my fib by showering, dressing, eating breakfast, and putting out food and water for the canine shadow that had been materializing in my yard over the past weeks. In fact, I'd named him Shadow. Although, I appeared to be the only one who recognized that as his name.

Ever since he'd sided with me against an interloper during the pursuit of Foster Redus' murderer, the dog no longer disappeared at the sight of me. On the other hand, he didn't come running when I called his name, either. Or when I put out his food and water.

"Morning, Shadow," I said.

He watched from a safe distance, approaching the bowls perched on the stump in the barren back yard only when I retreated to the steps.

I'd read a book about dogs last week that said some were praise-motivated while others were food-motivated or play-motivated. The first thing in training a dog was to figure out what motivated yours. The writer suggested paying close attention during all interaction for clues. Since Shadow avoided interaction, I was short on clues.

Most mornings I was in enough of a hurry that I'd go inside at this point. Today, I sat on the back steps.

He stopped. Stared at me, flashed a glance at the bowls, back to me.

I sat and waited.

Me, bowls, me. Then a shift. Not only was it bowls, me, bowls, but the looks at the bowls lingered.

He took a step toward the bowls, shot me a suspicious look, which found me innocently sitting in the same spot as the previous check. Took another step, looking at me. A third.

Then he turned away for several steps—presumably so he wouldn't run into the stump. Because as soon as he reached it, he pinned me with a long, assessing stare.

At last, he turned away and chomped on a mouthful of food. He watched me while he chewed. So went the entire meal. Although when the food was gone, he turned away long enough to lap up water. Finally, he turned to me again. His chocolate-brown eyes looking directly into mine, he belched.

I laughed.

Startled, he darted five yards away, stopped, and looked back at me, still on the steps, still chuckling.

"Glad you enjoyed it, Shadow. Have a good day," I called.

He stared for a long moment, turned slowly and loped away. But we'd made progress, I decided. Real progress.

Having been awakened early, I also had time to call Dex before I left the hovel, as I had come to think of this house. I timed the call to hit his morning break, knowing he'd be out feeding squirrels at the FBI facility in Quantico, Virginia.

"Do you know a forensic pathologist in Montana named Grenley?"

Most people would have responded to that opener with the conversational equivalent of an eye-roll: either "Good morning to you, too, Danny" or "I don't know every forensic pathologist in the country, you know." But I know my audience.

Dex said, "No. What agency?"

It was only part of why I loved him like a brother—better than a brother, since none of my brothers worked in the FBI crime lab. Best of all, although Dex worked at the FBI crime lab, he hadn't given himself over to the FBI crime lab's culture, which is why he'd talk to me. Most FBI crime lab types would rather drink every chemical in their arsenal than talk to a member of the media.

Dex never treated me like media. Early on, he'd called me Danny to mask my identity from his coworkers—a nickname that caught on with family and friends—but now I'm not one-hundred percent sure he remembers I'm with the media. By completely protecting him as my source, I give him no cause to remember.

"None. He's a civilian as far as I know. But some Wyoming counties and other places use him."

"Ah."

"Ah what?"

He ignored that. "Where?"

"Billings."

"I'll get back to you."

He hung up. There must have been a particularly hungry-looking squirrel. *Good morning to you, too, Dex.*

Chapter Nine

MY MORNING drive to KWMT was its usual uneventful self.

After commuting for years in New York City, and before that in Washington, D.C., that was a fact worth noting.

The uneventfulness allowed information about Keith Landry's strange death to roll around in the back of my head, while the front chewed on another issue. I needed a "Helping Out" segment.

I had a few in the can for my twice-a-week consumer affairs spot, but you never knew when you might need a few more. News Director Les Haeburn might start listening to me and add more slots each week. Or he might get the bright idea to use me for the kind of stories I'd done for nearly two decades before being exiled to KWMT after daring to a.) accumulate birthdays, b.) compound raises, and c.) call it quits with a news network-exec husband who knew the nasty pitfalls in my contract, because he'd written it and recommended I sign it.

Okay, miracles were unlikely. I still needed a "Helping Out" segment to keep my hand in at what I liked to think remained my profession. Especially since I'd turned down the lucrative change-of-life talk show offer my lawyer/agent/relative Mel had secured.

That reminded me of the Gift Card Burglars—don't blame me, I didn't name them.

Reports came through the Better Business Bureau about thieves with a simple yet effective ploy. They called a home where someone lived alone and said the person had won a gift card at a local store. But the card had to be claimed that day at the store. When the unsuspecting resident drove off to claim the prize, the thieves drove in, assured the house was empty.

The group had been working their way vaguely north, reaching northern Wyoming in these last days of June. This group concentrated on rural homes. The distance residents had to drive to get to town gave the thieves time to load a van with every valuable and semi-valuable item. No kitchen sinks reported stolen, but they'd taken TVs, computers, furniture, wine collections and refrigerators, complete with food.

I had taken three steps into the KWMT-TV newsroom, when I encountered the first hint that *something was going on.*

"Thurston's here," Audrey Adams, an assignment editor, said out of the side of her mouth as we passed in the hallway.

It seemed an odd response to "Good morning," but okay.

Jenks sidled up when I was heating water for tea in the mini-break room. "A certain somebody doesn't have an inkling of what's happening." He kept his side to me, to fool anyone who might suspect we were doing anything as nefarious as talking.

Add in a meaningful nod and wink from two participants from yesterday's sticky-note derby, and the superspy/espionage motif was complete.

To keep my cover intact, I placed calls about the Gift Card Burglars. Mostly leaving messages asking people to call me back.

A shadow cut the glare on my computer screen. I turned to find the pleasantly creased face and form of Needham Bender, editor and publisher of the Sherman *Independence*. While we exchanged greetings, I noted my fellow KWMTers' nonreaction. In most cities I'd worked, TV and newspaper folks are casually cordial on neutral ground, but don't visit each other's lair.

Mike detoured from the coffeemaker to join us. "Morning, Needham."

"I was about to tell Elizabeth that I dropped by to see if she—and you—are going to this news conference."

"And I was about to tell Needham we wouldn't consider it, since Landry's death is Thurston's story. Every shot, angle, frame and word." Needham's shaggy brows asked the question. I answered:

"Haeburn is on vacation and left Thurston in charge."

"That explains last night's newscasts."

"Speak of the devil," Mike murmured.

Following his gaze, I saw Thurston closing in on us.

"Did you see the rodeo queen release?" he demanded of me, ignoring both men. "Copies were to be routed to Les and me only."

It was less a question than an accusation. Apparently there was a big black market in rodeo queen news releases, and Fine suspected I was ringleader.

"I saw it on Les' desk during last week's meeting—long enough to see that it informed all media outlets that the queen would rein—r-e-i-n rather than r-e-i-g-n—over the festivities."

"They do have to show horsemanship," Mike murmured.

Thurston looked blank. "You didn't sit behind Les's desk."

Since that would have required sitting on the news director's lap during that meeting, I was happy to confirm. "Never did."

"So, you couldn't have read it then," he concluded triumphantly. "What I want to know is if you have the release now. Or know its current location."

I was tired of this game. "No."

"I'll just—" He reached toward files in a rack on my desk.

I stood and blocked him. "No, you will not."

We were six inches apart, close enough for him to see I meant it. Meant it with every degree of heat from a good dose of Irish temper. He stepped back.

I relented. "It was almost certainly sent electronically." Since he was notorious for screwing up the computer folder where such shared files were kept, I added, "Ask Jenny to print another copy."

"That *is* her job," he said huffily and stalked away.

Needham said, "You read the release upside down? Our TV star must have a deep, dark, secret newspaper past."

I nodded. "As a kid at our local weekly, run by the crustiest of old-time newspaper types. I learned to read upside down and backwards with old hot metal."

"Ah, sometimes in my dreams I smell the aroma of hot type. I kept the turtle with the *Independence's* last hot metal front page."

"Explain, you two old fogeys," Mike said.

"This electronic generation, no sense of history," Needham lamented. "You do know newspapers were produced before computers existed, don't you?"

Mike said, "Some gadget by Gutenberg, right?"

"Roughly. Between the centuries of building each line of copy by placing letters one by one and today's computer, typesetters used to type copy into a machine called a linotype, because it transformed liquid metal into lines of type. It took a while for the metal to cool, thus *hot type.*"

I took up the tale. "A printer placed type inside a form on a wheeled table—a turtle. One per page. Everything was backward so when ink and type met newsprint on a press it came out right."

Mike's frown cleared. "Like backward writing you can read in a mirror. But why upside down?"

"The printer stood at the bottom to see the page right side up. That left the lowly office gofer—"

"Or editor," Needham inserted.

"—standing at the top, reading upside down and backward to spot errors. I didn't mind. It's a useful skill for a reporter. Though it didn't pay off this time. All the release said was a local girl won a beauty contest—"

"Rodeo queen is not a beauty contest," Mike said. "You tell her, Needham. You're on the committee again this year, right?"

"The newspaper editor's on the rodeo queen committee?"

"Small-town journalism, Elizabeth. Different kettle of fish," Needham said. I wondered if he knew about the missing big shots. I doubted it. Or he'd have printed the story. It was telling that the county brain trust had included Haeburn but not Needham. The newspaper editor rose even higher in my estimation. "Each girl goes from collecting her horse, to full tack and saddle, then works calves. We ask questions all along—equine diseases, safety, grooming. Each girl also displays a talent associated with ranch work, western life or rodeo. This year's queen is a champion roper. Most impressive I've seen. Hope she gets to show it. This news conference . . . I've got a feeling about it."

Mike and I avoided looking at each other or him.

"I see," he said slowly. "Not going to the news conference? Either of you?"

"Have calls to make. Breaking consumer affairs story."

"I'm heading out on an assignment. Gotta go now," Mike said, giving me a look over Needham's head. Perhaps he should have kicked me, because I didn't get the significance. He seemed to realize that, because disgust tinged his parting look.

I offered Needham coffee. We chatted about the weather, the hay crop, tourists headed to Yellowstone Park, and how traffic would increase over the Fourth of July weekend. In other words, we covered all the top Cottonwood County news except yesterday's death of a prominent rodeo contractor.

Then Needham Bender sighed and shook his head. "I'm surprised at you, Elizabeth. Surprised and disappointed."

A burn in my chest jolted me. It took a second to register it as the burn of remembering my ex saying those words when I'd balked at a move. I didn't remember which move. Perhaps, he'd said it more than once.

Needham was still talking. "You did good work on the Foster Redus case, truly fine journalism." That salve helped, but the burn remained. "I must have told my wife a hundred times that this county will sit up and take notice with you here."

I have accepted professional awards and fulsome compliments with far greater aplomb than my mumbled, awkward thanks.

"I can only imagine Cottonwood County, Wyoming was not where you saw your career going. I wasn't aware of your divorce. Thelma told me—my wife keeps up with those things. I'm sorry, Elizabeth. Sorry for the personal difficulty of divorce and sorry the son of a gun took it out on you professionally."

I didn't manage even an awkward mumble.

"But I can't be sorry it brought you here. At least not if you practice the kind of journalism you did on the Redus story. However, if you leave stories like this death at the rodeo grounds to Fine, I will not be even a quarter as happy as I thought I'd be."

Needham Bender was the unvarnished truth kind of journalist I'd trained under. And he'd immediately treated me as a respected colleague, unlike much of the KWMT newsroom. I even rather liked his mix of barbs and compliments.

"I can't make promises about your happiness. Each of us is responsible for our own happiness," I lectured primly. "However, I do suggest you go to the news conference now. You want a good seat, so no one misses you when you start asking questions."

He looked at me for a good ten seconds. Then he grinned. All over. Every crease happy.

"Hot damn," he said. "Hot, hot damn."

✧ ✧ ✧ ✧

THURSTON FINE swept from his private office across the newsroom toward the door. Diana followed, carrying her new camera—well, new to her. Haeburn had replaced some of the KWMT shooters' most archaic equipment, but only with more recent used hardware.

Diana did not look happy. I knew why. I'd seen the assignment board with her name marked in for Fine's beck and call all day.

When he stopped abruptly in front of my desk, he caught Diana off guard. Her lowered camera goosed him a good one. She raised innocent shoulders in response to his glare. When a few titters sounded, Fine spread the glare to the mostly empty desks.

"I am leaving for the press conference at the sheriff's department," he announced. He always set my teeth on edge, but this was worse. I debated saying he wasn't going to a press conference. Not unless Alvaro allowed only the print media (not a bad idea.) If Alvaro let Fine in, as well as representatives of radio or the Internet, it wasn't a *press* conference. TV and radio don't use presses, so it was a *news* conference.

"And no one else goes," he added. "That is my express order."

"What about Diana?" came a voice from off to my left.

Fine twisted around to try to stab the speaker with his steely glare, but apparently couldn't identify a target. "I and Diana alone. The rest of you are instructed to work on your daily assignments."

That drew no response. What could you say to someone ordering you to keep doing what you'd been doing before he interrupted to give the order?

"Carry on!"

Once he was gone, "Carry on!" passed from one staffer to another. An assistant answered the phone, "KWMT. Carry on!"

The caller must have wondered why that produced laughter in the newsroom. I was too busy grinning to worry about confused callers. It was another small sign of camaraderie.

Good newsrooms balance on a knife's edge, with competitive on one side of the blade and collegial on the other. KWMT's newsroom had been settled into a dull plateau of neither. Every little bit helped to change that. It was nice that Fine contributed something to that knife's edge, little though he intended it.

With that happy thought, I popped up from my chair and waylaid Jenny, the newsroom aide I knew best. "I'd like you to go to the news conference," I said quietly.

"What? The one Thurst—"

"Yes. That one. Stay at the back, and he won't notice you. Even if he does, he won't raise a stink about you being there. After it ends, I want you to find out everything you can about calls to or from Keith Landry's cell last night. If they don't have details yet, find out when they expect them."

"I don't need to go to the news conference for that. I can get into the database and—"

I clasped both hands around her arm and dragged her into the ladies room.

"Wha—"

"Quiet." I checked the two stalls. Empty. First glance had assured me the rest of the tiny room was empty. "Are you crazy? Haven't you had any training? Have you not heard of journalistic ethics? Have you not heard of *News of the Day*? Rupert Murdoch? Hearings before

Parliament?"

She gaped at me. "I don't remember all those questions. You asked a lot really fast. But I think the answers were all no. Except . . . we don't have a Parliament, do we?"

"Britain's got Parliament. We have Congress."

"Right. I thought I had that right."

I blew out a breath. "You haven't had any journalism training?"

"Nope. But I read blogs."

Note to self: Weep later. "You work here. You must be intere—"

"My folks said they wouldn't pay for any more computer parts unless I got a job. I saw an ad in the paper, and I figured a TV station would have cool equipment. Boy, was I wrong. But a bigger station should be better, right? Only, first, everybody needs to call me Jennifer. It's more mature. That'll help me move up."

My head throbbed at career advancement based on fine-tuning a name, rather than having a background in journalism. But there wasn't time now. "Listen, Jenny—"

"Jennifer."

"Jennifer—you cannot hack into the phone company's computers to—"

"Oh, I wouldn't hack the phone company. I'd hack the sheriff's department. That's easier."

"No hacking!"

She blinked. "But if you need the information . . ."

"We'll talk about journalistic ethics, not to mention legalities later."

"Cool."

"But for now, I want your word that you will go to the news conference, ask if that information has come in—do it when no one else is around—and do not hack anyone or anything until we've had a long talk. Understand?"

"Okay."

"Give me your word."

Her eyes widened. "I gave you my word."

I felt like I'd insulted a Disney character or a Muppet. Something highly skilled at inducing guilt. "Oh. Well, you better get started."

She nodded with dignity. And then she left with dignity, sidestepping the incoming Diana with dignity.

"What was that about?" Diana asked when the ladies' room door closed behind her. "What was wrong with Jenny?"

"Jennifer," I corrected. "Apparently, I hurt her feelings."

She propped her hands on her hips in disapproval. It took dexterity to accomplish without hitting one elbow on the sink or digging the other into me. "How? Jenny doesn't hurt easily."

"I asked her to do something. Well, *not* to do something. She said okay, and I asked her to give me her word, and she said she had given me her word."

Diana dropped her arms. "She had."

"*Okay?* Saying okay is giving your word?"

"Yes."

"Don't tell me this is some Code of the West thing, where a man's word is his bond. Or in this case, a newsroom aide's *okay* is her pledge."

"Don't have to tell you, since you figured it out yourself. Now, get out of here. I have one bathroom and two kids at home. This is the only bathroom where I have any privacy."

"That's pathetic."

"I've seen the bathroom in that house you're renting. Don't go throwing rocks at pathetic houses."

Chapter Ten

I DETOURED outside to make a private call from my cell phone.

The parking lot of KWMT-TV was dusty, hot, and my dermatologist wouldn't approve of the sun beating down on me, but I would spot anyone approaching long before they could hear my conversation.

Not that I wanted to make this call. I would have preferred to ignore my parents' morning phone call and its implications. But with my family and my professional lives now connected through the rotund figure of my mother's cousin's daughter's husband, the implications had not remained in the mental lock-box of *Family*.

When I was shell-shocked from the revelation that my just-turned ex-husband was using his network clout to get me ousted from my job, Mel Welch had stepped in and taken over negotiations. Wes had wanted me out of TV news. Mel had arranged for me to come here, clinging to the edge of the business.

Mel was a lawyer in Chicago whose only media contacts I'd known about were Wes and me. Until a few weeks ago, when Jenny-now-Jennifer had mentioned a connection between Mel and KWMT's owners, I hadn't considered how it came about that I ended up at this particular station. I hadn't gotten anything out of him about that. Yet. But, then, I hadn't tried very hard.

Mel answered with flattering promptness after I identified myself to his assistant.

"Danny! How wonderful to hear from you." He, like many of my longtime friends, had picked up the Danny nickname started by Dex. Do you have something good to tell me?"

"I have something to ask."

"Oh?" Caution turned the syllable into a shifty figure diving for the shadows.

"You told my mother that the St. Louis job is still open. Since I turned it down, why would you keep tabs on it? Out with it, Mel."

"Uh, I haven't told them you said no."

"What? *What?*"

"I wanted to give you time to reconsider. For your own good. That job might truly be the best choice for you."

"Are *you* saying this, or my mother?"

"We both care for your welfare," he said stuffily.

"Mel, you have got to quit meddling in this."

"Meddling's what you pay me to do. I'm your agent."

"*My* agent? Or operating on someone else's orders?"

"I have no idea what you're talking about." His affronted dignity swelled with each word.

"We both know we're talking about *whom*, not *what*. And we both know exactly which whom. I'm not unsympathetic, Mel. I know what a force she is. But—" His mutter might have been *Like mother, like daughter.* "—rationally, she's barely even family."

"She *is* family, just like you are."

"Your wife's mother's cousin. And what could she do to you?"

That wasn't entirely fair. Catherine Danniher's cold shoulder was the worst, because she achieved it without ever leaving you alone. Her cold shoulder put her disapproval right there in front of your face until you begged for a good case of shunning.

His silence was glum. That was good, because it meant my displeasure was not entirely outweighed by his trepidation.

"You *are* my representative," I said, "and I expect you to follow my wishes. If you don't, I will be forced to share with certain members of the Chicago legal community that you are afraid of a small-town housewife. Wouldn't take me long to find out whom you would least like to hear that tidbit, and who's the biggest gossip."

"You wouldn't."

"All you have to do is stop meddling, stop trying to arrange things for what you—or my mother—think is my good. You'd think you didn't believe I could handle this, for heaven's sake. You know I did build quite a career once, and just because my ex's vindictive nature blew a crater the size of the continent in that career, doesn't mean I can't do it again."

Somewhere during that speech I recognized a quality to his silence that peeled part of my mind off to follow a separate track. A track paved with memories of time I'd spent with my family between finding out my ex had cut off oxygen to my career and starting my less than challenging duties at KWMT. Memories of truncated sentences, half-glimpsed looks, sympathetic tones, and words spoken too heartily.

"And *will* do it again. Even better this time," Mel said. Too heartily.

Ding, ding, ding, ding. The bells and whistles in my head were loud enough to be heard in the New York network executive suites.

You've been strained for so long trying to keep up with that career Wes put you in.

That's what they thought? My family, my agent? That Wes *put* me in this career, that *Wes* built it, and I'd been along for the ride? I'd realized Wes had thought he'd created me. But my family, too?

"Mel, I have to go."

"Oh, but—"

"Don't talk to anybody, anybody at all, until you hear back from me." I disconnected without waiting for an answer.

I stared at a line of distant cottonwood trees, my mind a blank. Then I shook myself, pocketed my phone, and headed inside. I'd pull a Scarlett O'Hara and think about this another day.

✧ ✧ ✧ ✧

WITH JENNY-Jennifer off to the news conference, I made more calls, tracking a rumor that a Cheyenne station had footage that would go with my Gift Card Burglars piece.

Stretching, I looked at my notebook page of jotted names, numbers, and notes. It was littered with triangles. Huh. I was doodling again, after at least a year of not.

Large triangles segmented by ever-decreasing triangles had been my doodle of choice ever since Advanced Algebra nearly proved my undoing in high school, although I hadn't realized all the ramifications until years later. Perhaps at first triangles had assuaged a homesickness for more graspable geometry.

After leaving a message for a contact at the Cheyenne station, the phone's message light blinked, indicating a call had come in while I was on the line. It was Mike, telling me to meet him.

This newsroom superspy stuff was getting out of hand. He didn't say why. *Where* was "the roadside turnoff where you had a conversation alone with a murder suspect a few weeks back." At least he didn't say the message would self-destruct.

✧ ✧ ✧ ✧

I ROUNDED THE last curve before the path reached a picnic table beside the Jelicho River west of town.

"Here she is," I heard Mike say. "Finally."

"And wondering why I got dragged out here by 007 Paycik," I stopped—speaking and walking—when I saw his companion.

Thomas David Burrell.

"I thought you'd follow me when I gave you the high sign," Mike said. "When you didn't, I left the message."

His words got me moving again. "You were entirely too subtle for me. What are you doing here?" The last, directed at Tom Burrell, wasn't my best question ever, I admit.

"When I didn't hear from you, I contacted Mike." *This* is what he wanted to talk to me about? Not that he'd shown up at my door, kissed me in a convincing manner, then walked away without a word in the weeks since?

"You didn't give me much time," I grumbled.

"Time's not on our side with this." Had he emphasized *this*? I'd need a voice expert to say.

"I jumped on his offer," Mike said. He sat at the end of one side of the table, Burrell in the middle on the opposite side. "To help us with background on the Keith Landry story."

"That's Thurston Fine's story. Talk to him. Don't look at me like that, Paycik. It is. He specifically ordered me not to attend the sheriff department's news conference. He's doing all the coverage."

"Coverage of a news conference informing the media what you two knew twelve hours ago," Tom said.

I glared at Paycik. The blabbermouth shrugged without remorse. "If we want background on the rodeo, we need Tom."

"Oh?" I turned to the man in question. "What does Tom get out of it?"

"I hope the rodeo gets the truth."

"You don't have confidence in Deputy Alvaro?"

He gave back a look as steady, as solid, and as unemotional as a rock. He had a long, craggy face that reminded me of a new and improved-looking Abraham Lincoln. "Not as much confidence as I have reason to have in you."

He was referring to the Redus case. I can't swear I didn't dig my toe into the dust in modest confusion, except I think I would have noticed dusty shoes later if I had.

"Richard Alvaro's a good man," Tom continued. "He'll do his best. But he's young and inexperienced. Even if he gets to the bottom of this mess, it will likely take longer than the rodeo has."

"What do you mean?" I took a seat on the same bench as Paycik, but at the other end.

"This needs to be cleared up before the Fourth of July Rodeo—a couple days before."

"Investigations into death don't run on some rodeo schedule."

"Any more uncertainty could push this over the edge. Look, this is for you two only . . ." Tom waited for a nod from each of us. "The rodeo's in financial trouble. That other contractor walking out last minute meant the rodeo basically had to give Keith Landry whatever he wanted. And he wanted a lot. Three times the normal fee. If we don't break attendance records, the rodeo will be bankrupt."

"How do you know?" I asked.

"I was a longtime member of the rodeo committee until other

events occupied my time." Like murder knocking at his door. "Other committee members still consider me a member. And . . ." His dark Abraham Lincoln eyes went to the river flowing past us.

Maybe George Washington could not tell a lie, but Abraham Lincoln Burrell could certainly sidestep the whole truth, and nothing but the truth. I'd known that from our previous encounters, but in those circumstances he'd been direct about what he'd tell me—mostly nothing. Evasion was new.

"Who are you looking out for?" I asked.

"Like I said, the rodeo."

I didn't believe it. Oh, he was concerned about the rodeo, sure. But there was a thread of the personal, too.

He blandly gazed back. "Don't you want to ask me questions about the investigation, Elizabeth?"

"What do you know?"

"Not much."

I jerked my hands wide. "Oh, this is a great partnership. How about what the shouting was about at Landry's meeting with the rodeo committee Wednesday morning?"

"Don't know."

"Can you find out?" That had a bite to it.

"I can try."

"Also find out who he was shouting at on the phone during the afternoon, and why, and what he and Oren Street were shouting about after Street arrived in town."

"I'll try on that, too. One thing I do know," Tom said in his unperturbed way, "is they've pulled the records off Landry's phone."

Mike shot me a told-you-so look. I avoided it, asking, "What did they find?"

"There were 28 calls to Newt—Stan Newton."

"Oh, yeah?"

Tom shook his head, negating the significance. "There were nineteen to Oren Street, fifteen to a cowboy named Evan Watt, fourteen to your friend Thurston Fine, thirteen to a guy from the next rodeo they're scheduled to work, and more than 10 to another half-dozen contacts."

"Butt calls," I said.

"In this case, bull calls," Mike said with a grimace.

"Exactly," Tom said. "The bulls' hooves kept hitting speed dial buttons until they smashed the phone. It lasted longer than might have been expected because of the cushioning material in the pen. Including the deceased."

My turn to grimace.

"Every call was to somebody you'd expect on Landry's speed dial. Alvaro's talked to them. Those who picked up said they heard only background noise. A few got the calls as messages. The sheriff's department listened to undeleted ones, and that's all we heard on those messages, too."

"We?"

"I was there when they listened to messages to one recipient."

"Who?"

"Not saying."

I glared at him, proving I could glare and ask questions at the same time. "No other noises?"

"Like what?"

"Like Keith Landry shouting for help."

"Not that I've heard mention of, and it does seem they'd have brought that up."

"Didn't people think it was odd they got so many calls from Landry?" Mike asked. Good question.

"Folks stopped answering after the first couple. Figured it was a malfunction and didn't think anything else of it. Nobody knew about anybody else's calls."

That was annoyingly logical. "The sheriff's department considers the calls a dead end?"

Burrell's head and shoulders shifted slightly in a suggestion of a shrug that also served as a *yes.*

"But Tom's going to help you on another angle," Mike said.

"Me? Why not help you?"

"Got to cover a summer baseball league playoff. Even if it never makes the air, I have to make an appearance. He's taking you to the Newton place," Mike said. "Stan Newton owns the rodeo grounds, and his son—that's Cas Newton—is real involved with rodeo locally. That should be good background."

As if his emphasis on the name Newton hadn't been enough, Mike gave me a look. One I had no trouble interpreting.

I had the impression Tom caught it, too. Though he gave no sign as he said, "We'll get lunch then head out—"

"I have plans for lunch and a call coming in right after. From back East," I added, bolstering the fib with detail, even as I wondered why I'd bothered.

"After lunch, then. Two-thirty? I'll come by the station."

"Fine." I smiled, professional and neutral, because further delay made no sense.

He stood.

"There's something else for you to check on," I said.

He stopped, looking at me politely.

"We have reports that Keith Landry was shouting at nearly everyone he came in contact with Wednesday. Yet he had what appeared to be a cordial lunch at the Haber House Hotel with Stan Newton, Cas Newton, and Heather Upton. What was different about that lunch from Landry's other encounters Wednesday?"

"Ask Stan and Cas this afternoon," Tom said.

"I want a better idea of the situation before I ask them about it. Think you can find out, what with all your connections?"

Tom lowered the front brim of his black cowboy hat in a leisurely nod—one motion that said yes, he understood the assignment, and yes, he expected to fulfill it, and yes, he recognized my undercurrent of snideness, and no, it didn't rile him any. He started for the path.

"Burrell?" I called, not prepared to be left with the laconic Westerner's nod. No reaction. "Tom?" He turned. "Do you know where the county's bigwigs have gone?"

"No."

I squinted at him. "But you knew they were gone."

"Yes."

"How?"

"Can't reveal my source." He said it deadpan.

"If your source knows where the big shots are, or how to get in touch with them, it might be a good idea to get them back here."

One finger nudged up his hat's brim. "You know," the drawl came thick and slow, "we talked about that, my source and I, and we think it's better to leave them where they are. Give Richard and you folks a chance to see what you can find out."

Chapter Eleven

I WAITED UNTIL I was sure Burrell was out of earshot, but not a second longer. "Paycik, did you tell him about Richard's doubts about this being an accident?"

"No."

"I don't know what you think can be achieved with this—"

"Like you said yesterday, asking questions, searching for inconsistencies."

"Yesterday I was fed up with Fine and more than a little bored."

"Has either condition changed?"

No, but maybe other things had. Damn. If not even my family believed I'd built my own success . . . No. I wasn't going to think about that now.

"If Alvaro confirms foul play, it's an official story. That makes it Fine's. Fighting that could mean a quick end for both of us at KWMT. And if Richard confirms it's *not* foul play, it's not a story. Yesterday we had wiggle room. Now we don't. It's going to be cut and dried very soon. Fine's story or no story."

"Soon, maybe, but not yet. Let's keep digging and see where it takes us."

"Paycik."

"Elizabeth." He gave me that smile the camera loved, with just enough self-deprecation to make you not hate him, even as you recognized everything he had going for him. "I learned more from you on the Redus story than I had in all the years of being interviewed and taking classes and my months here put together."

"I'm glad. Really. But, Paycik, you have got to realize modeling your career after mine is not a good plan. I had a husband rising through the exec ranks who brought me along for the ride and—"

"That's bull." He winced belatedly at his word choice, but kept going. "If anybody was along for the ride, it was him."

"I appreciate your loyalty, Mike, I do. But—"

"It's facts, Elizabeth. Look, I'm not an idiot. I did some digging in my own untutored way when Haeburn said you were coming here. I know your asshole ex-husband has you riding out your contract in the worst place he could think of. I can only imagine what it felt like for E.M. Danniher to show up as KWMT consumer affairs reporter, working with a dickhead anchor like Fine. But—"

"Oh, I've worked with dickheads before," I murmured.

It didn't slow him. "But," he repeated, "I also know you've refused to stay down. By doing good, professional work on this bullshit assignment, you're raising the work of everyone around you. What you did about Redus, and what you can do now is beyond what this station has ever seen. Or I've ever seen."

So one person thought I could do this work. Though the fact that his basis of comparison was KWMT didn't exactly put me in the ranks of world-beaters.

✧   ✧   ✧   ✧

"WHY, ELIZABETH, fancy you being back. I see you're picking up lunch." Without a breath, Penny added, "I was thinking about you and those calls on Keith Landry's phone. The ones the bulls—"

"How do you—?" I paused while unloading a salad, mini packet of dressing, mini-er packet of cheese, and can of green tea that had rattled around in a cart meant for cowboy-sized meat and potatoes.

"Oh, I heard last night about the bull calls." Of course she had.

I resumed unloading as slowly as possible, leaving long, empty gaps on the belt conveying my purchases to Penny. With so few purchases, I had no time to waste on subtlety. "What do you know about Keith Landry?"

"Now, I'm not one to speak ill of the dead, even one who drank that way, and I'm not saying he didn't do things that looked real nice at the time. It was only when folks came out the other side and looked back that they took to realizing what happened. Even smart women with a good head on their shoulders.

"And there I gotta give Heather credit for the sense to see what was what before she got sucked in like the others. I woulda thought ambition outweighed her sense, but there's the evidence. It mighta been her mama keeping that girl from following a path walked by a number before her."

"What path are—?"

"He wouldn't've had half the success he had with girls, even ones near half his age these days, if he hadn't polished that routine of his up bright. Act like he'd heal whatever ailed a girl to rush her off her feet, got what he wanted, then left her flat. Seen him do it here time and again, and I suppose other stops on the rodeo route, too," she said. "River don't stop being wet just because it's out of your sight."

It took me a beat too long to process that last statement.

"What is it that some women think a man who's been eatin' buffet all his life will suddenly settle in for the same menu every night once he tastes their cookin'?" She clicked her tongue. "Sonja was foolin' herself, that's all. 'Course she's not the first. But I've got a sight more sympathy for others than Sonja.

"Well, good to see you again, Elizabeth. Bye now. Hi there, Lisa, haven't seen you since your youngest got the measles. How is that red-headed scamp? Now, when Carol Sue's boy's oldest had the measles . . ."

I wanted to shout *Wait a minute! Tell me the rest! You can't leave me hanging.* But she could. She had. And the next customer in line appeared prepared to run me over if I didn't move along.

There was only one way to get more information. A reporter, a real reporter, not one whose career was built by a Svengali-wannabe husband, is not deterred by obstacles. I would pay the price for cookies.

✧   ✧   ✧   ✧

JENNY-JENNIFER came through. It wasn't her fault that Tom had given us the headlines first.

She'd also shown initiative by using her phone to snap pictures of the documents while the friendly deputy was out of the room—faster and more complete than note-taking. I thanked her profusely to offset not recognizing "okay" as a blood oath. With a smile, she scooted back to her desk to email me the images.

I chomped down on a cookie from Round Two with Penny. She had given me a few details on Sonja, Landry's conquest in Sherman two years ago. Sonja and her immediate family had moved to Seattle last year, hadn't been back to visit, and hadn't left a supplanted boyfriend nursing a grudge against Landry. Penny had said there'd been no Landry liaison last year. I'd run out of time and cookie purchases before I got a last name for Sonja.

I opened the file with the images and scanned the list of times, numbers, and names. Partway down the first page, I stopped, refocused and started over, ticking off calls to various names.

Burrell had been absolutely accurate—twenty-eight calls to Stan Newton, nineteen to Oren Street, fifteen to my scruffy cowboy acquaintance Evan Watt, fourteen to Thurston Fine, thirteen to someone named Baldwin from a town in Montana that was to have been Landry's next stop.

And yes, he'd been accurate in saying there were more than ten each to another half-dozen contacts. They included Landry's bank, Street's home number in Enid, Oklahoma, and former Judge Ambrose Claustel with eleven calls each.

The remaining three were more interesting. Twelve calls each to Caswell Newton and Grayson Zane. And fifteen to Linda Caswell, chair of the rodeo committee. Burrell, not knowing I had another string working on the phone records, had left her out of his litany, even though she should have tied with Watt.

Bingo. Something personal in this for Burrell.

The good news was my instincts hadn't atrophied into mush.

The bad news was that I saw another visit to Penny's checkout line in my near future, and that meant more cookies. The sacrifices I make for journalism.

✧ ✧ ✧ ✧

"I'LL DRIVE," I told Burrell as he held the door for me to exit KWMT.

I'd made him wait. But not long. The sight of him sitting patiently in an uncomfortable break room chair had worn me down.

"No."

"I'm working. I'll drive my car."

"It's dirt roads, and I don't want to be stuck when that tin can of yours has its underside ripped out by a rock. We're taking my truck. If you want to drive, drive my truck."

I snapped my mouth closed.

"Unless you can't drive a shift?"

"I can drive shift." And I'd driven a pickup, along with Jeeps, and once—memorably—a tank. But that had been a demonstration. The pickup driving had not been for years. Nor had it been a brand new truck with the owner sitting next to me. "I'll take you up on that another time," I said smoothly. "You drive this time. I'll prep for the interview."

Once on the way, I asked, "Why's Newton willing to have me come out asking questions?"

"You'd have to ask him."

"What aren't you telling me?"

He stayed silent half a beat, cut me a look, said, "A lot."

I felt as if this conversation had hit a patch of ice. It could go any-where from here. I tried to bring it back onto the main road safely. "What did you say to Newton to get him to say yes to my coming?"

"I said, 'Newt, how's about I swing by this afternoon with that smart lady reporter from the TV station and we talk about this some.' And he said, 'Okay, Tom.'"

"Smart lady reporter?"

"Yup." He cut me another look. "Which one you objecting to? Smart? Reporter? Or lady?"

I rolled my eyes and opened the file of material the newsroom aide had printed out for me.

The facts and figures confirmed what Penny had said. Stan "Newt" Newton had built an even greater success atop a foundation laid by his father. The file added dates to the family history, along with a couple pictures of Stan and Inez, who had stood straight and tall and three inches higher than her husband.

Other items showed Newton had bought the rodeo grounds four years ago from Cottonwood Drive. I learned that was the name of the Caswell family business, including a ranch, a small rodeo stock operation, and other enterprises. A sampling of letters to the *Independence* showed a general feeling that the rodeo wasn't what it had been under previous ownership. Between the lines I almost heard the mutter of *money-grubber.*

A series of articles followed Newton's effort to bar protestors from the gates of the Sherman Rodeo. He'd failed. Because the protestors weren't on rodeo property. Unless they found their way under the grandstand.

There were a dozen clips of Cas Newton's athletic exploits. Two included photos with the proud father beaming beside his son.

I closed the file.

"I've read the dry, boring stuff. Now tell me what this family's really like." I looked around and saw that by heading generally southeast, we'd come into high-desert-looking country. Arid range land stretched wide, broken occasionally by sharp hills, some with steep sides the wind had eroded into rust and dun stripes.

"Don't know them well enough to do that."

"If you're going to be discreet, you won't be one bit of use."

He flicked a look at me, but said nothing.

"Okay, I'll tell you what I've gathered, and you tell me if I'm wrong. Stan is proud as all get-out of his son. He's determined that Cas, being half Caswell, will give the Newton name the gloss, tone, and standing the Newtons haven't been able to acquire with money. Cas, being half Caswell and a teenager, wishes his father would drop into a hole. Except when Cas needs something, such as a slot in the Fourth of July Rodeo."

More nothing from Burrell. Although the very optimistic could view the new tilt of his cowboy hat as impressed.

"You're saying nothing, so I have it right," I said.

"All I know is that father-son relationships make me glad I've got a daughter."

"You don't want a son following in your footsteps?"

"Most sons don't follow in their father's footsteps. They run the other direction or do their damnedest to rub those footsteps out."

His voice held enough undercurrent that I steered a neutral course. "You're saying Wyoming isn't immune to teen rebellion?"

One corner of his mouth lifted. "That's what I'm saying."

"But you're not saying I'm wrong. And—" I turned to his profile. "—you're not saying what you know about the Caswells. I hear you're friends with Linda. Surely you know the family dynamics."

He did respond to that. He said, "We're here," and tipped his head as he turned left under a chopped-off goalpost structure like the one at the rodeo grounds, this one with a sign dangling from it reading "Newtons."

Chapter Twelve

HERE WAS AN exaggeration. But I didn't realize that until a good fifteen minutes worth of road had brought us to a compound that looked more like Hollywood's idea of ranch buildings than any Wyoming ranches I'd seen. For one thing, all the buildings were the same vintage, rather than historical strata that, like rings of a tree, showed an established ranch's years of necessity, boom, and bust.

It took a couple moments longer of peering at the set-up to realize another difference. The house was in the center, flanked by the ranch buildings. On most ranches, the ranch buildings stuck together while the house sat to one side, presumably to limit the impact of smells, dirt, and other potential inconveniences.

"Are the Newtons high-siders or low-siders?" I asked. I'd learned that residents in Cottonwood County's western part—closer to the mountains—were designated high-siders. Low-siders lived in the eastern area, where the land was flatter, drier, and tougher.

"Low-siders geographically. But Newt's got one of the biggest spreads in the county, along with the other businesses. Some would say high-siders for that."

"I'd have expected Stan would want high-side property."

"Nothing available when he bought. And he wanted big."

Tom steered the truck to the left, honked twice, and stopped.

Cas Newton emerged from a building that appeared to be a stable, with a trio of dogs trailing him. Tom raised a hand in greeting out the open truck window. Cas returned the gesture and started toward us. I read reluctance in his lack of speed.

"What breed are those dogs?" I asked. "They look like Shadow."

"Those are top-notch cattle dogs," Tom said as he opened his door, "and if Newt hears you likening that stray of yours to them, he'll throw you off his place before you can say another word."

I huffed, but contained myself.

As we approached each other across open ground that gave off a strong smell of sun-heated dirt with each step we took, I watched Cas. But all I got was that he had the Stoic Westerner demeanor pegged. Or else he didn't recognize me as the person who'd spotted him and Ms. Blue Hair under the bleachers. That was possible, considering the lighting and that my head had been thunking on the footwell like a dummy in a simulated car crash, which would make it hard to recognize anyone.

Tom said, "Hey, Cas."

He responded, "Mr. Burrell."

"Cas, I understand you met Ms. Danniher yesterday."

He confirmed with a "Ma'am."

"She's hoping you have more time to answer questions now."

"I got work, Mr. Burrell."

"I know. But the lady respected your time before competing last night, and she drove out here, so you can take a few minutes to answer some questions."

A few minutes? I'd have to set ground rules for Burrell being part of this, and that included not committing me to a deadline I might not keep. There was also the matter of how Tom knew I'd met Cas last night, as well as the tidbit about respecting the kid's time.

"I don't know anything," Cas mumbled with traces of sullenness.

"We won't know that until you hear my questions, and I hear your answers. You don't mind if I record this to make sure I get things straight, do you? For my use, not for broadcasting." I ran it together, wrapped with a cheerful bow, as I pressed the pocket recorder's button. "Has there been any trouble at the rodeo grounds in the past week or so?"

"No, ma'am. We most all know each other and get along."

"Anything unusual happen before Thursday morning?"

"No. Well . . . but that wasn't—"

"Go ahead and say, Cas," Tom said.

"Somebody got in my gear bag. I didn't notice until last night, and it wasn't a big deal. Nothing missing. Probably just one of the guys needing tape or something."

"You noticed Thursday night—when could someone have gotten into it?" I asked.

He frowned. "Wednesday night most likely. I'd left it with my ropes while I talked to somebody after my events, and when I came back, it looked like somebody'd knocked into my stuff. Didn't think anything of it, not until I saw things moved around last night."

"Any idea who might have done that?"

"No. It's just regulars around."

Tom shifted his weight. But I didn't need the hint. "That's not entirely true, is it, Cas?" I let that sink in. As red started up his neck—chagrin at being called on the fib, rather than anger—I added, "I've already talked with two cowboys from the circuit who don't usually compete here. I want to hear your side."

His eyes flashed to mine in transparent surprise. His first unguarded reaction. "Side? Nothing's happened between the circuit cowboys and us."

Sometimes a shot in the dark doesn't hit anything. "Outsiders have been around the rodeo grounds, however, right?"

"A few, I guess. Most circuit guys come later. And they're mostly not above saying hey to a local because they have their pro rodeo card and I—we don't yet."

"What did you talk to Grayson Zane about yesterday evening?"

"He wanted to get filled in, since he hadn't been here in a few years. Asking how the rodeo was run, who was in charge, things like that." The glow in his face now had nothing to do with chagrin. He basked in the memory of being asked anything by a champion.

"Like who the judges are? Chute men? Clowns?" Tom asked. I suspected it was more to fill in for me than out of curiosity.

"Sure, that. And about the committee, the front office."

"How about the stock contractor? Did he ask about him?" I resumed.

Cas shook his head. "No. He knew Landry was dead. Everybody'd heard by then."

"How about yesterday morning? Did you see Zane then?"

"No. I wasn't at the rodeo grounds in the morning." The jury was out on the truthfulness of that answer.

"What did you think of Keith Landry?"

"Can't say I knew him. Saw him a bit other years."

Not a word about the lunch. "Has there been any talk about this year's rodeo? Anything out of the ordinary?"

He shook his head.

"Have you heard rumors or stories about people involved with the rodeo that have to do with their personal lives?"

His eyes did the bad-liar flicker. On top of that, when he said, "No," he didn't shake his head, as he had with previous negatives.

Pressing or not pressing is always a split-second decision. This time my internal vote went for not pressing. If I wanted to talk to the kid later, better to play it friendly now. "How about non-rodeo people? Any issues there?"

"No problem with town folk." That was deliberately obtuse.

"What about the animal rights people protesting out front?"

"We ignore them."

That came fast and a little loud. He'd rehearsed it. But if he hadn't recognized me as last night's spotter—and I thought he'd be a lot more embarrassed now if he had—who had he rehearsed for?

"Must be hard to ignore every last one of them . . ." I held his gaze an extra beat. He tensed but didn't crumble. ". . . when they're shouting as you drive past the gates."

"Only when it spooks the horses we're trailering in."

"You don't mind animal rights activists saying rodeo hurts animals?"

The kid and Tom made eye contact. So much for Stoic Westerners. They might as well have shouted *Outsider Alert*. With a side order of disgusted *Women!*

"One of the jobs of a journalist is to ask questions the audience would ask," I said. "That's the image of rodeo for a lot of people. That you cowboys are having sport at the expense of pain to the animals. Prods and spiked straps and sharp spurs. That's what a lot of people beyond Wyoming think of when they think of rodeo."

"All against the rules," Cas said. "No prods allowed. Spurs got to be rounded, so they roll along the horse's hide, not dig in. And that's with a horse's skin seven-, eight-times tougher than ours. And flank strap's got to be padded with fleece or that rubber stuff."

"Neoprene," Tom filled in.

"Right, that stuff. So it's padded. But even if it weren't, you'd have to be some kind of fool to cinch it tight, because that would keep the horse from kicking up as much, and that's what you want because it's how you get points."

Tom nodded. The kid nodded back. They turned to me, probably to see if I was nodding. I wasn't.

"Besides, they aren't accusing us of doing those things here in Sherman," Cas said, volunteering something for the first time. "They got this loopy idea about animals roaming free. No riding horses, no keeping a dog on a leash, no having a cat inside. Most of 'em wouldn't know which end of a horse to feed, much less that they're individuals. You ever seen a bucking horse, ma'am?"

"Of course. I've been to the rodeo." Twice.

"I mean out, natural. C'mon." He struck out, with Tom right behind, neither looking at me. If I stayed put, I'd get left.

I didn't stay put, but I still lagged. Boots let them extend their head start while I slid around in the leather flats I'd worn while last night's shoes aired out. Who knew dust could be so slippery.

I joined them at a pasture fence. Two gray-muzzled horses ambled over, eyeing Tom and me with curiosity before focusing on Cas.

"This's Jammer." Cas pulled a baggy from a pocket. I was revising my view of him until I realized it held oats. He shook out a pile on a palm and extended it to the horse, which muzzled the food deftly. "He's bucked any soul who's tried to ride him."

He fed a bucking bronco by hand, and I couldn't get a dog to be in the same yard with me when he ate.

"Now, his full brother, Marble, here . . ." Cas fed the other horse. ". . . wouldn't buck if you set off a firecracker under him. Jammer came out bucking from the start. Threw one too many hands, and my grandpa wanted to sell him for dog meat."

Checking ingredients of Shadow's dog food shot up my to-do list.

"It was Dad who put Jammer in rodeo. Was in the NRF three years running," Cas said with evident pride.

Tom murmured. "National Rodeo—"

"Finals," I finished with all the confidence of someone who'd known that for nearly a whole day. "That's fine, but—"

"Wait," Cas said. "Watch this."

I followed the direction of his tilted cowboy hat in time to see Jammer kick out his heels, arch his back in a move a Halloween cat would envy, kick out again. He repeated the cycle, then trotted to us. I'm no expert on horses—or dogs, as I've proven—but I swear that animal was grinning.

"You showing off that old renegade again?" asked a sharp voice from behind us.

It was Stan Newton. He shook hands with Tom, who introduced me.

"Didn't think Cas did near good enough last night to have TV come out to talk to him. Nowhere near his potential." Not only was Newton one of *those* fathers, but he was playing games by pretending Tom hadn't called about my visit.

"That's Mike Paycik's beat." I blithely threw Mike under this bus. "I wanted to talk to Cas about information he might have concerning Keith Landry and his death, since Cas was at the rodeo grounds the evening before . . ."

I stopped because Stan had gone from fair weather to tornado in a heartbeat. He stepped toward me. I held my ground. Unnecessarily, Burrell interposed his shoulder.

I'd learned over the years that, unless he has a mob behind him, an interview subject who comes straight at you is seldom as dangerous as the ones who slither around behind you. That went for husbands, too.

"It's a good thing the sheriff's department has more sense than you do, Miss Big-Shot TV reporter. They know Cas had nothing to do with that poor excuse for a stock contractor."

"Dad. It's just questions."

"Poor excuse for a stock contractor? But you supported his bid last fall and more recently."

Stan Newton's lightning bolt gaze flickered. His expression backed down to merely stormy, and he retreated a step. Burrell returned to his previous position. "Learned things since."

"Like?"

"That's rodeo committee business, not yours." Newton wasn't done blowing hard. "I'll tell you who you should be asking questions of—those crazy animal people. I've always said they were nuts enough to cause real trouble. They ain't normal."

"Do you have any evidence that connects them to Landry's death?" I might have stressed *evidence.*

"What I've got is good sense. Those people yelling and screaming about things they know nothing about don't have a lick of sense. And they've never worked for anything. Those are the people you should be asking. That's the kind to up and throw a man into a bull pen to let him get stomped to death for no good reason. That's what I told that deputy this morning on the phone. Wanted to talk to the sheriff—*acting* sheriff since you liberal media types are driving out the real sheriff—but that Alvaro boy thought he knew better. Let me tell you, that isn't the way things were run under Sheriff Widcuff."

"No. Under Widcuff—"

Burrell's low voice talked over me. "What do you think, Cas?" And he was right. Arguing with Stan was not productive.

The boy stood tall and met his elder's eyes. "Deputy Alvaro seems all right."

"About the animal rights protestors," Tom pursued.

"They could stand to take more showers, sir." Red charged up his neck again. I wondered if he and Blue Hair had indulged in simultaneous showering. "And things'd be a lot better off if they used their mouths for something other than talking all the time."

This kid had *cajones.* If he knew I'd seen Ms. Blue Hair using her mouth for something other than talking with him—an activity that gave him ample opportunity to assess if she needed a shower—he had a major set of them. Even if he didn't know, to toss around those hot potato words under these circumstances was impressive. Or foolhardy.

"But mostly we ignore them," Cas concluded, glancing at his father. And now I knew who he'd been rehearsing for.

I looked at Stan, saw only satisfied pride. Then at Cas, straightforward, upright, and in all ways a young pillar of the community. This was getting us nowhere, and with Stan on guard duty there was no hope of getting into useful territory. I wrapped it up, leaving an opening for a return visit.

Once inside Tom's truck and starting the trek back toward the turnoff, I said, "If that Ma'am-ing and Sir-ing is what passes for rebellion in Wyoming, you folks need a course in tattoos, piercings, drug abuse, and foul mouths."

"Oh, we got those, too, but that's not always the most dangerous kind. Sometimes it's the quiet, hidden rebellion that can cause the most trouble. And heartache." Without looking at me, he added, "Go ahead, ask your questions."

"How'd you know I'd met Cas last night?"

"Linda. She'd heard some from Cas, some from Vicky Upton."

I grunted acknowledgement, then played back what I'd recorded, absently watching clouds pile up on the northern horizon—which, considering the distances out here, could mean it was raining in Canada—while I listened. When it completed, I said, "If one of those animal group people ended up dead, I'd sure want to look at Stan a lot closer."

"For an accident?"

I sidestepped. "Not sure it would have been an accident if it involved Stan and the animal rights people."

I played the recording again. The third time, I took notes. "Cas seems pretty sharp," I commented as we neared town.

"Yeah, I'd say so."

"I get the feeling he was hiding something."

"Kid that age? Sure."

I slanted a look at him, but his face gave nothing away. Did he know about Cas and Miss Blue Hair? More importantly, was there any way to find out without giving away what I knew? No.

"It's a lot simpler," he said, "if you just ask if I knew Cas was running around on Heather with one of those protestor girls."

"Why the hell didn't you say so earlier?"

"You didn't ask."

I forced myself to breathe in and out. "That is not how this works if you want to be part of what Paycik and I are doing."

"They're kids. I don't see their love lives being a factor in the rodeo's future."

"We don't know enough to eliminate *anything*. Cas Newton is running around with one of the animal rights protestors his father hates. Not to mention he appears to be treating this like a short-term hookup, and he sure wouldn't want to have Heather find out and lose his permanent good thing."

"You're pretty worked up about this. Maybe your personal history has something to do with that."

I stared at him, too stunned at his using *personal* after ignoring the personal elephant that had propped its butt between us since the night he'd kissed me at my door, to even pretend to fend off whatever it was he'd clearly decided he wanted to say.

"Your divorce. It's natural you'd see it from the point of view of the woman. Women scorned, you could say."

"Or not say," I snapped as we bumped into the KWMT lot.

"Want to talk about it?"

"You want to talk about my divorce, when you have not said word one about—about other things?"

Give him credit. He did not ask *What other things?* He did say, "Not up to me."

"The hell it's not."

His mouth twitched. The credit he'd accrued dipped. "You could have mentioned it."

"I—*I* could have!"

"Yup. Any time. If you'd wanted to."

I restrained myself, heroically under the circumstances. "Your actions, your responsibility for discussing it or not."

"I wasn't acting alone for long, as I recall."

I gathered myself and my dignity. "I'm working, and I'm going inside now."

"I'll walk you in."

Short of shooting him, I couldn't think of how to stop him.

Chapter Thirteen

INSIDE KWMT, it was a case of good news-bad news, which seemed appropriate.

The good news was Mike was back and nearly done with his regular work for the day.

The bad news was he said to Burrell, "Why don't you come with us to Elizabeth's place tonight. We'll pick up pizza and talk about where we are with this." That was bad news on multiple levels, including that I hadn't invited Paycik, and here he was inviting someone else.

Burrell said, "Not tonight. I'm picking up Tamantha from camp and only have a couple days before she heads to my sister's."

"Busy social life for a second-grader," Mike said.

"Third-grader," he corrected, leaving no doubt he was echoing his daughter.

Tamantha was the light of his life. And one scary short person. When it came to determination, she could make a Navy Seal look wishy-washy.

Burrell left, and Mike got back to work, while the good news-bad news trend continued on the "Helping Out" front.

The good news was the Cheyenne contact had called, leaving a detailed message at my work number after, he said, receiving a not-in-service message on my cell. More and more of Wyoming had coverage, but leaving both numbers was easy insurance.

The bad news was the details he left included that his station didn't have any footage similar to what I was looking for.

Good news—he thought Denver had run something, and he left

the name and number of a likely contact—bless him.

The Denver contact said, yes, they'd run footage of a house stripped of its contents by thieves. He'd check with his boss and see about our using it.

The whole conversation took about five minutes. And that included my tacking on that I'd be interested if he heard anything about a rodeo contractor named Keith Landry who'd been at a rodeo somewhere near Denver the weekend before. With that lack of specifics—did I have any idea how many towns around Denver held rodeos?—he was understandably pessimistic, but said he'd let me know if he got anything.

If the video came through from Denver, I'd need to supplement it with something local. There was no Better Business Bureau in Sherman, and I doubted Les Haeburn would approve a trip to Cheyenne to interview the state rep there. Maybe someone from the sheriff's department. But who?

That was the only reason I called Mike's Aunt Gee. Absolutely the only reason.

She gave me a name of an officer who would talk about how to prevent being victimized. She also gave me the name of two more Cottonwood County bigwigs who apparently completed the list of the absent. She had learned from an unspecified source that a.) not even spouses knew a location, b.) everyone had left Wednesday morning by personal vehicle, and c.) the exodus had been in the works for a week before that.

I took note of all this, thanked her, then dropped in an oh-so-casual question about what she knew of a Sonja.

"Sonja? Which Sonja?"

Damn, I'd banked on there being only one Sonja in Cottonwood County. "I don't know. Apparently she was involved with Keith Landry when he came through Sherman with the rodeo year before last."

"Oh," she said with significance. "Sonja Osterspeigel. She was rodeo queen two years ago. Not, perhaps, the committee's most inspired selection. I do recall her having a whirlwind romance with a competitor. Soon after, she began an association with that Keith Landry. Disgraceful. He was old enough to be her father. And he dropped her flat. She made quite a scene at the Kicking Cowboy. He left town the next day."

And then she had to go and move to Seattle, taking her whole family of potential suspects with her.

Sonja Osterspeigel further stymied me when Aunt Gee denied any knowledge of a phone number or address for the decamped Oster-speigels. They had been short-timers in Cottonwood County, having arrived only five years before her stint as rodeo queen.

I Googled Sonja as soon as we hung up. I found a couple items about her royal status, but no one by that last name was listed in Seattle or environs. Sonja was getting on my nerves.

✧ ✧ ✧ ✧

"**TELL ME ABOUT** the trip out to the Newtons' place. Anything interesting?" Mike asked that evening.

"Not a lot, but you can hear for yourself."

I played the tape while we ate. Yes, it was pizza. Yes, it was in the dismal living room of the hovel.

Mike abruptly interrupted his considerable consumption of pizza to say, "He sidestepped there. About knowing Landry. Didn't outright lie, but sidestepped."

"A definite sidestep," I agreed. "Good catch."

He grinned. "I've done it often enough on the other side of the mic. And he lied about there being no talk about personal lives. I thought you were leading up to asking about that girl."

"Blue Hair? No."

"Why not?"

"He would have lied with his father there. Besides, I didn't want to ask in front of Burrell."

I watched as I told him about Jenny-now-Jennifer's findings. I saw the bulldog in his eyes even before he said, "Tom might not have been given all the names. Or he could have forgotten those."

As a kid, Mike had developed a case of hero worship for high school basketball hero Thomas David Burrell, and it didn't seem to be out of his system. "Convenient coincidence."

"Could have happened," he insisted. But he turned the conversation. "Now, all these people out of town at the same time. That's not a coincidence."

I'd filled him in earlier on what Aunt Gee had said about the bigwigs and Sonja. He had no knowledge of the Osterspeigels, since he'd been away playing pro football when the family lived here.

"Also not a coincidence I believe in," I agreed, with an added slice of meaning that he ignored.

"Where do you think the bigwigs went?"

"Somewhere underground? Like one of those bunkers for government officials. That would explain no cell coverage."

"Don't have to be underground for that. Lots of places in the mountains don't get reception. But what do you think they're doing? All of them together, out of town at the same time."

"Back to the alien mothership to renew their human forms?"

He eyed me. "You're more interested in Landry, aren't you? I had a feeling this morning you were considering walking away from the entire Landry story, but not now. What was going on?"

"It's not our story," I sidestepped. Since I wasn't thinking about my career, past and present, I sure wasn't talking about it.

"Not the official one, maybe, but the one we're finding—that *is* our story."

Instead of answering directly, I said, "Let's go to the rodeo. More precisely, let's go almost to the rodeo."

"What does that mean?"

✧   ✧   ✧   ✧

IT MEANT PARKING along the highway outside the rodeo grounds gates, a hundred yards shy of the protestors' camp.

It's best not to approach groups like this directly. No plowing into the center and firing questions. I slowed Mike with a gesture that we should prop ourselves on wooden sawhorses that would be in their peripheral vision as they shook their signs at cars. It's also best not to interrupt such groups while plying their trade.

I told Mike this as we deciphered their signs, watched interactions with spectators, and observed the group's dynamics.

The guy who was in his early forties—or had lived even rougher than I'd factored in my estimation of his age—was the would-be leader. Would-be, because he acted like he was the leader, while few of the others acted as if he or anyone else were the leader.

Certainly Ms. Blue Hair didn't accord him leader status. She kept herself apart and kept most of the group between her and Would-be Leader. He tried to circle closer. Moves not lost on a tired-looking woman in her thirties whose sign-waving was perfunctory.

A half-dozen others appeared to be college-age kids doing their best to meld James Dean dissatisfaction, later-day-hippiedom, and a dash of Greenpeace. A gray-haired couple who smiled gently at the cars going past, asking the occupants to reconsider what they were doing, appeared to me to be the most effective.

With the entering cars slowed to a trickle, I purposely headed toward the college-age kids.

"Hi, I'm E.M. Danniher from the local TV station. We're considering a story on the protests, and we'd like background. What's your name?" I asked a redhead nearly a foot taller than me.

"My name? Jonathan—"

"Wait a minute, Jon," ordered a wiry brunette with a sharp chin. "What kind of story?"

"A piece for the evening news."

"Cool," came from one of the others.

Without removing my attention from the wiry girl, I was aware of Would-be Leader moving our way.

"Would it be on the Internet?" she demanded.

Which way to jump? Which answer would get me what I wanted? "Probably," I hedged.

"Cool," again came from someone.

"No," the wiry girl said decisively. "We know what we're doing is right, but it can be edited, taken out of context, and in this part of the country . . . no. If it goes on the Internet, it's there forever." She looked at Jonathan. "First, you get into law school."

"What's going on," came the rough voice of Would-be Leader, pushing to the front as the college kids melted away like ice at the Equator. Beside me, I felt Mike's higher level of alertness.

I repeated my spiel about TV coverage. Would-be Leader immediately switched to Major Suck-Up. Mike relaxed.

"Roy Craniston." He stuck out his hand.

I hoped the griminess was only from carrying signs. Oh, well, I've touched worse. I met his hand without hesitation.

"E.M. Danniher. And what's your name?" I asked Ms. Blue Hair, tossing a pleasant smile toward where she stood a yard away.

"None of your damned business."

"Is that n-u-n?" I asked sweetly.

That drew a sarcastic laugh from the woman in her thirties.

Roy snapped, "Shut up, Ellie."

She did better than that: She stalked off to a nearby camper, slamming its door.

Mike gave me half an eye roll and deftly caught up with Ms. Blue Hair, who'd headed in the opposite direction from the camper.

That left me with the gray-haired couple and Roy.

"It's about time the corrupt media began to pay attention to my work," he started.

Great way to sell me a story. But I nodded thoughtfully, listened for any place where what he said might overlap with what I was interested in, and kept the corner of my eye on the direction Ms. Blue Hair and Mike had taken.

Roy Craniston had shown no signs of running out of breath when I caught movement from that corner of my eye. Time to take control of this.

"Do you protest only rodeos?"

"Not at all. I believe that the panoply of society's ills—"

"You came into town when?" I interrupted.

"Yesterday," he said. The gray-haired couple had to be faster off the mark if they wanted to answer any questions. "As a symbol of Americana, this event called out to me to provide a conscience for those without one of their own. I have led protests in—"

"So far ahead of the Fourth of July Rodeo?"

His gaze flickered. Annoyance at not being allowed to list his achievements or something else? "I fel—"

"All of you came yesterday?"

"Yes. I set the agenda, the others follow."

Before he went on, I pointed in the direction Ms. Blue Hair had gone. "I saw her around before yesterday."

"Her? Yeah, I guess. She's just a little local. She's here all the time. I let her join us when we come in for big events."

"Oh, not local, dear," corrected the gray-haired lady. Roy scowled, which she appeared to take as interest in what she had to say. "You're thinking that because she knows where everything is, but she's from Oklahoma. From what I gather, she roughly follows the rodeo circuit. Not every event, but always rodeo. Since Sherman has this nightly rodeo, she has been here a number of times and knows it well."

"Do you know her name?" I asked.

"No, dear. She says names are stifling. We call her Pinky."

"Pinky?"

"Her hair was pink when we met. I do think the blue is more becoming."

I bestowed a huge smile on the woman. "Isn't that interesting," I said, as Mike—alone now—headed toward us. I turned to Roy with flattering attention. "It must be difficult when officials try to intimidate you into leaving. I understand you've had run-ins—"

"That blowhard who owns the rodeo grounds tried telling us we couldn't protest here, but I'd researched our legal rights—" The gray-haired man made a sound that called into question Roy's description of who'd done that work. "—and he had to back down. Another guy came around pretending to be interested, but he was only after some tail. I ran him off to protect my women."

I concentrated on widening my eyes and not letting my lip curl. "You did? What happened? Maybe Ellie can tell me . . ."

"No need to talk to Ellie. Didn't involve her. An old man going for a girl like—But I told him how things were and to get lost."

"I think I heard about that. There was a lot of shouting?"

He puffed up. "Yeah, shouting. That's all he was good for. When it got physical, he took off."

Mike arrived, and I dropped the wide eyes. "But that happened Wednesday, Roy, so you couldn't have arrived here yesterday. Which means you were here when the man you argued with died."

Roy grumbled his next words under his breath, but I have good hearing. What he said was, "Fucking little bitch."

Me? Or Ms. Blue Hair?

✧　✧　✧　✧

"NO NAME, BUT a partial thaw," Mike reported once we were in his SUV. "Which puts me ahead of you from the expression on Roy's face."

"I win friends and influence people wherever I go." I filled him in on the shreds I'd picked up. "So, what did you get?"

"Cautious yet cordial relations have been established. Cas was right about what she wants—all animals totally free. No leashes, fences, or other interaction with humans."

I considered him for a moment. "How did it end?"

"She said, and I quote, 'You're not as a much of a dickhead as you look.' She gave a slight wave, and the middle finger was *not* raised."

"Call the Nobel Peace Prize committee."

Chapter Fourteen

WE WENT INTO the rodeo grounds by a side gate Mike knew about. Since we weren't in a KWMT vehicle, the gatekeeper demanded IDs when Mike told him we were media.

He looked at mine without interest, but did a double-take at Mike's. "Paycik? Mike Paycik? I remember you as a kid. You were *tough*, man!"

I started to tune out, because how many times can you listen to people telling your coworker how wonderful he is? But he caught my attention by extolling Mike's skill at rodeoing, rather than playing football. Mike finally drove on, hunting for a parking space.

"You rodeoed, huh?" That vision of Mike in the butt-and-front framing gear of rodeo competitors rose up before my eyes again.

"Yeah."

"Which events?" I asked, partly to try to fight off the vision.

"All to start. Roping events later." He started to back into a spot, keeping his head turned from me.

"Grew out of it, huh?"

"No. I gave up rodeo to keep my football coach from having a stroke."

"You played in the NFL. You must like football better."

"It's not better than rodeo. It's different."

I put on the mental brakes. I'd hit a button. When you do that, it's best to figure out what the button's attached to before you mash down on it more. "Why's rodeo important to you?"

"It's ours," he said. "It didn't come from anywhere else and get imported here. We didn't adopt somebody else's sport and try to catch up. We started it, and we're the best at it, and we know it."

"We being Americans?"

"We being Westerners."

I snorted as we exited opposite sides of the SUV, punctuating my next statement with the door's closing thud. "Regionalist snob."

"Like the South and New England and the Coasts aren't?"

"Fair point. So that's it? Pride of ownership?"

He shook his head as we met behind the vehicle and started toward the arena. "It says a lot about the people who live out here—no, don't start spouting those lines from the anti-rodeo nuts. I've heard enough of that already tonight."

The booming announcer's voice indicated events were in full swing, and we were practically alone in a field of pickups.

"Touchy."

"No, fed up. They call themselves animal rights backers. Wonder how many of them have stayed up all night with a sick horse, or been out in a blizzard helping a calf get born, or chased down a cow that didn't want the medicine it needed to stay alive, or held a loyal old dog when he just couldn't stay with you any longer no matter how much he wanted to."

There was no doubting his sincerity. "Point taken, Mike."

He cleared his throat. "Anyway, there's another angle of why rodeo's important." He waited. I wasn't sure if it was to regain the rest of his composure or to yank my chain.

I responded only to the yank. "What is that angle, Oh Wise Western Sage?"

He grinned. "Sage—that's pretty good. Have you ever noticed that we say we play football, play baseball, play basketball, or tennis or golf or shuffleboard? But with rodeo that *is* the verb."

"Okay. What does that mean?"

"It's the same with running or swimming. They didn't start as sports, they started as work or transportation or survival. Rodeo started with on-the-job competitions. All the events were skills needed on a ranch or on the range."

I would accept that for timed events. And maybe in the old days for bronc riding. As for bull riding . . . It takes courage. And skill. And, yes, there's the thrill of danger. There's also the question of why? It's not like the bull will learn better manners.

But I didn't have the heart to point that out to Mike. Instead, I thought about Heather and said, "Even for the rodeo queen, right?"

"Exactly. Like Needham said, they have to show skills. Barrel racing, too. It's the ability to weave a horse around obstacles at speed."

"You've really thought about this, haven't you?"

"You think the only thing in this pretty head is how to block for an outside slant or recognize a blitz?"

"No, I think it also holds market rankings and sports anchor openings."

"True, but there's still room for philosophy and sociology and all the other —ologies. Besides, I did a paper on it in college."

"Oh-ho—a jock course?"

"Was not. Senior level sociology. And I got an A. Minus, but still an A."

"Well, excuse me, Mr. Academic—" I stopped myself and put a hand on Mike's arm to stop him, too.

"Mo-om." It was the teenager's exasperated, long-suffering, whined moan. It came from the next row over of vehicles. I saw no one, but recognized the voice.

"Heather," I said in a low voice.

"Put it on," commanded Vicky Upton.

"But I wore this last night. I'll wear the red—"

"You will not. You know we're saving that for the Fourth of July. So put this one on."

"Out here?"

"There's nobody around." Vicky clicked her tongue. "Well, you really, truly tore this. Took a chunk right out. We'll have to hope I have material left and can make a repair that won't be noticed."

"It's my favorite."

"That's because you look your best in that pink. Though the red will be perfect for the Fourth. What . . . take your hat off before you try to put this shirt on. You can't go over your head with . . ."

Mike and I looked at each other and quietly walked on, waiting until we'd reached the main path behind the grandstand, blending in with others passing by, before we both started chuckling.

"Can you imagine trying to pull anything over that hat?" I asked.

"I know. The tiara alone—"

This time I wasn't the one who interrupted him. It was a male voice shouting, "You idiot! You moron! Can't you count?"

Behind the concession stand counter under the grandstand, Stan Newton, red-faced with anger, had Evan Watt backed up against a pole. Two other workers pretended to be deaf and blind.

"Sorry, Newt. There were all these people. It happened fast—"

"It's coming out of your wages. If you ever manage to earn any. And quit your damned spitting back here. People lose their appetite when they see you spitting." Newt slapped his hand on the counter hard enough to make the napkin dispensers jump, not to mention Evan and the other two workers. He spun around and disappeared from view.

Watt saw us, tried a smile, gave up on it, and turned away to move something on the back counter with a clatter.

Mike and I had nearly reached the stairs to the grandstand when Newton emerged from a door under them, stopping just short of running into us. Coming face to face, it was only polite to say hello, so Mike and I did.

Newton, his face still red, said, "That sorry-assed piece of shit. I knew I shouldn't have given him a job. If he worked for Landry all the time like he said, why didn't Street hire him on?"

"Hope it's nothing serious . . ." Mike dangled artfully.

"It's serious, all right. Give that broken-down never-was idiot a chance to earn a stake, so he'll leave me short in concessions on the busiest weekend of the year, and what does he do but hand some wahoo forty extra bucks in change."

"How do you—?"

"I saw it. Saw it with my own eyes! I'd be better off having those morons outside the gate in here. At least I know they're trying to ruin me."

"Forty bucks—"

"Oh, it might not be much to you, Mr. Big Shot NFL player, or to some TV reporter from New York, but forty bucks is forty bucks. I've worked hard for every damn penny, and nobody's screwing me."

"Your son said—"

"My son says a lot of things. Thinks he's smarter than his old man and runs his mouth. I never had the advantages *Caswell* has had. I had to claw for everything. Work damned hard, and I'm not about to see a bunch of weirdos with signs, or half-witted rodeo bums, take any part of it away from me."

I wondered if he considered marrying Inez part of that clawing.

"And they're not taking anything away from my boy, either," he added with a sudden shift. "None of them."

What would he think of his boy canoodling with one of those weirdos? If he got this hot with a near-stranger over a forty-dollar mistake, how would he view his son's betrayal?

Before I could follow up, he said abruptly, "I heard someone say Grayson Zane got to town Thursday morning after Landry was dead. But that's not right. I happen to know that rig of his got to the rodeo grounds right around midnight."

"Oh? How do you know?" Mike asked mildly.

"Had a drink with a business associate at the Kicking Cowboy. Saw that rig of Zane's. Figured . . . It brought the rodeo grounds to mind is all, so I drove by, to see things were right. Followed them in. Zane, then the clunker that idiot Watt drives. Saw 'em set up, made a circuit, everything was quiet, and I took off," he said.

"Did you see Landry?" My voice appeared to snap Newton back to awareness.

"No. And I don't have time to stand here talking about this crap. I've got work to do." He strode off.

As we started up the steps, Mike said, "Not sure how clear you are on Cottonwood County's geography?"

"Kicking Cowboy's on the south end of Sherman. He drove from there to the west outskirts of town to come here to the rodeo grounds, before going back south and east to his place."

"Right. The other weird thing? There's no highway near the K.C. Nowhere Zane would be driving coming into town. Either Zane went out of his way or Newton—"

"Lied."

"Even without that, why would Newt follow Zane's truck onto the rodeo grounds and stick around while he set up?" Mike asked.

And be so focused on Zane that he didn't notice he'd put Watt in town several hours before Landry's death, too.

I glanced toward the concession stand. Or *had* he known he was doing that?

DAY THREE

SATURDAY

Chapter Fifteen

"**WHAT?**" **AT LEAST** that's what I tried to say when I answered the phone at an obscene hour Saturday morning.

"Danny, I have news."

"Dex? *Dex?* Do you know what time it is?"

"Eight-oh-six a.m."

I blinked at the alarm clock that wouldn't have gone off at all, since it was Saturday morning. *Saturday.* "That's six-oh-six here."

"Of course it is. You're in the Mountain Time Zone," he noted, clearly not getting the point.

"I was asleep, Dex. I'd like to still be asleep."

"Do you know what they say about those who can sleep when they're being questioned about a crime?"

"It's the sleep of the innocent?"

"Opposite. The sleep of the guilty."

"Guilty of killing people who woke them up?"

"It's not limited to a specific motive." He was serious.

I yawned and shoved another pillow under my head. "How do you figure it's the sleep of the guilty?"

"It's the experts—forensic psychologists—figuring, not me. For the innocent, being questioned is the high tide of anxiety and adrenaline. For the guilty, high tide was committing the crime. By the time they're being questioned, the tide's going out. They put their heads down and fall asleep."

"Lucky them. Phones must not ring in the middle of the night where they are."

I never knew if Dex didn't get the points aimed at him, or understood them but didn't consider them worthy of consideration. "You know, time's a funny thing."

"It frequently gets me chuckling," I muttered, expecting no reaction to that, either, and thus avoided disappointment.

"A crime's committed when it's committed for a reason. It's never truly random. Even what are referred to as random murders, there's a reason the act happened then. Most often it has to do with the murderer's pathology. The compulsion to kill has been building and building, and this is the moment it reaches critical mass. Other stranger-on-stranger murders can be because the victim was in the wrong place at the wrong time, perhaps a witness to something."

"Stranger-on-stranger doesn't seem likely here. Assuming this *is* a murder."

"Ah. That's even less likely to be random. Why it happened then and not another time will involve the old standbys—means, motive, and opportunity."

"So, working backward from the when might provide insight into the other elements? And possibly the killer?"

"Unlikely, but possible."

I huffed out exasperation. "Well, if it's unlikely, why bring it up?"

"It's another element you need to keep in mind. It's another piece that has to fit a solution."

"Thanks for that, Dex. But now that I know the guilty can sleep, and they commit their crimes when they commit them for a reason, I think I'll see if I can't get more sleep myself."

"Hey, I thought you'd want to know this." He sounded hurt. As only a squirrel-feeding FBI scientist can sound hurt.

"Know what?"

"There were ligature marks around your victim's neck."

For a moment, all I could do was stare at the mottled wall opposite my bed. "Ligature marks?" I managed at last. "Dex, in journalism that's called burying the lead. You couldn't have told me that right at the start?"

"I'm telling you now. There were ligature marks around his neck."

I sat up, swinging my feet out of bed. "He was choked?"

"Not by hands. Ligature means it was produced by something strung around the neck."

"What?"

"I said ligature means—"

"No, I was asking what was put around his neck to create the ligature marks?"

"That has not been determined absolutely."

"Not absolutely," I repeated. "But they have an idea?"

"Perhaps."

"And this idea, they might have shared it with you?"

"Yes."

"And you could share it with me."

"Oh, no. Not until the evidence makes it much clearer than it is now."

"Dex . . ." But he wouldn't change his mind on that. "So it's murder."

"That is not determined."

"C'mon, Dex. Ligature marks? You think he committed suicide?"

"That is not determined," he repeated.

He would not add more. Vintage Dex. Woke me up at six on a Saturday morning to tell me that while the apparent means of death was a bunch of bulls, the bulls were actually red herrings.

❖   ❖   ❖   ❖

MIKE AND I HAD agreed to meet at the station at eleven before heading for the rodeo grounds to poke around more. With my second straight earlier-than-I'd-intended awakening, I got there early.

I checked in with the senior citizen who served as security two nights a week and all day Saturday and went right to the KWMT library that would have made Edward Murrow feel right at home. I locked the door from inside, so nobody could get in without my letting them in. That precaution was the result of a lesson learned.

After nearly two hours with the clips and my Thermos of coffee, I emerged to find a spattering of weekend staffers around the newsroom. Mike and Jennifer sat huddled at her computer. I headed their way.

"What are you two doing?"

"Plotting out where Keith Landry's rodeo has been since the season started. I figured it was a better use of Jen . . . uh, Jennifer's skills than to start on the bankruptcy of some contractor who never came here," Mike said. Clearly he, too, had received the now-Jennifer edict. "The fact that Landry was killed here, probably means something different happened or came to a head. But to know what's different, first I have to know what was normal."

Although Jennifer wouldn't pick it up, his expression and a faint emphasis on the word *killed* telegraphed to me his belief that Landry hadn't died accidentally. Wait until he heard what Dex had said.

"Not bad—both of you. Not bad at all."

"But?" Mike asked. "I heard a *but* in your voice."

"Won't the sheriff's department have better resources for this."

Jennifer answered. "Nah. I did some work for them last winter. For Mike's Aunt Gee, actually. A hack of the program they bought to make their call center work better. The sheriff's department doesn't have anywhere near as good a setup as I've got."

"KWMT has a better system than the sheriff's department?"

She scoffed with a sound that consisted mostly of the letter P and a lot of air. "Not the station's. I'm hooked into my own setup."

I met Mike's eyes, then coughed. "Maybe you both could win points with the sheriff's office by sharing the info when you get it."

✧　✧　✧　✧

MIKE WAS SO full of theories about why the big shots had disappeared—none involved body-snatching aliens—that all I had time to tell him of this morning's call from my "federal law enforcement source" was about the sleep of the guilty before we reached the rodeo grounds.

Apparently, Mike had viewed Diana getting there before us Thursday as a challenge. His attempt to set land speed records tossed me from one extreme of the seat-belt's limits to the other.

We skidded to a stop. I was waiting for the dust kicked up by the vehicle to subside enough to get out without asphyxiation when I spotted Linda Caswell approaching the office from the direction of the arena.

"How about introducing us?" I asked Mike.

"Sure thing."

We intercepted her five yards from the rodeo office steps. She had a firm handshake, a pleasant voice, and worried eyes.

"I'm trying to get background and hoped to ask a few questions." Taking for granted that she'd agree, I added, "I read that you're also on the rodeo queen committee. It wasn't clear—are you also chair of that?"

She smiled. A lovely smile, with a dose of mischief in it. "Not at all. The permanent chair of that committee is Mrs. Parens."

I felt my eyebrows shoot toward my hairline. "Mrs. Parens?" Mrs. Parens was Aunt Gee's neighbor in O'Hara Hill and a retired teacher. Which told as little about her as saying Michael Jordan was a retired basketball player.

"Oh, yes. Didn't you know?" Linda Caswell's mischief graduated to deviltry. "Mrs. Parens established the scholarship. She was one of our early rodeo queens."

I shelved that to consider later. The rodeo queen committee had been an opener to pave the way for real questions. But before I could ask, she said, "I understand you talked with my nephew earlier. We're very proud of Cas." Her smile warmed, and I felt the tug of its charm in that otherwise plain face. "I consider him one of the good guys in training."

"Yes, we met." Would Heather agree with that good-guy-in-training designation if she knew about Ms. Blue Hair? "About this rodeo, I read you voted against Keith Landry when the committee first awarded the contract?"

"I did."

"Why?"

"His production—" She gave the word an edge of distaste. "—had become more theatrical and less traditional over the years. More flash, less substance. I felt, along with the committee's majority, that we should return to tradition with the annual rodeo."

"In the end, though, you must have been grateful when he rescued the rodeo after your chosen stock contractor went bankrupt."

"It was a choice between Landry's company and no rodeo."

"Yet your phone number was on Landry's cell phone," I said.

No smile now. "There was business to conduct. For the good of the Fourth of July Rodeo."

"Putting aside personal feelings—" I thought something flickered in her eyes at that. "—I understand you have a rodeo livestock business, Ms. Caswell."

She smiled. "A very small operation, Ms. Danniher. Nothing to rival Landry's. Though when the original contractor fell through, if I could have supplied the livestock for Sherman, I certainly would have. My grandfather started the Sherman rodeo."

"Why couldn't you?"

"Cottonwood Drive is a small operation, primarily to keep a tradition alive. I was surprised Landry could step in, even with so many more head."

A voice called her name from the rodeo office door. I looked around and saw Stan Newton. He raised a hand. Possibly in greeting, though quickly seguing to pointing to his watch.

"You'll have to excuse me, the committee's meeting. There's a lot to decide in light of . . . this horrible accident."

Mike and I said the right things. We watched her walk into the rodeo office, with Newton closing the door firmly behind them.

"Pick up anything?" he said.

"You mean that she didn't want Landry to be contractor, even after that new company left them hanging? But why was she so against it?"

He gave me a slanted smile. "I think it's time you have another History of Cottonwood County lesson with Mrs. Parens."

"I'm sure I will benefit greatly from such a lesson."

"Teacher's pet." He shifted tone. "You were a little cold about Cas."

"One of the good guys in training? She and Vicky Upton are selling what a good kid he is awfully hard." I looked around. "I have something more to fill you in on. Is there someplace to sit where we won't be overheard?"

"Sure."

He led me to a fence with a good view of the office, parking lot, and pens behind the arena. In one smooth move, he sat atop it, his boot heels hooked over a lower rail. "C'mon, you gotta learn the fine art of fence-sitting to get the most out of living in Wyoming."

"No fence-sitters among the people I've met here," I said.

"*Ta-dum-dum.* Good one. Now get your, ahem, self up here. It's not hard."

The climb wasn't difficult. But he was wrong about it not being hard. That rail was definitely hard. At least with the sky temporarily overcast, it wasn't a hot seat.

First, I told him he was sworn to secrecy.

"With Tom helping—"

"No. What I know changes things. If you don't agree to keep it to just us, I won't tell you." He was troubled, but agreed. Without revealing my source's identity, I told him what Dex had said.

Mike whistled. "How reliable—?"

"My source is 100 percent. His source? I'd say ninety-eight percent. My source wouldn't have told me if he didn't trust the information."

"And nobody knows except us?"

"Alvaro might. Through official channels, or through his sister. This explains why there was less blood than Richard would have expected. Landry was dead before the bulls started, so his blood wasn't pumping."

"So it's a murder. And not death by bull."

"Yet the body ended up in that pen with the bulls. So, a crime of opportunity? Or a body dump of opportunity? Was he killed in the pen? Or killed elsewhere then brought there?"

"That would be risky, wouldn't it?"

"Any riskier than killing him there?"

"Not many people around overnight. When the circuit cowboys start coming in, there'll be trailers and trucks and such here each night, but it was barebones that night."

I *huh*'d. "Except Grayson Zane and Evan Watt," I said.

"If we believe Newton."

"Right." I considered another aspect. "Was the damage the bulls did a lucky break? Or would someone who knew bulls, which appears to be everyone in Cottonwood County—"

"Except you."

"—except me, know they'd be displeased about having a body dumped in their midst and expect a fair amount of, uh, disruption to the evidence?"

"Expect, maybe. Sure couldn't count on it."

We sat for a moment. Mike in apparent thought. Me in contemplation that if fences were meant to be sat on, they would come with cushions.

I broke the silence. "You're awfully quiet."

"Thinking about how this murder happened with the community leaders out of town. Is that an angle of investigation? Where they are, and what they're doing?"

The network has a storied annual retreat for top execs. My ex had angled to be invited from his first job. Once he started going, he'd returned saying the decisions were super exciting, would change the industry forever, and would blow me off my feet, though he couldn't divulge any top secret details. I didn't want details. By that time, I'd been around enough to see that whatever *super-exciting, change-the-industry-forever, blow-me-off-my-feet* concept the brain trust conceived at these bashes were illusions.

I compressed that hard-won wisdom into a question to Mike. "Do we truly care where they are and what they're doing?"

"It's like your friend said. The timing was significant for the murderer. It's part of the planning, or the trigger. Otherwise, the murderer just happened to pick this time with all the big shots gone? Too lucky to be believable."

"I don't know that it's lucky for the murderer. If the bigwigs had been here, Richard wouldn't be in charge. And would any of the people who might have been put in charge have noticed something *not quite right?*"

"Probably not." He rallied. "But the murderer couldn't have known Richard's smart. That's another point—do we tell Richard what your source said?"

"No way. It would only distract him. Not to mention possibly putting my source in an awkward position. Richard's getting info from the official source, and we're not impeding his investigation." After another silence, I asked, "What are you thinking, Mike?"

"Thinking that no matter what, it would be a good idea to track down those bigwigs."

I huffed.

"You don't agree?"

"I don't *dis*agree. I just can't find it in me to go looking for Haeburn. But go ahead. Besides, you have connections, I don't."

His connections came in handy sixty seconds later, when Grayson Zane walked past.

Mike called to him. Zane smiled, started toward us, slowed when he recognized me, but kept coming. I used his approach as an excuse to descend from the fence.

Mike hopped down—showoff—and extended a hand to Zane. "Haven't had a chance to say hello, Grayson. Good to see you."

"Hey, Mike. Heard you'd come back to Sherman."

"Yeah, doing sports for KWMT. We'll have to set up a piece. You know my colleague from the news side, E.M. Danniher? Elizabeth, this is Grayson Zane."

We shook hands. "Apparently I'm the only one in the state who didn't know your championship status, Mr. Zane."

"Grayson, ma'am. And that's no problem. Truly, no problem." A twitch of his mouth seemed directed at himself rather than me. "I consider it even trade for you not asking about my name."

"I was holding off until now," I said. "I still get points, right?"

"Fair enough. My father kept wanting to name a baby of his Gray, to have a Gray Zane, for the writer Zane Grey, you know?"

"Yes, I know." I suppose I deserved his doubt I'd know of the famous western writer of an earlier age, considering I'd proved myself ignorant of current rodeo stars.

"Mama kept saying, no. Dad kept saying, the next one will be Gray. I'm the ninth, and after I was born, Mama said I was the last. Dad said okay, as long as my name was Gray. Mama got it to Grayson, but couldn't budge him more." He had a good grin.

I smiled back. "The name's well suited to rodeo."

He lifted his shoulders. "The bulls don't care what your name is when they try to stomp the stuffing out—" He cut it off in apparent memory that bulls succeeded in stomping the stuffing out of a man recently.

I nodded, acknowledging the shift to serious. "How did you get along with Keith Landry?"

"Fine." He was either a damned good liar or telling the truth. "In fact, I owed him. After my rookie season—"

I flaunted my homework: "All-around rookie of the year."

"After that season, I had a couple bad years—injuries, rig broke down, bad luck. Folks thought the good rookie year was the fluke, and the no-win years were the real deal. Would've been easy to slide right off the circuit for good."

Quite forthcoming for a man who'd evaded me, then given minimal answers Thursday. Why the change? Because he'd decided what to say? Because accidental death seemed the accepted view?

"But Landry got me invites," Zane said. "Opened doors I was fortunate enough to walk on through. I got back on the upswing."

"That sounds very generous of him."

"Contractors and cowboys got what you call a symbiotic relationship."

Knowing how to pronounce symbiotic and use it in a sentence did not cross him off a list of potential murderers. "Meaning?"

"Meaning we need them, and they need us to make the show go," he explained. Score one for the cowboy. He not only knew the meaning, he'd wrong-footed me. "The animals are like the third leg of a three-legged stool. The whole thing falls over without them."

"Yet the protestors—"

"Them! Listen, Ms. Danniher, just because we wear cowboy hats doesn't make us stupid. And we'd have to be stupid to abuse the animals that provide our livelihood." I groaned. He ignored it. "If these animals aren't fit and treated right, we don't get the ride that gives us the points that put the dollars in our pockets."

"Please, I've already heard that refrain enough to hum along."

"You saying I'm preaching to the choir?"

"I haven't formed a judgment, except to know I've heard the line frequently enough to not want to hear it again."

"Fair enough. Got to get along now. See you later, Mike."

His grin carried a self-deprecating twist, which gained him far more points than his argument had. He tipped his hat, turned and started away, displaying a rear view made for jeans ads.

"Zane . . . Grayson!"

He stopped, turned. I waited. He didn't budge. Ignoring Mike's curiosity bubbling beside me, I closed the gap. Mike kept pace.

"You hadn't been to this rodeo for several years. Why not?"

"Just the way the schedule fell those years."

"But you used to come to Sherman every year."

"Most years." He was cautious, not on edge.

"Did you have an emotional attachment to the area?"

He dismissed that. "Nice enough place. Like a dozen or more I see most years."

"Other emotional attachments? Say dating someone?"

For less than the intake of a breath, his body and face stilled. Then he relaxed it out of existence. "Nope."

"Never dated anyone from here?"

"Now, Ms. Danniher . . ." The drawl was back. ". . . if I considered every girl I dated in every town an attachment, I'd be attached all over this country."

"I'm not interested in every town, only here. Have you dated any-one in Sherman?"

He was shaking his head before I finished. "Can't say as I recall. Sorry, ma'am."

He started to tip his hat. I cut in. "When did you arrive here?"

"Thursday morning."

He had that right on a technicality. Even Newton said his arrival was about midnight. "What time?"

"Can't rightly say. Got here when I got here."

"Did you see Keith Landry when you got here?"

"No, ma'am." With his calm apparently unruffled, he tipped his hat and departed once more.

Mike and I stayed put until he disappeared around a truck. This time I don't think either of us was considering Grayson Zane's jeans-wearing assets.

"You saw that?" I asked Mike for confirmation.

"Yeah. But I don't get it. Why would the question of dating around here put him on edge?"

"And make him not want us to know it put him on edge. Both very interesting questions."

Chapter Sixteen

SHERIFF'S DEPARTMENT vehicles began rolling in before Mike and I had a chance to return to the torture seat on the fence.

"Ligatures?" Mike asked.

I understood his shorthand. Did I think Richard Alvaro was having another go at the scene, now that he knew it was a crime scene? Or as Dex would say, now that Richard knew it was a scene consistent with a possible crime having been committed. "Yes."

"Shall we go see?"

"Better not." Barely were the words out of my mouth than Alvaro peeled away from assigning deputies to specific areas of the pen and strode toward us.

"What are you two doing here?" he demanded.

"Hey, Richard. We're waiting on the rodeo committee meeting," Mike said with great presence of mind. "To find out if they've decided about going ahead or not."

I focused on keeping my face a pleasant blank.

Alvaro gave us a solemn survey. "I don't want you poking around the investigation."

"What are you investigating, Deputy? Anything new?" I asked. Because not to have asked would have been very suspicious.

"No," he said shortly.

The guy needed lying lessons, but he had the law enforcement do-what-you're-told stare mastered. After issuing his order-by-facial expression, he walked away.

I watched what was going on in the pen as closely as I could without seeming to stare. To keep it believable, I let Alvaro see me watching a couple times. They were going inch by inch over the ground as well as the tubed panels that formed the pens.

The problem was, they were working on the chute that opened onto the arena and then a couple of the pens closest to it. There were about four other pens between us and where they were working, with all those panels obstructing our view.

Mike had his phone out, taking photos. I turned my back to the pens, facing him so he could aim over my shoulder and look natural. "They've got something," he said. "Go ahead, look. Richard's occupied."

I turned to see Alvaro climbing a ladder to look at something being pointed at by a deputy on another ladder. Between them was the crossbeam of the wooden chopped-off goalpost structure that divided the permanent structures from the movable pens.

"Getting anything?" I asked.

"They're looking at the beam's top and sides. Won't know if there's more to see until I get the pictures on a bigger screen."

"When will—Richard," I warned.

Mike shifted the phone to one hand and had it behind my head before the deputy faced our way as he descended the ladder.

But apparently Alvaro had a suspicious nature, because we heard him order his people to get out tarps and put them up. While they started that, another deputy climbed the second ladder and took photographs of something on the beam.

The tarps had covered about half the enclosure when an excited call came. "Got something, Richard. I got something."

With nothing to lose, Mike and I angled across the open area to cut the distance to what was going on. His longer stride got him there first, taking pictures as he went. By the time I got to where other pens stopped us, all I saw was a gaggle of deputy uniforms around the base of one of the wooden uprights.

Alvaro told everyone to lower their voices. He turned toward us and glowered, but didn't need to do more, because the tarp between us rose with perfect timing.

"Spoilsport," I muttered. "See anything?"

"No detail. It looked like the guy held something between his fingers, but no idea what. Again, maybe a bigger screen . . ."

"Or maybe you could worm it out of Lloyd."

"I might be able to do that. If I can get him alone, and in the right frame of mind."

✧ ✧ ✧ ✧

"HERE COMES your friend," Mike said, looking toward the office.

Turning away from the now shrouded pen, I saw Oren Street step off the porch.

"Good heavens, it's like that café in Paris, where they say you see everyone you know if you sit there long enough." I considered the surroundings. "Only without the café, or the wine, or the other amenities."

"That's Sherman, Crossroads of the West. That's the thing about rodeo, too. People always on the move, coming and going. Hit a new town every week. Those climbing up, and those sliding down the ranks."

Street stopped and stared at the tarped pen.

"C'mon," I said to Mike. "Fair's fair. You rehabilitated me with Zane, I'll rehabilitate you with Street."

Oren Street shot a wary look at Mike as I executed introductions as if they'd never met.

"What's going on over there?" Street tipped his head toward pen.

"Sheriff's department is sifting through the pen again. It's routine." I hurried into a question to steer his thoughts away from what looked far too much like a crime scene for the chatty mood I hoped for. "Is there a decision about the Fourth of July Rodeo? That's what the committee talked with you about, isn't it?"

"It's what we were talking about, but if there's a decision, they haven't told me."

His sourness struck me as unfair. They'd hardly had time to decide, much less inform him, since he'd left the meeting. But I shook my head in sympathy. "I'd think with the livestock already here, it would make sense to go ahead."

"That's what I've been telling them." His gloom, which had lifted a bit, returned in full force. "I'm not the talker Keith was, though. He's the one knew how to make folks see things his way."

"But you're expecting the committee to vote in favor of going ahead with the rodeo?" Mike asked in friendly tone.

Street shot an uneasy look at him. "That Linda Caswell never has liked this company. Didn't want us when we started coming here, didn't want us when we bid this year. And she's the only one voted against it when Keith said we'd step in when that other company backed out on 'em."

Interesting. She'd made it sound as if she'd voted for Landry, though out of necessity.

"When was it you started coming here?" Mike asked, apparently taking to heart what he said I'd said about giving people questions they don't mind answering before getting to tougher ones.

Street's gaze swept across us to the masked pen. It lingered before traveling to the front gates, then toward the mountain-top horizon to the west. "Let's see . . . It was the year before my baby was born. I missed her birth to be here for our second year, so it's twenty."

"No trouble before now?" I asked.

His eyes flickered. "Not with the stock. Nobody's ever had any problem with my livestock."

"But with Keith Landry?" I speculated.

"He could talk the birds out of the trees when he wanted to."

"What if he didn't want to?"

He cut me a look. "He didn't waste much time with those he didn't want something from."

"And what did he want?"

"Hell if I know. I ain't no mind reader."

"What did he pursue?" I kept my tone mild. "You knew him for a lot of years. You must have seen what he went after."

"Power. Money. Women." He paused a moment. "Not like he's

the first or'll be the last."

I had to agree. It wasn't an original list.

"You said no trouble with the livestock," Mike said, not challenging, "but it was unusual to have them here this early. Why bring them so early?"

"Why? Because Keith hollered at me on the phone that I better get them to Sherman right away and forget resting them the way they need. Hollering about how I baby them worse than my kid, and when I tried to say anything, he kept hollering to get them here. Didn't matter it was tough on the animals, or I had to scramble and change everything.

"Sure as hell, things went wrong. Truck with the pens didn't show, so's we had to use pens left from the night's rodeo. And that was after holding stock in the trucks for near two hours. All around it was a full-blown shit storm. Sorry, ma'am."

"What did Landry tell you about why he wanted the stock here early?" I asked.

"Tell me? Didn't tell me nothing. Explainin' wasn't his way."

"You must have a guess."

He shook his head. "Something with the rodeo committee. That's all he said. Bottom line is, livestock's here. Top-line livestock. We can give Sherman a damned good rodeo for the Fourth like we agreed to. If you're looking for a reason that wouldn't suit certain people, check the grudge somebody's been holding for twenty years."

With that, he turned and marched toward the tic-tac-toe pens, heading down one of the corridors toward the arena, but well to the east of the area tarped by the sheriff's department.

When he was out of earshot, Mike said, "Might as well have pointed a finger at Linda Caswell, but wonder what that stuff about a grudge was?"

"Not being subtle doesn't mean he's not on to something. I'd like to talk to her again."

"More waiting. At least it hasn't been dull," he added as we returned to the fence.

With my mouth open to respond, I spotted another familiar form.

Good heavens, it *was* a crossroads. "There's *your* friend now." I tipped my head toward Ms. Blue Hair emerging from the next aisle west from the one Street had taken.

"Like I said, Crossroads of the West," Mike said.

"Listen, Mr. Chamber of Commerce, go see what progress you can make with Ms. Blue Hair."

He grunted assent and headed off to intercept her.

I climbed the fence and used the added height for a better view of the pens bounded on the east by the grandstand, on the south by the arena, and on the west by the sheriff's department's tarps. Oren Street was almost out of view to the east. About the same distance to the west, and just skirting the tarps, was a cowboy in a black hat. He turned, giving me his profile. Cas Newton. I looked to where Mike had caught up with Blue Hair.

As a rough guess, each of the three had traveled about the same distance. As if they'd come together at the center of the triangle they now formed, then bounced away.

Had Street come upon a moment of star-crossed love and turned away in embarrassment? That would fit his personality from what I'd seen.

And Cas and Blue Hair? Maybe they didn't want anyone to know about their meetings . . . though in that case the stock pen maze didn't seem the best place for a rendezvous.

Street, as a partner in the stock contracting firm, had contact with Stan Newton. Was that who Cas and Blue Hair were sidestepping? Or Richard and his cohorts? Or maybe it was *anyone* they didn't want to know. Because if word reached Heather, or her mother, the safest place for young Caswell Newton might be inside the rodeo arena with hard-charging animals.

I smiled when I spotted a familiar figure over by the concession stand, talking with a couple workers I didn't recognize. Needham Bender, plying his trade. At least he knew his story would make the newspaper, since he owned it. What Mike and I found might never see the light of day.

Mike ambled back, talking on his phone as he came. He hung up before he reached me. "Got to get to that tournament. You want the report with or without profanities?"

"Without."

"That'll speed things up. She was in the rodeo grounds to take a shower because she doesn't want to stink like your friend Roy and his, uh, companion. But she also doesn't have the money to throw around like those, uh, dim college kids.

"But—"

"Yeah, she'd need a grounds pass. I mentioned that. She said it was none of my business how she got in."

"Did you ask her anything about Cas Newton?"

"No. I want to be able to keep talking to her."

"That's great, but there's a time when you have to risk open lines of communication with a source in order to push for information."

"Did you push Oren Street?"

"No. I—"

"I'll push her if I think it'll help us. And now, I've got to get going, or I'll miss that tournament final. Coming?"

"Not yet. I'll get a ride to the station from somebody."

"I'll give you a call tomorrow." He started off. As a sight to watch, his rear view held its own with Grayson Zane.

The rodeo office door opening pulled my head around. Linda Caswell came out, followed by Burrell.

Fat lot I'd get out of her with him being all protective. I'd try her later. So I went after Mike, to catch a ride to the station.

✧   ✧   ✧   ✧

ON THAT EVENING'S foray to the Sherman Supermarket, I selected new dog food—after checking ingredients—paper towels, and glass cleaner. The last qualified as a talisman of faith that I'd get enough paint off the bathroom's glass surfaces someday to need glass cleaner. Feeling virtuous with not a single package of cookies in my cart, I chose my spot in Penny's monologue on how the rodeo wasn't the same under Newt and rammed in my question.

"What was that you said before about Grayson Zane, and something happening years ago, and not giving the heart orders, but he should have done right? Did he date somebody?"

"—but give the devil his due, he dotes on that boy. Dated Linda Caswell, five years back." It took a second to realize she'd shifted from Newton to Zane. "Now there's a good woman. But not the least bit glamorous. Not even pretty. Surprised everybody when Grayson Zane took up with her for that spell. Didn't surprise nobody when he dumped her, because it would take a brain to see her quality, and those rodeo cowboys wear their jeans so tight they're forever squeezing the parts that do their thinking."

She clicked her tongue. "Men an' snakes. Sometimes it's hard to tell them apart. Even for a woman like that with a good head on her shoulders . . ."

Penny went on, but I was stuck on that phrase. *A woman with a good head on her shoulders.* She'd said that before. She'd said it in connection with someone being taken in by—

"Penny!"

". . . maybe he loved her, maybe not, but he never treated—"

"Penny!" I nearly shouted it.

Her eyes opened wide, but she stopped talking.

"Who all dated Keith Landry?"

"Like I said, I don't know other places he's—"

"From here. From Sherman. Sonja, you said. And he was pursuing Heather Upton. Who else?"

"Like I said, the rodeo queen if it was anybody. He goes way back with that. One way or another, it's always a surprise the girls who go with him. Now when Mike Paycik goes with a girl—"

"Who else did Landry date from around here?"

Miracle of miracles, my question changed the direction of her flow. Like a twig turning the Mississippi.

"Vicky Upton at the start. That surprised some, brought up strict the way she was. Jolie Graf a few years after that, then Barb Duncan, and Chrissy Barctski. Then Linda five years ago. Like I told you, that had jaws sagging. First off, she wasn't no rodeo queen, and him going

after rodeo queens had got to be a joke, and why she . . ." The flow
went on, around and past me.

Linda had been romantically involved with both Zane and Landry.

"Elizabeth! You forget something?"

I blinked myself back to the present. My groceries were bagged.
Penny was ready for the next customer.

"No. I . . . I just had an epiphany. Sorry." I hurriedly paid, and
pushed my cart out to my car.

Next thing I knew, I heard my name again. "Elizabeth?"

Once more I blinked back to the present. This time to find Tom
Burrell standing beside me, with the trunk of my car yawning open.

Chapter Seventeen

"ARE YOU OKAY?" Tom asked.

I blinked a couple more times, pulling myself back to the here and now. "Fine. Thinking about potatoes."

His mouth quirked. "Care to share?"

"Too long and complicated for the Sherman Supermarket parking lot."

"Then how about a drink at the Kicking Cowboy?"

My mind skittered sideways at that. "Where's Tamantha?"

"Sleepover. Like I said, she's got quite the social life."

"Aren't you here to shop?"

"I can skip it. But if you have things you need to get home?"

Abruptly, I realized he probably wanted an opportunity to come clean about his editing job on the phone call list. Everything settled into place. "We could go to my hovel. I have wine."

"Better not."

"Why, Thomas Burrell, are you trying to protect my reputation?"

"Yes." He was serious. "Or at least to protect your choices."

I sheered away from that. "Okay, let's go."

"What about your groceries?"

"Dog food, paper towels, and glass cleaner. They'll keep." I dropped the trunk closed. "See you there."

I didn't wait for a response. When I pulled into the parking lot, he pulled in right behind me.

Inside the Kicking Cowboy, I paused, getting my bearings. A bar stretched along the left side, but tables were occupied by solid citizen types, mostly in couples.

"Not what you expected?" Burrell put a large, warm hand briefly to the small of my back and leaned close to be heard over music from a speaker directly above us. "Table in the back corner."

I headed that way. "I had imagined a wilder scene."

"Come by during rodeo week." He received and returned hellos from several solid citizen types sitting at tables. "On second thought, don't. It can get rough."

"Hey, Tom. Good to see you here." That greeting came from behind the bar.

"Hey, Badger. Good to see you, too. How about a draft and . . ." He looked at me.

"Vodka tonic." I preferred wine, but VT was my fallback, figuring no one could mess that up.

"Vodka tonic," Burrell repeated, as if the bartender wouldn't have heard me. Sometimes chivalry is downright weird. "At the back table."

"Sure thing."

The bartender's response coincided with the last notes of a man's song about writing a letter to his younger self.

A slurred voice rose from a huddle of young men at the bar near the pool table. "—only been dead a month. And here he comes walking in with somebody new. It ain't right he's cattin' around!"

"They've been divorced for years, you moron."

A woman's voice added, "And if you want to talk about catting around, Mona Burrell—" A new song opened with a hard drumbeat, smothering the voices.

Burrell's face showed no expression.

I felt like an idiot. I shouldn't have pushed him when he'd reconsidered being seen in a social setting with me, especially here, since this had been a favorite of his ex-wife.

"Don't let that jackass bother you none, Tom," said the bartender as he delivered our drinks. "More beer than sense in him. Already took his keys."

"Thanks, Badger." He went for his wallet.

"After all you been through, it's on the house."

Tom thanked him again.

Turned out, I was wrong about not messing up a vodka tonic. With the bartender—Badger—beaming at us, I fought a grimace at the first sip of liquid so sweet he must have added sugar by the tablespoon, and managed a smile for his good intentions.

After his departure, silence ballooned between us.

I broke it. "Explain why having a drink with you in a bar is better for my reputation—" I skipped the topic of *choices*. "—than a civilized glass of wine at my house?"

"Because everybody can see what we're doing. And not doing. Now, what's this about potatoes—growing, eating, or cooking?"

"Cooking." I'd rather get right to his apology over withholding some of the phone records, but perhaps he needed to ease into it. "First, for background, I am a decent cook. Some things I do quite well. Cookies, brownies, things like that. And you should taste my lemon bars." Did that sound like an invitation? I slid my glass to the right, watching condensation trail behind it, took another swallow, and regretted it. "Plus, I can cook the complete Danniher Thanksgiving turkey dinner. That was self-preservation after I tasted restaurant turkey my first year away from home."

"Never understood the big deal with turkey. It's dry. Give me a steak."

"Gee, could that be because you're a cattle rancher? But no Danniher turkey is dry. Everybody loves it. However, early in my—" I skidded around the word *marriage*. "—cooking career, I had gaping holes. Especially baked potato. Yes, I know, it's basic, it's easy—"

"Tamantha—"

"Oh, no you don't. You can't make me feel bad by saying Tamantha can do something. That girl probably could have designed a suspension bridge in the cradle if it had occurred to her that she wanted to."

Fatherly pride shifted his Abraham Lincolnesque face closer to craggy handsomeness.

"Anyway, if I tried to bake a potato, it came out like a rock. Oven, microwave, toaster oven, it didn't matter. Potato rock. Wes took to calling me *Potato* the way couples call each other cabbage or muffin." I caught myself before venturing deeper down memory lane.

"And here's where my epiphany starts. One day I was helping a co-worker put a Band-Aid on his hand. I kept a supply, because he was always hurting himself. Later he nearly got shot by a kid in Indonesia on assignment, and it shook him up enough he finally got into AA, so—But that's not the epiphany. I'm putting the Band-Aid on, and he says something about getting this puncture wound while pricking a potato with a fork before baking it."

I sat back. Burrell raised his eyebrows. "And?"

"I grabbed him by the arm and demanded, 'Pricking? What's this about pricking a potato?'"

"You didn't know about that?"

"No." I moderated my voice. "No, I didn't. Not until my co-worker said that. And there it was. The trick nobody had told me, because everybody thought everybody knew it. The one small trick that you have to know in order to make sense of what you're dealing with."

He regarded me with those depthless eyes. "And?"

"I can now bake a potato like nobody's business."

"That wasn't what had you staring into your car trunk at the supermarket like it held the answers of the universe. What do you know now that makes sense of something?"

I was listening, but I wasn't looking at him anymore.

I would have sidestepped the answer, anyhow. Learning to bake a potato, yeah, I'd tell him about that. But he was inviting more. And I wasn't accepting. Especially since what I knew now that made sense of several things involved his good friend Linda and her love life. It certainly added another dimension to Street's hints that Linda held a grudge against Landry and his company.

And now I had the perfect excuse for a change of subject.

A familiar figure had caught the corner of my eye, and I tracked him to a seat at this end of the bar, with his back to us. Without waiting for an order, Badger put down two large doubles of something amber-colored, unpolluted by water or ice.

Stan Newton upended the first in one long swallow, followed by a healthy draw on the second.

I turned to Burrell. What I saw in his so-often unreadable expression said this was why he'd brought me here. "Been going on every night for nearly a month," he said in his usual, unhurried voice. "Including Wednesday."

Had Stan lied about seeing Zane and Watt arrive at the rodeo grounds? Or, fueled by alcohol, had he gone there and had a confrontation with Landry?

"The cause?" I asked Tom.

He hitched a shoulder. "There's talk of money. That's not new. The pendulum has always swung back eventually. Usually going higher than where it started."

"Anything else?"

"He passed a comment to someone when he was well into one session that a conscience was a detriment to a businessman."

Considering that Newton's body language sent off waves of *Leave Me Alone*, I felt safe in assuming that *someone* was Badger—the one person Newton wouldn't want to scare off.

"Suggestive, possibly. Not conclusive."

"Not at all." Without comment or fuss, he emptied most of my vodka tonic into his water glass. "You want something else?"

"No, thanks. I better get going." Newton was among the few who didn't watch us leave.

Tom walked me to my car door, holding it open. I got in. "Thanks for the drink."

"You didn't drink much of it."

"I've had sweetened ice tea in the South, but that's the first time I've had a sweetened vodka tonic."

"Badger's idea of a girly drink. We'll get it right next time."

"Not if he thinks I drank it all."

"No point hurting his feelings right off." He stood there. Not closing the car door. Looking at me.

"Something more, Burrell?"

"Yeah. I was waiting to hear you say that your epiphany was about how your ex-husband calling you *Potato* showed what a bastard he is."

He punctuated that by closing the door and walking away.

✧ ✧ ✧ ✧

MIKE HAD LEFT a voicemail.

"Elizabeth, I was looking at the pictures I took. I can see that the deputy who hollered was holding something with a pair of tweezers, but can't get detail."

DAY FOUR
SUNDAY

Chapter Eighteen

THE KNOCK was at the hovel's front door, shortly after eleven o'clock Sunday morning. I'd had no nasty ringing phone wake-ups today, thank heavens. I heard the knock, but felt no obligation to answer. There's no law I know that you must answer your door just because someone knocks on it. Besides, I was sitting on the back steps, waiting to see if Shadow would return to eat while I was there.

Some people's pets do tricks. This dog's only trick was disappearing.

After Friday's progress, I'd left Saturday before he ate. This morning he'd been halfway through his food when I came out, and he'd immediately vanished. Talk about persona non grata. Just the sight of me put a starving dog off his food.

Yes, I was having a pity party.

The track my mind had followed during the conversation with Mel had gotten fed up with being ignored and woke me this morning with its unvarnished conclusion: My family—including my professional representative—thought/believed/feared my success in broadcast journalism was thanks to my ex-husband.

Morning is not my best time, which is why that conclusion had found the opening to mug me. Perhaps, too, my resistance had been weakened by the potato epiphany Burrell had forced me to see. *Potato* had not been an affectionate nickname. It had been a reminder of a failure.

Now, there sat the conclusion, no longer ignored, but instead lodged in my head and fully-armed. My success was not mine.

My ex had pushed. Prodded. Watched for opportunities. I would have stayed at our first jobs out of school, where we met. Wes had provided the kicks up the career ladder. Beyond that—?

Tom Burrell came around the corner from the front driveway with his usual long-legged gait.

Most people would have started talking right off, about how he'd knocked but nobody answered. He said nothing as he approached me at an unhurried pace, his gaze taking in the half-full food dish, the dogless yard, and me. He sat beside me without permission. Also without talking.

After a few minutes, I realized it hadn't been that I didn't want company, I just hadn't wanted conversation.

A minute more, and I realized that with Burrell there, the examination of my ex's role in my career had settled back into its corner. Sure, it growled a little, but it stayed there.

Then Shadow emerged from behind the garage. He stopped and looked from me to Burrell and back. He sniffed the air audibly. Slowly, he approached, coming at an angle that brought him closer to me than Burrell.

"What kind of dog do you think Shadow is?" I asked.

"Male."

"I guessed that when I saw him peeing standing up. I meant what breeds do you think he has in him."

"As many as he could get."

I grimaced.

"Best you could call him is a Wyoming ranch dog," he said.

"Is there such a breed?"

"More of a generic than a breed."

"Don't you think he has collie in him?"

"Like Lassie?" He ended the question on a cough that sounded suspiciously like it covered a laugh.

"I'm not saying purebred, but those ranch dogs often look like they're related to collies. A ranch collie. Look at him, the way his ears tip, the markings around his ruff, the long nose. And I'll bet he'll have a good coat when he's cleaned up."

"*If* he's ever cleaned up."

"I think he has a certain panache." There was silence beside me. I looked over. "Don't you think so?"

"I think it's a damned good thing you already named him Shadow, because any Wyoming dog would starve himself to death rather than be called Panache."

I laughed. Shadow skittered toward the garage. It was something he'd have to get used to, because laughing was something I wanted to get used to.

Tamantha Burrell came around the corner from the direction of the driveway, determination in every line of her narrow face.

With dimples and curls she might be called cute. Tamantha had ears that poked out between straight, almost lank hair, and extremities that tended to stick out of whatever she wore, as if she'd grown since she got dressed that morning. She's called bossy.

Chances are she won't outgrow the label. In fact, in another fifteen years, as she climbs whatever career ladder she decides on—and if Tamantha decides to climb those rungs will get climbed—she'll surely pick up the other "B" tag: bitch. If she reaches grandmotherdom, her decisiveness might, finally, become "character."

When she spotted Shadow, her expression shifted from disapproval to admonishment. I was cravenly grateful it was directed at her father. "I wouldn't have waited this long if you'd said there was a dog. What's his name?"

"Shadow," I said, since the question had been directed at me. "But he doesn't like people. At least not yet. He's been on his own a long time, and it seems he might have been treated badly. We have to be patient and give him time to get used to us. Don't rush him. Don't try to be friends with him until he's ready."

She listened until I stopped, then turned and looked at the dog. Then at me. Then her father. It was the last two looks that had the hair rising on the back of my neck.

"Daddy says some people are like that, too, and we should treat them just like what you said. Be real patient with them, wait for them to come to us. Not rush them. You know, people like you," she said.

I snapped my neck around to glare at the father of the pint-sized know-it-all. The move hurt my neck, as well as giving little satisfaction, because the brim of that all too useful cowboy hat hid his eyes, and the rest of his face was expressionless.

"Daddy said we had to be patient—"

"Tamantha." Father and daughter looked at each other. This time, father won.

I would not stoop to pumping a second-grader for information about what her father might have said. However, now that she was heading into third grade . . . but it would have to wait until the father wasn't around.

Tamantha turned to the dog and said, "I won't hurt you, so don't be silly. Come, Shadow."

And he did.

Or almost. A heck of a lot closer that he'd come to me with the exception of the one time he'd assigned himself as my guard dog.

"Good dog," she said. "Now eat your food."

She came and sat on a lower step between her father and me, extending her legs in front of her, emphasizing that her pants were even shorter on her than they had been when I met her at the start of May. She wore a top with bright red and yellow stripes that had to be new because the sleeves almost covered her wrists.

Shadow ate. Whenever he glanced toward us, it was directed to Tamantha, and I'd have sworn the message was *see how good I'm doing at exactly what you told me?*

When he finished, Tamantha said, "Good dog. Now let's go see what's in this yard."

"I don't know—"

"She'll be okay," Tom said to me. To his daughter he added, "Don't bring back any live snakes."

She stood and started off. Shadow stared at her a moment, then trotted along parallel to her, though ten feet to the side. He wagged his tail. It was the first time I'd seen him wag his tail.

I found myself grinning stupidly. "Your daughter is terrifying."

"Tell me about it."

I turned to view his profile. "Single parenthood tough?"

"Not her doing. It's the wondering if there are better ways, or things you're forgetting or never knew." His mouth did that quirk thing. "'Specially woman things."

My opinion was that Tamantha would be better off learning *woman things* from the man sitting next to me than she would have been from her mother, but it wasn't my place to say that. "You've got time. And I'd imagine your sister will be a big help."

"Yeah, she will." He stretched one leg, seeming to signal a shift in the conversation. "Best tell you what I've learned while we have the chance. The shouting at Wednesday morning's meeting with the rodeo committee was over Landry saying he wanted yet another bonus, or he wouldn't bring in the stock. The committee'd about decided they had no choice but to pay, when Street arrived with the stock trucks. Best guess is that Landry was shouting at Street about the timeline of his arrival, taking the teeth out of his grab for another bonus. Less clear what Street was shouting about. One person who heard claimed Street said something about it was one thing with strangers, but Landry'd known him twenty years."

"What was *one thing with strangers?*"

"No idea. The person didn't stick around, though the shouting went on. Between the committee in the morning and the showdown with Street, I got three reports of Landry shouting on the phone. One, telling somebody they owed him and better rethink their high-and-mightiness. Two, telling Evan Watt he didn't care what he'd said before, Watt better get his sorry ass to Sherman, pronto. Three, telling a liquor store they damned well better deliver."

That all fit.

"Couple folks I talked to mentioned Landry was drinking hard," he added. "They'd known him from other years, and they said this was new. And bad."

"Why didn't you tell me this last night?"

"Didn't know last night."

I felt my brows hike. "You've talked to people since last night?"

"Couple folks who work at the rodeo grounds go to the same church as Tamantha and me." He tipped his head to indicate his daughter's approach. Shadow stopped well back. "Had a chance to talk a bit about what's been happening at the rodeo grounds."

I understood and would cooperate with his inclination to cloak what was going on with generalities such as *what's been happening at the rodeo grounds.* Though it wouldn't have surprised me to discover his daughter knew more about the situation than we did.

She announced, "I'll be rodeo queen when I grow up."

"Will you?" Tamantha is not a girl I would have expected to have that ambition. For one thing, she's not a pretty or even cute child. More important, I would have expected her not to waste her ambition on anything smaller than running several countries. On the other hand, Mrs. Parens had been a rodeo queen.

"Yup. Probably a bunch of years in a row."

"Usually in these things, once you win, you can't enter again."

She cast me a disdainful look. "Real queens rule forever, and I'll be a real queen."

As I said, several countries. Come to think of it, Tamantha, Mrs. Parens, and Heather Upton might be sisters under the skin.

Burrell stood, resting his hands on his daughter's thin shoulders. She leaned back against him, as content as I'd ever seen her. "Time we got going. Tamantha and I—"

My phone rang. I put a hand on it, but didn't pull it out.

"You'd best get that," Burrell said.

It was Mike. "Elizabeth. I've got something."

I didn't move to make this private, and the Burrells stayed where they were. "The pictures you took?"

He sighed. "Can't see much except blurs on the beam. Otherwise, most of what I got is a bunch of deputies' backs. In the one I mentioned on the message, you can see a deputy's hand holding something with tweezers. What's being held is mostly a pixilated squiggle. Maybe a thread. Maybe something else."

"Too bad. It was worth a try."

"I suppose. But here's what I do have. Aunt Gee has good information that Stan Newton is in trouble financially."

Technology let us down with the pictures, but Aunt Gee's grapevine worked fine in confirming what Burrell had presented last night. I needed to tell Mike about that. "How much trouble?"

"That's not clear yet." That *yet* meant Aunt Gee remained on the case. "The other bit of news is that Jenny—"

"Jennifer."

"*Jennifer* is emailing us a list of rodeos Landry's company has worked the past five years—places, dates, contact names. Sending it to Richard, too. Since she's done with that, she's going to dig on that contractor going bankrupt."

"That's great."

"Listen, how'd you like to come to Sunday dinner at Aunt Gee's?"

My eyes flicked to the Burrells, then away. Had Tom been about to issue an invitation? Had I wanted him to? "Uh . . ."

"We can see what else she knows."

"I thought I'd go see Mrs. Parens today."

He made a sound that might be spelled, "hmm," but carried as much warning of danger ahead as the loudest train whistle.

Mike's Aunt Gee and Mrs. Parens were next door neighbors and rivals. Rivals for what wasn't clear, unless it was uncontested Empress of Cottonwood County. Mike had claimed he didn't know the history and was neither brave enough nor stupid enough to ask.

This from the man who'd faced down NFL defenders for enough years to build a nest egg and a reputation. The nest egg had bought him a ranch in the county; the reputation was going to help him secure a spot in big-time broadcasting when he chose.

"Better see Mrs. Parens first this time," he said, referring to a visit a few weeks back in which we'd had lunch with Aunt Gee, then answered Mrs. Parens' summons to visit her in her front parlor. "That way, she gets to feel good about our going there first, and Aunt Gee gets to feel she stole us away."

"You make it sound like negotiating a cease fire between World

War II combatants."

"At least they had the Geneva Conventions. Pick you up at one-thirty." We hung up.

Burrell said, "Dinner at Gisella's?"

"Yes."

"Can't do better than that. I suggest you leave room for chocolate pie."

How could he think there'd be room left for anything after being fed by Aunt Gee? "Chocolate pie? The Haber House Hotel?"

"Yep. Sit in Kelly's section. But don't go until Sunday rush is over. I don't know her, she's just signed on this summer, but I'm told she won't give you any time if you interfere with her tips."

"Why do I want Kelly's time?"

"Because of who she served lunch to Wednesday."

Chapter Nineteen

ONE-THIRTY LEFT me wallpaper-chipping time before getting cleaned up. The bathroom of this rental house featured *Night of the Living Dead* green paint covering the light fixture and window, plus wallpaper with platter-sized cabbage roses of purple and black.

As a break from the tedious paint-chipping, I had started removing the wallpaper, only to discover that behind this layer were previous layers, each covered in paint. So, my break from tedious paint-chipping had become tedious paint-covered wallpaper chipping. Ah, the glamour.

But first, I called Matt Lester at his home in a suburb of Philadelphia. His wife, Bonnie, answered.

"Danny! How are you? I hate you being off by yourself in the middle of nowhere living in what sounds like a shack."

"Hovel," I amended under my breath. "But how do you know about my living quarters?"

"Oh. Uh, you know, I, uh, heard."

"Good God, Bonnie, did my mother call you?"

"No!"

"So it was Mel."

Silence greeted that stab in the not-so-dark. "Actually, I called him. He is your agent now. He was so nice those times we'd met him and . . . We'd heard nothing for so long, I was worried."

Guilt surged as it could only for someone trained in the Catherine Danniher School of Guilt-Riddenness.

Bonnie and Matt had taken me in for several weeks during the first shock-waves of my life upheaval, but I had steered clear of them until a few weeks ago when I'd called asking Matt for Philly-related research. And here I was, doing the same thing.

"Bonnie, I'm good. Well, maybe not all the way to good, not every day, but better. Really, truly, and honestly."

"I'm glad," she said simply.

"And I will be better about staying in touch. I will. I promise."

"Except that right now you need to ask Matt questions."

I chuckled. "You are the ideal wife for a journalist, you know that?"

"I remind Matt of it several times a day. Here he is."

"Hey, Danny. Bonnie giving you a hard time about not being in touch?"

"A little, but—"

"Good. You deserve it. So, what can I do for you?" That was the way Matt wrote, too—to the point, but never belaboring it.

"You did a series of pieces on animal rights protestors a while back, didn't you? Two years ago?"

"More like four. But, yeah."

"If you've still got the contacts and can find out anything about a group out here led by a guy named Roy Craniston, I'd appreciate anything you can get. On him and his associates."

He repeated the name, clearly noting it and the descriptions I gave him of the others. "Sure thing. I'll make calls tomorrow."

And then we said good-bye, so he could get back to his family. And I could chip more painted wallpaper off the bathroom wall.

✧   ✧   ✧   ✧

NOT MUCH WALL had been freed of wallpaper when my cell rang from the pocket of the sweater hooked on the bathroom doorknob.

Caller ID allowed me to answer with, "Hi, Mel."

"I'm glad I got you, Danny. I feared you might have left Friday's call with a mistaken impression."

"No, I don't think so."

"I have great respect for you. I don't want you to think for a second otherwise. You have always been so impressive. And even when you and Wes were moving frequently, driving so hard, I was impressed with all that you did, how much you achieved. Have achieved . . . are achieving. Impressive. Achievement, I mean."

When Mel beat a word into the ground, it was a clear sign of discomfort. When he stuttered around tenses, it was serious.

"Thanks, Mel." I crunched that out. *I* achieved? Or Wes achieved through me? "But—"

"But," he nearly shouted over me. "But things have changed now. And you seemed so unhappy when we saw you. Perhaps it's time for something new, something different. Different priorities."

"Of course I was unhappy at Christmas and before I headed out here—I'd been demoted from New York to Sherman, Wyoming."

"Before that."

"I wasn't—"

"Yes, you were," he said, stubbornly. "And we . . . I hate to think of you all alone out there. If you moved closer—"

"Forget the St. Louis talk show. And I'm not alone."

That stopped him. But not for long. "You're not? Well! That's splendid. Already! I know . . ." He broke off into coughing.

When it subsided, I said, "I seem to have acquired a dog."

I hadn't missed that *I know*. But he was on guard about it now. Far better to pump him later.

I let the silence stretch, until he said, very carefully, "A dog? Well . . . that's good. That's very good. Isn't it? What breed?"

"Possibly collie."

"Oh, those are beautiful dogs."

"Don't start thinking Lassie, Mel," I scolded, remembering Tom's laughter and grinning. "I'm told he's a . . . a ranch collie."

"Is that like a border collie? They're very intelligent."

"There are similarities." Four legs, two ears, a nose and a tail.

"Where did you get . . . him, you said?"

"Yes. It's more like he got me."

"A stray?" Mel and his family had segued from a Dalmatian to a lab to a golden retriever, each with a lineage more impressive than Queen Victoria's. "Are you certain that's a good idea?"

"Sure. Everyone deserves a chance at a new life, right, Mel? I'm fortunate that the owners at KWMT were willing to give me one. You know them, don't you? The Heathertons. Val Heatherton, I understand, is the real power, and she named her son-in-law Craig Morningside the station manager. You might not know him, because I hear you called Val, went right to the top when you—"

"Danny, I . . . oh. Just a minute, Eileen!" He called away from the mouthpiece. I had not heard a peep from his wife in the background. "Sorry, Danny. Got to go now. Eileen's calling. We'll talk again. Soon."

"Okay, Mel. Give Eileen my love."

"Of course, of course. Bye."

I grinned at the phone. As much as I like getting answers to questions, it might be worth delaying finding out precisely what Mel Welch was up to for the pleasure of tormenting him.

✧   ✧   ✧   ✧

"I KNOW FINE'S officially got the story, but I'm glad we're doing this," Mike said abruptly. We'd been driving toward the mountains and O'Hara Hill, which sat in a narrow valley just east of them, in easy silence. "Besides, it's another chance to have you mentor me on a big story."

He coated the last line with nearly enough dryness for me to pretend he hadn't meant it seriously. But not quite. "I am not mentor material. You do not want me as your mentor, Paycik."

"Yes, I do, along with other things. And you already are," he added, which allowed me to ignore the other phrase. He'd indicated interest, but hadn't been pushy about that. And it wasn't that I was *un*interested. It was just one more thing I wasn't ready to think about quite yet. "But tell me why I wouldn't want you as a mentor."

Under the direct challenge, I skidded sideways. "I'm hard news, and you're sports."

"You think sports is just scores and what happens on the field?

Reporting sports, really reporting it, means knowing exactly the things I'm learning from you. Digging for facts and putting together the truth. It gets my goat when people don't realize sports reporting is everything in hard news, *plus* keeping score."

"Keeping score," I repeated. "That has a lot of appeal, doesn't it. Knowing exactly where you stand. I wonder if that's some of the appeal of sports. The clarity. No wondering if you've done okay or not. It's all there to see on the scoreboard."

"Not all sports."

"But rodeo . . ."

"Cut and dried in rodeo. If you don't win, you don't earn anything. Period."

"Is it hard to figure out if you've done a good job—played a good game, I mean—when you're on a football team?"

"Not really. Each player has a specific assignment on each play. Watching film, you see if you did the job or not. Were you at the right spot at the right time, did you make the right move, did you accomplish what you were supposed to do? And if you don't see it," Mike went on, "the coaches will point it out."

"What if the coach isn't . . . impartial?"

He slanted a look at me. "Like I said, it's there on the film."

There was no film, no replay for me, except in my own head.

"Your teammates know, too. That's what a lot of people outside of football don't understand. It takes the team to make any individual player look good over the long haul. A team can have a top quarterback, and if his offensive line doesn't give him time to throw, if his receivers don't hold onto the ball, if the coach doesn't put in the right plays, heck, if the equipment guys don't get the right shoes, it can all go south."

"Can an individual coast on the ability of his teammates?"

"Some. More often the individual pushes himself to play better than he has before to match the rest of his team."

I considered that. I'd worked with some of the best in the business. Maybe I'd pushed myself to match them. I could live with that. "What about the other way around?"

"The whole being greater than the sum of its parts? Sure. But there's got to be a level of competence. Otherwise, it pulls down the team eventually."

I hadn't dragged down my team. That I was sure of. There was a zing, like hitting the sweet spot on a tennis racquet, when your team produced good work, and I'd had that zing plenty of times. Too many to have been a fluke.

"Sorry. Chewing your ear. You shouldn't get me on to football."

"You miss it, don't you?" I asked.

"Probably about as much as you miss big-time TV news."

"More."

I saw my response surprised him nearly as much as it surprised me.

✧ ✧ ✧ ✧

MRS. PARENS welcomed us and led us to her front room, which doubled as a Cottonwood County archive. Each wall was filled with maps and photographs.

"You never told me you were a rodeo queen," I complained after greetings.

She tipped her head. "My dear, Elizabeth, I have lived a good many years. I have known you for a short period of time. I am entirely certain that there are any number of my activities of which I have not informed you."

It was reasonable and reasoned. Why did I still feel as if she'd been holding out on me? I said, "I would be interested in hearing anything you'll tell me about the rodeo or those involved with it."

"That's far too wide a net. I would have you and Michael here for more time than would be comfortable for any of us."

"Tell her about Cottonwood Drive." Mike received a reproving look from the woman who wasn't much taller than his elbow. He added, "Please."

"Rupert Caswell drove a herd of longhorn cattle up from Texas as the open range was ending. He was the first to bring his herd to this area of what was then Wyoming Territory. He was reported to be quite a . . ." An uncharacteristic hesitation from the former teacher. ". . . forceful man."

"Shot homesteaders he said were on his property," Mike said.

"That was never proven in a court of law," Mrs. Parens said.

"And sheepherders when he was over ninety."

"Flesh wounds," she clarified. "He was nearly blind." I wasn't sure if she was excusing his shooting people or merely wounding them. "He guarded his legend. As an element of that, he named his ranch Cottonwood Drive, to forever serve as a reminder that his cattle drive had given the county its start."

"He was Linda Caswell's grandfather? He started the rodeo?"

"Rupert was her great-grandfather. His son, Rupert Junior, began the Fourth of July Rodeo. Cottonwood Drive provided the livestock each year from its beginning, until Keith Landry's company won the bid twenty years ago. That was the end of an era. Walter was bitter about that until the day he died. Didn't set well with any of the Caswells." She squared her shoulders. "Yes, Rupert Junior was quite a different sort of man from the original. Linda is much more like him than her own father, or certainly Rupert Senior. I recall Rupert Junior fondly from my youth. Indeed, he crowned me as rodeo queen."

It was the opening I'd hoped for. "About this year's rodeo queen and—"

"I never had Heather as a student. I know little of her outside the screening process."

"What about her mother, Vicky?"

"She was a student when I was principal. I knew of her but not as I would if I had taught her."

"You were on the rodeo queen committee that selected her?"

"Yes."

Remembering things Vicky had said, I hazarded the guess, "But she didn't use the scholarship money?"

"No."

Guesstimating Vicky's and Heather's ages, having a baby might have been the reason.

"Did you know Heather's father?" I asked.

"He was not from Cottonwood County," she said, "and to my knowledge never resided here. So I cannot give you information on him beyond what you likely know."

"I know Heather Upton's father died—" A tiny nod acknowledging a correct answer. "—when she was quite young."

A tuck appeared between her brows, quickly smoothed away.

"He didn't die when she was young?" I turned to Mike, passing on the blame. "You told me her mother's been a widow a long time."

"She has been. Long as I can remember."

"You have made an incorrect assumption, Michael."

"It wasn't an assumption. People said it. *Vicky Upton is a widow.* My Mom said it. Everybody said it."

Mrs. Parens cleared her throat. "At times a certain amount of delicacy has been valued over absolute accuracy. In addition to delicacy, there is a responsibility in discussing personal lives. In that regard, I place greater reliance on both of you than on our county's officials."

Ah. I'd wager a dollar or two that Mrs. Parens was Tom's source about the big shots being out of town—and his guide in deciding it was better to let them stay uninformed of recent events.

"I see Elizabeth wondered and now has drawn the correct conclusion," Mrs. Parens said.

We both looked at Mike.

He looked back. "Don't look at me like I'm stupid. What . . .? Oh. She was never married?"

"That is accurate to my knowledge," Mrs. Parens said.

"Why did everybody say she was a widow? It's not like other women around here haven't had kids without being married."

"True. However, in Vicky's case, there were circumstances that inclined much of Cottonwood County to accept the account of a deceased husband. Vicky was a late-in-life baby for her parents, who were from a generation not as open about such matters. They sent Vicky away. When she returned after more than a year with a child, a wedding ring, and an account of a husband's tragic death, it was not questioned. I don't know if Vicky has maintained that construct since her parents' deaths out of respect for them, or because she has no wish to disturb her own standing."

"I wonder if she's told her daughter?"

Mrs. Parens gave me a searching look. "That would be between mother and daughter, Elizabeth."

"So, who's the father?" Mike asked. "Does anyone know?"

Her disapproval was clear. "I should imagine that Vicky Upton knows. She was never of a temperament to not know such a thing."

Neither Mike nor I pushed.

"Now, we should depart for Gisella's house, or we'll be late for dinner," Mrs. Parens said. "Ah, I see you're surprised, Elizabeth. Gisella has her faults, but she is generous, as well as being an excellent cook." A glint of humor lit her eyes. "I allow her the pleasure of demonstrating her skill and her generosity by having me as a dinner guest."

Chapter Twenty

MRS. PARENS WAS not the only additional guest next door. Donald from the sheriff's department dispatch staff and his wife Doris were there, along with Jack, a gray-haired ranch foreman Mike had worked for in his youth. Also a woman named Connie and her three teenage sons.

It was a close-run thing whether those three eating machines or Aunt Gee's colossal spread would hold out longer. Aunt Gee won.

While we watched the final rounds of that battle, Connie came and sat beside me, surprising me by starting her remarks with, "I'm pleased to have this chance to thank you for what you did."

Unless a "Helping Out" segment had saved her from a travel scam or taught her how to get her toaster fixed, I couldn't imagine how I'd helped her.

"I work in the office of Burrell Roads," she said. That was the name of the road construction company, started by his father, that Tom Burrell ran in addition to his ranch. "My husband's not well, and Tom insisted on keeping me on full pay even when there was so little business this spring that he told me not to come to the office. I couldn't have gone on that way, but thanks to what you did—you and Mike and Diana—making it clear Tom was innocent, we should be back to full capacity next season." A smile lifted the lines of her face. "I just wanted you to know the good you did."

I uttered useless, but socially acceptable phrases. She smiled again, patted my hand, and went to talk with Aunt Gee. From across the room, Mrs. Parens gave me a small, approving smile.

Only after the other guests left, and Aunt Gee allowed Mike and me to carry dishes into her surgically clean kitchen, did we have an opportunity to pick up information from her. She allowed us to provide no other assistance.

We heard that Aunt Gee was pleased that Richard Alvaro was in charge of this big case because, "He's a good boy." Mike and I looked at each other, but neither of us had the answer to whether Aunt Gee knew it was murder, and neither of us asked.

We also heard that Stan Newton had two major balloon loans coming due later this year, while a number of other enterprises, including the rodeo grounds, were experiencing dips. If nothing else went wrong, the expectation was he'd survive, though likely need retrenchment. If more problems arose—say, the rodeo grounds' biggest weekend being a bust—the outlook wasn't as optimistic.

She had no further information for me on Sonja Osterspeigel. Nor had Keith Landry's time of death been narrowed from between midnight and when Thurston Fine discovered him shortly after seven a.m.

Finally, we heard that county leaders were a pack of fools who thought scurrying off to a hidey-hole and weaving grandiose plans about how to keep the people of Cottonwood County in the dark was what passed for leadership.

"You tell 'em, Aunt Gee," Mike said, while I clapped.

With great severity, but a smile in her eyes, she kicked us out of her kitchen and sent us on our way with leftovers stowed in twin cool packs for each of us, along with another set for Jenny-Jennifer "because that poor girl's stuck out there at the station without any way to get a meal." I was past being surprised that Aunt Gee not only knew everyone in the county, but also their work schedules.

I drifted off as we headed back to Sherman. The amount of food Aunt Gee provided, the comfort of Mike's four-wheel drive, and the warmth of the sun starting to beat back the overcast had me drowsy. Mrs. Parens' teacherliness might have influenced the direction of my thoughts.

I'd been a good student all through school. Except in math.

Oh, not arithmetic. I can do that well enough for ordinary life. My checking account balances. I can double or halve a recipe, figure percentage off for shoe sales, or appropriate tips in my head.

No, I'm talking about Mathematics. After the first mid-term in Advanced Algebra, my teacher, a soft-spoken man named Mr. Gladner, called me in. He sat beside me in the otherwise empty classroom and asked me to solve a few problems on the spot. With each one, he looked more perplexed.

Finally, he pulled out my mid-term. "I don't know how to grade this, Elizabeth. Your answers are almost all right, but the only time you had all the right steps, your answer was wrong."

What did the steps matter? If the answer was right, it was right. If the answer was wrong, it was wrong.

"How do you do that?" he asked.

"Um, I sort of look at the problem to get a big picture. Then I do a few steps, and then I just sort of *see* it—the answer."

"See it? Before doing the other steps?"

"Uh-huh."

He looked at me so long I remember heat coming into my cheeks. "Elizabeth? Do you like math? Algebra?"

"No." All those boring steps.

He murmured something that sounded like *Thank God.* "Since you've more than fulfilled your requirement, I suggest that after this course you consider taking no more Mathematics. I'm not sure we're ready for you."

I was more than happy to take his suggestion.

It wasn't until years later that I abruptly realized that quiet Mr. Gladner must have at least wondered if I was a remarkably slipshod cheater. That's why he'd asked me to do problems while he sat beside me. It had never occurred to me before. I'd been focused on the resolution—no more math!—not the steps to reach it.

In journalism, the steps do matter, though not the way they do in Algebra. And I've become adept at supporting my answers while digging for the right solution.

Still, that's the way I've mostly operated, grasping the outlines of the big picture long before the details are in order. Then testing and checking that big picture as I add details. Being alert to the chance that new details might wipe out the big-picture sketch.

That wasn't how things had worked this spring however, when I'd been tracking a missing sheriff's deputy. I'd never gotten a full grasp on the big picture until it almost was too late.

Somehow, this issue of Keith Landry's death felt more familiar. As if I had started, if not getting back into the groove, at least walking on solid ground.

✧ ✧ ✧ ✧

WE SWUNG BY the station to deliver Aunt Gee's bounty to Jennifer. She dug in, but between bites told us, "Didn't find a single bankruptcy in that name—Sweet Meadows Rodeo Stock."

"Damn. I suppose it was too much to hope," Mike said.

"But I did find a DBA. That's Doing Business As. In Oklahoma."

"Sweet Meadows was doing business under another name?" I asked.

"No. A person was doing business as Sweet Meadows Rodeo Stock. Betty Gates. She's the widow of a minister."

"Why on earth would the widow of a minister do business as Sweet Meadows? And what about the guy who came here to make the bid? Could it be a family business?"

She shrugged at each of my questions. "I found her right before you came in. I'll keep digging."

"Thanks, Jennifer. Something else . . . I've done the basic searches, but do you have other suggestions for finding someone? With a last name like Osterspeigel, you'd think I could find her."

She turned. "Sonja Osterspeigel?"

How on earth . . .? "Yes. Do you know her?"

"She was in my homeroom in eighth grade. We keep in touch."

"Do you have her phone number?"

"No, but I can IM her and ask for it. Want me to?"

"Yes. See if there's a time I can talk to her this evening."

"Sure thing. I'll let you know when I hear back."

Mike smirked at me and said under his breath, "The pleasures of small-town journalism."

✧   ✧   ✧   ✧

MOST TABLES AT the Haber House Hotel's dining room were empty when we arrived.

The Haber House celebrated its status as a historic hotel with quantities of red plush that seemed more in keeping with a historic bordello. But the food was several steps above Hamburger Heaven, and the chocolate pie was worthy of acclaim. Though not after an Aunt Gee meal.

While I contemplated how to find out which server was the Kelly that Tom had mentioned this morning, Mike applied his smile to the hostess and had the answer. Kelly was the black-haired young woman heading out a side door.

We were slowed by people exchanging greetings with Mike. I was antsy she'd be gone, but when he opened the door onto a closet-sized space nearly surrounded by brick walls, she eyed us through cigarette smoke and heavy eye makeup. She might have given off a goth vibe, if she hadn't been wearing a white blouse and a frilled red apron with black slacks.

"Customers aren't supposed to be out here. Employees only."

"We'd like to talk to you a few minutes," Mike said with a smile. "Hope you can help us out with something."

For the first time, we encountered a female who did not appear entranced with the prospect of helping Michael Paycik with anything and everything.

"I'm on break." She took a last, deep drag on the cigarette, dropped it to the ground, and stepped on it at the same time she pulled out a pack of gum. "Hate this crap, but tips go to hell if your breath smells like smoke."

Ah. That book on dogs I'd read might not have been a waste of time after all. We'd established Kelly was not Paycik-motivated, but adding in what Tom had said, she just might be tip-motivated.

"We realize we're taking your time. We'll compensate you for what you're losing in tips." I ignored that she'd have missed out on tips regardless, since she was on a cigarette break.

She ignored that piece of logic, too. "Yeah?"

"Yes. That is if you can give us information about the lunch Wednesday that included Keith Landry, the rodeo contractor who was killed." She continued to look blankly at me, so I added, "The lunch the sheriff's department asked you about?"

"Oh, yeah. You don't want to know like what the people ate or anything, do you, because that was days ago, and about a million tables ago. I have no—"

"Not what they ate. But did you hear what they said?"

"No. Deputy asked that, too, especially if there'd been any yelling. That I would've remembered, especially considering all the yelling that guy did at dinner when the manager told him to get out. But there wasn't anything exciting about the lunch. Like I told that deputy, I was too busy doing my job and avoiding that dead guy's roving hands. Not that he was the dead guy then. Though I wouldn't have minded if he had been, because his hands wouldn't have been all over. And I wasn't the only one. That girly-girl could've used a fly swatter to keep his hand off her leg. The boyfriend would've used a shotgun if there'd been one handy."

"How do you know if you don't remember what they said?"

She rolled her eyes. "Like you have to memorize words to get the atmosphere. You gotta be good at reading people to get good tips. Like reading body language shit. Know when to leave 'em alone, when to ask if they want more. I'm good. I get *great* tips."

"So, what was the atmosphere?"

"Nasty. Real, real nasty. Like a big pot of nasty stew."

"Can you be more specific?"

She cracked her gum and stared at the side of the building. "Girly-girl was pissed at Boyfriend, but as the lunch went on, she was even more grossed out by Mr. Hands. When he wasn't trying to feel me or Girly-girl up, Mr. Hands was trying to get Boyfriend to do something, and getting fed up with Boyfriend not toeing the line.

"That was all said hush-hush between the two of them. No, don't ask. I didn't hear any of it, and besides, I'd've forgotten it along with the rest by now." She frowned slightly. "Wasn't clear if Boyfriend was dense or being a Boy Scout."

"How about the other man at the table?" Mike asked.

"Oh, yeah, Mr. Double-Double-and-Keep-Em-Coming. He was trying to drown something that was eating at him. And from a couple looks Mr. Hands sent that way, he was the one doing the chewing, and ready for his next big bite. Mr. Hands was no slouch on the double-doubles, either, by the way. Boyfriend was split between worried and disgusted with Mr. Double-Double. Seemed like he thought he was on his own to handle Mr. Hands."

We asked a few more questions, but it was clear these impressions were all she had.

I forked over a twenty, got a smile and a blast of wintergreen riding on a wave of cigarette smoke.

✧   ✧   ✧   ✧

WE SAT IN THE hovel's driveway in Mike's four-wheel-drive and went over what we had. His vehicle was considerably more comfortable than the couch inside.

After a pause, I summed up, "It could be anyone we've talked about. And it's not impossible it's someone we know nothing about."

"Yup. And the rodeo folks will scatter when the Fourth of July Rodeo ends eight days from now. Unless it's canceled, then they go any minute. What do we do?"

"Go back to the beginning to find more inconsistencies. Hope we scrounge up more leads to follow. Hope Jenny—"

"Jennifer."

"Damn, I was doing so well, too. Hope *Jennifer* comes through. And hope my law enforcement source has something wonderful for us."

"That's a lot of hoping."

I agreed and said good-night.

✧ ✧ ✧ ✧

ONE HOPE WAS fulfilled. Jennifer texted me Sonja's phone number.

"Hi, Sonja, this is E.M. Danniher with—"

"Oh, hi! Jen said you couldn't find me because of the name." She giggled. She did that a lot in the next forty-five minutes. This, the first giggle, was for the fact that she'd changed her name to her step-father's last name of Davidson when her mother remarried last year. "Because, really, Osterspeigel? Do you have any idea how many ways people mess up a name like that?"

I did after she spent five minutes telling me.

I broke in to ask—to try to ask—about her experience as rodeo queen. I had to break in to that answer to say I'd understood she had a relationship during her reign as rodeo queen.

She giggled. Then she sighed. Then she told me her version of what Penny Czylinski had conveyed in a few succinct sentences.

A circuit rodeo cowboy whose name meant nothing to me (but which I noted to check with Mike or Diana), had swept her off her feet two days before the rodeo started. "The best sex ever. I mean, ever," she said, and giggled. It had continued as an intense, whirlwind relationship until immediately after the rodeo. She had then heard from a third party, a jealous bitch of a third party, whose expectations of being rodeo queen had been laughable, that her cowboy had told others he intended to leave town without a word of farewell.

She had rushed to his camper . . . it was gone.

She'd been sitting in her truck by the empty spot, bawling over the tarnishment of her crown—her phrase—when the passenger door opened and Keith Landry got in, gathered her in a hug, and offered her the solace her lacerated heart required—again, her phrase.

Then ensued a period of six days, spent mostly in a motel room. To my relief, she did not describe these days or the sex, other than to say that was what had occupied them.

Until the evening Landry left to get takeout, he'd said, but he'd been gone an awfully long time—and Sonja received a phone call. The same jealous bitch of a third party informed Sonja that Landry was at the Kicking Cowboy talking about her.

Sonja had arrived at the Kicking Cowboy in a swirl of righteous anger. There'd been shouting. There'd been glass breakage. There'd been a slap. There'd been remonstrations from Badger. There'd been a law enforcement escort out for her.

"I was so young." She giggled. "And such a fool."

I thanked her. She giggled. I told her Landry had died. She said she'd heard, then giggled, though it sounded nervous. She said to call back if I needed anything more. And giggled.

I went out, sat on the back steps to look at the light-pricked expanse of sky over my head and to listen—not to silence, because there were the usual night sounds of trees and animals moving, two voices, a car-door closing at a distance. But no giggling.

I spotted Shadow living up to his name as he slipped around in the darkest patches, yet somehow giving me the sense he was keeping me company. Maybe it was wish fulfillment, but I don't think so.

Sunday ended, and I had not gone to the Sherman Supermarket once.

Penny Czylinski is off on Sundays and Mondays.

DAY FIVE

MONDAY

THE PHONE ON my desk rang as I walked into the KWMT newsroom Monday morning.

The Denver contact had come through, getting approval for me to use their video. We finalized arrangements, including the courtesy super that credited his station.

"Oh, one last thing—that rodeo contractor you asked about?" he said. "Turns out a rodeo committee nearby was in deep trouble because the new contractor they'd hired evaporated at nearly the last minute, and your guy mounted a rescue mission."

That was *not* the last thing in our conversation, considering the similarity to Sherman's situation. I had dozens of questions. He only had answers to two—the town's name and a possible contact.

It was intriguing, but I forced myself not to jump to a conclusion, because that was a sure way to prematurely close mental doors.

In a rendition of the time-honored Pass the Reporter game, the possible contact sent me to someone else, who in turn referred me to the committee chair. I had partially dialed the number for the committee chair when my cell rang.

It was Dex.

I stopped dialing, told Dex to hold on a minute, and headed outside. No way was I talking to him inside the KWMT newsroom.

Chapter Twenty-One

"**THEY FOUND FIBERS,**" Dex said as soon as I reached the parking lot and told him to go ahead. The sun was beating down on my head. I should have worn a hat. And a vat of sunblock.

"Fibers from somebody's clothes?"

"No. Fibers that could be consistent with the appearance of hanging."

I had a vivid image of the wooden beam that had so interested the deputies Saturday. "He was hanged, and that's what caused the ligature marks."

"Fibers were found that could be—"

"Fine, fine. Consistent with the appearance of hanging. So, fibers were around his neck."

"The area of the neck that would be consistent with hanging was too compromised. But fibers were found inside his collar and on his chest."

"But not around his neck? Then how would fibers get on his chest and inside his collar, and remain there to be found?"

"Very good, Danny. They could be expected to come from whatever was used to hang him, both as he was yanked to a hanging position and during a period of struggle, which would be expected. That friction would cause fibers to detach. Fibers also would have been around the neck initially, but, since that area was exposed, those fibers would have been dispersed by the bulls. Fibers that slipped inside the front and back of his collar, however, were afforded more protection, being caught between his clothing and his body."

Remembering how little protection his clothing had provided parts of his body, I said, "Were there many fibers left?"

"One can be enough," Dex said. "And there were more than that, because they were protected by the multiple layers of fabric. The collar and placket were less disturbed than areas covered by a single layer of fabric."

Compromised. Dispersed. Disturbed. Somehow the euphemisms were worse than the fact.

"They're trying to identify the fibers?"

"Yes, indeed. Looking first for class characteristics, then individual characteristics for a specific identity."

"Talking generally—" At his disapproving sound, I amended it to, "For the layperson, these fibers would be consistent with rope?"

"In the broadest, least useful terms, yes."

"Thank you, Dex." And I meant it, because I knew it pained him to talk in such terms. "Anything else? The autopsy—"

"Showed compression of the carotid arteries that is consistent with hanging."

I whistled soft and short. Score one for Richard. Actually, score a couple thousand for him. If this evidence hadn't been found to back his hunch, he would have been hip deep in agricultural byproducts for a very long time when the big shots returned.

"Could it be suicide?"

"Marks from the knot are wrong to be consistent with most suicides, and that region was not as severely compromised."

"Okay, Dex, I hear it."

"Hear what?"

"That smug tone that says you've got something you know you'll enjoy telling me. Spill it."

"Your deceased was strung up."

"Strung up? Is that the scientific term?"

"It fits," he said primly. "Either he stood still in that pen of bulls and let someone slip a lasso over his head, then let himself be strung up—"

"You like saying that, don't you?"

"It sounds so *Western*. Or," he picked up, "someone very good with a rope tossed it so it went over that beam—"

"Wait a minute. How do you know about the beam?"

"I've seen the crime scene photos, of course."

"The guy—your contact—sent them to you?"

"Professional courtesy."

"Since it's not an FBI case, you could send them to me and—"

"Oh, no. That would be a slap in the face to a colleague who shared them with me."

I knew he wouldn't budge on that.

"As I was saying," he resumed, "either he let someone put what was in essence a noose around his neck then toss the loose end of the rope over the beam, or someone very good with a rope tossed a looped rope over that beam in such a way that it came down around his neck. Either way, the person used the beam to yank him off his feet."

"But when Landry was found, there was no rope." I'd have to triple check with Jenks, but I hadn't seen one in the footage, and no one had mentioned a rope.

"Nevertheless, a rope, or similar implement, was used. A definitive quantity of fibers was found."

"That throw would be pretty tricky, wouldn't it?" Like champion-caliber roping. Unless, as Dex had said, the roper lassoed Landry first and then got the rope over the beam. No. Landry would have realized something was up and fought. "Somebody threw a rope over the beam and around a human head with all those bulls trampling around there?"

"It was only after he was dead that he was dropped and the bulls did damage," he said without much interest.

He wouldn't dismiss those bulls so readily if he'd seen them up close. Or, perhaps, that aspect wasn't geeky enough for him.

He added credence to my second conjecture when he added, "But you're not asking the most interesting question, Danny."

"I give. What's the most interesting question?"

"Was he dead or alive when he was roped and strung up?"

"That is an interesting question," I conceded. "Which was he?"

"They don't know yet."

"Dex!"

"I said it was the most interesting question, not the most interesting answer. It's quite fortunate they found evidence of the ligature considering the condition of the body, that he appears not to have been suspended for long, and the fact that he was—"

"Strung up," we concluded together.

"Danny, there's something else quite interesting."

"Oh?" I asked cautiously. Dex's *interesting* often was other people's *disgusting*.

"As one would expect, there are rope marks on the beam."

"From when he was strung up."

"Those, yes. Also others. The marks from the hanging are angled and quite deep. There are other, as yet unexplained marks, at a 90 degree angle to the beam and not as deep."

"Made before or after the, ah, fatal marks?"

"That has not been determined. Further tests will be required."

"Dex . . ." I closed my eyes. Sometimes, I swear, this mild, rather sweet scientist was the biggest tease on the planet.

✧   ✧   ✧   ✧

I CALLED MIKE inside KWMT and told him to meet me outside. While I waited, I called Jenks, on assignment covering the opening of a new exhibit at the local museum, footage that wouldn't air unless Fine unexpectedly lifted his all-Thurston edict.

"No rope," Jenks said in response to my question.

"Positive?"

"Positive. Unless it was shredded."

I thanked him as Mike approached.

"The question is, who could have roped him," I said at the end of my report. Mike had whistled when I'd described the throw over the beam. "That has to be an extremely difficult throw, right?"

"It's not one I'd ever expect to make."

"Good, that narrows the field. I know we watched Cas Newton

win that tie-down roping. And Heather Upton is a champion roper,
her mother bragged—why are you shaking your head?"

"The field's wider than that. Think about it. Who taught Heather
to rope?"

"How should I kno—oh. Her mother?"

"Yup. And Newton taught Cas. Linda's real good with a rope.
Don't forget Grayson Zane."

"I don't suppose Evan Watt's a horrible roper?"

He shook his head again. "Not Zane's or Heather's level, but good.
So's Oren Street. Most times, most places, I'd say that throw narrowed
the field a lot. But these are people who know how to throw a loop.
I'm not saying all of them could hit it every time, not even half the
time. But every one of them would have a chance."

"So it's still any one of them." I looked at my watch. "I've got to
go. I have an interview for a 'Helping Out' segment your aunt set up.
Diana's probably already there."

"Give me a call when you're done."

I agreed and was in my car, turning to head out, when he ran up
beside the driver's side, asking something I couldn't hear with the AC
on and the window up. I opened the window.

"Poly or nylon?"

"What?"

"The rope—was it poly or nylon? Knowing that would narrow it.
And if they know the twist—"

"He said rope." Actually, he hadn't. But I was paraphrasing.
"Rope. Fibers. Hanged. That's what I concentrated on. I've got to go."

✧ ✧ ✧ ✧

DIANA AND THE subject were waiting.

The subject wasn't the least bit annoyed, because Diana had kept
him talking about himself while she set up. If *she* was annoyed, she
didn't show it.

The interview went great. Walking out, I told Diana she was such a
good set-up person I'd have to be late all the time. She said, "No," in

her mother-of-two voice, and I apologized sincerely. She forgave me enough to let me follow the Newsmobile on a shortcut to the station that avoided what passed for traffic in Sherman.

I called Mike, but it sent me to voicemail. I left a message.

In the newsroom, Jennifer told me the Denver tape was in.

Even though it consisted of a cameraman walking through a house, it had impact. The place resembled an animal carcass picked clean.

With the interview fresh in my mind, I roughed out the package in record time. A little polish, a lead-in, and I'd have another deposit in my "Helping Out" bank. With this gang working its way through the region, I logged it in as the first to be used. And hoped the all-Thurston-all-the-time programming wouldn't last much longer at KWMT.

✧ ✧ ✧ ✧

AFTER A MOMENT'S hesitation, I accepted Burrell's telephoned last-minute invitation to lunch.

If he wasn't going to come clean about his editing job on the bull calls from Landry's phone on his own, I would use this opportunity to bring it out in the open myself. It was way past time.

But when he picked me up at the station, he announced he was glad I'd said yes because I'd have a chance to get to know somebody. So, lunch was out for raising the phone calls. And the drive to the Haber House Hotel didn't allow enough time before joining his not-so-mysterious third party.

In the cool dimness of the restaurant, the hostess walked us to a corner table with one occupant. Linda Caswell. Suspicion confirmed.

Our server was Kelly. She showed no sign of remembering me.

"Linda's real busy with the rodeo and all," Burrell said after reaffirming our introductions, "but like I told her, she's got to eat. Thought you two could get to know each other this way."

I would have preferred to interview her without a buffering presence. But I wouldn't let this opportunity go by. Except it became clear as the meal progressed that to get in serious questions, I'd need to make the opportunity happen.

First, a steady stream of people stopped to say hello to Tom or Linda or both. One or two acknowledged me.

Second, when the stream faltered, Tom fed Linda lines like "Tell Elizabeth about how your family got started in Cottonwood County" and "Tell Elizabeth how the Fourth of July Rodeo started" and "Tell Elizabeth about the state Claustel left the committee in."

Considering those puffy lead-ins, her responses were relatively restrained, though they covered ground I knew and took up time.

"Excuse me," I interrupted after Linda had refused Tom's suggestion of dessert. I suspected that even if I ordered a slice of chocolate pie, she would plead the press of business and leave us. "I want to get the server's attention to be sure the bill comes to me."

Tom frowned. "You're not paying."

"Oh, KWMT will pick it up." In the ultimate proof that I was not Pinocchio in a previous life, my nose remained its same size.

"You are not paying," he repeated, placing his napkin on the table and standing.

"Really, the station—"

"No." He strode off in search of Kelly, whom I'd seen slip out the side door seconds before I'd started this diversion.

"What do you want to ask me?" Linda asked.

So she'd recognized my ruse. Good. That saved time. "How does your former romantic relationship tie in with the Sherman Rodeo?"

She gave me a hard look. "I thought you might be going to ask me about Tom. But I'm not entirely surprised you're curious about that aspect under the circumstances," she said with dignity.

It was the dignity, nothing else, that persuaded me to go for honesty. "Specifically, I'd like to know what about your relationship with Grayson Zane would make him tense up about it five years later?"

"*Grayson?* I thought . . . He tensed up?" Sad eyes and a slight smile added wistfulness to her plain face. "No reason he should."

"But he broke it off?"

"Yes."

"There was nothing—?"

"No." Now the eyes and mouth erected a fence with a *No Trespassing* sign plastered on it.

I went around. "You thought I was going to ask about your romantic relationship with Keith Landry?"

I couldn't swear she'd flinched at the word *romantic*. There was no flinching in her answer. "Yes."

"Tell me about that."

"It started quickly, lasted somewhat longer than—" She cut herself off, looking away for the first time. "Ended just as abruptly. And the same way. As you probably already know. There are no secrets in Cottonwood County."

Dumped by Grayson Zane. Dumped by Keith Landry. Definitely coming down in the world. "Must have been hard to see him the next year." My *him* could only refer to Landry, since Zane had not returned the next year.

"It wasn't. What mattered then is what matters now—the Fourth of July Rodeo. So, no, it wasn't hard."

"What difficulties have there been over the years with Landry? In your capacity as a member of the rodeo committee, I mean."

She frowned, possibly a result of trying to remember. Or not. "I don't recall any. I was simply another committee member."

"You voted against Landry's company this year?"

"I voted *for* Sweet Meadows, as did a majority."

"But you voted against Landry, even when there was no other choice. Sounds like a personal grudge." I caught a tall figure closing in from the corner of my eye.

"My vote is always what I think best for the rodeo."

"Why did you want the livestock brought in early this year?"

She frowned deeper. "I didn't. I had nothing to do with that. Why would I?"

"That's what I'm asking." Tom drew his chair back, then stopped as I added, "I have a source who says you demanded Landry get the livestock in by Wednesday night."

"Your source is wrong."

"Elizabeth—"

I ignored Burrell. "My source has no reason to lie about it."

"I have no reason to lie."

"Don't say any more, Linda," Burrell said. "This is over. Go on, and we'll talk later. Elizabeth and I'll sit here a bit."

She obeyed his order, I didn't.

After skirting tables and people in my way, I followed her out, wanting to ask more, though not at the expense of making a scene. Since she had longer legs, a head start, and a clearer and closer path to the door, she was in her truck before I hit the parking lot.

Burrell arrived at a leisurely pace as she drove away.

"I'll take you back to the station," he said in his impossibly even voice.

When he opened the truck's passenger door, I climbed in, grabbed the handle with both hands, yanked the door out of his hold, and slammed it shut.

The trip to the station was accomplished in silence. His silence seemed to have the limitless calm of outer space. Mine felt like the inside of an industrial dryer—hot, jumbled, and crowded.

When he pulled to a stop in the KWMT parking lot, I had my purse strap on my shoulder and myself under control.

I cracked the door open before facing him. He was slewed in his seat, his back partially against his door. His mouth and dark eyes were impassive.

"Don't ever do that to me again," I said.

"You were asking—"

"It's my job to ask questions."

"Not questions like that."

"Exactly questions like that."

"It wasn't necessary to ask personal things to protect the rodeo and—"

"First, you don't decide what's necessary or not necessary for me. Second, protecting is not my job, Burrell. And it's not what we're doing—Mike and me, and ostensibly you. You agreed to help with this. That doesn't mean picking and choosing what can be looked into. And it doesn't mean erecting barriers to protect the rodeo or the people you like. It's the truth that matters. The truth. And you can't screw around with it. When you do, things happen."

He held his silence for half a beat. "Are we still talking about Landry's death? Or are you talking about your personal past."

I got out, closed the truck door—firmly, but not a slam—and leaned back in the open window.

"*I* am talking about the arrogance of Thomas David Burrell, who thinks he always knows best. That arrogance got you arrested for murder, and maybe that can be overlooked because you thought you were doing what was best for Tamantha—though I don't think you were right—but this time there's no such excuse."

"Elizabeth—"

"No. You said you were in on this investigation, but you're not. Not when you, in your infinite wisdom, have decided some people should not be considered suspects. And have—"

"Suspects of what?"

"—decided you don't need to share what you know, despite saying you would. And I'll tell you suspects of what, Burrell. Murder. Keith Landry's death was not an accident. It was murder."

I pushed off from the truck, turned around, and walked into KWMT-TV, knowing that I had, for the first time, seen Tom Burrell absolutely surprised.

Chapter Twenty-Two

INSIDE THE BUILDING, I stopped for a drink of water, and that was when the satisfaction of surprising Burrell gave way to regret that I'd told him Landry had been murdered. Damn. I should have kept my mouth closed.

Are we still talking about looking into Keith Landry's death? Or are you talking about your personal past.

Both, you jackass. Both.

The one I could *do* something about was Landry's murder.

After a moment's thought at my desk, I dialed Mrs. Parens' number and said I'd like to ask a few more background questions.

I should have eased into it, letting her give me another history lesson. I wasn't in the mood. "You've known Linda Caswell for a long time? I understand she had a rough time, growing up and with the death of her sister."

She gave me a skeletal outline of Linda's life. Her version was basically little more than I could get from reading clips and devoid of Penny's flourishes. Except once. When she talked about the aftermath of Inez's death.

"Linda and that boy held each other up in their grief," she said. "It made a true bond. Cas Newton loves his father, but he's a Caswell, through and through."

"Linda's never married?"

"Not as of this date."

"But I understand she was involved with Grayson Zane a few years back."

A tiny sound came from Mrs. Parens. Perplexed? Disapproving? Whatever it was, it didn't seep into her precise, cool words. "I believe they did keep company for a short time."

"He broke it off?"

"That is my understanding. What—"

I covered the objection I felt coming with another question. "She immediately began seeing Keith Landry, didn't she?" I gave her only a beat before I followed with, "She told me she did."

"What does this have to do with your inquiries, Elizabeth?"

"I don't know. But one thing I learned early in reporting is to follow the anomalies. Something that doesn't make sense at first, usually will make sense if you look at it from a different angle. But you have to follow it long enough to know which different angle it needs." I considered my words. "If that makes sense."

"It does, although it could have been expressed with greater economy."

"Yes'm," I said before I could stop it. I redeemed myself by adding, "A woman like Linda Caswell having a brief relationship with a rodeo cowboy, then with a rodeo stock contractor immediately after, is quite an anomaly, wouldn't you agree?"

The silence vibrated with something I couldn't put my finger on. Disapproval yes, but something else as well.

"My agreement or disagreement is immaterial," she said. "However, if you want to follow the anomaly of Linda's personal life, you will need to do so from another source."

She gave me nothing more, unless you count what sounded like a sincere wish that I have a good day.

Mrs. Parens was one of those sources a reporter loves to hate, or possibly hates to love. When she told you a fact, it was golden. She might tell you what she knew of a person's character, but she didn't volunteer much and rarely ventured into the oh-so-profitable realm of speculation or downright gossip.

I reviewed Sunday's conversation . . . and recognized one fact she had told us: Vicky Upton was not a widow.

Interesting. I focused on precisely what Mrs. Parens had said.

There was something about that conversation. I felt my forehead contracting in concentration. To hell with the wrinkles. There was something . . .

I straightened.

Mrs. Parens had practically *volunteered* the information that Vicky had never been married. At least she'd made me stand still in front of the puzzle long enough to spot the pattern.

Why? Because there had been another puzzle she didn't want me zooming in on? What had we been talking about?

Heather's father. He was dead. But hadn't been dead for a long time. Vicky had been a rodeo queen before she was a mother.

I snapped my head up. Jennifer was across the room, and at her fingertips were the facts I needed to test a new surmise.

But between us stood Thurston Fine.

If I went to the newsroom aide's desk, he was close enough to eavesdrop. If I called her over, he'd follow. If I messaged her, he could read whatever appeared on her computer screen . . . as he seemed to be doing this very moment.

I grabbed the phone off the empty desk behind me—in case Fine's eyes were good enough to read Caller ID on Jennifer's phone—and hit the numbers for her extension.

"Don't say who it is and don't look around," I said quickly, "but if you have anything on your computer screen you don't want Thurston to know, switch screens right now."

"I know *that*," she said with something close to disdain, which evaporated into confusion. "But who is this?"

"Elizabeth."

"Ohhhhh." As if that explained everything, which apparently it didn't, because she added, "Why are you calling me?"

"Because Fine's right over your shoulder, and I don't want him to know what I'm about to ask you."

"That makes sense. I'd already taken care of that from this end when the issue first arose." In other words, she'd been aware of Fine's arrival and switched to something innocuous on her screen.

"Good. I want to know a couple things, and I don't want you to write this or type it—again, because of Fine. Understand?"

"Well, *yeah*. It's pretty obvious, isn't it?"

"I suppose it is. And you're not to tell anyone anything about this information. Understand?"

"You always say that."

For good reason, since she'd spilled the beans to me a couple months back that Fine had spread rumors that I'd been demoted from the network because of drug use. But, as far as I knew, Jennifer hadn't blabbed anything she'd learned from me.

"I know. It's important. It might be very important to figuring out why that man died at the rodeo grounds, but even if it's not, it will be important and very private for the people involved."

"Got it. What is it?"

"I need to know when Heather Upton was born. And if Keith Landry was in Sherman about nine months before that."

"Nine—? Oh. *Oh*. Okay."

"Can you find those things out?"

"Easy. As soon as . . . as soon as I can."

"Excellent. The last thing, Jenny—"

"Jennifer."

"Yes, I'm sorry. Jennifer—be careful when you give me the answers. For the same reasons."

"Sure thing."

✧ ✧ ✧ ✧

TRIANGLES APPEARED beside the names I'd written on a pad.

The names were Vicky Upton, Sonja Osterspeigel, and Linda Caswell with a question mark. Also the name Keith Landry, surrounded by lots and lots of triangles.

I wrote *rodeo queen*. Then *not every year*. Finally, Oren Street's list of three things that mattered to Landry: money, women, and power. I wrote one on each leg of the biggest triangle around his name. I drew a triangle around each word: money, women, power.

I had my hand on the phone to redial Jennifer, when it rang.

"I'm on my way to the station to get you," Mike said.

"Oh? Are we going somewhere?"

"Yes. I finally got Lloyd Sampson off by himself, fed him lunch. And got some info about the beam. The experts think the straight marks were made before—probably shortly before—the angled ones. They hedge it around with a lot of scientific stuff, but that's what it amounts to. Also, they believe the angled marks were from when Landry was hanged."

"Good work, Mike." *A far more productive lunch than mine.*

"There's more, and it's better. I told Lloyd that I saw what they found caught in the wood post. Told him I saw a piece of green string held in tweezers." He drew in a breath. "He said it wasn't green. It was pink."

"*Very* good, Mike."

"Just wait. A shred of pink shiny cloth, like it was torn off a piece of clothing. Like maybe a girl's fancy shirt."

I recalled the conversation we'd overheard between Heather and her mother Saturday night. "The famous torn pink shirt."

"My thoughts exactly. So do we tell Richard? Or what?"

✧   ✧   ✧   ✧

FROM DOWN THE street, we watched Cas Newton's truck pull into the sun-dazzled Upton driveway, Heather emerge, an exchange of waves, Cas drive away.

Vicky was at her job as a guide at the big museum in town. Heather was home for her customary break between her part-time job at the Sandwich Shop and her evening duties as rodeo queen. As always, Aunt Gee's reconnaissance was one hundred percent accurate.

Heather swung the door open with an air of impatience. "I told you—" She broke off when she saw who was at the door.

"Hi, Heather. We want to talk to you for . . . for a story."

Her eyes sharpened. "This is in addition to the one Leona is doing for next weekend, right?"

"Yes." And it was not a lie. Leona D'Amato was KWMT's fluff

specialist. If a story came out of what Mike and I were pursuing, it would be completely separate from what Leona did.

"I don't have long. I need to rest before tonight's rodeo or I'll look as old as . . ." She let it die after flicking a look toward me. Clearly, tact was not a required element on the rodeo queen committee's checklist.

The house seemed familiar. From the front door, we looked straight ahead into the kitchen where an ironing board was set up. It was the only element out of order. To the left was a hallway that presumably led to the bedrooms. To the right, the living room.

Heather led us three steps to a couch under the front window. An out of date TV sat across from it. On the end wall, surrounded by plaques and awards, was a two-by-three-foot framed photo of Heather, complete with tiara. Vicky had wasted no time.

"How can you do a story with no camera. Not that I'd be on camera like this."

"You look great," Mike said with his smile. "But this is background, so no camera."

She nodded wisely. "Background. Like about me growing up and how hard I've worked to be rodeo queen."

"That's more for Leona," I said, keeping my tone light. "What we'd like to know is what you saw and did Wednesday night at the rodeo grounds."

Her eyes flickered, and the color in her face washed out. But she did not buckle at the knees. "It was like any other rodeo night. I did my run-through for the queen, because my first warm-up queen's ride was the next night—Thursday. Though I won't do it for real until the Fourth of July. That's the important one. That's—"

"On Wednesday—"

"I placed second in barrel racing." She emitted a dissatisfied huff. "Should have won. My concentration wasn't—"

"Later that night, Heather. Much later. After everyone else was gone."

"I wasn't there. I left and came home like always—"

"You and Keith Landry were by the bull pens."

"—and stayed here. I—"

"We know you were there, Heather."

"You're wrong. I wasn't. I told you—"

"The tear in your pink shirt proves it."

She froze with her mouth open.

I kept on. "A piece of fabric the sheriff's department found at the scene will precisely match that tear." It was a bit of a gamble, but not much.

She closed her mouth, her eyes remained wide.

"You have a choice, Heather. You can tell us what happened for background, with no camera, just as we said. Or we can take what we know to the sheriff's department right now, and you can tell them, a conversation that will *not* be on background, and certainly will be on the news."

I didn't mention that no matter what, at some point very soon, we'd have to tell Alvaro about the matching torn shirt. Especially if he went public with discovery of the pink fabric. Because then we could not pretend we didn't know what he didn't know we knew.

"That shirt is not the only item that shows you were there." I avoided the word evidence for now. "And what you did."

"I didn't—"

"You did. But why you did what you did can make all the difference in how this plays out, Heather. We want to know why. Why you did it."

"I . . . I was caught."

"Caught?" I repeated when it seemed she might not say more.

"On that pole, the old one, the wood one."

It took me a beat to realize she was answering my *why you did it* with an explanation of how her shirt ripped. "What were you doing there?"

"It was because of the bulls. I couldn't go straight through, because the bulls were in those pens. I don't know why. They shouldn't have been there . . . and he was coming at me."

"Who?"

"*Him.* The one who died."

"Landry? Coming at you? Threatening?"

"Yeah." She'd gone pale, her lips even paler, like she might be sick to her stomach. "The things he was saying, and that smirk. It was bad enough at lunch when he'd pawed at me, but then . . ."

Again, she seemed about to get stuck. I nudged, "So, you're by the chute, and Landry is coming at you . . . But how did it start? He didn't just start—what?—leering at you and coming at you."

"Yes, he did! When he saw me, he did. That's exactly what he did."

"Back up, where were you when he first saw you?"

"I told you. Stuck by that chute. I'd tried to slip away when I heard him, and that's when my shirt—"

"You heard him. Doing what?"

"Yelling at somebody. On the phone."

"About what? Do you remember anything he said?"

"Something about damn well get your ass here, and do it now, and do what you were supposed to do or there'd be hell to pay," she said with some of her customary snap.

"Did you get any sense of who he was talking to?"

"No."

I eyed her. I wouldn't have bet a nickel either way. "Then what?"

"He must have spotted me, because he hung up fast and started in that awful, slimy voice about wasn't I the eager one, and no need to be shy, and this was even better than he expected and . . . and the other stuff."

"Other stuff?"

"What he'd . . ." She swallowed audibly. "Do."

"What happened then?"

"I told him he was crazy and disgusting, and I'd never—I kept yelling at him, but he wasn't listening. It was like . . . He wouldn't stop. And the flounce from my shirt was caught in the wood of those old posts. I tried pulling away, heard the material start to tear, and knew Mom would skin me alive. But I had to stop him. I had to, because . . ." She sucked in a breath. "I'd done a trick over a bar to rope a cow. I knew I could make the toss. Got him first time."

Mike twitched. I empathized. Was this girl such a rock-hard killer that she took pride in putting the rope around a man's neck on her first try? But if she wasn't such a rock-hard killer . . .?

Don't get ahead of yourself, Danniher. One question at a time. "What happened next?"

"I tied off the rope—"

A damned casual way of saying it if she meant she'd yanked the rope tight until a man died from hanging.

"—so I had both hands to get the shirt out without tearing it worse." Yet left a fragment of pink fabric. "I got out of there. With him yelling at me the whole time, saying he'd see to it I was dumped as queen, and I'd have to give back the scholarship, and there'd be a scandal and everything."

"Yelling?" I repeated.

"Yeah. He started off sort of laughing, you know, when I swung the loop and it settled over him, like I was being . . . *cute* or something. When I snugged it up, he started yelling."

"He could yell?"

She frowned. "Sure."

"Heather, where was the rope?"

"I told you, tied off on the chute."

"The part of it around Keith Landry—where was that?"

"Around him, like I told you."

She sounded impatient, and I felt the same way, but I didn't want to put words in her mouth—or take them out.

She resolved the issue with a hunched shoulder gesture that might have been part of a shrug, except she drew both elbows in tight to her waist and clamped her hands to her sides. "Like that," she said.

"Because the rope was . . .?"

"Around his waist, holding his arms in tight. I saw him trying to work his arms to loosen it up, but he would've still had a ways to go." Her chin wobbled. "I suppose that's why he didn't get away from the bulls, though why—"

"None of that's clear yet," I said firmly. I couldn't tell her the truth. If she wasn't innocent, it might help a murderer go free. If she was innocent, it could compromise the investigation. And either way, if it ever got back to Quantico that I'd shared details with a suspect, I would not only never get another piece of information from Dex, he'd probably feed me to the squirrels. "Let's get this straight. Landry walked through the bull pen, and—"

"Through? No way. He'd've been an idiot to do that. He came down the aisle next to it, toward the chute. That's what I don't understand, how he got in the pen. It doesn't make sense. When I left he was in the aisle. Why would he go in there?"

I shook my head to say I had no answer.

"What were you doing there that late?" Mike asked.

Her face changed slightly, her mouth went mulish.

"If you were meeting Landry, it's not—" he added.

"No! I wasn't meeting him. I didn't want anything to do with him, not ever. I—I'd left gear behind. I didn't sleep for remembering it and went to get it."

"What time?"

"I don't know."

"Heather—"

"I *don't* know."

"Were the security lights on?"

"Those, and ones around the office, where . . . *he* had come from."

"Was there a light on in the rodeo office?"

"I don't know. I wasn't paying attention to that."

I gave Mike a chance to ask more, then picked it up. "Last question: Why not rope him regular, instead of over the bar?"

A flicker of You-Stupid-Easterner expression appeared. "Roping's for pulling something toward you, or dragging it behind. That's what a regular throw would've done. But I wanted to stop him coming toward me, and I sure didn't want him dragging behind. I wanted to slow him down enough to get out of there. And that's what I did."

✧   ✧   ✧   ✧

MY PHONE RANG as we drove to my house to talk this through—no way could we discuss it a KWMT, not with Fine prowling.

"It's the person who put together your computer," came a hushed voice.

"Jen—Jennifer?"

"Shh, don't say. For the usual reasons."

"Jennifer, if Fine's near you, he already knows who you are."

After a pause, she said, "Right. I won't say—you know—the other part."

"Good. Don't name me or anything to give away what we're talking about."

"Yeah . . . Yeah, okay. So," she said in her normal voice, practically blasting my ear because I'd been listening closely. "That *birthday* party we were, you know, *planning*? That'll be on April 20. To celebrate *his* eighteenth birthday *next* year."

"Heather Upton's birthday is April 20."

"Right."

"She'll be eighteen next year. Was Landry involved with the Fourth of July Rodeo the year before she was born? That would be nineteen years ago this month."

"Exactly! Right the *second* time."

"That was the second year he was stock contractor here?"

"Perfect. That'll be a perfect present." I heard a male voice in the background. "Gotta go."

"One last thing. Can you come by my house tonight? Remember where it is? After you get off? When is that?"

"Nine. Yeah, I can. And, yeah, I remember."

She hung up, and I turned to Mike.

"Got it," he said. "A good chance Heather is Landry's daughter. He couldn't have known, not going after her the way she said. God, he couldn't have known."

"No idea. The other two questions we don't have answers to are if she knew he was her father, and if she was telling us anything like the truth."

✧   ✧   ✧   ✧

"**KEITH LANDRY** was outside the bulls' pen with the rope holding his arms tight around his waist. Then what?" I demanded of Mike, as we sat in my rental's living room.

"Sounds like Colonel Mustard in the library with the wrench. Okay, quit groaning. It wasn't *that* not-funny. Of course, that's assuming Heather told us the truth."

"True. But would she have told us anything if she'd hanged him? I'd have expected her to throw us out. Deny, deny, deny."

"Could be an act, to make us think the way you're thinking."

"True again. Though if she's that good, forget rodeo queen, she should be on Broadway. Also, her story explains things we hadn't understood."

"Like why Landry let himself get roped at all."

I nodded. "Sounds like he thought it was some sort of foreplay at first. On the other hand, her story leaves new questions. Like how did the rope go from his waist to his neck, which it had to do for him to be hanged? What happened to the rope? How did he get in the pen with the bulls?"

"Still assuming she's telling the truth, whoever got the rope from his waist to his neck probably took it. In other words, the murderer."

"Maybe, but not necessarily. And how would he or she get it while the bulls were—you know. Plus, another new question, who was he meeting there?"

"Again, probably the murderer."

I repeated, too. "Maybe, but not necessarily. Let's start with the first question, how the rope got from his waist to his neck. I have an idea."

Chapter Twenty-Three

THE KNOCK AT the door came at the worst possible moment.

"Stay there," I ordered Mike. "Don't move."

"Forget it. I'm sitting . . . if I can."

Impatient, I opened the door. Tom Burrell's tall form filled the frame.

"Elizabeth," he said. I saw him focus over my shoulder, then back to me. "Looks like I came at an inopportune moment. I have something I think you'll want to hear, but I can come back later."

"You can come in and rescue me," Mike called from the other side of the living room, where he sat on the edge of a wooden chair.

"I don't want to interrupt if you two are uh, otherwise tied up," Burrell said, his tone what my grandmother called half-kidding, whole-earnest. His eyes became serious when he met my look, and he said very low, "It's not as black and white as you—"

Mike called, "Oh, for heaven's sake. Let him in, Elizabeth."

With reluctance, I let the door swing wide. Burrell entered with a glance at me that acknowledged this was not done.

"No more tied-up jokes, Tom," Mike added.

"Well, you can understand my wanting to be a bit delicate with . . . what is that you're tied up with?"

"Extension cord," I said. "We're recreating what might have happened with Keith Landry."

"I didn't think an extension cord figured into it," Burrell said.

"I tried to tell her . . ."

"We had to improvise," I said firmly, heading off a resurgence of that dispute.

"You've gotta hear what we found out, Tom," Mike said.

I shot him a look, but he wasn't looking at me, and I could hardly complain, since I'd told Burrell it was murder.

Mike recapped what Heather had told us, and how that led us to the question of how the rope went from around Landry's waist to around his neck. Which led us to this demonstration.

At the end, Tom gazed at the extension cord tied around Mike's waist, pinning his arms to his sides, for a long moment before saying, "Elizabeth, you know a lot more about the world outside Wyoming. But I know a sight more about things here."

I gestured to acknowledge that and to indicate he should get on with whatever he was driving at.

"A rope's a whole different animal from an extension cord. Not to mention you're about to cut off circulation in Mike's hands."

"Thank you," breathed Mike.

It was that male allies thing, and it drove me nuts. Even though I was far from ready for any zinging, and might never be, there was the promise of a definite zing with each of these men. So shouldn't they be at each other's throats, instead of going all buddies and teaming up against me?

"I wanted to simulate the restriction of movement. All you had to do was say it hurt." I started undoing the knotted extension cord. Maybe I had been overzealous.

"I did. You said that would have been more motivation for Landry to try to get free. I couldn't offer rope without going out to my place," Mike said to Tom, "and she didn't want to wait."

"I wasn't the only one, Mr. Gung Ho Investigator. You—"

"I have rope in my truck."

Tom was dispatched to get it, while I finished freeing Paycik.

"I am sorry," I said.

He rubbed his arms briskly. "I know you'd have let me loose if I'd really hollered, Elizabeth. I just didn't want to really holler."

His grin twisted, and I responded with a mock severe, *"Men."*

A brief knock announced Tom's return. "This is old ranch rope.

It'd be better if we knew what kind Heather throws. Did your expert say, Elizabeth?"

"Just a rope."

They both looked at me as if I'd blasphemed.

"First off, like I told you, there's poly or nylon—they've pretty much replaced the old hemp or rawhide," Mike said. "They're less changeable in cold or wet, so you know what you're throwing no matter the weather."

"Then come the real choices," picked up Tom. "Right twist, left twist, treated, untreated, what scant you like, what kind of lay. 'Course that depends a lot on what you're roping. Softer for calves. Stiffer if you're heeling."

Back to Mike. "And the length. Too long, and you got that extra weight. Too short, and you're compensating. And there's the *feel*. Got to work it, see how it fits your hands, how it throws a loop. 'Course, there's also braided—"

"Mostly bull riders," Tom said.

"Heather Upton was *not* riding bulls," I said. "Can we—"

"True," Mike said—to Tom, not me. "The kind of hondo, too."

"Hondo?" I repeated. "What on earth?"

"The eye of the rope, to make the loop," Mike tossed over his shoulder to me before returning to Tom. "A breakaway hondo would have popped open under the pressure when he was hauled up."

"Good point, Mike. She must have been using a regular hondo. That would narrow which of her ropes—"

"All right, all right," I said. "If they ever find the rope, you two have convinced me they'll be able to positively ID it as Heather's and probably determine when, where, and how that specific chunk of rope was made. But in the meantime, can we do something with *this* rope, or do we have to wait for a twin of the rope she used—grown from the very same plant or—"

"Like I said," Mike started, "poly and nylon have—"

"—mostly replaced plant ropes. I swear, I'll study ropes—but *after* this murderer is found."

"Sounds like a trip to King's is in order," Tom said.

"Good idea," Mike agreed.

"What's King's?"

"King's Saddlery and Ropes in Sheridan. It's a great place for an education on ropes."

"Fine. I'll go, I'll take a class or—" They chuckled. This male bonding had passed the annoying threshold a while back. "—or whatever. If we can get on with this, forget the delightful nuances of all things rope, and return to trying to find a murderer."

"Your rope's a lot closer to whatever she used than that extension cord," Mike said to Tom.

He nodded back. "And without that wad of knots."

I had a strong urge to blow them both raspberries, which I do well, having had a great deal of practice in my youth in commenting on my siblings' doings.

"There's no room in here to throw a loop. And I doubt this is a demonstration you'd want in your yard for neighbors to see?" Tom made it a question with one raised brow to me.

"No thanks. Don't want Neighborhood Watch after me."

"So, we'll place it like it would have ended up on Landry. You've done your turn, Mike. Why don't you do the tying, and I'll take the role of Landry."

Mike shook his head. "Your rope, you do the roping. Besides, I've got experience now."

I noticed neither offered to let me do the tying. The wad of knots on the extension cord hadn't been *that* big, though Tom was significantly more efficient handling the rope than I had been with the extension cord.

The rope had a small loop tied at one end—a hondo, I realized. The rest of the rope had already been passed through it, so all Tom had to do once he'd passed that bigger loop over Mike's shoulders and down to his waist was tug the loose end to tighten it.

"He couldn't get out of this?" I asked. "Spread his arms and open the circle wide enough that it drops, and step out of it."

Mike shook his head, demonstrating by trying to stretch his arms. "If she uses a leather burner, that would add friction and make it harder for the ropee to release it," he said.

"The angle, too." Tom looked around. "Mike, if you kneel by the door to the kitchen, we might be able to mimic some of that."

Mike prepared to kneel without a murmur of protest—despite having bad knees that ended his NFL career.

"Wait a minute." I grabbed a cushion from the ratty couch and put it directly under where his knees would hit. "Kneel on this."

"I'm okay."

"Use it, you bull-headed—"

"Sorry, Mike, I forgot. We'll switch and I'll—"

Before Tom or I finished our protests, Mike was down, but at least he was on the cushion. "This doesn't bother them much."

"All those knee surgeries and this doesn't—"

"Elizabeth, if you'd move out of the way." Burrell's interruption was a barely veiled order to shut up and quit lecturing Mike.

I moved. I shut up.

Tom passed the rope coil over the open kitchen door, then disappeared behind it. I followed. He was tying off the rope around a chunky leg of the kitchen table. We returned to the living room.

"Can you move?" Tom asked Mike.

"Not much. Going over the door and being this low made it harder. Would have been even more so going over that beam." As he spoke, he worked his shoulders forward and back, tried to pull out one arm, then the other.

"Is that loosening the rope?" I asked.

"Some." He frowned in concentration. "Very little."

"Enough to get out?"

"Not any time soon."

"Landry did it somehow, because the rope went from his middle to his neck."

"Mike can't reach the hondo. If Keith Landry could, that would have helped," Tom said.

"That's an *if* and a *could*. Not the strongest material to work with," I said.

Mike stopped trying to pull his arms up, instead trying to slide his right elbow to the middle of his back. His motion had his shoulder rotating in a way shoulders should not rotate. "Mike, you'll pull something out of its socket if you don't—"

"Almost . . . there . . . almost . . . Got it!"

I'd been watching his elbow and shoulder. I hadn't noticed the tips of his fingers slide inside his front jeans pocket, scissoring his phone out. Now he manipulated it into his palm and pressed a number.

"Brilliant, Mike—his phone. Of—" I was interrupted by my phone ringing.

Mike grinned. "No need to answer. Just demonstrating."

"Some guys keep their phone clipped to their belt," Tom said. "If Keith Landry did, that would have made it easier."

"Much easier," Mike said. "Unless he had a lot of time to work free, the phone might answer the issue of how the rope got loose. Because it had to be loosened to get from his waist to his neck."

"A friend?" Tom said. He put a hand between Mike's back and the rope and tugged. It loosened the loop. Mike started to maneuver it toward his shoulders. "Not yet, Mike. Leave it where it was."

As soon as Mike complied, Tom went around the door, and the rope went taut again.

Tom came back to our side of the door. "Didn't take much."

"The cell phone records," I said. "We have to get a look at those records—the complete records."

Tom said, "You're thinking early calls could have been made by Landry. At least one, the call Heather heard when he arranged to meet someone before he spotted her—"

"If she's telling the truth," Mike inserted.

"—or, if he got to his phone the way Mike did, then a call to someone asking for help after Heather left."

"Exactly," I said. "Whoever he calls arrives, loosens the rope, and Landry starts to pull it up to get free."

"But his *friend* has left the rope over the beam and at the right moment, yanks it tight," Tom picked up. "The friend stands in front of Landry, holding the end of the rope. He'd see exactly when to do it. As soon as it was tight, Landry didn't have a chance."

We were silent, all envisioning the scene, I suspected.

"You think a woman could have done it?" Mike asked Tom.

"Hard to know for sure based on this experiment, but a strong woman, used to ranching . . . I'd think so."

"Especially one fueled by anger, adrenaline, or both," I said. "There's one problem—at least one. We don't know how Landry ended up in the bull pen."

"I've got an idea about that," Mike said. "Tom, go back in the kitchen, give me a count of three, and give the rope a good, hard pull."

"Why? What—"

"Just watch, Elizabeth," Mike ordered.

Tom counted. On *Three* the rope went taut, hauling Mike up several inches.

He tucked his legs like for a cannonball into a pool. For three seconds he swung, held only by the rope around his middle. The rope eased, and he came back to the floor.

"Did you see that, Elizabeth? Did you see it?"

"Yes."

Tom came around the door. "See what?"

"He swung. Mostly sideways."

"The angle across the beam," Mike said. He stood, and Tom loosened the rope. "Not only was Landry yanked off his feet, but he was yanked sideways. Over the bull pen."

"Would it get him over the top rail?" I asked.

"It could take some doing," Mike acknowledged. "The height of the beam would make a difference. And the strength of the person pulling."

I brought a chair over, stood on it and looked at the top of the door. Faint marks ran perpendicular to the door's face. A deeper groove cut into the edges at an angle from when Mike let the rope take his full weight.

"Grooves. Similar to what Lloyd described to you, Mike." I removed a chip of paint loosened by the experiment and shook my head. "The sacrifices I make."

"All in the interests of justice," Mike said.

"And at the expense of my security deposit."

"Good lord, you paid a security deposit on this place?"

My cell and the landline rang almost simultaneously. I answered when I saw it was Audrey from KWMT. By habit I checked my watch—four twenty-seven. Before I finished hello, she shouted, "He's short! Thurston. He's short. He says a minute, and Warren can fill in on the weather. But I've looked at it twice, and it's five fifteen short. *Five-frigging-fifteen!* Maybe more. And he won't do—"

As the wail continued in my ear, I covered the phone's mouthpiece and said, "Problem at the station. Paycik and I have to go right now."

"—anything about it. And there's nothing from yesterday I can grab because—"

"Hole," I said to Mike's questioning look. "Five fifteen."

"Holy shit!" He rustled through notes on the coffee table for his keys.

"—it was all him, and this is all him, and he won't approve using anything from the feed, and oh, my God, we're going to have six minutes of dead air, even if Warren gives the weather from around the entire fucking globe!"

"Audrey, calm down. And you can stop calling my other number now."

"Oh. Right. But five-fucking-fifteen! He won't listen. Just walks away. How will we ever—?"

"We'll be right there. Paycik's here. He can do something. And I have 'Helping Outs' in the can."

"I know. I checked, but the one booked for first says it's not done."

"I can get it done in time. And Audrey, you're the producer. You are the *producer.*"

She gulped in two shaky breaths. "Okay. I'll be okay."

"Good. We're on our way."

All three of us were out the door and down the steps before I turned to Tom. "We forgot. You came to tell us something."

"It'll hold. Go fix your hole."

Chapter Twenty-Four

WE DID. BY THE skin of our teeth. And with no help from Thurston Fine.

He insisted the time would be fine, and Audrey was panicking. Kept insisting it, despite the numbers consistently coming in at more than six minutes short. Stubbornly insisted on it with another refusal to approve Audrey or Mike using anything from the network feed. Went on insisting it while I gave the Gift Card Burglars package a lick and a promise, and Mike knocked together a sports report.

Serenely insisted on it, until the instant when he took back the toss from Warren Fisk after the shortened weather segment allotted under the Thurston Fine regime . . . and saw he had nearly seven minutes of airtime left.

He blanked. Utterly. Completely. Potentially fatally.

Temptation to let him stew in his own hubris rose. Professional instincts won out. I slid into the seat Jerry, who served as both floor director and cameraman, had set up over Fine's protest, and launched into my solo lead-in.

The piece looked better than I had any right to hope it would. With Fine still apparently comatose, I did the wrap-up I'd written for him and ad-libbed a toss to Mike for his teaser.

In the commercial break before the meat of Mike's report, I eye-balled Thurston. He blinked twice. Presumably he was still in there.

"Can he do the close?" came Audrey's disembodied voice.

Jerry and Mike looked at me. I looked at the control booth and said, "Ask him."

After a pause came a tentative, "Thurston, can you do the close?"
Nothing.

"Elizabeth, is he conscious?" Jerry asked.

Now on the camera side of the anchor desk, I went close and bent to look into his face.

I don't know what came over me. I reached across the desk, grabbed his suit where one lapel crossed the other and yanked him forward until his ribs must have connected with the desk, because he stopped abruptly.

"Thurston! You are doing this close, you hear me. You will sign off this show like a professional, or you sitting here like an idiot will go viral faster than you can say former anchorman."

"Coming back, in five, four—"

"He'll do it." I wasn't sure if it was a prediction or a threat.

"—three, two, one."

Mike came through beautifully. He turned it back to Fine with only enough time for the simplest of sign offs.

We held our breaths as one second went by and a second started— a lifetime in live TV.

"That's all from KWMT-TV news until your updated report at ten p.m. I'm Thurston Fine, saying I'll see you then."

"And we're clear."

Fine walked off the set without once looking at anyone.

As soon as the set door closed behind him, we saw a pantomime of jubilation through the window of the control room.

✧   ✧   ✧   ✧

WE ALL TROOPED out to a hurried but giddy dinner at Hamburger Heaven. All except Thurston and one poor soul left to man the phones.

Surviving near-catastrophe is a rite of passage for any newsroom with pretensions to being a true working news unit. Even those who had not been here tonight would catch the reflected glow of overcoming the odds.

Back at KWMT, Audrey gave instructions for the late news with a new crispness. She said she was covered for the half-hour, which would include the shorter version of the package I'd prepared, and we didn't need to stay. She thanked us again and strode away with purpose.

"A producer is born," Mike said under his breath.

Jennifer hurried up, clutching her laptop to her chest. "Elizabeth, are you leaving?"

"I guess so." I gave Mike a questioning look, but he didn't respond.

"Can I come to your house to do the next part of . . . you-know-what?" Her voice dropped to a hoarse whisper. "While we were at dinner, Fine asked Dale how to track employees' Internet searches. It wouldn't matter even if Dale told him and Fine managed it, because I'm not on the station's system, but it's . . . creepy. And I can't go home because Mom's got bunco, and even with headphones I can't shut them out. Those women are *loud*."

"Sure. What about you, Mike? We'll go over—"

"Sorry. I've got something I've got to do. I'll call you in the morning. 'Night, Elizabeth, Jennifer." And he was gone.

I did wonder . . . but he was entitled to a personal life. Though this was not the most convenient time. And it was his damned rodeo.

Jennifer rode with me. She said her father drove her to work, and she would have gotten a ride home from Dale, who I realized was the tall, skinny aide who walked with his head tucked, as if afraid it might hit the ceiling.

She came out back with me while I put out fresh water for Shadow, though there was no sign of him.

Back inside, Jennifer settled in on the couch, opened her laptop, and poised her hands over the keyboard like a pianist. "Want me to keep working on the DBA woman or something else?"

"Something else right now. Use the list of where Landry's been as stock contractor and find the names of women who have been rodeo queen in those places the years he's been there."

This had been the upshot of my earlier triangle doodling with the women's names and Landry's pattern. I'd been about to ask her to track this when Mike's call about Heather took precedence.

Her eyes widened. "Oh. You think he's been going after rodeo queens from way, way, way back when it was Heather's mom right up to Sonja. And not just here?"

I wasn't sure Vicky would appreciate that many "ways." I didn't correct Jennifer in thinking Sonja had been his last Sherman rodeo queen target. Apparently, Jennifer didn't subscribe to the Penny News Flash, or she'd have known about his chasing Heather.

"I'm wondering." My phone rang. "And I'd like to know," I added, before answering.

It was Matt. I took the call in the kitchen.

He confirmed most of what I'd suspected. Roy Craniston was a bit player at best among hard-core animal rights protestors, viewed as an opportunist, rather than a true-believer. As a bonus, Matt said his sources acknowledged they'd never protested the Sherman rodeos— nightly or the Fourth of July—because they *weren't as bad as the worst*. "Pretty high praise from these folks," he inserted.

Craniston's usual female companion was Eleanor Redlaw, who came from El Paso, Texas. Matt's sources said she was the brains, and Roy was the ego of the outfit.

I rewarded Matt by asking him to find out about a girl in her late teens/early twenties with a wide streak of blue in her hair who protested at the Sherman rodeo and other, unnamed, rodeos.

"Gee, why not make it really challenging," he grumbled.

"C'mon, a swath of blue in her hair. Used to be all pink. Said to be from Oklahoma. That's hardly a challenge to the mighty Matt Lester."

"Yeah, I love you, too. Call you if I get something."

"*When* you get something," I said, catching a corner of a chuckle before the line clicked dead.

✧   ✧   ✧   ✧

AFTER JENNIFER had a few names, I searched for phone numbers on my laptop, then started calling. The first two acknowledged only a vague recollection of Landry as the stock contractor the year they were rodeo queen. The next wasn't available.

Then I hit a familiar story.

An attractive rodeo cowboy pursued the rodeo queen. After the queen's favor had been won, attractive cowboy dumped her abruptly and with no warning. Landry swooped in on the heartbroken as the understanding and comforting older man. He'd enjoyed the spoils, then performed a similar dump. Like a vulture swooping in to snap up what was left over by the wolf.

That wasn't my image. It was Mandy Abernathy's. Call Number Seven, Confirmation Number Two.

After Mandy, we switched to possibilities in the Pacific Time Zone because it was getting late to call in the Mountain Time Zone.

We found three. The first Pacific Time Zone woman was another in the pattern. The next hung up when I said Landry's name. The third vaguely recalled the name.

The math in my head felt like it might be about to give me an answer, then came another incoming call.

"Elizabeth." It was Mike.

"Hey. We've made progr—"

"I've got to talk to you. Wanted to be sure you were home so I didn't waste time." He sounded both shaken and resolved. "Can you be ready to go when I get there?"

"Go wh—? Yes." The question was reflex. The *yes* was in response to his tone.

"Good."

I'd given Jennifer the run of the house, grabbed my bag, and opened the door before his vehicle pulled in to the driveway. I was in the passenger seat, and he was backing out with no wasted time.

He also wasted no time in explaining. "I was at the sheriff's department, trying to get more out of Lloyd. They were keyed up about something, but wouldn't tell me what. There was a report on the counter—where that hallway leads back to the offices."

I nodded, but wasn't sure he saw.

"It was upside down. I wouldn't have thought of it if it hadn't been for what you and Needham said, but I read enough of it. It was about the fibers found on Landry, what kind of rope those fibers would've come from. There was a list of names—people who'd bought that kind of rope. One name was circled."

We'd expected Alvaro to arrive at this point. We'd just expected the piece of material snagged on the post to be the breadcrumb he followed. And we'd hoped for more time. "Heather's."

"No," Mike said. "That's just it. It was Cas Newton's."

Chapter Twenty-Five

VICKY UPTON'S small truck was in the drive, and she answered the door.

"Absolutely not," she said to my request to see Heather. "She's in bed, and I will not disturb her."

I considered her determined face. Persuasion wouldn't cut it. I stepped past her into the house. "Heather!" I shouted, giving Mike a look.

"Be quiet! What are you—?"

"Heather! Heather Upton," Mike thundered, pulling the front door closed behind him. "We have to talk to you. It's about Cas."

A door down the short hallway opened. I suddenly realized why the house seemed familiar. It was the mirror image of the house I rented—mirror image, well-maintained, and painted more than every four decades.

"I'll call the police right now if you don't leave immediately," Vicky said.

"It will be better for your daughter if we talk to her before the police do, Vicky," I said. "If we don't talk to her, we're going straight to Deputy Alvaro, who's investigating the murder of Keith Landry."

"Murder—? That's—"

"What about Cas?" Heather demanded from the doorway.

With no makeup and her hair pulled back in a scrunchy, she looked better than I'd ever seen her before. Except for the fear and worry in her eyes.

"You go back to bed, right now," Vicky said. "I'll take care of this."

Heather ignored her mother and repeated to me, "What about Cas?"

"The sheriff's department knows about the rope. They have Cas at the sheriff's department right now."

"How could they—?"

"What are you talking about?" Vicky demanded.

I answered Heather. "They identified fibers and connected it to Cas' rope."

"But they can't *know*."

"They know Cas' kind of rope was used to lasso Landry," Mike said. "They can tell the fibers and the twist. They know."

"Was what you told us all a lie to protect him?" I demanded.

"No! It was the truth. It was all the truth."

"Except you didn't mention using Cas' rope."

"I never meant—I'd grabbed it when . . . I didn't even think about it."

"Heather, you are not to say another word."

"You had to know it wasn't your rope," Mike said, overriding Vicky.

"Of course I did, but I never thought—are you sure they know it's Cas'?"

"Yes. What they don't know is that you threw that loop."

"No!" Vicky shouted. "She didn't! She couldn't have. I tell you, she was here, right here all night. You're lying. I'll tell the police you're lying."

"I can't let Cas take the blame, Mom," Heather said, apparently contemplating her bare feet.

Vicky sucked in a breath, and it seemed to restore her usual calm. "You're not going to do this. Cas will be okay. His family's powerful. They have money. They'll take care of him. There's no need for you to do this. To risk . . . There are things—" Her gaze cut to Mike and me. "Private things."

"We know," I said.

"You can't." Vicky's voice lost its usual certainty on the next words. "Nobody can. Nobody can know. Ever."

Her daughter raised her head. She looked both older and much younger than Rodeo Queen Heather Upton. "*I know.*"

"I told you only because . . . only—"

"Because you were afraid I'd have sex with my father."

"*Heather.* Don't."

"Like I'd have sex with that gross old man." She turned to us. "It was like I told you. He tried pawing at me, and I had to dodge him all over the place, and that night he was just *there*. And he was coming after me, only now I knew he was my *father*, and it was . . . *sick*."

My stomach lurched with contagious nausea. "Why didn't you tell him?"

"I *did*." She sucked in a breath. "He said there was no use lying, and all he wanted to do was make me feel better since Cas had dumped me." A frown tucked between her brows. "I didn't understand that. Cas and I'd had a fight, but we didn't break up, much less him dumping me."

"What was the fight about?"

"How many buttons I had open on my shirt for the program pictures. He said I was showing too much." She pivoted, tossing over her shoulder, "I'll be right back."

✧ ✧ ✧ ✧

ALONG WITH HER clothes, Heather must have donned some of her Rodeo Queen armor.

Her head was high (though hat- and tiara-less) and her posture perfect when Richard escorted her and her mother into Interview Room Two. Vicky's surface was ruffled, but I had the sense her inner resolve wasn't dented.

It had taken persuading to get Lloyd Sampson to interrupt Alvaro and tell him we had important information.

Alvaro had come out of Interview Room One, looking as if he'd like to bite off our heads and swallow them whole. That didn't change much when I said Heather had something vital to tell him, though after a glance at the girl, he gestured for her to go ahead of him. Over his shoulder, he glowered at Mike and me. "Don't go anywhere. I'll talk to you two later."

We'd been sitting on an uncomfortable bench across from the counter that divided the deputy on duty from the public for 14 minutes when the door to Interview Room One snapped open.

"—and you can't stop me, Deputy. I demand to see Alvaro. I agreed my son could talk to you without a lawyer to clear up this crap, but not if we're treated—"

Stan Newton's voice preceded him. Once outside the door, he looked down the hallway, spotted us, turned red, and jumped back into the room, slamming the door behind him.

The next hour's tedium was relieved only by Alvaro emerging from Interview Room Two and entering Interview Room One without glancing our way. Nineteen minutes later, he reversed the process.

Early on, Mike started to say something, but I cut my eyes toward Deputy Sampson, and that was the end of confidences in the sheriff's department waiting area.

Mike had driven the Uptons in their car, to make sure there weren't any detours on the way to the sheriff's department, and I spent my time speculating on what might have been said during that trip. I also fell asleep.

Whispers woke me. I doubt if I'd have stirred for a full-voiced conversation, but whispers do it every time. That's what comes of having older brothers who planned deviltry in whispers.

I elbowed Mike awake. Alvaro was finishing his whisper with Lloyd by the door of Interview Room Two. He gave Mike and me a brief, threatening death-stare as he went to the door of Interview Room One, then gestured to Lloyd.

Sampson opened the door of Interview Room Two. Heather came out.

Alvaro swung open the door to Interview Room One, said, "You can go," and stood back.

The timing was perfect.

Cas stopped dead in the doorway of Room One as Heather sailed past.

Beyond the teenagers, the parents gave each other wary looks, unsure if secondary alliances conflicted with the primary allegiance each held to a child.

Before anyone else reacted, Cas ran the two steps after the girl and grabbed her by the arm to spin her around. "Heather? *You?* You used my rope? I thought maybe—" He bit it off, but it was too late.

"You thought it was that skank you've been buying flowers for."

"Once. I got her flowers. Once. For her nineteenth birthday."

"That bitch. You yell at me about a couple buttons open on my shirt, and you're with *her.* That fucking Pauline." Heather made the name sound like more of a curse than the f-word.

Cas paled. "You know her name? How do you know about . . . and the flowers? How do you know?"

"Do you think I'm stupid, Caswell Newton? Do you think I've known you all your life without figuring out when you're hiding something?"

She turned her back on him and walked out without looking left or right, with her mother hurrying to catch up.

✧ ✧ ✧ ✧

"**—AND WITHHOLDING** evidence—"

"We did not withhold evidence," I said. "We withheld conclusions. You had the pink fabric. You had the marks on the beam."

That stopped Deputy Alvaro. Or else he'd stopped for breath after a comprehensive lecture about interfering in an investigation. Even giving him the list Jennifer had developed of where Landry's rodeo had been didn't soften Richard.

"And as for interference, we've actually provided assistance," I said. "As soon as we knew evidence had led you to Cas—"

"How *did* you know that?"

I ignored him. "—we went right to Heather to demand she talk to you and straighten it all out. Without us, you'd have followed the wrong path for days. Although I did wonder what motive you thought

Cas—"

"Landry wasn't exactly making a secret of going after Heather." Alvaro glowered at me. "As you already knew."

"How would I know?" I dropped the innocent act at his look. "Penny?"

"Deputies buy groceries, too, you know." It was the closest he'd come to looking human since we'd walked in. "What else do you know?"

He looked at Mike, who shook his head, then at me. I raised helpless hands. He rubbed the back of his neck, and I realized some of his glare was from being dead tired.

"Listen, Richard," Mike said, "we all want to solve this. And it's clear we're not putting stuff on air that would interfere with your case."

"Thurston Fine won't let you get on the air."

"We could if we felt it was necessary," Mike said.

Even if we had to lock Fine in a storeroom . . . which had a lot of appeal. "But we're not," I added, both to Alvaro and to end my storeroom daydream. "What we are doing, is gathering information to try to figure out an answer to this as fast as possible. You're short-handed and pressed for time and—let's be honest—not experienced with investigations like this."

"But Elizabeth is," Mike slid in.

"We could help," I said, "if we had more information."

Alvaro was silent a long time before, "Like what?"

I was ready. "Where was Landry's phone found?"

He gave me a quizzical look. "In the pen. Where'd you think?"

"Still in a pocket?" I felt Mike tense, but didn't look at him.

"No. It wasn't still in a pocket. Why?"

"How close to the body?"

"It was in pieces. Trampled."

"The pieces were where? Do you know? Did you keep track?"

"Yeah, we kept track," he snapped. "They were most a fair distance from the rest—from the remains."

"How far?"

"I don't remember precisely, not without looking at the report again. Four, six feet away."

I sat back. "Ah."

"Ah, what?"

"*Ah* that removes a potential stumbling block to a growing theory."

"Which is?"

"I'm not prepared to say right now."

"You can't withhold evidence."

"Not evidence. Theory."

"Elizabeth. If you know—"

"We don't *know* anything. We're feeling our way."

"Ms. Danniher, as an officer of the law—"

I raised one hand. "I swear, Deputy Alvaro, if we know something for sure, we'll come to you and tell you the whole thing."

"And not go after the murderer yourself? Ignorance can be damned dangerous in a murder case," lectured the cop who was the age of some of my nieces and nephews.

"We'll keep that in mind. In the meantime, it would be helpful if you'd let us have a look at the detailed phone records."

"The phone's card is in Cheyenne. It'll be a while before their forensic tools finish with it."

Well, well. Young Richard had become subtle. What he'd said was no doubt true. What he left out was that they already had preliminary phone records from his brotherly connections. "When you get the information, you'll share it with us?"

"I'll think about it."

✧   ✧   ✧   ✧

"SO THAT'S WHY Heather was at the rodeo grounds so late—trying to catch Cas with the other girl. What did the Uptons say during the drive here?" I asked Mike as soon as we were in his night-cool vehicle.

I needed to fill him in on what Jennifer and I had been doing before his call, but I was too tired to do it tonight—or, technically, this morning.

"Not much that you don't already know. Heather said she grabbed Cas' rope by accident."

"Ah, jealousy. I bet that was her in Cas' bag Wednesday night. That's when she found a receipt for the birthday flowers for Blue—uh, Pauline. She's rooting around in the bag, sees Cas coming, grabs up her stuff, mistaking his rope for one of hers, and gets out of there."

Mike's thoughts seemed to be on a different track. "He has a point—Richard—about this being dangerous. You and Diana were nearly killed last time. Murderers are nothing to fool around with. Maybe you shouldn't—"

"Stop that. You're feeling guilty again, and you have no reason to. What happened was not your responsibility, not mine or Diana's either. I refuse to feel guilty or have anyone else feel guilty because of what a murderer did."

I doubted I'd persuaded him, but he didn't argue it now. Instead, he said, "Where the pieces were found is consistent with Landry pulling out his phone to use it *after* Heather lassoed him, but why'd you ask for phone records when we already have them?"

"Richard doesn't know that. He'd wonder if we didn't ask. Besides, we don't have the phone records I'd really like. Jennifer got pictures of the list of calls made with the bulls stomping on the phone. But what matters is the last call *before* the bull calls. We can't know that until we see earlier calls—the ones that went through. With the complete list, we could narrow who he might have called to meet him or get him loose from the rope Heather threw."

❖   ❖   ❖   ❖

I SWUNG MY front door open and stifled a gasp.

I'd forgotten about leaving Jennifer there. And apparently she'd forgotten about leaving.

She had found the cookies. Also the chips, pretzels, popcorn, bread, and peanut butter. All were scattered over the coffee table that would have cost a fortune in Manhattan as reclaimed wood, but was actually just old. In the center were her laptop and a legal pad with pages flipped back.

Jennifer sat on the couch, hunched over the laptop. It took me a long moment to realize she was sound asleep.

DAY SIX

TUESDAY

Chapter Twenty-Six

I TOSSED SHADOW a piece of popcorn.

Having popcorn for breakfast was my rebellion against being awake far earlier than I would like. The popcorn was a little stale, but it had other things going for it. It was made and had been sitting on the coffee table, waiting for me to grab the basket and walk outside with it.

Jennifer was still asleep on the couch. Which said something about her ability to sleep anywhere. She'd barely stirred the night before when I'd brought a pillow and comforter and nudged her to lie down.

Shadow plucked the popcorn out of the air with greater aplomb than a number of outfielders the Cubs have employed, and swallowed.

"Good job."

His ears flickered, but he stayed back. I sent him a few more high fly popcorns, and he was errorless. Gradually, I brought them in closer, until I was down to the last few, and he was swallowing infield flies.

I'd called KWMT while still in bed and let them know I'd be in after lunch, but was reachable by cell. I figured measuring by stress-per-minute, I'd put in a week's worth of time yesterday in preventing the Live at Five news hour from imploding. The day-shift assignment editor who'd answered said the phones had been busy because word had gotten out that the sheriff's department believed Landry was murdered, most likely by hanging, and it looked like it would be another all-Thurston day on-air.

Next, I'd called Matt Lester and told him I was taking all the fun out of his search by giving him a first name—Pauline.

I'd also called Mike and told him to come over because we had things to talk about.

"Oh, yes, we do," he said, all mysterious. Which miffed me. Not only had he already been awake and cheerful, but he'd expressed no interest in *my* mysteriousness.

So I didn't tell him on the phone what Jennifer and I had been working on the night before when interrupted by the Heather-Cas drama. That would teach him.

I tossed another piece of popcorn to Shadow. This one overshot. When he lifted his head to try to grab it, it slid down the back of his head and nestled in the fur at the top of his back.

I reached out, snagged it, and presented it in my open palm. He slurped it up, with an additional, delicate slurp of my palm for any residual popcorn atoms.

We stared at each other.

It had all been so quick and automatic, it was only then that I remembered my decision to be careful around this dog. Because I had no idea of his past, which meant I had no idea how he would react to unfamiliar movements, especially quick ones.

Apparently he reacted fine to quick, unfamiliar movements, as long as they ended with popcorn in his mouth. Or, perhaps he'd reacted as unthinkingly as I had, with his caution forgotten for that instant. His big, dark eyes looked more surprised than cautious.

Not looking at him directly, I put another piece of popcorn on my palm and held my hand out. Not under his nose as I had unthinkingly a second ago, but within reach.

Caution came back into his eyes. His focus went to the popcorn. He licked his lips. His gaze flicked to my face, to the side, back, away again.

I could put it on the ground partway between us, let him come that half step. No, not unless he refused this.

My hand started to bob from the double effort of keeping it steady and not thinking about his teeth.

He took one step forward, did the face-gaze flicking again. He stretched his neck toward me until I began to think he was part giraffe.

He didn't so much eat the popcorn as put his muzzle near my hand and suck it in without making contact. He retracted his neck, stepped back, and swallowed.

Two pieces left. I could repeat that maneuver, but I wasn't sure either of us could take the tension. I flipped the first piece to the side. He had to move for it, while cutting the distance between us. The last one was closer to me than him.

With that one swallowed, he looked at the basket.

I raised my hands. "All gone. You can have more another time." He started trotting away. "See you later, Shadow."

He stopped, looking over his shoulder in my direction, his head tipped, as if contemplating my words.

"I know. Crazy human. But you've got to admit, I've got good eats." He licked his chops, gave one wag of his tail and headed away again.

The wag *might* have been the movement of his tail from turning and trotting off. But I don't think so. I really don't think so.

✧   ✧   ✧   ✧

NO ONE EVER said Mike Paycik is all stupid. He brought coffee and pastries. He also brought Thomas David Burrell, so not all smart, either.

I discovered this when I came into the living room after taking a quick shower and putting on jeans and a plain white shirt.

From behind them, Jennifer ostentatiously looked from Mike's back to Tom's, sent her eyebrows toward the ceiling, and popped her eyes out at me. To tamp down the gossip speculation I saw going on behind her eyes like a pinball machine gone wild, I began introducing her to Burrell.

"Oh, I know Tom," she said. "My Uncle Rob—that's Dad's youngest brother—has been his best friend since, what? Middle school?"

"Before that," he said, taking the comforter that had been more mashed than folded from her hands. "I've known Jen since she was less than a day old."

"Jennifer," I corrected.

They both looked at me blankly. I wasn't fool enough to try to explain. "Don't you need to get to KWMT? You said you were working early today, right?"

She dug her phone from her pocket to check the time. "Yikes. Gotta go. I'll see if I can get those final dates and names and get back to you."

"Thanks for everything, uh, Jennifer." I held the door and waved her off.

"Good thing she has the early shift. I only got three coffees," Mike said, seated on the couch and pulling containers from a bag. In the same tone he added, "Tom's got something to say."

I sat on the wooden chair across from the couch and selected a bear claw. I needed to get in there fast, because Mike had already consumed one and was trolling for a second choice. "Okay."

Tom placed the comforter, now contained in a well-folded bundle, on the scarred table between the front door and short hall with doors leading off to the bathroom and two tiny bedrooms. He took his time getting back to the couch and taking a seat.

"Stan Newton accepted a bribe from Keith Landry. I got it confirmed this morning. I had a strong suspicion yesterday, but—"

"What?" I stood, three-quarters of a bear claw in hand. "*That's* what you wanted to tell us yesterday? You said it would *keep*."

"You and Mike had to leave." He calmly sipped coffee.

"We could have waited another minute to hear that. And all that time you were here with the ropes and the door, and you never said a word."

"I told you I had something I thought you'd want to know."

"I thought you were going to come clean about the phone calls."

Comprehension dawned in his eyes. "Ah." He looked at Mike. "You knew, too?"

"Yeah." Though why Mike should sound abashed, I didn't know.

He wasn't the one who'd withheld information.

"I applied my judgment to the situation based on what I knew then," Burrell said.

"Your judgment has been crap on this," I said. "First, in lying by omission. Worse, because you indicated you were giving us the full info. Second, by not telling us about Landry bribing Newton. No, this isn't working. Burrell's out of this investigation. We shouldn't have included him at all."

I crossed my arms—the gesture somewhat hampered because I still held the bear claw—and waited for him to leave.

Slowly, he stood.

But instead of leaving, he took off his cowboy hat, hooked it on the wooden knob that decorated the top left corner of the couch, and sat again. "First, I acted based on the information I had, which did not include that Landry had been murdered. Second, you need me in this investigation. You wouldn't be so fired up at me not telling you about the bribe yesterday if it wasn't important, and there's more to tell."

"He has you there," Mike said, unhelpfully telling me what I already knew.

"And," Burrell added, a glint in his eyes I didn't like, "you won't know what else I have found out, or could find out, if you don't keep me in."

So, Thomas David Burrell was willing to play dirty. "What's the more you have to tell us?" I asked.

"You'll tell me what you know?"

"I'll tell you as much as I tell Mike."

"Hey!" protested Mike.

"Deal," said Burrell.

"You don't tell me everything?" Mike demanded.

"Have you told me everything?"

"Haven't had a chance to yet."

I shook my head. "Not just this morning. You don't tell me everything. Certainly not what Ms. Blue Hair said to you and—"

"Not word-for-word, but I told you the important stuff."

"—not what you saw in those photos you took that made you feel it was worthwhile working Lloyd Sampson as a source after you told me there wasn't anything there."

A flush rose above his collar and into his face. "It was a hunch. Nothing solid. I wanted to see—"

"Exactly. We each have bits and pieces we hold back, waiting to see if they develop or fade into nothingness."

"I'm not holding anything back on purpose," he insisted. "And to prove it, I'll tell you that I had another chat with Ms. Blue Hair and heard all about how her parents don't understand her, never have. That her father is particularly heinous, and she will never reconcile with a monster who delights in torturing her by being a carnivore and indulging in brutal practices—not against her. I did get her to confirm that. From what she said, her family's in the cattle business, and she's been in full-blown teen rebellion since age six. I'll also tell you Aunt Gee called and said the big shots are at a retreat in the mountains. They wanted to keep it quiet to talk about how to repair the county's image—especially the justice system—without anybody knowing what they're doing."

"Where are they?"

He shook his head. "Nobody knows. Not even Aunt Gee can get a line on it. Richard's been trying, too."

I turned to Burrell. "And what about you?"

"Like I said, I've heard from two people I trust, and one I don't, that Newton took a bribe from Landry."

"Gives Newton motive for murder—to keep the bribe quiet," Mike said.

I added, "And that means Cas has motive—to protect his father. Heather, too."

"To protect Cas' father? Isn't that stretching it?" Mike said.

"How about to protect Cas? Along with the possibility of protecting herself. Remember that rodeo scholarship. She said Landry threatened to yank it. Well, what would happen to the rodeo—and the funding for her scholarship—if word got out that Landry bribed his way into getting that contract with all the lucrative bonuses. It was as important for her that a bribe be kept secret—"

"Hold on there," interrupted Tom. "Couple things. First, the bribe wasn't kept secret. I found out. Others would have, too."

"No one with a motive to keep the bribe secret could know that for sure. Even if word does come out, it could still have been a motive." I finally took the next bite of my slightly mangled bear claw.

Tom stretched his fingers and rested the edge of his hand on his leg, gesturing to put that aside for now. "The second thing is that what I've been told isn't all about Landry bribing Newton to get the last-minute contract."

"He bribed Newton for his vote last year, when the contract went to Sweet Meadows?" Mike asked.

"It's not that clear-cut. Sounds like money changed hands late last year, but I can't pin down what it was for." Tom frowned. "There're conflicts in what I've got. I'll go back to the first person and see if I can get it clearer."

"What about the third source? The one you don't trust."

He raised his open hands, let them fall. "He says there were two bribes. He got cagey about what the recent one was about, but talked free about the first one. But, then, he wasn't entirely sober."

"Getting sources drunk isn't—"

Tom interrupted me. "Wasn't a matter of *getting* him drunk, it was a matter of finding him in that condition."

"Great. Real reliable."

He shrugged.

"Your turn, Elizabeth," Mike said.

I hesitated, then told them what Jennifer found, and what I'd learned from talking to the women.

"The sonovabitch did the same thing over and over—sounds like all those women had a motive," Tom said grimly.

Mike took another pastry. "Maybe motive, but not opportunity. Has to be someone who was here. Unless we find out one of those women was visiting Sherman . . ."

"That's another thing." I made a note. "Why the murder was committed here can tell us something, as well as why now. Both good questions to pursue."

"Tell Tom—"

I cut off Mike. "You tell him. If we want any shot at another pastry, we need to keep your mouth otherwise occupied."

Both men grinned, but I noticed Tom did grab a bismarck as Mike gave the gist of Dex's points about there being a reason a murder is committed at a certain time. I'm no fool, I took a raspberry Danish.

"Let's see where we are." I pulled over a legal pad and pen to list the names we'd discussed. "Who should we start with?"

"Remember what Jenks said about seeing a woman that morning?" Mike asked.

I countered, "Vague memory, off to the side, and that was when Landry was found. He'd been dead a while."

"We don't know for sure when he died."

"Had to be early enough for the bulls to do their worst before Jenks and Thurston arrived. Why would the killer stick around?"

"Retrieve evidence," he said promptly.

"No evidence was found that was worth retrieving."

"Maybe. But the murderer couldn't be sure of that without checking. I think Vicky's the top suspect. Keeping Landry away from her daughter permanently is a strong motive. And that fits with why the murder happened now. Landry's sexual advances on Heather had to be her worst nightmare. After Heather ropes him, he calls Vicky—"

"Why would Landry call her after all the years of silence?" I asked.

"Because Heather told him he was her father," Tom said. "He calls Vicky and demands to know what that was about. And her second-worst nightmare would be if he tried to take Heather away."

Mike and I exchanged a look. Tom's personal history skewed his view on this. "Maybe." Now I met Tom's gaze. "But did Landry strike you as somebody who'd embrace fatherhood?"

He tipped his head in half a nod, conceding.

"But what about this?" Mike said. "What if Vicky followed Heather there and saw what happened?"

I kept going with my devil's advocate role. "And didn't do anything but watch it unfold while her daughter's father made lewd proposals?"

Mike grimaced. "So, she got there in time to hear the end of it, enough to get the gist, but didn't need to intervene because Heather temporarily neutralized Landry with her rope. After Heather ran off, Vicky decided permanently neutralizing him would be a lot better than temporary."

"Keep going."

He sat forward. "Look at the motive. What's stronger than a mother protecting her child? That's Vicky's primary drive. All Heather's life, she's done everything in her power to make a better life for her than she had."

His *hers* and *shes* were jumbled, but I followed him—watch out for Mama Bear if you start fooling with her cub.

"Landry was the worst possible threat, with no good outcome. If he kept pursuing Heather, Vicky could not be a hundred percent certain her daughter wouldn't fall for it the way she had—and commit incest. So, she told Heather the truth to prevent that. But what if Landry found out he had a daughter? He could lavish all the things on Heather that Vicky hadn't been able to."

Mike thumped his hand on his knee. "Heather said she was yelling at him about being his daughter as he came after her. She takes off, but he's still roped, starts thinking about what the girl said. Vicky shows up and—boom!—it hits him square between the eyes what the girl meant. He threatens to take Heather away or maybe to tell the world the truth or—whatever, and Vicky decides to put an end to it. She grabs the rope—"

"A rope she would have thought was her *daughter's* rope." I said. "In your scenario, she'd have seen Heather throw the rope. After everything she's done for Heather, she'd use a rope traceable back to the girl? I don't see that."

"But it was Cas Newton's rope," Tom protested. I eyed Mike, who shook his head, denying he'd spilled that tidbit. "I've got sources, too," Tom said, a glimmer in his dark eyes.

"Vicky wouldn't have known it was Cas' rope," Mike said. "If she arrived at the end of Heather's encounter with Landry, she'd see her daughter throw a rope and assume it was hers. She took the rope after he died because she thought it was Heather's. She didn't know fibers would lead to what kind of rope. She'd think taking the rope was enough."

"Maybe," I agreed reluctantly. There was something . . . something . . . "So, she kills Keith Landry, takes the rope afterward to protect her daughter. No, wait . . . That's it. Remember me saying she'd told me about Heather's roping ability? Bragged about it. Saying her daughter was even better than she was? No way would she have done that the day Landry was found, knowing Heather's roping ability set up the murder."

"She didn't tell you anything you wouldn't have heard anyway. Everyone would tell you Heather could do that trick. Besides, we didn't know then that he'd been roped that way."

"*We* didn't. But if she killed Landry, *she* would have." I shook my head. "No way would she have drawn attention to her daughter's roping ability. No way would she have been the one to put that in my mind for when it did become known—not if she had the guilty knowledge that what she thought was her daughter's rope had been used."

"What if Vicky comes later. Finds Landry, but doesn't know Heather is the one who roped him. After he's dead, she takes the rope, thinking to protect herself. That could explain the bulls, too. Trying to disguise any evidence."

I considered that. "Maybe. She stays on the list."

"You go through this for anyone you think might be a suspect?" Tom asked.

"Yes." I looked up from the list. Was he wondering if we'd done something similar when he was accused of murder? We had.

"Amazing, isn't it—the way Elizabeth sees the holes," Mike said.

"Yes," Tom said evenly. "Who else is on your list?

"Cas Newton," Mike said. "He fits the same scenario—whether Heather killed Landry or left him tied up the way she said. And he'd take the rope, too, thinking it was Heather's."

"Landry didn't call Cas," Tom said.

"No, but if Cas followed Heather—"

"Other way around," I said. "Heather followed Cas, trying to catch him with Blue Hair, or at least get more info on her. On the other hand, there *were* calls to Stan Newton earlier. Maybe Cas intercepted one and went to the rodeo grounds to have it out with Landry to protect his father. Sees Landry trussed up, thanks to Heather, and seizes the opportunity."

"That's assuming Cas knew about the bribe," Mike said.

We both looked at Tom, hoping for more on what Cas might know about the bribe. We got about as much response as we would from the Lincoln Memorial in D.C.

"Or," Mike picked up, "Stan got the call—maybe he was the one Heather said Landry was yelling at to get down there. Or Landry called him for help getting free after Heather's rope trick."

"Why would Stan take the rope or put Landry in with the bulls?" I asked.

"To confuse the issue," Tom said. "Same goes for anybody."

I put my pen down. "We're not eliminating anybody. Or zeroing in on anybody. We need more information."

"Like what?" Mike asked.

"A clearer picture of everybody's movements that night. See if you can pin down Zane and Watt about when they came in. More on that bribe."

Mike nodded at the first assignment, Tom at that second.

"I still want to know why Landry wanted those bulls brought in early. It's—"

"An anomaly," Mike filled in.

"Yes. Mike, see what you can get from Stan on that. Ask Watt and Zane if they know anything, too. And I'll try to get more detail from Oren Street. And those women Jennifer's found—the ones I didn't talk to last night, and any others she finds. I also want to talk more to Linda. But right now, I've got to get ready for work."

"I've only got to swing by for a couple hours today," Mike gloated, "since I worked Saturday night, and Fine's back to not allowing me on the air. How about if we meet back here tonight to go over things?"

I grimaced. "You're volunteering to come to the hovel?"

"It's ugly, but it's a lot more convenient than my place or Tom's.

And the refrigerator works. That's the most important thing."

Tom chuckled. "Works for me."

"Terrific." I stood. "Any questions?"

"Yes," said Tom. "Who is Ms. Blue Hair?"

I turned. "You seem to know everybody around here—do you know any of the animal rights people? The protestors by the gate to the rodeo grounds."

He shook his head. "Not from around here. Is that who Ms. Blue Hair is?"

I left Mike to confirm that. I went to get ready for work.

Chapter Twenty-Seven

"I BEEN CALLING you since eight o'clock this morning," said the grumbling male voice on the other end of my KWMT phone line.

"I'm sorry, callers were supposed to be connected to my cell phone number to reach me this morning."

"I don't hold with those cell phones. Told that girl if she tried it, I'd hang up. You shoulda been *there*. What kinda job you got that you can wait half the day before startin' in to work?"

The kind that kept me working half the night and *all morning*. I dearly wanted to snap that. Instead, I repeated the phrase I'd started with: "May I help you?"

"You can tell me if you're that 'Helping Out' gal using letters."

It took a second. "Yes, I'm E.M. Danniher. May I help you?" I automatically jotted the number from Caller ID in the notebook I kept on the desk. No name displayed.

"No. But I can help you. I'd've told old Needham Bender if he hadn't written those things about me a while back. But I ain't giving him no scoop. Bring your camera out here this afternoon and see me blow a hole through some crooks."

Excuse me?

I turned to the computer and started typing in each word he'd said. "What's your name, sir? And address?"

"Why you wanna know?" Suspicion etched the words.

"Have to know an address to bring a camera crew." I jettisoned the name request without hesitation. With an address and phone number, I could get a name. I'd have a good shot with only the phone number from a reverse directory, but an address would help.

"Camera crew, huh?"

"Absolutely. If you're going to, uh, catch crooks, KWMT wants to be on hand to bring that news to the people of Cottonwood County." He was mulling. Drawing in a slow breath, I coached myself to go easy. "What kind of crooks are these?"

"The kind you been talking about. Calling people, saying they won a prize at some store. She told me first I won this gift card, but I had to claim it at the store by three o'clock this very afternoon. Told her I didn't want any gift card—don't trust those things. Give me money, real cash money. That's the only thing that means something. And she squeaks right up with how I'd get cash instead, only I had to come into the store at three."

I double-checked the time. Depending on where he was in the county, that might be cutting it close.

"That *could* be the scam I reported on last night. But—"

"Could be? It *is*. I don't enter no contests. Don't have my name on no lists. It's them. So, are you coming or not? I got things to do around here, and I don't have no more time to waste talking with you. Gotta check my guns and such to set a trap for these crooks."

"We're coming. Give me the address."

"The Poppinger place."

Before I could ask for a road, he hung up.

I spotted Jennifer and hollered to get Mike, who'd come in at the same time I had, and Diana—with equipment—here immediately. Heads turned in the newsroom, but no one said a word.

I dialed the sheriff's department—not 911, because I didn't want to try to get past a dispatcher unless I absolutely had to. I asked for Deputy Alvaro, saying, "Tell him it's Elizabeth Danniher from KWMT, and it's an emergency."

While I waited, I typed the phone number into the reverse directory. It gave me Hiram Poppinger and an address.

Alvaro's voice came on. "Elizabeth, I don't have ti—"

"Neither do I. Listen, Deputy. I received a call four minutes ago from a man who did not identify himself." I was writing the name and address and phone number in the fresh notebook as I spoke. "He said he received a phone call saying he'd won a prize at a store in town. He's certain it's those thieves who have been working the area. He was told he had to—"

"That's great, but—"

"*Listen*. He has to pick his prize up by three today. He told them he would, but he plans to double back and set a trap for them." The fresh notebook, a spare, and three new pens went in my bag, which already held my digital recorder. "He asked if I wanted to come see him—and I quote—'blow a hole through some crooks.' The reverse phone number says the name is Hiram Poppinger."

Deputy Alvaro said a word that the FCC gets very cranky about having on the airwaves. "He'll do it, too."

Mike and Jennifer were coming across the newsroom at a good pace. "Have you got all the information, Deputy?"

"I have it. But—"

I was on my feet, said, "I have to go," and disconnected as I grabbed my bag and went to meet them.

"Diana?"

"Said she'd meet you outside," Jennifer said.

"What—?"

I cut Mike off. "I'll tell you on the way. Jennifer, stay by my landline. If it's Hiram Poppinger, keep him talking and transfer him to my cell, but don't tell him that's what you're doing, or he'll hang up. Anybody else, tell them you can't reach me. That includes the sheriff's department." We were at the door. Diana drove up in the Newsmobile. "Got it, Jennifer?"

"Got it."

I pushed Mike to the front seat, while I climbed into the back. If any navigating was required, he'd be a lot more useful than I would.

"Where to?" Diana headed toward the highway without waiting for the answer she didn't need quite yet.

"The Poppinger place. Do you know it?"

"Hiram Poppinger?" she asked, as she and Mike exchanged a look.

"Yes. I have an address."

"No need. I know it."

She turned onto the highway going east and drove at a generous interpretation of the speed limit, while I filled them in.

When I'd finished, Mike said, "One question. What am I doing here?"

"Are you kidding? After all the hand-wringing you've done about not being on-hand when Diana and I had our little *tete-a-tete* with a murderer, you think I'd leave you out of this? Besides, if Hiram happens to mistake us for the crooks, you make a bigger target than Diana or I."

✧   ✧   ✧   ✧

MY CELL PHONE rang as we made the third turn since we'd left the highway.

Fully prepared to ignore a call from Alvaro, I saw the ID and answered. "How nice of you to call back," I said, as Mike turned to stare from the front seat.

It was the committee chair from the Denver rodeo, and I wasn't letting him go without asking my questions. Besides, what else could I do while Diana indulged in off-road racing? Taking notes, though, was out of the question.

Bob Lewis was chatty, but cautious. The chattiness came to the fore as I asked about the difficult situation his rodeo had encountered and heard an eerily familiar story. The rodeo had received a hard-to swallow bid from their established contractor, Keith Landry. They accepted a much better bid from a new contractor, though *not* Sweet Meadows. A few weeks before the scheduled rodeo, they received the startling news that the new contractor had gone bankrupt and vanished. Landry came to the rescue—for a hefty fee.

This Colorado rodeo had been held, cleared a tiny profit once Landry was paid, and the contractor headed for Sherman with fat pockets.

The Colorado rodeo committee chair's caution took hold when he connected what he'd been telling me with the newsworthy death of a stock contractor at a rodeo in Wyoming. But I had what I needed.

Another possible pattern. Another task for Jennifer.

"Did you get that?" I asked the front seat's occupants.

"No," Diana said. "Concentrating on driving."

"Thank God," I muttered as I hit buttons on my phone and prayed for coverage.

"The gist," Mike said. "What are you doing now?"

"Getting—Jennifer?" I interrupted my explanation when I got her. "I have another layer of research for you to add."

"Good. I'm tired of finding rodeo queens. I'm back almost twenty years. You know, I'd find all this stuff a lot easier if I—"

"No hacking."

"Mike read that paper upside down," she protested.

I glared at him, but he'd turned back to face front, so the glare missed its target. "There's a difference between looking at something that's out in the open and rooting around for it. Have you heard of an expectation of privacy?"

"No."

"We'll talk later."

✧ ✧ ✧ ✧

"BUMP," DIANA said by way of warning as she turned north once more.

Which was rather like looking at the Grand Canyon and saying "dip."

Despite my tightened seatbelt, my head brushed the roofliner, and the return trip jolted me back into the seat. "Where on earth are we going?"

"Shortcut. Coming in the back way."

I looked around. "We're in a pasture."

"Yup."

"Consider this Hiram Poppinger's back door," Mike said. "And we're not the only ones to think of it."

I scootched down to look out the front windshield and saw a ball of dust ahead of us.

"The thieves?" Diana asked.

"I don't think so. They've been using vans, and I can't imagine them driving on this."

The road curved sharply to the right, and Mike squinted out the side window at the dust bomb. "Sheriff's department."

"If we can see the dust, so can the thieves," I said.

"I suspect the deputy wouldn't mind if the thieves took off. Better than having Hiram shoot somebody again."

"Again?"

"Hiram got himself a horse thief when I was in high school."

"What happened?"

"Not much. He didn't kill the guy, and the guy was a horse thief."

It was a true you're-not-in-Kansas-anymore-Dorothy moment. Not in Kansas, or St. Louis, or D.C., or New York, Elizabeth. I mean, I know that. Every day when I wake up in the hovel, when I drive with the mountains as the true West on my mental compass, when I produce my packages with throwback equipment, I know I'm not—as Thomas David Burrell once said to me—anywhere I'd ever been before. But something about bumping through a pasture with Mike talking calmly about Hiram Poppinger shooting a horse thief crystallized that recognition.

The sheriff's department four-wheel drive ahead of us slowed. The dust plume subsided, and we saw the vehicle take the right fork of a Y that divided around an abrupt rise of land.

"What's he doing?" Mike said. "House is to the left."

"Barn's to the right," Diana said. "I think it's Shelton."

"Oh."

Not only wasn't I in Kansas anymore, apparently I *was* in a land where *Shelton* had meanings hidden to me, and *Oh* conveyed much more than those two letters.

I checked my watch for the forty-third time in twenty-five minutes. It was twelve minutes to three.

The vehicle bore sharply to the left, so sharply it appeared the mysterious Shelton would drive straight into the hill. Instead, the vehicle disappeared from view for a moment, until we followed through a gap that opened to a gathering of ranch buildings.

The sheriff's department vehicle had parked behind a battered blue truck, along the side of a large barn. Beyond the end of the barn, a corner of a weathered house was visible at a distance of a hundred feet or so. Diana drew up as the third vehicle in the row, leaving enough room for the deputy to get his out. We started along the line of vehicles toward the house.

We didn't get far.

The deputy had his door open with his legs out the side and a shotgun pointed at us.

"If you don't get back in that vehicle . . ." Pronounced *vee-HICK-ul.* "I'll be forced to take extreme measures. Yeah, I got it. Alvaro told me to expect you vultures. Hey, Diana."

He began hitting buttons on his cell. His erratic conversational style made sense with the *got it* reference directed to whoever was on the other end of the radio.

Before we responded beyond Diana's "Hey" back, he said, "Hiram, it's Wayne Shelton. Pick up the phone. I know you're in there. Pick up the phone. I saw you sneaking in your back door a minute ago. I'm out behind your barn, and I'm coming in. You know me, and you know I mean what I'm saying. Don't do anything stupid, or I'll be arresting you instead of those thieves."

Over the phone, we heard the clunk-click of someone picking up a call that had gone to an answering machine, then the man who'd called me said, "Too late. They're turning into my road." Hiram sounded both gleeful and cranky. "Don't go scaring them away now."

"I'm coming in the back," Shelton repeated. "And these TV vultures are here with me. If you shoot one of them, you can get in real trouble, Hiram, and if you shoot me, I'll kill you. So don't be stupid."

"I don't need no help."

Deputy Shelton hung up on him.

Shelton stood—barely as tall as the vehicle. It didn't dent his air of command one bit.

"Paycik, your daddy had a good head on his shoulders, and you better have the same. You stay here, and when you see them drive in, pull that KWMT vehicle crosswise behind them so they can't pull out. Let 'em take stuff first, or the charges won't stick. You two girls stay put. I'm going in."

"We are, too," I said.

He growled. "Hiram's got a gun, and he's a crap shot. I said stay put."

And he was gone. Dodging behind a rusted out tractor and a man-high attachment that seemed to grow out of the ground, he made his way to the back door.

"I'll see what I can get of them coming in." Diana shifted her new, smaller camera to fish out the keys and gave them to Mike. He trotted back to the Newsmobile. He'd be closer to the action but able to see only the front door. I decided to go with Diana and keep watch on both doors.

We went in a side door of the barn, into dim, dusty heat. Staying well outside the shaft of light streaming in from the open front doors, Diana maneuvered toward the corner that would give her the best angle and be least visible. I followed.

Outside, I heard Mike start the Newsmobile. That was smart—that way he'd avoid having a new sound possibly alert the thieves.

"Here they come," Diana said, looking through the viewfinder.

I peered over her shoulder. A plain white van notable only for the amount of dust it carried slowly cruised toward the house, going straight to the porch, before making a circle. Three heads inside turned this way and that, apparently looking for signs of life. After one complete, slow circle, the van pulled around again, facing out, with its back doors at the steps.

Two men and a woman, all in jeans, black T-shirts, and black cowboy hats, got out quickly. They went to the back of the van. The woman opened the doors, the men positioned a ramp straight across from the porch into the van.

"Spares wear and tear on the knees from going up and down steps," I whispered.

The smaller man went to a window. I thought it was to check

inside, but he barely looked before getting to work with a tool. He had the window open, was through it, and was opening the front door to his compatriots practically before we drew a breath.

Diana mouthed a word we would have had to edit out if she'd given it any volume.

After a brief pause, the men came out carrying a mammoth wide-screen TV. From inside, the woman's voice said something about silver.

As soon as the men went back inside, the Newsmobile came around the barn and pulled across the van's front. Not only could the van not get out, but Mike couldn't either.

My attention snapped away from his efforts to scramble over to reach the passenger door when shouts, followed by a shot, erupted from the house.

Instinct had me running back through the barn, then following the path Deputy Shelton had taken, since it offered some semblance of cover. Diana came right behind me.

We cleared the tractor and dashed to the unidentifiable farm implement. And came face to face with the black cowboy-hatted female of the band of thieves. She made as if to dodge us.

"Stop!" I shouted. "We'll shoot!"

Diana made a sound, but I was distracted by the appearance of an ill-tempered gnome at the open back door with a shotgun that had to be as tall as he was.

"If they don't, I will!" shouted what could only be Hiram Poppinger, as he advanced on us.

The woman threw her hands up. "Don't let him shoot me. He's crazy!"

"Oh, for Pete's sake, Hiram, put that thing down," commanded Deputy Shelton from the doorway. He grabbed the barrel of the gun and neatly wrested it away as he walked past the rancher. "If you shot at her, you'd hit those TV vultures, and what'd I tell you about the world of trouble you'd have?"

Poppinger grumbled, but was distracted when Mike emerged from the house and asked, "Everything okay?"

"Just peachy," Shelton said. "You and Hiram keep an eye on those two in the front room."

"Mike Paycik! You're Michael Paycik!" shouted the gnome as they disappeared inside. Hiram no longer appeared to be a threat, unless his adulation distracted Mike enough that the two male thieves got away.

Shelton held out the shotgun. "Here, hold this, Diana."

"I can't, I'm shooting."

The thief jerked in alarm, but Shelton clucked and turned his glare on me. "You ever handled a gun?"

"Ever? Yes."

He looked at me from under bushy brows and muttered a curse that would never make the air—not that I planned on any of this being in our package.

He pointed the gun toward the unoccupied distance. "Come over here and hold it like this. Whatever you do, don't point it at any living creature, especially not me."

I accepted the shotgun and the strictures, watching over my shoulder as he handcuffed the thief.

"Now," he said, "let's get back inside."

He started off with a hold on the thief's handcuffs and Diana shadowing them from the side, filming all the way.

"What about me?" I called.

"I'll be back."

Chapter Twenty-Eight

HE TOOK HIS time about it, but he did come back and relieve me of the shotgun.

"Suppose you'll insist on going inside, joining those other two," he grumbled.

"Since you already charged me the price of admission by leaving me out here, you're damned right I do."

He grunted, but I caught a glimmer of humor.

Mike appeared in a doorway at the far end of a kitchen that would give a location-finder for a 1930s drama and an HGTV designer heart palpitations for opposite reasons. "Deputy Shelton, they're talking."

Diana and I reached the door in a dead heat, with Shelton handicapped by tugging the third evil-doer. Poppinger shuffled along last, apparently losing interest now that shooting was out.

I let Diana go ahead, since she had the camera running, and found myself off to the side in a room that was overcrowded by the two male thieves and Mike, and threatened to burst with the addition of Diana, me, the deputy, his prisoner, and Hiram.

Deputy Shelton read them their rights, while they protested it was all an honest mistake. No standing on their right to remain silent for this trio. Theirs was a well-told story. Each had a part and a few key phrases. They were passing through the area, and they'd promised a buddy they would gather items he'd left behind when he moved out last year.

"No buddy of yours ever lived here," interrupted Poppinger.

"Oh, we can see that now," said the woman, going wide-eyed. "It's so embarrassing."

This buddy was, perhaps, the worst direction-giver ever—a veritable anti-GPS in human form—and here they supplied a pair of examples that caused the trio to chuckle in fond remembrance.

Poppinger gave them a narrow-eyed glare. "You had my silver coins. Ain't no one told you to pick up my silver."

"He did say he'd left money," the bigger guy inserted.

"What's this buddy's name?" Deputy Shelton asked.

"Tom Johnson," supplied the smaller guy.

"Nobody by that name's lived in this country since I've been here," Deputy Shelton said, deadpan.

I found that hard to believe, since it combined two of the more common names in the United States without stooping to John Smith. Apparently the three thieves found it even harder to believe.

The big guy recovered first. "Good God, we must be in the wrong county!"

"Then why'd you call me first with that malarkey about winning a contest? That was you, missy." Hiram stabbed a stubby and dirty finger toward the woman.

She did the eye-widening bit again. "I never called you. I don't know what you're talking about."

While Hiram replied—I don't think he used a single air-worthy word—I stepped to the side to relieve my hip, which was being pierced by the corner of an old cabinet, and to get a better view of everyone. Apparently that gave the smaller of the male thieves his first look at me.

"Hey, I know you," he piped up. "You're that lady on TV. Saw you on the news last night talking about us."

He smiled at the camera, as the other two groaned.

✧   ✧   ✧   ✧

WITH AMPLE backup from the sheriff's department having arrived, and the routine well underway, I cornered Deputy Shelton.

"Can we ask you a few questions on camera?"

He heaved a capitulatory sigh. "Where do you want me, Diana?"

Without wasted words or long pauses, he delivered exactly what we needed like a pro.

When we finished, Diana headed to the Newsmobile, where Mike was being peppered by reminiscences from Hiram, joined by deputies.

I put out a hand. "It's been a pleasure, Deputy Shelton."

"Not sure I'd go that far." He met my grip with one that would have turned my bones to dust if it had lasted much longer.

"Do you find it surprising that they'd seen the story on KWMT last night, knew the community was warned, and still tried to pull it off?"

"Nope. Once they've done it a few times, some of them just can't stop," Shelton said. "Doesn't matter that sense says they'll get caught. There's something talking a lot louder in their heads, telling them they can get away with it. It's ego, but it's beyond ego. It's like they can't *not* do it."

I nodded slowly. "You're right. They can't not do it."

"And this time ego caught them real good, because of you putting that report on TV."

"Why, Deputy Shelton, I thought we were vultures."

"Vultures serve a purpose in nature," he said, in perfect deadpan. "Besides, Michael Paycik was one hell of a ballplayer." He nudged his hat brim. "And this'll get Thurston Fine's goat for sure."

✧ ✧ ✧

FINE SPUTTERED A few protests about airing the report on Hiram Poppinger and the thieves on Live at Five, but his heart wasn't in it. I knew that, because he barely turned dark pink, and the veins in his forehead didn't throb.

Well, maybe one twitch. I said on-air, all in a rush, that it was due to Fine breaking into the coverage of Keith Landry's death the previous night to air my piece that Mr. Poppinger had been fore-warned, allowing the sheriff's department to lock up these dangerous criminals.

Fine then had to say he'd aired it for the good of the community, and that the action today was an important story.

A nice moment, compounded by Cheshire Cat grins from a number of staffers outside the studio afterward.

Jennifer, who'd already finished her KWMT shift, called and said she'd found two more towns with the same scenario as Sherman and the town near Denver—one in Texas and one in southern Colorado, both last summer. She was still digging. She also would email us the list of names of rodeo queens from towns where Landry had run the rodeo right back to the beginning.

Diana and I put together a shorter package for the late news with backseat editing by Mike. I was debating whether to do my intro live when another call came in for me.

Linda Caswell. Asking me to come to the rodeo grounds this evening. I said sure, in an hour.

I taped the intro. Mike and I ate at Hamburger Heaven, while Diana headed home to no doubt fix a nutritious and balanced meal for herself and her two kids.

Along with dinner, we chewed over why Linda might want to see us. "Not us, you," Mike said with a touch of chagrin.

"To confess?" I suggested.

Mike frowned. "Tom says—"

"Spare me. But I agree confession's a longshot. More likely she's found out word of the bribe's gotten to us—"

"You."

"—and wants to spin that to us."

"You."

✧ ✧ ✧ ✧

WE ARRIVED AT THE rodeo grounds along with the evening's influx of entrants and workers, but well ahead of the spectators. The protestors didn't bother to get out of their lawn chairs.

It reminded me of Thursday evening, with the arena, rodeo office, and pens stretching long shadows across the open areas. The population of vehicles had swelled with the continuing arrival of competitors for the weekend events. A few vehicles ranked as decidedly upscale—in the Grayson Zane category.

Linda met us outside the rodeo office. She gave Mike a dismissive greeting and said she was glad I could come.

He faded away graciously with only an I-told-you-so look. She led me around the far side of the office, and across a scrub area to a picnic table amid cottonwood trees by a creek a couple hundred yards away.

She sat on the attached bench, with her back against the table and a view of the dry creek bed. I sat beside her, the seat warm, but the shaded spot otherwise pleasant.

"I want to talk with you." She didn't say *woman to woman*, but it drifted between us.

"I prefer asking questions. Let's start with the end of your relationship five years ago with Grayson Zane."

She was ready for that. "As I said yesterday, he broke it off abruptly, but there'd been no promises or pledges."

"What about heartache?" I asked.

This smile was rueful. "Entirely self-inflicted from falling from castles I'd built in the air all by myself. As I said, he made no promises or pledges, so he never broke any." Then she went a step too far. "I can look back now and say we had a wonderful time, and wasn't I fortunate to have had such an experience."

"I don't know how anyone can feel that way when they've been kicked in the teeth by love."

"I heard you're recently divorced, Ms. Danniher."

Ouch. "Yes. As I said, I don't know how anyone can feel that way when they've been kicked in the teeth."

She relented with an expelled breath. "You're right. I was much less philosophical at the time. I became quite . . . low. That's when Landry appeared."

Clearly not a woman who enjoyed talking about this, so why was she? Trying to lead me toward something? Or only away?

"You immediately started dating Landry on the rebound?"

"Rebound . . . yes. Though *dated* is more than it deserves. He showed up right after Grayson left. Keith offered a shoulder to cry on. I thought a kind shoulder, to pick up the pieces of someone shattered by another man. I suppose I needed someone . . . to tell me—show me—I was attractive. As attractive as I've ever been."

I let the silence extend. Some people over-explain in situations like this, giving more information than they ever intended.

"We had sex," she said succinctly. "Frequently over the next week and a half. That was all we did. I finally took a look at myself, what I was doing. I didn't like it . . . I invited him to a cookout with friends. It seemed a logical step toward a more normal situation. He was gone the next morning. I was humiliated."

"Your friends . . ."

She waved that away sharply. "Humiliated in my own eyes."

"By Zane, as well as—"

"No. He made no promises. Landry did. With Zane, it just ended. But with Landry . . . He'd done it deliberately. Some things he said, about my family, about getting back at the Caswells for never thinking he was good enough for our rodeo . . . I was sure."

Did she recognize her words gave her additional motive to murder Landry? Did she care?

"I didn't hear from him again until we were looking for someone to take over after Sweet Meadows folded. Then it was strictly in my role as committee chair."

"Why didn't Landry get this year's contract to start? He'd had it for several years, right?"

"Yes, he had. But his fees had mounted at a rate that had already pushed us, and this year they jumped significantly. We looked at other bids, and Sweet Meadows won."

"What did you know about the company?"

"I can't tell you how, or if, their references were vetted, but they were glowing. When I became chair, I tried to reach them, without success. That was worrying, then with the bankruptcy, we were left with no choice . . ."

"But to give Landry whatever he demanded. Why do you think he'd raised his fees so much to start with?"

"I only saw the finished bid. For how Landry reached that number, you'd have to ask Oren Street. He might know."

"Only might? Street was Landry's partner."

She looked off to the side, narrowing her eyes. "That strikes me as the same category as an abused woman being called the abuser's partner," she said. "*Partners*, because they're married. Yet, it's not only not a true partnership, it's a mockery of the concept."

"In what way—for Landry and Street, I mean?"

She hitched her shoulders. I thought it carried impatience that I'd requested clarification. "Certainly financially, but you already know that, don't you? I'm sure even less homework than you do would have revealed that."

"And beyond financial?"

"Landry spoke for the company, did the negotiation, set the schedule. Oren carried out the orders, handling everything to do with the livestock."

"Did Keith Landry consult Oren Street? Perhaps behind the scenes?"

"Not that I ever saw. He made decisions on the spot." She considered. "No. The way he talked about Oren was dismissive. Slighting. The way he talked *to* him . . ."

"Taken altogether, you're saying Street has a motive for murdering Landry."

"That's not . . . No." Denial, but not shock at the accusation. It had been in her head somewhere. Possibly at the forefront.

"From what you said, it's a natural conclusion. And," I added deliberately, "saying so makes sense from your standpoint."

"Why would I . . . oh. Oh, yes, I see. I would be attempting to get out from under a truckload of assumed guilt dumped on me by heaping it on to Oren Street."

"As I said, it makes sense from your standpoint."

She regarded me for a long, silent moment. Long enough that I felt the drag of it tugging at words from the back of my mind, even though I know that trick and use it.

She saved me by saying, "I wouldn't want to live in a world where that sort of sacrificing of others for self-gain is expected."

"Might not be expected, at least by some, but you *do* live in a world where it happens. All the time. Wyoming's not exempt."

Still looking at me, she said, "Tom Burrell speaks very highly of you. I wonder why."

"I could say precisely the same thing to you, Linda."

"I don't know what—"

"Yes, you do. You either killed that man, or hope to protect someone who did. Either way, you're making a mess of it. Tom says you're intelligent. Well, intelligent people should know that telling lies during a murder investigation is stupid. A lie—any lie—turns a spotlight on the liar. That spotlight doesn't care what it lights up. If you try to dodge around underneath it, hiding this or that, you and anybody you're connected to looks all the more guilty."

I stood. She did not.

"I am cooperating completely with the police," she said.

"Are you? Have you taken Deputy Alvaro into your romantic confidence the way you did me?" I didn't try to curb the skepticism. "You know, I missed one option earlier—in addition to the possibilities that you killed him or that you're protecting the killer, you might be protecting someone you *think* murdered Keith Landry. And if that's so, this half-baked effort to distract me with the tale of the heartbreak Landry handed you—but Zane didn't—could put the person you're trying to protect in an even deeper hole."

Her mouth worked, but nothing emerged.

"If it's Door Number Three—you're protecting someone you think murdered Landry—who? Stan Newton? Your nephew Cas? Or perhaps Zane? Are you truly that forgiving that you'd protect him?"

She stood, picked up her bag, placed the strap deliberately on her shoulder, and walked away. Not once looking at me, or displaying any emotion or hurry. Leaving me with my questions unanswered, except by my own, entirely unsatisfactory responses.

Did I think she'd killed him? Maybe.

Did I think she was covering up for someone she knew killed him? Maybe again.

Did I think she was covering up for someone she thought might have killed him? Probably.

Did I think that the person she was covering up for *had* killed Landry? Or have an idea who that person might be? How the hell would I know?

Chapter Twenty-Nine

IN THE TIME we'd talked, the sun had dropped behind the mountains. There were no artificial lights near the picnic table, but the ones around the rodeo grounds started to glow.

As I walked toward the office and the activity beyond it, Linda reached the porch. The office door opened, and Street stepped out. They stood there, in what from this distance appeared to be neutral conversation.

Something drew my gaze to the side, and there was Grayson Zane in the shadow of a truck, looking toward the office.

Over by the arena, I saw Mike talking to Stan Newton. Newton appeared edgy. His gaze traveled past Mike to the office, the parked pickup trucks, the grandstand, the pens.

Cas was back where I'd seen him the first night, preparing for competition. This time his hands were still as he stared at his father and Mike, though he was too far away to hear them. When Stan's gaze made another circuit, I saw Cas' follow the same path.

Linda and Oren parted. She went inside, he stepped off the porch toward the arena.

Zane flicked a look toward me, then turned on his heel.

Beyond him, I saw Evan Watt dart behind a pickup truck.

I headed after Watt, praying he hadn't used his concessions earnings to buy chewing tobacco.

Once I cleared the rodeo office's corner, I saw Street's back as he passed two female figures by a patiently standing horse. The Uptons, mother and daughter.

At that moment, Vicky looked up and spotted me. She headed toward me. Looking determined.

If I kept after Watt, what were the chances of his talking to me with Vicky on my tail? About as good as my chances of shaking her off.

"Ms. Danniher."

"Please, call me Elizabeth," I said with a charming smile.

"Ms. Danniher," she repeated. Apparently not as charming a smile as I had hoped. "I want to talk to you about the privileged material you obtained last night and—"

"There is no privilege, Vicky. I'm not a member of the clergy or the bar. I'm a reporter."

"You will not put any of that from last night on TV." It had the air of a threat more than an order.

Still, I replied with sweet reason. "I will if it has a bearing on Landry's murder."

She opened and closed her mouth twice, in an apparent attempt to swallow my sweet reason. "It does not have any bearing."

"If you or Heather murdered—"

She gasped loud enough to stop me, and that was only a precursor to snapping, "How dare you?"

"Oh, I dare. You're strong suspects. Both of you."

"My daughter had no reason—"

"C'mon, Vicky. That won't fly. By her own admission he was coming after her, and she roped him to put a stop to it. She could have taken the roping farther than she's admitted—taken the final step. Or—"

"She did not—"

"—you could have done the deed yourself."

"Ridiculous. Why would I?"

"As much as you seem to hate Landry? That's easy. Of course, we only have your word for it that Landry *was* Heather's father."

"You think I'd claim *him* as sperm-donor if it weren't true?"

"You never told anyone who the father was before telling Heather last week?"

"Why should I? It's nobody's business."

"It was his business."

"He dumped me, didn't want anything to do with me."

"You could have gotten help from him."

"No."

"A paternity test to prove he was the father, and you'd have gotten child support."

"We didn't need anything from anybody. I've put away money from the time Heather was born—even before. Sometimes only a couple dimes a week, but every single week, no matter what. She's worked hard, too. To be rodeo queen and get that scholarship."

"You can seek money from the estate. For college . . ."

"No." Two letters. As cold and vehement as I've ever heard. She collected herself. "I didn't want anything to do with him while he was alive, and I don't want anything to do with him now that he's dead."

She turned on the heel of her cowboy boot and stalked off. One very determined woman who had absolutely wanted her daughter's father out of their lives.

✧　✧　✧　✧

NO HOPE NOW of tracking Evan Watt, but I still wanted to know what he'd been able to see from where he'd stood.

I reached the spot and turned for a survey.

It told me that even with the waning daylight, he'd been able to see everything I had seen—more accurately, everyone. Zane, the rodeo office porch where Linda and Street had stood, where Mike and Newton had talked, Cas' preparation spot, and the Uptons.

I stepped to the side, mimicking his dart. Fat lot of good that did me. It appeared to put him out of sight for every one of—

"What were you talking to Linda Caswell about?"

I spun around at the voice behind me, already knowing I'd see Grayson Zane. I took my time before answering, watching him. "You. What happened five years ago."

He didn't look away. He didn't explain.

"Tell me your side of it."

"Nothing to tell."

"Then we have nothing to talk about, Zane."

He put a hand on my arm—"Wait."—and withdrew it as soon as I stopped. "You can't be thinking she's a suspect in this."

"I can be," I said. "Why would you care?"

"Don't want to see the wrong person blamed."

"Who's the right person? You?"

"I didn't kill Landry."

"We know you and Watt got to the rodeo grounds well before you first said you did. Closer to midnight than as the sun came up. Plenty of time to see and kill Landry."

He gave no evidence of falling to his knees and confessing. "That wasn't me saying the time, it was Watt."

"You're capable of making the throw over the beam that put the rope around his neck, aren't you?"

Not a flicker indicated he might know the initial throw was ostensibly accounted for, and it was the neck part that mattered. "Yes. But like I said before, Landry gave me the opening that let me get my career back on track."

"What did you do for him in exchange?"

He looked at me. These silent westerner types were a pain to interview. Give me Hiram Poppinger any time.

"What do you know about Landry telling Street to bring the stock in early?"

"Not a thing."

"You know more about what's been going on than you're saying, Zane."

"I got nothing to tell you." Which in no way denied that he did know more than he was saying.

✧　✧　✧　✧

DRIVING BACK TO the station, I gave Mike my rundown on the conversation with Linda Caswell.

He reported that Stan Newton had denied pretty much everything.

Newton said he wasn't at the fairgrounds when Landry was killed, having stopped just long enough to swear Zane and Watt had arrived before zero hour.

He said Cas went to bed at eleven and stayed there, and became snarly when Mike pointed out that by Newton's own account, he hadn't returned until after one o'clock and hadn't checked his son's bedroom.

He said the lunch at Haber House the day before Landry died had been a social occasion and a pure delight. No undercurrent of lechery from Landry toward Heather, disgust from Heather toward Landry, smoldering anger from Cas to Landry, coolness between Heather and Cas, or animosity between him and Landry.

He said he had not heard a single word about under-the-table dealings concerning the choice of a livestock contractor—that was as close to raising the bribe rumors as we'd decided Mike would go. For now.

Finally, Newton said he'd had no role in Landry bringing in the livestock early and couldn't venture a guess as to who might have or for what purpose.

Mike had even less success with the others. Cas did his melting trick. Mike caught a glimpse of blue hair in the vicinity of that melting.

Oren Street said he had nothing new to add, and he had more work to do than he had hours in the day.

Mike also encountered Evan Watt. Not a pleasant olfactory experience from Mike's description.

"Talk about funky—as in, a man in a total funk—that's what he smelled like. Sweat and old booze and unwashed."

"Got it. What did he say?"

"Not much. Asked him about what time he and Zane got in last week, and got no straight answer. He was jittery as all get-out. Talked about not sticking around for the Fourth. I said the sheriff's department might have other ideas. He turned gray. I asked how it was going in concessions. The gray got more sickly, and he said he wasn't doing that anymore. When I asked if he was working for Street—it seemed a natural question, since he'd worked for Landry and made no secret he needed cash—I thought he'd pass out."

We'd reached KWMT. I parked beside Mike's four-wheel-drive and turned off the engine. With the sun setting, opening the windows to let in the breeze made it comfortable.

"I asked when he'd eaten last, and it was like I was talking a different language," Mike said as he fiddled with the seatbelt. "I, uh . . . Maybe it wasn't the right thing to do—I mean for a story, but I felt bad for the guy. I gave him a twenty."

"You don't tell about my twenty to Kelly on Sunday, and I won't tell about your twenty to Watt today. At least yours was for food, not cigarettes."

"Unless he spends it on booze," he said.

"Or chewing tobacco."

He grinned. "We're going to your place, right? Tom'll be there later."

"Wait a second. I also saw Vicky Upton." I recapped that.

"Well, she must have wanted something to do with Landry at one time," he said, "or they wouldn't have had a kid."

I snorted. "That feeling is long forgotten. Besides, it was on the rebound, like his others. And Landry dumped her. That's quite a one-two punch. Ask Linda or Sonja or the others Jennifer found. That's not a scenario that engenders fond memories."

Mike followed me to my house, parked on the street, and wasn't far behind as I walked up the steps.

For a second night in a row, Jennifer scared the socks off me when I opened my front door. This time with more justification, since I hadn't left her in my house.

Once again, cookies, chips, candy, and pretzels covered the coffee table.

She looked up. Her eyes held the empty stare of someone trying to focus at a new distance after too many hours devoted to the computer. The screen's light gave her face a waxy glow as she said, "I found something."

Chapter Thirty

I LOOKED AT MIKE. He looked back at me. We both looked at her.

She said, "Your dog really likes those bacon treats. He practically licked my hand raw."

"He ate from your—" No. What a stray dog ate, and how he ate it, and whether he seemed to like anyone and everyone better than the person who was feeding and watering him and had given him a name wasn't the point. I changed the subject to, "I swear the door was locked when I left."

"It's a junk lock," she said with scorn.

"That is no . . ." Her earlier words hit. "What did you find?"

"First, I found two more towns for that list I gave you at the station, all before last year. Then I found something *really* good." Judging from her smirk, she was not referring to my cache of junk food. "Remember that woman who was registered as DBA for Sweet Meadows Contracting?"

"Yeah," Mike and I chorused.

The impression that things were near to adding up in my head to produce an answer—even if I didn't know the steps—returned. If I hadn't been going full tilt, would it already have surfaced?

"I went back and looked at the location of her home address," Jennifer said.

"It's not a town Landry's rodeo has been," Mike said quickly. "I'd have recognized the name. I'm sure I would. I've looked at that list so many times . . . It isn't, is it?"

"Nope. But . . ." Jennifer drew it out in triumph. "It's four miles from where Landry's rodeo was June, three years ago."

"That's when Sweet Meadows was founded," Mike said.

"Yup."

"Good job. Can you get background on this woman? As much as you can get legally and ethically," I added for safety.

"What does it mean?" Mike asked. "Was she in on this with Landry, or did he use her as a front, and she didn't know?"

"Don't know yet, but it's another piece of string to tug on."

I started to walk away, but Mike lingered, saying, "Jennifer, that information you found about other towns having trouble with a new stock company backing out at the last second, can you put that together for us to look at?"

And I thought I saw the answer.

At least to this sub-issue. But we'd still need to work out a lot of steps to have the proof.

"Excellent, Paycik. Your instinct about the bankrupt contractor was right all along. Jennifer, see if you can find out if any of those other bankrupt contractors are DBA situations. And if there are more DBAs, check their locations against Landry's schedule."

Her eyes went wide, and she started to grin. "Cool!"

"And—" My mind jumped ahead. "See if that minister's widow has a daughter who was rodeo queen when Landry was in town."

"You think . . ." Mike said. "But why?"

"Think? Yes. Know? No. But it's sure worth having Jenny—uh, Jennifer check."

She didn't notice my slip. She was already typing.

✧ ✧ ✧ ✧

TEN MINUTES later, Tom arrived.

"You all look half dead," said Mr. Charm.

"Comes from an afternoon spent with one of your county's solid citizens," I said.

"I heard about that dust-up at Hiram Poppinger's place."

"You saw our coverage?"

Tom's mouth twitched. "No. Wasn't watching TV. Got a ranch to run. Taking advantage of long daylight. You should be home asleep," he added to Jennifer.

She didn't look up, her fingers didn't slow. "Not yet. But if you're going to talk, I'll go somewhere else."

At that, she did look up—at me.

I offered, "Kitchen, bedroom or bathroom—though I can't recommend the bathroom unless you want to think you've come down with the plague."

"Kitchen," she said, balancing her open laptop on her forearm like a waiter, leaving a hand free for a bag of chips, pen, and paper.

With her gone, Tom turned to Mike and me, and I read the intention in his eyes.

"Oh, no you don't. You haven't known us since we were born. You can't order us around."

"Well, actually, he has known me . . ." Mike started. Tom chuckled, and Mike joined in. "Not that I would leave."

I was not in a chuckling mood. "Good. Then let's go over this."

"You'd both be better for some rest," Tom said. "Why not come to it fresh in the morning?"

"Because it's Wyoming's version of a snow-bound English house party crime scene," I said.

"Excuse me?" Tom said.

"Crossroads. Tell him, Mike."

He did, then said, "But I don't get the English house party connection."

"All the suspects are gathered only as long as the storm holds them in place. Once the storm's over, they disperse. No solution. Same here, except no snow, no English countryside, no house party, no lords and ladies, no servants."

"Other than that, exactly the same," Mike muttered.

I ignored that. "You told me if the rodeo is canceled, there's no reason for out-of-towners to stay, and no reason for locals to be even as cooperative as they have been. So, you can leave, either or both of you, but I'm going over what we've got so far."

"Staying," Mike said, reaching for pad and pen.

Tom sat, took off his hat, hooked it on the corner of the couch frame again, and said, "What did you two pick up today?"

I took that opening. "Linda Caswell called me to the rodeo grounds this evening and proceeded to tell me a.) details about her romantic relationships with Zane and Landry, b.) what a bad relationship Landry and his partner had."

"Interesting."

"Isn't it just. After all the effort to tell me the least amount possible, while portraying them as nearly-forgotten episodes in her distant past, suddenly she takes me into her confidence. And she piles on details about Street and Landry's business that a couple days ago she knew nothing about."

"And that has you thinking what, Elizabeth?"

"It has me thinking that she called me out to the rodeo grounds for the express purpose of telling me those things in order to redirect my attention from something or someone. In other words, covering up for somebody."

"Could be."

"I'm so glad you think so," I snapped.

His mouth twitched. But it was dead straight when he said, "Ask what you want to ask."

"Did you tell Linda about Newton bribing Landry?"

"No."

"Was she one of your sources?"

"No."

I believed him. Partly because of those damned Abraham Lincoln eyes. But also because of who else might have told Tom about a potential bribe and told Linda about telling Tom. Cas.

Mike stepped into a silence. "If Linda was covering up for somebody, can we eliminate her as a possible suspect?"

"No," I said. "Might be an effort to throw us off. I'd have expected her to be more subtle."

"She's not accustomed to being subtle about things like murder," Burrell said.

"If you can't keep an open mind—"

He interrupted me. "I'm not going to pretend I think Linda murdered anybody."

"You don't have to," Mike said. "Elizabeth and I don't always agree on who's a likely suspect. Just don't interfere with thrashing out the possibilities."

Tom nodded. "Okay. Here's what I got today. One source I trust added a couple of tidbits of information, which is the end for what that one knows. But it led me to the second source I trust, and I did more digging. It seems Newton didn't get one bribe, but more like a series of kickbacks from Landry."

"For what?" Mike asked.

"For his vote on the first go-round, like we thought. And for voting to bring in Landry last-minute, with all those bonuses. Which, by the way, put him over what he'd asked for to start last fall. Then there was an additional payment in there, too."

"If he'd heard rumors about Sweet Meadows going under, probably for word if it pulled out so he could get the jump on a last-ditch contract," guessed Mike.

"That makes sense. Except it sounds, from what my source says, like it was for getting hold of documents and destroying them," Tom said.

Mike raised his eyebrows at me. I replied with the smallest shake. These vague documents didn't necessarily have anything to do with Sweet Meadows' DBA status. What Jenny—*Jennifer*—had told us was so tentative, so new . . . We'd have to see where her research and this conversation took us before trying to make connections.

"What documents?" I asked.

"No idea. Source swears to that. It was right around the time Sweet Meadows pulled out. Can't pin down if it was before or after. I could use some coffee. Mind if I . . ." He tipped his head toward the kitchen door.

"Help yourself. Mugs are in the cabinet above the coffee maker."

Mike stood and said, "I need a refill, too. Elizabeth?"

"No thanks, I'm fine." More accurately, caffeine wasn't going to help what was bothering me.

I studied the list of women I'd talked to, going back ten years. Then the list of towns where Landry had been with the rodeo. Of course, the rodeos were where he'd met the women. But there was something else . . . a connection like an echo . . . or *something*. It was right there on the edge of the jumble in my head. If it would just come a little closer . . .

The kitchen door swung open, and I became aware I'd been hearing more activity from there than coffee required.

Tom came out with Jennifer in tow. "She was sound asleep with her head on the table. I'm taking her home."

She muttered a weak protest, which he ignored. She did look tired. I thanked her, and she said she'd finish in the morning.

At the front door, Tom said he'd be back in a few minutes, because she lived nearby. I felt vaguely guilty for not knowing that. Or much of anything about her.

Mike set his coffee cup down and settled into the couch as the door closed behind them. "I know you play your cards close to the vest, but you can trust Tom."

I wasn't so sure. I didn't believe he would overtly betray confidences, but he made no bones about having divided loyalties. What I said was, "It would be nice to get more facts before we launch into that. Besides . . ."

"Besides?" he prompted.

"I have a feeling about all those powerful emotions swirling around."

"But look at what we've found out about the business. Landry was cheating the rodeo left, right, and center."

"You're right. It's a possible motive."

"But you think his relationships are at the core of this?"

"*Relationships* is awfully high-tone for the sleaze he pulled."

He raised his hands in surrender. "No argument here. Definitely slime. Okay, I buy it's a possible motive. After all, look at what they say about hell having no fury like a woman scorned. In this case, multiply that by all the women we know about so far."

"Oh, God, you, too? And that's not the correct quote. It's 'Heav'n has no Rage, like Love to Hatred turn'd, Nor Hell a Fury, like a Linda Caswell scorn'd.'"

He eyed me. "My apologies to Shakespeare."

"Not Shakespeare. Congreve." I'd looked it up Friday after the discussion with Burrell on the drive back from the Newtons'. "And you notice the sequence of events here? The guy does the scorning. Not just a heartfelt, sorry, this isn't working for me any longer, but outright *scorning*. That deserves more than a little fury. That deserves a capital F-capital U."

My mind had followed a different path while I talked, one hitting the replay button on an unexpected track. Grayson Zane. That first conversation. The one time his calm held an edge.

Men like Landry take the sure thing. And if there's not a sure thing to be taken, they rig it so there is.

"But you say to chase the inconsistencies," Mike said. "And the business side—"

"That's it. That's *exactly* it. The inconsistencies disappear if he knew—Oh, my God. He *knew*. Look at how Landry did things. He didn't leave things to chance. When he wanted something, he arranged it. He stage-managed situations to make sure things came out exactly the way he wanted. The women, the contracts."

I scrambled out of the chair—an effort hampered because the foot I'd tucked under had fallen asleep, as my mother always warned. I grabbed my phone in one hand and found the list of names and contact info with the other.

"Elizabeth? What—"

"Sequence of events. Maybe. If—Sonja? It's Elizabeth Danniher from KWMT-TV. I won't take much of your time. I have just a few questions. Before you started, uh, dating the rodeo cowboy who swept you off your feet when you were rodeo queen, how was he doing in the rankings?" I jotted notes as she talked.

I had to break in to get in my next question. "After you broke up, how long before Keith Landry, uh, became part of your life . . . Found you crying that night, huh? . . . Uh-huh, uh-huh. I absolutely do understand your feelings. One last question. Did you happen to notice your cowboy's career after he broke off with you? . . . Yes. Uh-huh. Right. Got it. Thank you. Thank you very much."

I disconnected and started dialing the next number.

"You're thinking it was more than Landry picking up after their hearts were broken?" Mike said. "But how—"

He broke off when I held up a hand to indicate my callee had answered.

Give Paycik full marks. He jabbed a finger to the third name on the list, grabbed his phone, and headed to the kitchen.

✧ ✧ ✧ ✧

SEVERAL DIDN'T answer. But in less than half an hour, we had the same story from other women in other rodeo towns where Keith Landry had had a fling with the rodeo queen.

We sat on the couch and looked at each other.

"Why? Why would he do that to those women?" Mike asked, and his bafflement made me like him even more. "Okay, he might not have been with rodeo queens, especially not in recent years with him getting older and seedier, but—"

"It wasn't about sex. It was about power. Sex was a way to keep score. To let him know he'd won and made them lose. Remember what I told you Street said about how for Landry it was all a game, and he not only had to win, he had to *beat* the other person?"

"Holy shit," Mike said.

I agreed. "Same sequence of events each time. A rodeo cowboy down on his luck rushes a woman—mostly the rodeo queen. After a brief fling, the cowboy breaks it off abruptly and in a manner sure to break a woman's heart. Keith Landry swoops in for a week or two of consolation sex—"

"With a woman who wouldn't otherwise have looked at him," Mike pointed out.

"Afterwards, the cowboy gets invitations to rodeos he otherwise couldn't have afforded to enter. Gives him a chance to win some, and his career picks up."

"Though in Evan Watt's case, it slides back down," he said.

"This can't possibly be a coincidence. Not the same sequence every time. Landry wasn't simply an opportunistic vulture or an emotional ambulance chaser, he was arranging it."

Chapter Thirty-One

TOM CAME IN and sat while we were absorbing what we'd found. He looked from one to the other of us. "What's happened?"

Mike's gaze met mine with the same question as earlier. This time I nodded. Tom shot me a look but focused on Mike when he spoke.

"Tom, we've spotted a pattern in Landry's activities."

Tom's brows rose. "In the time I was gone?"

"Yes." I said to Mike, "The rodeo first."

"If Landry *is* Sweet Meadows—"

"*What?*" Tom demanded.

Mike backed up and explained what Jennifer had found and what she hoped to confirm with other rodeos and other DBAs.

"It would have worked something like this. He would come in as Landry, make a real high bid. Maybe a few times a year, just with the rodeos he thinks might be getting restless," Mike said. "If the rodeo accepts the high bid, fine, he makes his money. If the rodeo balks and asks for more bids, he sends in a bogus company to undercut everyone else. His bogus company gets the bid, then goes belly-up—not hard, since it never existed except on paper.

"When the bogus company disappears, it leaves the rodeo in the lurch. Landry comes back to save the day. Gets bonuses piled on top of bonuses, making even more than he would have with the first, inflated bid. The next year, the rodeo pays what Landry asks."

Tom remained silent so long that the urge to over-explain that Landry had arranged the whole thing in order to swoop in and take advantage financially nearly overwhelmed me.

Twice, Mike and I exchanged looks—each said, "How long do we wait?" and "I don't know"—before Tom spoke.

"If you want, I can do some checking without raising suspicions. Maybe back up whatever Jen found."

"That would be real helpful, Tom," Mike said.

"There's more." I pulled out the list of women's names that had started with towns and dates and phone numbers, and now had the names of rodeo cowboys added. "If Keith Landry operated like this in business, what are the chances he operated the same way in private?"

I explained why we thought the chances were excellent.

"That son of a—" He bit it off. "You're going to report this? Make public what happened to those women? Pile on more embarrassment?"

"They have nothing to be embarrassed about—any more than someone who's the victim of a robbery has cause to be embarrassed. But, no, we're not planning to report on this. Unless one of them is a murderer," I said. "But we need to confirm that what we think happened *did* happen."

"Why?"

"Because if we need it as a lever to get information on anything else, or if it turns out to be the motive for Landry's murder, we're not likely to have time to work the angle later. Or access." I looked at the list again. "What I don't understand is why he selected some rodeo queens and skipped others."

"I do," Mike said slowly. "I think I do. Seeing the list of women and their rodeos got me thinking." He dug a paper from the pile on the table, held out his hand for the list I had, then set them side by side.

"Landry's schedule. The women he went after. He pulled his shit on the women only when he had a schedule break. When he had to move on to another town right away, he didn't have time. That's why he pulled it here some years and not others."

A quick look showed he was right. Tom muttered something. I didn't catch the words, but I shared the sentiment.

"What we have to look at now is who knew about this, and if that knowing gave them a motive," I said.

"The women knew," Mike said. "At least part of it. If any of them figured it out . . ."

"You don't have proof any of them figured it out," Tom said.

"We don't have *proof* of much of anything," I said. "We're gathering possibilities for motive. Not everyone could make that initial throw over the beam, but assuming Heather left Landry tied up as she described, most of Sherman has opportunity and means. So, we have to look at motive, and there'd be motive for any of the women who figured out what he did. But they also have to be here in Sherman, so that means Linda Caswell and Vicky Upton."

"This long after the fact for Vicky?" Mike asked.

"Hey, you were the one backing her earlier. But, yeah, I think Vicky would have no statute of limitations on Landry's crimes."

Tom said, "Anyone who cared about the women involved—if they knew."

"That lengthens our list considerably." I was lamenting, not disagreeing. I added a line to the list to include the category.

"Including Stan Newton," Mike said.

Tom agreed, but I was in the dark. "Why would he kill Landry over his sister-in-law?"

"Cas is her heir," Mike said. "Aunt Gee told me that. If Linda took up with a man serious, he could become her heir. Not out of the question that she'd have a child of her own, too."

"Stan was not happy when she was seeing Landry," Tom said. "Or Zane."

"Wait a minute," I protested. "That would be a motive when Landry was seeing her, but what motive would Newton have after Landry dumped her? Especially after a few years." Could that be why he'd checked on Zane's arrival here? Worried that Zane and Linda would rekindle something? And what if his tirade Friday night about a cowboy taking things away from him had not been aimed only at Evan Watt's forty-dollar mistake?

"Honor of the Caswell name," Mike said promptly.

"Oh, c'mon. He's not a Caswell. He makes a big deal of being a self-made man. Why would he care?"

"His son's a Caswell," Tom said.

Sometimes I felt as if I'd stepped back a century. Or stayed in this century and ventured to another continent. But just because it was foreign to me, didn't mean it wasn't valid. Besides, if we considered only motives for murder that weren't foreign to me, our suspects would be limited to ex-wives of men who took the Jack Nicholson character in *Heartburn* as a role model.

"What about Oren Street?" I asked. "They didn't travel together, but they overlapped at most rodeos. He must have seen Landry in action."

"The rodeo was the set-up," Mike said. "The payoff didn't come until after the woman had been dumped, and Landry was there for the rebound. By that time, Street would have moved on."

"After all those women, over all those years, he'd have to start noticing something. He can't be *that* blind to anything other than livestock." They looked back at me. "Okay, maybe he is. But I'm leaving him as a possibility. What about on the business side? Street emphasized he didn't know anything about the business, and what Linda and Newton have said backs that. So, who else?"

"Evan Watt," Mike said. "Several of the women named him, and, remember, he said early on that he'd worked for Landry, being real cagey about exactly what he did."

"Landry was using Evan Watt . . .?" Tom looked as if Abraham Lincoln's good looking cousin had bit into a wormy apple.

I shrugged. "Some women go for that type. A walk on the wild side."

Mike muttered something about the unwashed side.

"Watt's on the list, along with the other men Landry hired or bribed to be his setup man," I said. "But, just like the women, they had to be here to have opportunity. That means Watt and Zane."

"I can't believe it of Grayson Zane," Tom said.

"Setting up a woman for Keith Landry? Or murder?"

He gave me a long, level look. He wanted to say both. And he knew I knew it. He also knew I would refute half with ease. "Murder."

"Ability to ride a bull or rope a steer does not equate to a stellar moral center," I said. "As he proved with Linda."

"No one can know for sure what he—"

"She knows." He had no response to that. "Anybody else either of you think might have known what Landry was up to?"

"Penny," Mike said promptly. "She knows everything."

As our chuckles fueled partly by tension faded, Burrell said, "What do you want me to do?"

"Give us your thoughts on which of these guys is our best bet to talk to," I said. "With Landry dead, that's our only way to confirm what was going on with these women."

Burrell's gaze held mine a moment, then deliberately shifted. From where he sat, he must have been looking at the irregular, roundish blot on the living room wall I hoped was the result of a bad job of washing red crayon. He looked grim. The room was enough to make anyone grim, but I didn't think it was the decor.

Finally, Burrell leaned forward, transferred his gaze to the list on the coffee table that we'd gathered from the women and directed one long finger to a name.

Grayson Zane.

"Talk to him," he said.

"Even though we only know of one time with him?" Mike objected.

"One of the men who's not here might be more open to talking, since they're not a murder suspect," I said. "On the other hand, Watt was the most frequent, uh, introductory act among the women we talked to. If we get him to talk, it opens the floodgates."

"That's why he won't talk," Tom said, withdrawing his pointing finger. "Too much to lose."

"Seems like Zane has a lot more to lose," I protested. "Being a big shot in rodeo, I mean. It would be a big story."

Tom shook his head, not denying what I said, but indicating something outweighed it. "He did it once and never again."

"Because his conscience bothered him," Mike supplied. Tom nodded, and they exchanged a look.

I interrupted their Code of the West moment. "Or because he didn't need to repeat because his career took off. You can't know—"

"Elizabeth, you were the one who pointed out his reaction," Mike said.

"Possibly embarrassment or fear of being outed. If we appeal to his conscience when he's thinking about protecting his own hide, we lose any hope of getting him to open up."

"You'll get him to talk."

"Gee, thanks for the vote of confidence, Burrell, but you're saying it doesn't make it so."

He picked up his hat, as if his proclamation settled the issue. "Because his conscience bothers him," he said, echoing Mike. "Also, because it was Linda. She's a fine woman. He knows it. And he knows he did wrong by her."

And damned if Mike didn't nod.

Tom rose. "I'll say good-night now."

"You'll get back to us about the business angle?"

"Yes." He kept heading for the door.

He had closed it when I rose, said to Mike, "I'll be right back," and followed Tom out.

"Burrell," I called from the crooked steps. He kept going, around to the driver's door of his truck, parked behind my car. I jogged after him. "Tom."

He turned at that, releasing the door handle.

"If we get Zane to talk, it gives Linda double motive—business and personal." I don't know why I felt the need to give that warning.

"She didn't kill him."

"How can you know?"

He looked at me with those Abraham Lincoln eyes. "I know."

I threw up my arms. It didn't fluster him one bit. "Even assuming you're 100 percent right, it could be miserable for her."

"I considered that before I gave my opinion of which one of those boys to talk to. I've had cause to think about the matter," his eyes glinted at me from under the brim of his hat, "and I don't believe a murderer should go free."

"You had different ideas when you thought your wife—"

"Ex-wife. And since then, I've decided I was wrong. I wouldn't have been doing Tamantha any favors."

I blinked at him.

If I'd been asked to rank Thomas Burrell on a stubborn-o-meter, I'd have said he would break the thing. Yet here he'd changed his mind about a vital matter, and admitted it. More than that, he'd admitted he'd been *wrong*—not that circumstances were different or any of those other face-saving phrases, but that he'd been *wrong*. And he was prepared to back his words by helping dig into Keith Landry's business practices.

"So, you go on inside now, and you and Mike get back to work finding a murderer, Elizabeth Margaret Danniher." He reached out as if to brush hair off my cheek with the back of his fingers.

"Elizabeth!" came Mike's call from the open doorway. "Your cell. ID says it's Watt—Evan Watt."

Aware of Tom following, I jogged up the walk and inside to hear the phone still ringing. I scooped it up from the coffee table and answered in one motion.

Chapter Thirty-Two

THE NIGHT'S RODEO had been over for hours. We rolled right up to the entrance.

I'd tried to persuade Tom and Mike that I should come alone, since Watt had said he had something to tell *me* because he *didn't hold with that sort of thing.* He wouldn't elaborate on the phone. Said he'd tell me when I came. Paycik said no way was I doing this alone. Burrell said his truck was behind my car, and he wasn't moving it. Paycik drove all of us in his four-wheel-drive.

The number of protestors had swelled with the Fourth of July nearing and the news coverage of Landry's death. But they were clearly off-duty, sitting in rackety lawn chairs around small fires contained in cut-off barrels. Some were roasting marshmallows.

In the prime spot closest to the gates were the familiar faces of the original group. I waved.

Mr. and Mrs. Gray-Hair waved back with smiles. Ellie and Pauline, the protestor previously known as Ms. Blue Hair, gave me nearly identical scowls. Roy Craniston gave me the finger.

As we pulled past the protestors, a small truck heading out slowed to clear the gates.

"Vicky and Heather," Mike said from the driver's seat.

I turned, caught a glimpse of mother and daughter looking straight ahead, not acknowledging us or any protestors.

Mike pulled into a spot between a rusted pickup and a motorhome that out-swanked the presidential palace of several countries I've been in.

"Stay in the car, you two," I ordered as I reached for the door handle.

"No way," Burrell said from the back seat.

"There are lots of people around. I'll be fine."

"Wonder if Landry thought that," Mike contributed.

"Watt won't show himself, much less talk to me, with you two lumbering along."

"You said he sounded like he'd been drinking," Mike said grimly. "Lowers inhibitions."

"So he'll talk more. Which is exactly what happened with you, right, Burrell? Watt's your source you don't trust on the bribe."

"Yeah."

"See?"

"Alcohol can also lower other inhibitions," he added.

"See?" Mike retorted.

"Oh, c'mon, Evan Watt?"

"Hey, he took part in Landry's sleazy dealings with women a number of times we know of. Who knows what else he did. And this place is emptying out fast."

"I'll be fine." If Watt talked, we'd have absolute confirmation that Landry set up these women. I got out. They each did the same. "This is ridiculous. Do you have any idea the places I've been?"

"With a camera crew and bodyguards," Paycik shot back.

Not always. I started off, and they started behind me like big, cowboy-hatted shadows.

I stopped, hissed, "Stay back. Don't let him see you," and started again.

"Do not get out of our sight," ordered Burrell.

Watt had said to meet him by the concession stand. Just this side of it were the easternmost pens, with an alley left between them and the grandstand structure. The animals from this first tic-tac-toe column were gone, likely back in their distant, more spacious pens for the night. Their odor lingered, no doubt from agricultural byproducts. Judging from some faint sounds, animals remained in pens farther to the west.

I turned my back on the pens, focusing on the concession stand.

Watt had said he had something to tell me—needed to get it off his chest was how he'd put it. My logic said it was not to confess to murdering Landry. My logic said Watt was not dangerous. My heartbeat wasn't convinced.

The wait didn't help. I must have stood there half an hour—or at least ten minutes.

Maybe he'd seen my bodyguards, though I couldn't see them in the shadows.

Maybe he'd changed his mind.

Maybe he'd had more to drink and wasn't mobile.

Maybe—

I heard something behind me. Not close. I spun around, staring toward the sound. Through the shadows, I caught a glimpse of motion, down close to the arena. Something moving slowly, even stealthily, from east to west, probably along the open path between the pens and the arena chutes. I moved cautiously into the more deeply shadowed alley, with the grandstand on my left and the empty pens on my right, heading toward the arena, closing in on the figure.

It stilled, and so did I. Waiting.

It started again. If there'd been an aisle leading to the west that paralleled the figure's path, I would have followed it, but there wasn't. Our paths were at right angles, but I was moving faster, cutting the distance.

I was maybe twenty feet away when the figure seemed to look up the alley. I stopped, not wanting my motion to catch attention.

The figure moved again. A slant of light from a distant security pole gave me a second's impression of size, shape, and walk. Possibly Evan Watt. Or not.

I'd started moving when the figure's head jerked around—toward me? I couldn't tell. And I didn't stop to consider it, because the figure was running to the west. I ran, too. Down the rest of my aisle, a right-hand turn to follow the figure along the corridor between the chutes and pens. My flats slid on the dirt, as they had at Newtons' ranch. I should have worn my still stinky shoes.

I saw the figure in front of me.

And then I didn't.

I kept moving, now just past the end of the arena, reaching the spot where I thought I'd last seen him.

Straight ahead was the truncated wooden arch structure and the police-taped crime scene. To the left were the timed event boxes attached to the western end of the arena. To the right was another alley parallel to the one I'd come down, this one with pens on both sides. On the alley's east side, the pens were empty, on the west side, judging by the sound, animals were being held.

I had nothing to go on. Nothing. No movement. No sound, except the animals. Surely they would've reacted to an interloper.

I'd lost him.

Then I heard it. Clanking that announced something was happening with a section of portable fence. It came from the alley to my right, back among the pens. I ran toward the noise.

I spotted a figure ahead, atop fencing that formed the right boundary of this alley. It turned toward me, then dropped out of sight on the far side, into one of the empty pens.

"Watt! Evan Watt! Wait! I want to talk to you."

I reached the same spot and started up the fence, catching glimpses of the figure running diagonally across the pen.

From my perch, I saw that portable panels blocked the end of the alley that usually opened up to the rest of the grounds, creating a deadend. I also saw the figure reach the far fence and start climbing. The narrow-waisted back and cowboy hat stood out as a darker silhouette against the sky's faint lightness for an instant.

I dropped into the empty pen and ran. Climbing the far fence, though, I saw the figure's diagonal path across the next empty pen now angled back toward the alley, completing the first zig of a potential zig-zag route.

I followed. But I was losing ground. My flats gave me no purchase on the ground or the panels' rungs.

Climbing as fast as I could, I spotted the figure at the fence on the far side of the alley. So not zig-zag. What was he doing?

I dropped from the fence back into the alley. This time, my tired legs sent me stumbling forward and down hard on my knees. I scrambled up, refusing to consider agricultural byproducts left by previous passers-by as I brushed off my hands without slowing my angled route toward where the figure disappeared.

I heard a metallic clank from behind my left shoulder and some distance back down the alley, like someone messing with panels, followed by yelling in an unidentifiable voice.

But that didn't hold my interest long. Because then I heard something else.

Something living and breathing. Breathing with a low, asthmatic rumble.

Something on the move and headed right toward me.

I ran.

DAY SEVEN

WEDNESDAY

Chapter Thirty-Three

I DIDN'T TURN my head, because I didn't need to see them to know what was coming at me. I heard them and smelled them. I also felt the vibrations through the ground as their hooves hit.

By instinct I started running toward my destination—the spot where the figure had disappeared.

Two steps in, and a shout came from my right. "Elizabeth! This way!" Mike.

I caught a glimpse of two figures silhouetted atop the fence farther down the alley and on the right side.

"Here!" came a second voice. Tom.

Even as I turned toward them, trying to run despite the thick, slippery ground, one figure dropped down, no longer silhouetted.

"Here!" shouted Tom again. Closer.

His hand closed around my arm, swinging me almost off my feet, toward the fence.

"Up! Climb up!"

I grabbed for a rail, tried to get a foothold, but my shoe slid off it. Tried again. Got up one rail, a second.

The thunder came nearer and nearer.

From above, I felt Mike pulling my arms and shoulders. A hand on my butt pushed me hard, and I was hooked over the top rail.

Mike grabbed my leg and pulled it over and around, shifting my center of gravity. Now if I fell off the fence, I'd fall into the empty pen, not the alley.

"Okay?" he asked.

"Yes," I panted. "But—"

He was gone. He'd dropped down into the empty pen. Tom was still in the alley with the bulls.

And now I could just barely see, from my position hanging over the top rail like a useless old rug, that he stood with his back to me, waving both arms—one extended by his cowboy hat—and shouting. He was a good three feet away from the fence.

"Tom! Get out of there!" I shouted. It was lost amid the other sounds. "Tom!"

The first bulls came up, shifting away from the human waving and shouting. But I'd seen video of Pamplona. Not all the bulls would be that polite. And as the bulk of them reached this spot there wouldn't be anywhere for them to shift to.

"Tom!"

Another voice shouted his name, too. "Tom! Now!"

Tom seemed to launch himself at the fence. Not at the section where I still hung, but the next one nearer to where the bulls were coming from. He didn't make any effort to climb. Why didn't he climb? He had to—

"Up!" I shouted—I saw a dark mass coming—"Tom!"

For an instant, the fence seemed to disappear, then I heard a slam, felt the reverberation through the rail I still clung to, and he was gone. Nowhere.

"It's okay! It worked." It was Mike. Below me, catching me around the middle, half lifting, half assisting me down.

"Tom?"

"He's right here."

And he was. Standing in front of me. The faint light adding caverns to that Abraham Lincoln face no longer shadowed by a hat brim.

"Lost my damned hat," he said.

I sat down. Hard.

✧ ✧ ✧ ✧

"I DON'T UNDERSTAND." Not the first time I'd said it.

My knees were doing a decent job of holding me up. Now. Mike had wrapped his arms around me and hauled me up from the ground earlier, and I hadn't objected that he hadn't let go right away, leading me to the open area just past the pens, with the rodeo office diagonally to our right and the permanent fence Mike and I had sat on diagonally to our left.

My hands shook slightly. My breath wasn't even. I refused to consider the agricultural byproducts that my senses told me clung to my jeans. Although some of the smell might have come from the bulls now peacefully milling in the fenced-in alley behind us. They needed a breath mint the size of Lake Michigan.

A half dozen new figures had arrived, apparently drawn by the noise. They asked if everything was okay, offered help, and demanded to know what happened. Most appeared to be cowboys staying on the grounds in vehicles parked on the far side of the open area. I didn't recognize any. Certainly none was Evan Watt.

"When you took off," Mike said, with disapproval vibrating in his wonderful TV voice, "we lost you for a while. It was only when we heard the fence rattling that we realized where you were."

That must have been the illusive figure's noise . . . which also stirred up the bulls. Started to stir them up.

"Someone shouted," I said.

"We heard," Mike said grimly. "Tom kept the lead bulls to the other side, to give you a chance to get up. Once we had you out of there, I went and undid the fastenings between the next two panels and swung one side in—didn't want to do the near end, because the bulls would've streamed out. But doing that end meant they'd have to make a U-turn to get out."

I put a hand on the nearest arm of each of them. "You—you both . . . You two were—" I couldn't get anything else out.

Mike put his hand over mine and squeezed.

Tom leaned forward and said, "You ever take off like that again, and we'll leave you to the damned bulls."

Paycik laughed.

I snatched my hands back, but Burrell and Paycik were saved from more when shouts reached us from opposite directions.

Two figures were coming toward us from our left, from the direction of the arena, coming up the next open aisle among the back pens. And they were shouting something about the bulls.

A lone cowboy was coming from the direction of the rodeo office to our right. He had more ground to cover, and his shouts weren't words yet.

"What about the bulls?" demanded Tom of the figures coming from the arena.

"The gate that should've kept them out of the alley is wide open. Wide open!" As he neared, I recognized the irate speaker as Oren Street. "Never should have been that way. Never seen it that way. Don't know why it would be that way. It was like somebody swung 'er open and ran off. Never seen anything like it, I tell you. And then to have the end blocked off that way—it's crazy."

Tom asked a technical question about the gates, but my mind had jumped ahead.

Two people working together? Or was the figure I'd chased innocent—at least of this—and the bull-looser had grabbed the opportunity. Had the target been me? Or the running figure? Was that why the figure was running?

Street's words caught my attention again. "Bulls shouldn't've been there at all. Watt was supposed to have moved 'em on back. I heard the regular contractor give him the job. Don't know what's wrong with that no-good, broke-down excuse of a cowboy. Even if it wasn't my bulls this time, there's no trusting him anymore. I'm telling you right now. Evan Watt—"

". . . Evan Watt!" came the shout of the cowboy approaching from the right, just now near enough to hear. He shouted more, but it was lost among questions and comments by the gathered cowboys.

"Quiet!" Mike commanded in a voice that needed no microphone. "What about Watt?"

The cowboy, coming to a panting stop, got out, "Needs help. Zane said . . . get help."

"Where?" came from all the cowboys.

"Behind office. Trees. Creek."

Mike started in that direction. Tom grabbed the newcomer by the arm and followed, demanding, "Show us."

The rest of us strung out as our speed—or lack of it—dictated. Having already put in an all-out sprint, along with fence-climbing tonight, I was at the back of the pack.

Past the rodeo office, the scene resembled an anthill in the dark. Figures ran toward a large dark shape near the trees where Linda and I had sat this evening. Other figures, who must have heard the alarm first, were now running away from the trees, apparently going after more help.

As I neared the trees, stumbling over unlit and uneven ground, I heard engines behind, and headlights came on from trucks being driven toward the center of activity. So that must be what people had been running to do, to bring trucks to provide needed light. I changed my path to get out of the way for the first truck. Its lights showed the back of an old pickup with a camper shell at the center of activity.

A figure froze at the left edge of the light. A man in partial light, maybe twenty feet in front of me, went to his knees at the pickup's bumper, shouting something about *out*, his head turned toward that frozen figure.

Then the figure moved. Slipping away into the darkness.

A second truck adding its light made the man at the bumper identifiable as Oren Street and made sense of his motions—he pulled at something stuck in the tailpipe, struggling in the shadow cast by his body.

"Help me with this! I can't seem to get the duct tape off." he called. His earlier shout must have been a plea for help to get the thing out of the tailpipe—a hose, I realized, and started reaching for my phone as I jogged closer.

Stan Newton passed Street by, shambling toward the driver's door, but Cas stopped. Stared for a heartbeat, then knelt beside Street.

Against a backdrop of confused calls of "Get him out! Get him out!" and conflicting orders, another truck pulled in with its headlights pointed at the front of the old pickup. It illuminated Grayson Zane and Mike heading toward the passenger door. A sound had me wondering for a split second if it had started to rain. No. Glass shattering. They'd broken the passenger window.

Zane reached in. The door opened.

I pulled up, hitting 911 on my phone.

✧ ✧ ✧ ✧

RICHARD ALVARO proved he knew his community that night. He went where the people were. He established his incident room in an unused office near the hospital waiting room. Every soul who'd been on the rodeo grounds, along with a couple dozen more Sherman residents, showed up in the waiting room. It looked like a convention of black cowboy hats.

Alvaro also proved he was a humanitarian by letting me go home to change and shower before questioning me—but only after getting initial information from Mike, Tom, and me that we'd been together for all but a brief time.

"And we heard her floundering around for some of that," said Burrell.

I was too tired to even glare at him.

Even that alibi didn't prevent Alvaro from having Deputy Shelton drive me home and wait in my living room while I showered and changed. He also let me put out fresh water and food for Shadow, since I didn't know when I'd be back.

Shelton put all my dirty clothes in paper bags, which was more than a little creepy. But I couldn't fault Alvaro for being thorough.

When we came back to the hospital, Jenks was getting into his KWMT four-wheel-drive. He *was* in Fine's doghouse to be called out at this time of night for a few general shots.

Under those circumstances, it was considerate of him to first ask me how I was before complaining about the crappy assignment.

Inside the waiting room, I saw Heather and her mother had arrived, sitting across from Stan Newton. Needham Bender was taking notes as he talked with a man I recognized as a rodeo committee member. Linda Caswell had been there when I left and was still there, along with Street, Zane, and all the others.

As Shelton and I came in, Cas Newton entered from the opposite side with a tray of Styrofoam coffee cups. I crossed the room to intercept him before he got in amongst the chairs and couches.

"Was it you?" I demanded.

"Was what me?" This kid didn't lie worth shit. No wonder Heather had known he was cheating with Pauline.

"Who led me into the ambush."

"Ambush? I don't know anything about—"

"You were skulking around the pens, and you ran when I called to you."

"No," he said.

"Thanks. I've got all I need." I pivoted and went to where Mike had made room for me on a couch.

His raised eyebrows asked the question.

"He says no, but he's lying. He was the runner," I said just above a murmur. "Probably heading for a visit to his little friend." Who was not present, I realized. "But probably not involved with the ambush."

In an equally low voice, he said, "Richard's talking to Tom now. No update on Watt."

But it was no secret what had happened to him, not with a dozen and a half witnesses who'd seen the set-up as they helped get him out.

He'd been found in the locked cab of his pickup, with a hose roughly duct-taped to the exhaust pipe and fed in through a back window.

Breaking the passenger window and dragging him out to fresh air might have saved his life—too soon to tell—but it would have been moot if the pickup hadn't run out of gas and stopped pumping carbon monoxide into the cab before it was spotted.

The truck was spotted by Grayson and the messenger cowboy I now knew was named Bucky. Bucky had just arrived in Sherman, having driven in from another rodeo. They'd encountered each other near the office and were passing the time of day—or night—when Zane spotted the pickup, off by itself. He'd ordered Bucky to get help, and he'd run to the pickup.

"Why?" I asked Alvaro, when I was called in to give my account after Burrell.

"Why? No, never mind that. I'm asking the—"

I overrode his objection. "Why did Zane treat it as an emergency immediately?"

"It *was* an emergency."

"He couldn't have known that." Or shouldn't have known. "The pickup wasn't running anymore. No way could he see the hose or Watt in the cab. Why did he react that way?"

"He says instinct." Our eyes met for a flash, before the law enforcement officer veil dropped over his. But I'd seen. He wasn't satisfied, either. "Ask him yourself," he added gruffly. "Now, about your movements . . ."

Oh, I will ask Mr. Grayson Zane that question. That question and several others. Yes, I will.

We went back over my movements, starting with the phone call, in which, I repeated, Evan Watt had *not* given any indication of what he wanted to talk to me about. To Alvaro's further credit, he didn't allow himself more than a solitary Stupid Easterner smirk over my encounter with the bulls. When other characters appeared in my narrative, he listened carefully, jotting notes as I told who I'd seen where doing what.

"You're a very good witness, Elizabeth," he said at the end.

"I'm a reporter. But I know eyewitness accounts are suspect—even from reporters. So, you don't think this is a suicide attempt?" I tried to keep my voice casual, but he still went official on me.

"That has yet to be determined. Until it is, in light of what else has happened, we need to get as much information as possible. Now, let's go back to this figure you saw off to the side. Street says he doesn't remember seeing anybody before Cas."

"But he looked right at her and—"

"Her?"

My mouth opened in surprise. "I don't know why I said *her*, Richard, I truly don't. Maybe it was subconscious, something about the movement or . . ."

I stared at the table's gray surface, felt my eyes lose their focus. Instead, seeing Street drop down by the tailpipe. The figure. Frozen. The faintest motion. The lights. The figure, turning, leaving—"Blue."

"What?"

"The figure had a streak of blue in her hair."

✧   ✧   ✧   ✧

THE NIGHT dragged on. Needham asked us to unburden our souls to him. I responded by asking him to copy all his notes and share them with us. He chuckled almost silently and moved on.

The crowd thinned out, with many leaving after their time with Richard. Vicky and Heather were among those. As they left, Heather shot one look at Cas, who was watching her.

But what caught my attention was Vicky giving me an I'll-get-you-later glare. How unfair was that? Both Mike and Tom had told Alvaro about seeing the Uptons depart the rodeo grounds with enough time to have rigged Watt's truck. All I did was corroborate that they could have loosed the bulls on me by parking somewhere and doubling back on foot.

I went to find coffee, but got distracted.

Beyond the bank of vending machines, I saw a deserted, half-lit cafeteria, and beyond that a patio. I went out, letting the door close softly on the broom handle someone had placed on the floor to keep the door from locking.

A few tables and chairs populated the patio, but I chose to sit on the low wall bordering one end, my feet dangling above the ground. I was glad I'd grabbed a denim jacket as I left the hovel. Even the hottest climate can feel relatively cool in the middle of the night. In Wyoming, it's not just relative.

I felt more than saw the mountains' bulk off my right shoulder. A different volume of darkness began to present their shape as my eyes adjusted. Looking to the south, I almost thought I recognized the peaks of the Tetons. But that was imagination, because they weren't visible even in daylight.

While the mountains on my right gave a sense of solidity, the horizon toward my left ceded nearly all the space to the sky. It was almost too big, too star-spattered, too teeming and too empty at the same time.

"Elizabeth."

I jerked my head around. I hadn't heard anyone open the door or approach. Yet here stood Linda Caswell.

I brought one leg back over the wall to the patio side. "Yes?"

"I've been thinking about what you said earlier. About lying in a murder investigation. What I told you about Keith Landry and me, that was all true. But I was trying to distract you. Make you think along other lines."

"Because you knew I knew Landry bribed Stan."

That stopped her for a long breath. "Yes." She sat on the wall, facing the patio, leaving me her profile. "Tom's right, you are smart. You have no reason to believe me, but I knew nothing about the bribe until earlier today. Yesterday now. I still don't believe Stan murdered Landry."

We sat in silence a moment. "So, I'm smart, and you have a knack for dealing with difficult people. Your father, your sister, your brother-in-law, and the rodeo committee."

That drew a huff of delicately blended disgust and self-deprecation. "Which made me all the more susceptible to the most shopworn line of flattery."

"You were emotionally vulnerable."

She made the sound again, turning to me. "Because the dried up old maid is always emotionally vulnerable?"

"Because of your sister's death."

She looked past me. Out to the horizon. That ever-mirage horizon of Wyoming where things look much closer than they are.

I thought about Linda and her sister. And then I thought about the two brother horses her nephew had showed me, one born bucking, the other not.

"This county. This damned county." She spoke as evenly as someone asking for the salt shaker at dinner. A jolt like holding a frayed electrical cord went through me. There was emotion there, yet even more control.

Once more giving me only her profile, she stated, "You know the Caswell history, I'm sure. My father, his lost romance and late marriage, and how he drove my mother to her grave in his quest for a son." The scoffing sound returned, quieter, but harsher. "She died of cancer. She refused treatment because of the pregnancy. They didn't want to say breast cancer then. The same cancer my sister died of. When Inez got the first diagnosis, she asked me to research the family medical history before she decided on treatment. We never knew . . . Inez decided on a double mastectomy and aggressive treatment. That's almost certainly why she had those two years. Before it came back."

Stillness weighted the long silence before she spoke again.

"Has anyone you loved died of cancer yet?" Her final word sent an atavistic shiver through me. She turned, looking for my answer.

"No."

"They tell you to celebrate each day—the support people, the doctors. They tell you to enjoy the life while it's still there. What they don't tell you is that every second of celebration, every instant of enjoyment has its dark twin of grief. It's a marathon of mourning. Every waking instant—more, because even dreams . . .

"You try not to show it to anyone else, in the hope—prayer—that they're not feeling the same way, yet you know they are. You still don't share it, though, because you can't risk robbing them of even a breath of the good moments by mentioning the bad ones you're facing. Or maybe that's all bullshit. Maybe it was all just pride. And fear.

"It's a siege. The outside world recedes, becomes stranger and stranger. It's hard to tell if they withdraw or if you shut them out. I remember going to the drug store, and there were familiar faces. People Inez had known, had helped, had worked with. They were all saying what a lovely person she was, asking how she was doing. I said,

'She's dying.' Just like that. They melted away. I'd broken the rules. I'd made them see. Nobody wants to see.

"Not even Inez. Maybe especially not Inez. She fought to the last second. She died trying for one more breath. No deathbed benediction, no peaceful parting words.

"And when it was over, there was nothing left in me at all. I'd used up every bit of love, of grief, of strength, of hope, of prayer—everything. If it hadn't been for Cas . . ."

She looked at me, gave a slight smile.

"That's right," she said. "Not my father. Certainly not my brother-in-law. They needed greatly, too, but I only cared for Cas."

I wanted to put my hand on her arm. I wanted to tell her she should not carry that burden. But I was talking to her as a reporter. And who was I to tell anyone such a thing?

"Whatever I had, I gave to Cas. It wasn't much. I was hollowed out. Spent. Bankrupt. I buried my father not long after, and I felt nothing. Nothing. That was the woman Grayson Zane found.

"What it comes down to is this, I didn't commit suicide because of Cas. I started living again because of Grayson. It was a short time, really, though it didn't feel like that while we were together. There was—I thought there was—a restfulness between us." She laughed sadly. "I suppose I made it simple for him by neither demanding nor asking anything."

When she didn't say more, I asked, "Made what simple for him?"

She looked at me. Direct and open. "I believe you know, E.M. Danniher. But I will say it for you. Grayson Zane swept me off my feet, romanced me in his own way for a brief time, left me abruptly and without explanation. He did all of that at the behest of Keith Landry, and in return he received Landry's assistance getting his career back on track. And when Grayson was gone, Landry, in turn, swept in to scoop up the remains."

I stared at her. "How long have you known it was a setup?"

"Almost from the beginning. No, perhaps that's not entirely accurate. I *refused* to know almost from the beginning. I let myself know only a few months after it was over."

"You know about the others?"

"Others?"

"It's far too late for crappy lying, Linda."

Her mouth shifted. Not quite a smile, but an easing. "I strongly suspected. Landry had said something. A reference to my being a departure from his usual, and something about rodeo queens. It was only when I began using my mind again that I put it together. At first I thought perhaps I was the only one, because of what my family represented. He had a lot to say about that at the end," she said dryly. "About my family, and about how I thought I was too good for him. But he'd said other things, too. Things about how these other women thought they were so hot, but he had complete power over them. *Power.* The way he said that . . ."

"I warned Sonja Osterspeigel when I saw a cowboy rushing her and caught a . . . an expression on Landry's face. Sonja did not listen. I was relieved to see the experience showed no sign of diminishing her, ah, exuberance."

"And this year?"

"I asked Vicky Upton to lunch the day Landry arrived. Among other talk about the rodeo, I dropped in what I hoped would be a subtle hint. She . . ." Her eyelids dropped slowly. When they raised, she met my look. ". . . she left the table and vomited before she reached the ladies' room."

Had Linda suspected before that lunch that Vicky had been an early point in Landry's pattern? That Landry was Heather's father? She certainly suspected now.

She stood, and something shuffled to the front of my brain to get asked in case her mood of cooperation disappeared.

"The first time we talked, you said you were surprised Landry could supply the livestock for the rodeo. Why?"

Her eyebrows rose. "I thought I said. The Fourth of July holiday is the busiest time for rodeo contracts—except for those who send stock to the NRF."

By this time the initials were almost as familiar as NATO, UN or POTUS. "And that would affect Landry . . .?"

"I would have expected that he had all his stock committed long ago, with contracts to other venues." The eyebrows dropped into a frown. "He must have held some out, but that didn't seem like him. He told me the Fourth came first for a rodeo contractor, and every animal better earn its keep then."

The wheels in my brain turned, though I was too tired to know exactly where they were heading.

"There's one more thing I want to say," Linda said. "I have not a single doubt that Grayson did *not* kill Landry or try to kill Watt. It's just not possible."

✧   ✧   ✧   ✧

LINDA'S HIERARCHY of suspects was clear. Stan got an I-don't-believe-he-committed-murder. Grayson graduated to absolutely no doubt. Cas wasn't even a possibility, so wasn't mentioned.

I watched her go inside, walking through the cafeteria toward the hallway that led to the waiting room.

Gradually, I became aware of another presence on the patio. Still facing the cafeteria, I shifted focus to the side. In the deepest shadow. A tall figure in a cowboy hat. Grayson Zane.

It reminded me of that first day at the rodeo grounds. Zane staying close enough to see what was going on, but keeping a distance. I'd had to run him down and corner him.

Now, he was so busy watching Linda's departure that I wouldn't have to corner him. But what if I tried to run? Could I reach the door before him? No. Could I jump from my wall and get around the building to the ER entrance before he caught me? Probably not. Would he try to stop me from doing either move? I doubted it.

If he killed Landry and tried to kill Watt to prevent his sordid story from coming out, Linda was in far greater danger than me.

"Did you hear what you wanted to hear?" I asked, loud enough not to be ignored.

He turned toward me in no hurry. "Couldn't hear the words from this end." It was no apology, more a comment of dissatisfaction.

"Do you think Watt tried to commit suicide because he killed Landry?"

"No." That was either honest, or very smart.

"Did you try to kill him because he saw you string up Landry?"

"No." What else would he say?

He moved nearer, so light from inside caught him, the top of his face shadowed by the ubiquitous black cowboy hat, while the jaw showed stubble in the stark artificial light.

"You can quit following her around, wondering when she'll tell what happened. Your secret's out. A lot more people than me know it," I added quickly.

"Ma'am?"

"That's what Linda was telling me— although I already knew you'd been one of Landry's front men. The big break Landry gave you the year you were down on your luck, that wasn't a favor. Whatever he gave you was paid for in full, though Linda Caswell was the one who paid."

He didn't react to that, either. I prodded more.

"I suppose that's how you and Watt got to know each other, being studs in Landry's stable." No reaction. I kept spinning speculation, hoping I'd hit something that got a response. "Landry called you, demanded you come back to Sherman and serve again as his frontman. Threatened to spread the story far and wide about what happened five years ago.

"It would be a hell of a story. Tarnish that image of yours, scare off sponsors. And he'd have done it. He was taking more risks, drinking heavily. You knew he'd do it. So, you went to meet him after you arrived here. Maybe to reason with him, maybe to accept his demands, maybe with other intentions. You found him struggling to get free of a rope. He got it from his waist, to his chest, to his neck.

"It was there—right there. So simple, and it would be over. The hold he had on you. What he was doing to those women, to the rodeos. It would all be over. A pull—not hard for a man of your strength. That's what you did, isn't it, Grayson? Tell me. Tell me what you did."

Slowly he lifted his head, the hat's shadow receding before the light. He looked like he'd aged a decade. "I told him to do his worst."

"Landry wouldn't give up that easily. He—"

"He didn't. He called Watt and demanded he get his ass over to the arena because there was work to do. Watt was too drunk to hang up his phone, much less go anywhere. I'd gotten Watt into his camper when Landry called me again. He was so sure I'd bow to his threats. I told him to go to hell, left Watt's camper, and went to bed. That's all I did. With this happening to Watt, I wondered . . . But no way he could've gotten to the arena that night."

"You wondered if Watt killed Landry?"

A single shake of his head. "Saw something." He turned on his heel, heading for the door.

"Grayson, I need to know—"

"I got nothing more to tell you, E.M. Danniher," he said without turning back or pausing. He stepped inside and was gone.

Damn. Damn. Damn.

He'd confirmed his role—Landry pressuring him to repeat by threatening to reveal his past, the phone call—but without giving me a pry bar to use for further information.

I sat there, seeing the convention of black cowboy hats, the unidentifiable individuals under those hats coming together and moving apart in an intricate and unrecognizable pattern that became a square dance that involved Gary Cooper, John Wayne, Joel McCrea, and Jack Palance. Their hats turned white, striped, then back to black as they danced.

✧ ✧ ✧ ✧

I WAS STILL sitting on the wall when Tom came out and handed me a cup of coffee. "You okay?"

"Sure. Where's Mike?"

"Volunteered to run a couple of the rodeo committee to their cars at the rodeo grounds." He tipped his head, and I could tell from the angle and gleam of his eyes that he was watching me. "I didn't mean to intrude on anything between you and Mike."

"Oh, for heaven's sake, the extension cord was to see how a rope—"

"I didn't mean that. Meant overall."

I said nothing. Because there was nothing in my head. Not an answer, not a thought. Except a vague idea that if I were lucky, he would let it drop.

I wasn't lucky.

"Is there something between you and Mike Paycik?"

Now well-worn words and phrases about colleagues and interests in common and working together tumbled through my mind. None of them came out of my mouth. "I don't know. Maybe there could—I don't know."

He sat back a little, still watching. I knew the instant he decided to let it rest, even though it took another minute before he spoke.

"Okay. So, what are you doing out here?"

"Thinking." I might have dozed, too. "About the murder. What's been happening at the rodeo," I added.

"Any conclusions?"

"Not one. All I see are black hats. Doesn't anybody around here know only bad guys wear black hats? Are the bad guys the ones emulated even in cowboy culture? I thought you guys were all about the cowboy way, and being gentlemen and having honor."

"We are."

I threw up the hand not holding a coffee cup in exasperation at that succinct and unhelpful answer. "Then why don't they wear white hats if they want to be thought of as good guys?"

He regarded me for a long moment. Such a long moment that I had tensed for his accusation that I'd displaced frustration onto cowboy hats. I'd started composing a devastating response to such an observation, when he said, "Seems to me you're overthinking this, E.M. Danniher."

"Oh, yeah?" That was not my devastating response. I had to ad lib. He'd thrown me a curveball, especially since I had a feeling he was applying his observation about my overthinking to more than the topic at hand.

"Want a straightforward answer? Ask the straightforward question."

I toyed with allowing my bubbling anger to flare and slamming him for condescension. Instead, I asked the straightforward question.

"Why doesn't anyone wear a white cowboy hat anymore?"

"Dirt."

Chapter Thirty-Four

I LAUGHED. I laughed until tears started to flow. He gave me a napkin, went inside for more napkins to mop up the flow and a bottle of water to replace what I'd lost.

"Better?" he asked.

"Better."

Definitely better. I'd said I hadn't reached a single conclusion, and that was true, but pieces had begun to settle into loose groups. I thought I saw the murky shadow of a solution . . . but was it right? I was tired. Very tired. And sore. And rattled. Still . . .

I blinked.

"Back?"

I blinked again, and Tom came into focus beside me. "Sorry?"

"You'd gone off some place. Pretty sure you'd come back. Didn't want to disturb you if not."

"Thank you." And I *was* grateful for the time to put together my thoughts. Though it made me feel exposed that he'd sat there beside me, letting me forget his presence. I needed time to work this through. Time when I wasn't tired and sore and rattled. And when I was alone. "I think."

He smiled. A smile with a hint of self-satisfaction in it. "No problem."

✧   ✧   ✧   ✧

"ELIZABETH?"

I woke with a start. Mike sat sideways on the waiting room couch, facing me where I'd drawn up my knees and rested my head atop the back cushion. I rubbed a crick in my neck. "What's happening?"

"Richard says to go home."

Behind the counter that kept ravening hordes of waiting room waiters in place, there was a stir of activity. Through vertical blinds on a window facing east, the sky was startlingly brighter.

"Watt?" I asked.

"Not conscious. There won't be an update until later today un-less . . ." Unless it was bad news. I rubbed harder at my neck. "They seem to think he's got a chance. Tom left a while ago, caught a ride with a friend to pick up his truck at your place. He's driving Tamantha to his sister's. He said to let you sleep, but . . ." He looked away from me, across the nearly empty waiting room.

"But?"

"You said something in your sleep. Like a bad dream. I didn't want . . . I woke you up."

I didn't remember a dream. But I certainly preferred being awak-ened over sleep-talking in a public place, even if Paycik was the only one to hear whatever my subconscious spewed.

"Thank you. Let's go."

Out in the hospital parking lot, the eastern sky was well past the first blush of dawn and into its rosy stage.

"Want to get breakfast or—"

Mike broke off his question to check his ringing phone, which he'd just turned back on. We'd all been asked to turn off our phones in the waiting room. "Diana," he informed me before answering.

His end of the conversation consisted of "I can barely hear you," followed by "She's here with me. We were at the hospital all night because of Evan Watt," a few grunts, a "Right now?" another grunt, then "Diana? Diana?"

He disconnected. "Diana says we should get to the station right now. She was whispering and talking really fast. Said she's being sent out to the rodeo grounds to get B-roll. Then the line went dead. Go to the station?"

I straightened from an exhausted slouch. "Yes."

✧ ✧ ✧ ✧

I WAS SHAKEN. Definitely shaken.

Evan Watt was not one of nature's noblemen. He was scruffy, at best. Lacked a few essential morals, as well as a crucial amount of calcium where his backbone should have been, and he chewed tobacco. But did I think he deserved to suffocate in his own ratty truck?

No, damn it, he didn't.

The shaking of my calm shifted to a higher gear when we pulled into the KWMT-TV parking lot, where a gleaming dark blue four-wheel drive that somehow seemed to repel Wyoming dust sat in the prime parking spot.

"Oh, shit," Mike said, expressing my sentiments precisely.

The big shots were back in town, at least our very own big shot was.

✧ ✧ ✧ ✧

"I ORDERED THEM to leave my story alone, and they've been secretly reporting it. The whole time—the whole time!" Thurston squeaked in a range that should have been audible only to bats.

"Not the whole time," I said. "There were those seven-plus minutes on Monday."

Fine blanched.

Mike used the opening to say to Haeburn. "Are you aware that since Friday, Fine has logged almost every minute of airtime?"

Haeburn's eyes goggled, and his mouth opened, but he caught himself before uttering anything useful. "I will review the aircheck from while I was gone, as usual."

"I was in charge!" Fine bleated. "I was in charge, and even when I'm not, my contract says I get the top news story. I cover it, and I do the on-air. All of it. And they were doing it again, stealing my story."

"You weren't *covering* the story."

"I was! I was covering the accidental death of Keith Landry, and you were ordered—"

"Deputy Alvaro has been investigating a murder—"

"Deputy Alvaro was ill-advised to take such extreme steps," Haeburn interrupted. His pinkened scalp showed through thin hair, indicating he'd spent time in the sun lately. Golf? Swimming? Other recreation at this high-powered retreat? "When the county leaders were apprised on our return of this situation, we all agreed on this."

I swung around to him, letting pass for now that he'd counted himself among the elected and appointed officials it was his job to report on. "Extreme? It's only through his careful pursuit of a suspicious death that anyone knows it's a murder."

"You jumped to thinking it was murder because you hate men," Fine said. We'd given Haeburn the general outline of Landry's activities in hopes of getting the story covered adequately. Since Fine clung like a barnacle to Haeburn, that had meant telling him, too. "You and all those women who want revenge. You always stick together, dragging down a man's reputation, spreading rumors about him after he's dead. Just a bunch of emotional, hysterical—"

"I am not being emotional or siding with the women because those of us with ovaries always side together. My opinion has been formed based on Keith Landry's actions. This guy was slime. What he did was the emotional equivalent of a roofie in their drinks."

"What are the names of these so-called women who are saying this?" Fine demanded.

So-called women? I restrained myself from addressing that. "I'm not giving you names of my sources in a murder investigation."

"Murder," Fine scoffed. "It would be better left as a suspicious death."

"Better for whom? The murderer? It's not a matter of picking which you like. It's a matter of what is."

"Better for this community!" Fine's face went blood-vessel-popping red. "Something you know nothing about. The Fourth of July Rodeo means everything to this county, to this town. And the rodeo must . . ." His mouth closed, opened, and closed again, like his teleprompter had gone blank.

"What? The rodeo must what, Thurston? Go on? The rodeo must go on?"

Haeburn covered Fine's inability to speak. "You can sneer at the rodeo all you want—"

"Not the rodeo."

"—but you can't get away from the fact of its importance to this community. A community that has suffered greatly from losing its civic and judicial leadership." He glared at me, as if reporting the truth of what had been going on had been the problem.

"That was—" Mike started in our defense.

Haeburn talked over him. "The county's leadership has put together a plan to bring Cottonwood back to its preeminent position." So Aunt Gee's report that the bigwigs had repaired to a mountain hideaway for a secret conclave on the county's future appeared to be correct—no surprise there—and any recreational scalp pinkening was purely incidental. I could hardly wait to hear the details. "Having the rodeo's reputation damaged would be harmful to the economy—segments of the economy."

Certainly Stan Newton's economy. I wondered how many bigwigs at the exclusive weekend getaway had financial ties to Newton or benefited from the Fourth of July Rodeo.

"Deputy Alvaro is not impeding the rodeo. He—"

"Deputy Alvaro is no longer in charge of—"

"Of all the idiotic—" Mike inserted.

"—the investigation. Because—"

"Richard Alvaro has done better work this week than all those so-called leaders produce in—"

"Because," Haeburn shouted over me, "the leadership of this county is confident Watt's attempt to take his own life resolves the matter."

"*What?*"

"His attempt at suicide screams his guilt."

"Suicide? With no note?"

"No need for a note," Haeburn started.

"Because his so-called suicide attempt was busy screaming?" Mike scoffed.

"He was remorseful for killing Landry. It might even have been an accident."

"What about siccing the bulls on me?" I demanded.

"He also felt remorse about thinking he'd killed you," Haeburn added with ill grace, clearly not recognizing that Watt couldn't have loosed the bulls on me. He wouldn't have had time to get back to his truck, run it long enough to pass out and run out of gas before Zane found him.

"Or he was remorseful that he didn't succeed in killing you," Fine muttered.

Which, I admit, was a good line. But I ignored it and him. "It's all wrong. If he killed Landry and made some half-hearted attempt to kill me, he would have waited to see if he succeeded before attempting suicide. No . . ."

But I said no more. The gears of my brain had engaged. What was I thinking, gifting Haeburn and Fine with logic? They didn't have the first idea what to do with it.

I turned and walked out. Diana followed. Mike remained.

Once I hit the parking lot, I turned to Diana. "Have you ever heard such absolute rot?"

She lifted one eyebrow. "Was it? Absolute rot, I mean."

"Yes."

"Or," she went on evenly, as if I hadn't snapped at her, "are you reacting to the messenger more than the message."

"I am not—" I bit it off. Forced air in and out of my lungs a few times. "It is hard to see the clowns take over again."

"True. But we knew he'd come back."

"A nice, localized avalanche would have improved the quality of life at KWMT. Although we'd have to get Thurston under that avalanche, too."

"Wrong season. Is that really what has you worked up?"

I paced away, along the building's blank side. When I made the turn to start back, I saw Mike come out, buttoning a clean shirt from the stock he kept at the station. They exchanged a few words as I neared.

"Alvaro," I said to Diana, figuring Mike would catch up with the conversation. "He went out on a limb, and they're more than willing to saw it off behind him."

"You think you pushed him out on that limb?"

"Certainly didn't discourage him."

"Richard made his own decisions," Mike said. "He wouldn't thank you for taking that on your shoulders. Besides, Watt's so-called attempted suicide can't change the fact that Landry was murdered, and Richard was right. Nobody can say otherwise. Well, they can *say* it, but they're idiots."

"Do you buy that what happened with Watt was an admission of guilt?"

"He might have done it to divert suspicion."

"Do you think Watt has it in him—that sort of fancy touch?"

"Once you know the principle, it's not difficult. Can't imagine he doesn't know the principle—all winter there are reminders around here not to let your tailpipe get clogged if you get stuck in snow. Beyond that, it's a matter of putting together the hose, funnel, and duct tape. One pass through the rodeo grounds, and you'd find everything you'd need. One-stop shopping."

"I meant the diverting of suspicion. Do you think if Watt thought he was in trouble he'd stick around and try to divert suspicion? Or would he run?"

Paycik considered that. It was one of the things I liked about him. He listened, and he considered what other people said before giving a response.

"Run."

I liked it even better when he agreed with me.

"Me, too. And the one-stop shopping you pointed out goes for anybody who'd want to fake a suicide to get rid of Watt."

They both frowned, apparently assessing what I'd said.

Mike asked, "You started to say no-something in there. No what?"

"No, it wasn't Watt sending the bulls after me."

"Not enough time," he said immediately.

"Exactly. Plus, the only thing that makes sense is if the bull attack was meant to scare us away. And the reason to scare us away was to give the carbon monoxide time to kill Watt."

"You think somebody tried to murder him? Somebody who wanted him to take the fall?" Diana asked.

"If he wasn't trying to commit suicide, that's about the only other option. He didn't accidentally attach a funnel onto his truck's tailpipe and unthinkingly wrap duct tape around it and a hose that he absentmindedly stuck into his truck's back window."

Mike's mouth twitched. "No, not even Evan Watt. Which means there's a murderer loose. And—" he added with a jerk of his head toward KWMT-TV. "—Cottonwood County's brain trust isn't looking for him."

Chapter Thirty-Five

"I'VE GOT TO GET to the rodeo grounds." Diana grimaced. "Haeburn wants shots of the case wrapping up, the rodeo returning to normal."

"Normal." Mike snorted. He stretched, arms overhead, yawning hugely, impressive abs pressing against the front of his clean shirt. "More like figuring out how to go about calling off the Fourth of July Rodeo for the first time. The rodeo committee's getting cancellations left and right. They're meeting with Street this morning about how to pull the plug."

"Then everyone will go their separate ways—taking different routes from the crossroads," I said. "So, we'd better get back to the rodeo grounds, before we run out of time."

He groaned. I didn't blame him. I felt like groaning, too. The hovel had never seemed so alluring.

✧ ✧ ✧ ✧

MIKE DROVE US to the rodeo grounds, pulling in behind Diana.

On the way, I'd filled him in on the substance of my patio encounters with Linda and Grayson from the previous night. He told me what little he'd learned while chauffeuring rodeo committee members to their vehicles, though he suspected one of them of being one of Tom's sources on the bribe.

"So, what now?" he asked as he parked his four-wheel-drive.

There were new holes among the ranks of parked pickups and campers, and I saw a few groups who appeared to be packing up. Beyond the rodeo office, police tape encircled Watt's pickup truck and the picnic table.

"I think it's time to hit Zane harder. He's—" My cell interrupted. Caller ID said Mel Welch. At this time of the morning? "I've got to get this."

"I'll tackle Zane," he offered, and headed off as I answered.

Mel sounded frantic. "Are you all right? I tried and tried to call you last night, but you didn't answer, and you didn't return my calls."

"I'm sorry, Mel, I was at the hospital and—"

"*Hospital?* You're wounded. Oh, my God, I'll never forgive myself. We can get a flight out and—"

"No! No, Mel. I'm fine. I was at the hospital's waiting room. A suspect in—" I edited myself in time. "—a crime might have tried to commit suicide."

"In jail?"

"No, in a pickup."

"But they were arrested."

"Who was? Mel, what are you talking about?"

"That horrible shootout you were in the middle of yesterday."

It took a couple beats to remember the episode at Hiram Popping-er's ranch. That couldn't possibly be just yesterday afternoon . . . but of course it was. What also threw me off were the words *horrible* and *shootout*.

"How on earth did you hear about that?" Another implication hit me. "You *cannot* tell my parents, Mel. If you say—"

"Good God, no."

That held such genuine horror, I didn't press the point. "How did you hear about it?"

"I saw your report. A very nice young lady at KWMT-TV sends them to me electronically." I was impressed he knew how to watch them. "That was an excellent story. Frightening, but excellent. And that other reporter with you . . . he's, uh, quite good-looking, isn't he? Do you work together a lot?"

I heard the echo of Mel's wife Eileen behind that probe. "Paycik? He's sports. I'm consumer affairs."

"Oh, yes, of course, of course. I was shocked they tried to pull that scam after you'd aired your first report the evening before. How foolhardy." He made other comments that proved he'd not only watched those reports, but others. It was touching. Less touching was when he segued to a familiar strain. "Are you really staying there? I know you said so, but . . . What will you do with yourself?"

"My job. The job you got me."

"I wish I hadn't. You know that talk show in St. Louis—"

"Mel. I'm staying to work out my contract, and to sort out . . . things." Like what kind of reporter I truly was. "Maybe eventually I'll decide talk show is a direction to go, but I'm not ready to commit now. Tell them I don't want the job." I'd have loved to add *tell my parents*, too, but I wouldn't foist that on him.

"If I were a better agent—"

"Hey, if it weren't for you, I wouldn't have a job."

"Some job for E.M. Danniher. Twice a week? You'd be climbing the walls if it weren't for these burglars and that murder in the spring."

"How do you know . . . Never mind. What matters is that you cannot tell my parents."

He snorted. "You think if your mother knew I'd still have any skin?"

"You make her sound like Hannibal Lecter."

"Scarier. But I can't blame her or your father, since I sent you out there."

"No, you didn't, Mel. I'm responsible for my being here and what I do while I'm here." I said that off the top of my head.

A beat later I realized its truth. I'd been numb when Mel set out my options last winter, so I couldn't claim coming here as an active choice. But I *had* chosen to stay.

And I was responsible for what I did here. Not Wes the Ex. Me. Wes had pushed me, and for that, I might thank him—at least in my head—at some point when I thought of him without grinding my teeth. But *my* ability had made the most of each new situation.

I laughed.

"Sure, you can laugh," Mel said morosely. "You're several large states away from your mother."

I laughed more. "Not only that, but it's a sunny, blue-skied Wyoming day, and I've been doing some damned fine reporting. I'm doing you the favor, Mel, of not telling you any more about it, so you have full deniability."

"Oh. *Oh.* Thank you." Catherine Danniher would never fall for that ploy and would give him heck for it eventually. Mel, poor baby, was caught between a rock and a hard place—two Danniher women. "Well, you sound good. But how will you keep yourself occupied?"

"There's that dog I've acquired. And my job and attending the local rodeo." No sense mentioning I was attending because of a murder, an attempted murder, and a give-it-a-shot try aimed at me. "And I might take up cooking."

"You've always been a great baker, but do you think that's wise? Your father is concerned about that house's oven."

"Poor Mel—I told them it was my choice entirely. But as a matter of fact, I'm talking about cooking, not baking. Go to the Farmers' Market each day for fresh ingredients, grow my own vegetables. Real Earth Mother. I might stop coloring my hair and let the gray show."

"You color your hair?"

"Oh, Mel," I said through laughter, "Eileen should not let you out alone."

✧   ✧   ✧   ✧

STILL SMILING after hanging up, I checked my messages, phone and email, guiltily deleting the ones from Mel. Among all the usual detritus was an email yesterday from Jennifer with the subject line of *Rodeo Queens Complete List*.

As I looked around for Mike or Zane, I opened the message and skimmed down the list, starting with the familiar names of the women from the past eight years, then unknown names before spotting Vicky Upton near the beginning.

I was poised to close the list when a niggle of delayed recognition hit. I scrolled more slowly back up the list.

And there it was. An entirely unexpected connection.

I whistled softly.

I looked around again, saw plenty of activity, including a glimpse of Richard Alvaro talking to someone on the rodeo office porch, but no Mike or Zane.

Before I decided where to try, I heard shouting from near the arena and headed that way. Raised voices guided me, though no words came through. The next shout was either a man or a woman who shouted like a man.

"Go to hell!" came another shout, this one definitely female. Pauline's blue-streaked hair showed as she ran away from the concessions stand area toward the front gate.

I took off after her. With less speed, but a better angle, I cut her off before the gate and grabbed her arm.

"Get off me, bitch!"

"I see you're your usual charming self this morning, Pauline."

She froze at the name. Then she resumed snarling, "Let go of me."

"First, I want to know what you were doing by Evan Watt's pickup last night."

"No idea what you're talking about."

"The guy who almost died of carbon monoxide poisoning in his truck, behind the rodeo office. I saw you there."

"Yeah? So what? Everybody was there. Wanted to see what all the excitement was about."

"You disappeared. Didn't stick around to help."

"Wasn't anything I could do. He—Somebody was pulling that thing out of the exhaust pipe. People were all over. That Newton guy who owns the place, the cowboy, and that TV guy. So I split."

I was a little slow in responding because I was taking in something I should have spotted earlier. "The police want to talk to you, Pauline."

"Don't call me that. And why would they wanna talk to me?"

I debated pursuing the animus toward her name, but decided for this first girl-talk session I should avoid more conflict. "Your buddy Roy Craniston got in a shouting match with Keith Landry last Wednesday. What was that about?"

She sneered. "That old man came sniffing after me, like I'd ever let anybody that creepy touch me." She and Heather had more in common than they knew. "I had it handled, but Roy butted in like always. Assholes." That dispensed with both males.

"Do you remember anything they said?"

"Roy shouted some stuff about telling the world the creeper's history if he didn't leave Roy's women alone. Made me gag." Her eyes narrowed. "Why do the police want to know about that?"

"Landry was killed the next night. They want to know about any disputes he had."

"From what I heard that's all he had." Gee, I wondered who her source was on that? "The police can go—"

"They want to talk to everybody who was around last night."

"Shit."

It was uttered in such a resigned, disinterested tone that I dropped her arm. "You should go see Deputy Alvaro now. He's by the rodeo office."

"I'm not supposed to be in here," she said with curled lip. But beneath the curl, there was more. Hurt? Or was I hallucinating from lack of sleep?

"Was somebody yelling at you about that? Is that what sent you running?"

"Yeah." Lie.

"Or is there trouble with love's young dream?"

She looked up. "What the fuck are you talking about?"

That was a genuine reaction. "You and Cas. I notice you didn't mention him, though he was around last night, too. Protecting your love?"

She made a derisive sound. "Love. Yeah, right." She sidestepped me and headed toward the gate.

"Police still want to talk to you."

She gave me the finger without turning around. Or maybe the finger was for law enforcement. That thought gave me a nice cozy feeling about the progress of our relationship.

❖   ❖   ❖   ❖

As I HEADED back toward the rodeo office by another route, I spotted Stan Newton supervising removal of crime scene tape from where Landry's body had been found. It seemed the man might have wadded up a bunch of tape himself. Instead, he was supervising two other men doing it.

Richard Alvaro stood a few yards away, dressed in the Wyoming uniform—jeans, boots, plain shirt, and black cowboy hat—rather than his deputy's uniform. He looked glum.

"Deputy Alvaro, I'm glad to see you. There's something—"

"I'm off duty and off the case. In fact, there is no case. Except an attempted suicide."

"I heard. I'm sorry, Richard."

"Not your fault."

"What are you doing here on a day off?"

He still didn't look at me, but the corner of his mouth lifted. "Same thing you're doing here. Trying to solve the damn case."

"I have something you might be interested to hear. Pauline—she of the blue-streaked hair—just went out the front gate and is likely to be with her fellow protestors. Unless she's fleeing the law."

His head jerked around toward the gate.

"I told her," I continued, "the cops want to talk to her. I didn't happen to mention that some idiots think there's no longer a case."

He gave a quick nod, strode toward the gate.

At the same time, Oren Street appeared at the edge of the warren of pens.

"Good morning, Oren."

"Good for some," he snapped. "Oh, yeah, this time they're fine with letting the bulls move, since they belong to the *regular* contractor. But mine they kept separate like they'd got a disease or something. A day or more it was they kept 'em isolated. But since it's the *regular* contractor, it's all hunky-dory to take 'em back and let 'em rest. I'm not saying they shouldn't rest after they got run like that—they should. But my stock got—"

"I'm fine, thank you for asking."

He stared at me without comprehension.

"Tom Burrell wasn't hurt, either. Although he did lose a favorite hat, I understand." Still the blank stare. I added, "When the bulls tried to run us down last night. Bulls. Hooves. Trample. Human beings."

He blinked. "Oh, yeah. It's good you're okay. Sorry. Got a lot on my mind. Got to get this fence ready for loading and my animals on their way, or they won't be fit for the next rodeo."

"Has Sherman's Fourth of July Rodeo been called off officially?"

"Not official. But there's no sense keeping livestock with half the entries pulled out."

"How do you—"

My phone rang. As I pulled it out, he muttered, "Got to get started. Truck'll be here for these," and hurried off.

I didn't even get out hello. Jennifer said, "Elizabeth! I've found two more DBAs that went bankrupt, leaving rodeos in a bind. Just like here and Denver. These two and the one near Denver—every one of 'em listed in the name of a relative of somebody Landry dumped."

My heart rate kicked up the way it often did when a pattern started to look like a solution, even if I didn't yet know the final answer. "Great work."

"Thanks! I found a couple DBA applications online, and I swear he forged them. Not even a halfway decent effort." She went on, describing what she'd found and how she'd found it.

As she spoke, I watched Street pull up a pin from hefty metal loops welded to the fence panel's upright. One at the top, one at the bottom. Next, he swung that first panel around to lean against the second. On to the third panel in no time at all.

That must be what Mike had done last night to get Tom out of harm's way, swinging the panel only part way. Thank heavens he'd been quick about it and had the presence of mind to open the correct side, so the bulls hadn't been able to follow Tom and—

"Oh, my God." I didn't pull an Archimedes, sprinting through the streets shouting, *Eureka!* But I did enjoy knowing I had more pieces of the puzzle. I looked around, but no one was near enough to have heard. Except Jennifer on the other end of the phone.

"What?" she asked.

"I've got to go. Keep at it, get as much confirmation as you can, as many supporting documents. You've done great work, Jennifer."

Chapter Thirty-Six

I WENT IN SEARCH of Mike and came across Cas begging Heather to listen.

She gave every sign of not listening. She appeared to be buffing the side of her horse, though there's probably another name for it.

Her mother, a few feet away and fiddling with equipment in a large canvas bag, murmured a critical, "Heather."

And got a sharp, "Be quiet!" in return.

"Heather, please, let's just talk. I can explain."

I wrapped a hand around Cas' upper arm, realized there was too much muscle there for one hand, and joined it with the other.

"Don't bother," I said. "She won't listen to you. But I will. Talk and explanations are exactly what I want." Along with questions and answers.

He might have given up on Heather listening, because he followed along.

"Hey! You leave him alone," Heather commanded.

"Oh, no, you can't drop him then prevent anybody else from picking him up." I saw in her eyes when she recognized how that shot applied to Pauline.

With the picnic table off-limits, I steered Cas to an open spot near a fence. Nobody could get within hearing distance without us seeing them.

Perhaps to prove Heather hadn't sucked all the spirit out of him, he said, "I'm not saying anything."

"Yes, you are." I was way past subtle. "What was the deal Keith

Landry offered you?"

"How did you—Nothing. I don't know what you—"

"Forget it, Caswell Newton. You're a lousy liar. Landry thought you'd broken up with Heather. No, don't deny it. She told us he said that. So, was breaking up with her your deal with Landry?"

"No! That was never—and I told him I wouldn't do the other thing. I told him no way."

"That was later. First you said you *would* do it. Because he what? Said he'd get you in the Fourth of July Rodeo?"

"It'd be my big break," he muttered.

"So, you said you'd get Pauline to fall for you, then dump her."

Color surged up his neck and face like a time-lapse sunburn. "He took me aside the day he got in town, and I thought—but he started in about how I was too young to be tied to a girl, and if I broke up with Heather and stayed away from her a few weeks, he'd get me in the rodeo.

"I told him—I told him he was crazy. No way. I'd heard how he dumped the older sister of a friend a couple years ago. Then he said there was this other girl, somebody I didn't know, and all I had to do was, you know, talk to her. I said I'd meet her. That's all—I swear. He said a lot things, but that's all I said. I went by where she was, and we started talking, just talking."

The color turned up a notch. "But . . . well, she's older, and she's not like Heather and . . ."

"What about Landry? Did he know?"

He looked sick. "He . . . he must've seen or something. At that lunch he slapped me on the back, said things. Dad didn't notice, but Heather . . . She gave me this look. Then he—Landry—started in about all he could do for her in rodeo, real oily. Creeping her out. I took her hand, even though she was mad, held it so he saw, and he backed off.

"After lunch he got me aside and said it was clear I'd decided on the other one—Pauline, and I said, no, not either of them. And he got . . ." He met my eyes. In his, I saw relief at unburdening himself, and was reminded how young he was. "He said he'd ruin Dad—that's just what he said, ruin him. Said if I didn't dump Pauline by Friday night he'd be sure Dad went to jail and lost everything. I didn't know what he was talking about, and he was saying weird things about moving up his timetable and not waiting around like he used to for— well, crude talk about women."

"What did you do, Cas?"

"Nothing! I swear I didn't—"

"Cas. Slow down. I mean, what did you do when he told you that?"

"I told him he was crazy and left him swearing a blue streak. I didn't do anything after, either. I was working out what to tell Dad. Then Landry died."

✧ ✧ ✧ ✧

MIKE FOUND ME still standing by the fence, well after Cas had left. I had no idea how long I'd been there.

"Zane says he doesn't know anything about why Street was asked to bring the stock early. He doesn't think Watt does either. I double-checked with Newton, and he absolutely denies asking Landry to bring them in early. Tom says Linda does, too. He says he looked into it closely."

"In other words, he asked her and took her response as gospel. And Newton? Since when do we accept his word?"

"Newton, sure. But Linda *and* Tom? I don't believe it. I suppose if Linda told Tom, he'd accept it, but why would she lie? And to lie with Newton?"

"She'd protect him. For Cas' sake."

"Maybe, but I still don't see why they'd want to deny asking Landry to bring the bulls in early once we knew the bulls didn't kill Landry. Except for the fact that it's a stupid move. Absolutely no upside for the rodeo."

"Yet they demanded it for some reason, and now they're covering it up. Because it has something to do with the murder we're not seeing, or because they'd look stupid. If we figure out why they feel it's worth covering up . . . It's the cover up—always the cover up—that does in politicians."

"Cover-up of what?"

"I don't know. That's what's bugging me. When a cover-up is . . . Unless . . ."

"Unless what?"

Thoughts and fragments clicked into place. And I knew. In fact, I realized, I'd known for a while. Maybe since last night. I just hadn't known I knew. Just like Algebra.

Also like Algebra, I didn't know precisely *how* I knew. Only this time, I didn't have a bemused and understanding teacher. I had the decidedly un-understanding legal system to deal with. I needed to recreate my solution in a way other people followed.

"Unless what?" Mike repeated.

"Unless it isn't."

"Isn't what?"

I faced him. "I've got it, Mike. At least . . . No, I've got it. The solution. But not all the steps. Not the proof. That will take time. Maybe a lot of time."

Wait. There was something else. Something Mel said on the phone . . . Oh. About the thieves pursuing their plan even after the report aired. Deputy Shelton and I had passed a couple comments about the same thing. About how they could not *not* do it.

Then it clicked. The reason it had resurfaced now.

It was what Keith Landry had done with rodeos. It was what he'd done with women. He'd been an emotional scam artist. He'd set up his scam and worked it so many times, he couldn't *not* do it.

Yet on his last day, he'd been stymied every way he'd turned. His old standby, Evan Watt, would arrive late and likely too drunk to serve. Zane didn't buckle under blackmail. Cas withstood the lure of a boost into the big-time of rodeo and the threat of harm to his father, and refused to help with either of his marks.

Landry had become increasingly less discreet, less subtle. Jennifer's findings that he'd pulled the DBA scam more frequently, even going back-to-back with the Denver rodeo and here, were evidence. It was the same with his sexual scam. The scene at the Haber House Hotel demonstrated that. So did his approach to Pauline, which resulted in the fight with Roy Craniston, with Roy shouting about Landry keeping away from his women.

So, driven by who knew what, Landry went after Heather direct-ly . . . only to be told she was his own daughter.

What did that do to Landry? Would it make him give up? Not likely. What would he do? How would he get what he wanted?

"What sort of proof?" Mike asked.

Yeah, that was the problem. I had to have proof, and the English country house visit was about to break up, with the suspects going on about their lives, instead of being centered here on the rodeo grounds where—

Wait a minute . . . No, I didn't. I *didn't* need them to follow my solution step by step. Law enforcement needed that to satisfy the legal system, but all I needed was to have them trust me long enough to persuade them that my solution was the right one. That would slow the scattering enough for law enforcement to find the step-by-step solution.

That was a heck of a lot easier than Algebra. Thank God.

"Elizabeth? Elizabeth." But I was already dialing a number.

The collected voice answered, and I said, "Linda, this is E.M. Dan-niher. I need all the people involved with this brought together and—"

"The sheriff's department—"

"No. Richard's been pulled off the case. The county leaders want it to go away. If it does, so will some of the people. But the questions— the questions never will go away. You can say you don't care about yourself, but you do care about Cas. What about Stan? What about Grayson? Or Vicky and Heather Upton? Do you want all of them to go on living with suspicion? And the rodeo will suffer, this year and beyond. Do you want that? This has to be settled."

There was a pause, so silent that I wondered if she held her breath. "What do you want?"

"I want you to get everyone together. There. In the rodeo office. Right away. Most of them are around anyhow."

Another pause. This time I held my breath.

When Linda spoke again it was clear she wasn't talking into the phone, but to someone there. "It's E.M. Danniher. She wants me to get everyone concerned together."

Thomas David Burrell said, "Do it."

✧ ✧ ✧ ✧

FIRST, I CALLED Richard Alvaro and asked him to bring Pauline, Roy, and Ellie. He had questions, but I held him off. In the end, he said he would bring them.

Next, I called Diana. She'd started back to the station. I asked her to do a U-turn.

"Will this get me in trouble with Haeburn?"

"Probably."

"Is it a great story?"

"Maybe. I hope—"

"Will it piss off Fine?"

"Definitely."

"I'll be there."

Mike and I went to sit in the top row of the otherwise empty, sun-drenched grandstand, to watch the arrivals at the rodeo office. I told him what I thought—no, what I knew.

He confirmed a couple technical elements for me. We smoothed over some rough spots, leaving others.

That couldn't be helped. Shock treatment was the only shot at doing it now. Otherwise, they'd disperse, and it was unlikely the officials would pursue the evidence.

Burrell called three times. I let it go to voicemail.

✧ ✧ ✧ ✧

DIANA MET US on the office's porch, eyebrows raised. I ignored her unspoken questions.

Because I'd just thought of another question of my own to ask.

I stepped down from the porch, aware of Mike and Diana looking at me, then each other, as I hit speed dial. "I need to see if I can get Jenks. Something he said when we came out here Thursday . . ."

Jenks answered. I asked my question and got my answer. I thanked him, hung up, and said, "Let's go."

Mike opened the door and gestured first Diana, then me in ahead of him.

The grumble that started at Diana's entry with a camera melted away as all but two sets of eyes swung toward me. The exceptions—Heather and Pauline—glared at each other.

Besides Diana, Mike and me, there were a baker's dozen: Linda Caswell, Tom Burrell, Stan and Cas Newton, Vicky and Heather Upton, Oren Street, Grayson Zane, Richard Alvaro, Pauline, Roy Craniston, Ellie Redlaw, and a man I recognized as a rodeo committee member.

I didn't waste time on preliminaries like thanking them for coming or saying why they were here—that would just give them a chance to protest. About being here, about me, about the camera. No sense in that, especially since Diana had slipped behind the counter at the side of the room, where no one seemed to notice her.

"Let's start with last night and Evan Watt's near-death." I turned to Pauline, slouched against the wall beside Richard, pulling sullenly at her bottom lip. "You were there."

"Yeah? So what. So were a lot of other people. You accusing me of trying to off that old has-been?"

"Did you?"

"I'm not saying anything."

"No problem. I'll say. You were there. When Oren Street—" Her eyes flicked toward him. "—got down behind the truck and started trying to pull the hose out of the tailpipe, he called to you, asking for help. Didn't you, Oren?"

"I tried to pull it out, and I hollered for help, but I couldn't say I saw this girl or anybody in particular."

I didn't need his confirmation. "We'll leave that for now, because what was at the core of all this was Keith Landry. Who he was. How he operated. The pattern he followed—in business and with women."

Chapter Thirty-Seven

"**KEITH LANDRY** didn't just take advantage. He set up situations so that taking advantage was a sure thing."

A faint stir let me know some of my audience didn't know what I meant.

"Let's start with business. He played hardball in getting rodeo contracts—everyone's acknowledged that. We have found proof he did more. He paid bribes, and—"

Newton tensed, but the protest came from my left, from Oren Street. "Hey!"

I held up a stop-sign hand. "You'll get your opportunity to speak. But there is proof." I glanced at Richard. "I'm sure law enforcement will look into it carefully. But at this point, none of the paper trail on Landry's fraudulent business activities implicates Oren Street."

I addressed the broader group. "Landry began setting up dummy businesses at least four years ago. Presumably using a hired front man, he would have the dummy business offer an unmatchable bid for a rodeo. As the rodeo neared, the dummy business informed the rodeo committee it was bankrupt, disappeared, and left the rodeo committee in a bind. Landry would reappear, prepared to rescue the rodeo by providing the livestock for a hefty bonus. Sound familiar? It should, because Sweet Meadows was one of his shell companies."

"Oh, God," came Linda's voice, along with other mutters.

"This fraud could mean a motive for murder for anyone who cared about the Sherman Fourth of July Rodeo. Or it could be a motive for murder to mask a role in the fraud. Even with potentially incriminating documents destroyed—"

I caught a small motion, then saw Tom Burrell place a large, calming hand on Cas' shoulder.

Everyone else's attention was on Street's interrupting shout. "I don't know anything about this. I don't know anything—"

Again, I addressed Richard. "We have the paper trail well-started, and you'll add official documents we couldn't access."

More accurately, that I'd told Jennifer not to hack into. No sense worrying Richard about that. Especially considering the bluff I was about to pull.

"We'll have to ask Watt what he knows about this fraud," I said. "What he *does* know about is another of Landry's patterns. This one involved women. Oh, didn't I say? Evan Watt's regained consciousness and is talking."

The stir in the room rose quickly, threatening to swamp me if I didn't gain control. Richard took a step forward, then stopped.

"Yes," I said loudly, "Watt has admitted that numerous times Landry paid him—and others—to woo a girl, dump her abruptly and viciously, leaving Landry the perfect set-up to have his own fling with a girl who would not otherwise look at him.

"Maybe it happened fortuitously early-on. At some point, though, Landry decided not to leave it to chance. He liked the power too much. He's worked his scam for years. He planned to work it again this year in Sherman.

"But nothing was going right for Landry last week. Oren Street showing up early put a cramp in his plans. How could he squeeze one last bonus out of the committee to get the stock here when it was already here? Plus, he was crumbling by this point, drinking heavily, and shouting at everyone he came across. He had a physical fight with Roy here."

"Hey! He started it," Craniston whined. "He was going after my women."

"*Your* women," Pauline muttered in disgust.

"Trying to protect you," he grumbled.

"Her? Or Ellie?" I demanded.

Every set of eyes turned to the faded woman. Roy glared at her, his order that she keep quiet apparent to everyone in the room.

"Ellie's legal name is Eleanor Redlaw. Eleanor Redlaw was a rodeo queen in Texas fifteen years ago. At one of the rodeos Landry put on. Isn't that right?"

"I don't know anything about that," Roy said. "I don't have anything to do with it. I don't know her past or anything. We just hooked up—"

I interrupted. "Is that true that you just hooked up, Ellie?"

She met Roy's gaze as she said, "No."

"You b—"

Richard held up a hand that quieted him. Ellie looked at me with a tiny smile at the corner of her dry lips.

"Landry came after you fifteen years ago in his usual routine?" I asked her.

"Yes."

"And you told Roy."

"Yes. I recognized Landry in a newspaper clipping this spring and told Roy. Told him everything. We talked about using that to get media coverage for our protests. After that, Roy kept track of where Landry was. But we couldn't afford to go down to where Landry was at the time. We had to wait for him to come farther north. This was our first opportunity."

I turned to Roy. "You came to this rodeo this year because Landry was here, you lied about when you arrived, and you fought with Landry."

"I didn't even hit him—I missed!"

No one paid that protest any attention. Richard shifted so he could keep an eye on Roy.

"We'll leave that for now and look at what was happening with Landry. Watt was going downhill as a setup man, and he was delayed getting into town to start the scheme working. Landry tried to pressure other people into playing the role." I felt Alvaro's sharp look, but didn't return it. "But they wouldn't cooperate, despite his best blackmailing techniques. Finally convinced they wouldn't do his bidding, Landry called Watt and said to get to Sherman right away no matter what."

If my listeners had the impression that Watt was the source for this information, all the better.

"Then Landry stumbled on to an opportunity to take matters into his own hands. That did not go well for him. The episode left him humiliated and confined by a tightened lasso. Phone records that investigators have in their possession will prove he managed to call someone he fully expected to release him, so he could continue to pursue . . . his goals. Instead, the person saw an opportunity and used it to be rid of Landry for good by stringing him up," I finished, as a small nod to Dex.

I let that sink in. Most of the people in the room knew who these oblique references were to, but I'd decided it was smarter to tip-toe around naming names for now.

"The motion of hanging shifted Landry's body close to the bulls' pen. Maybe that gave the murderer the idea. When Landry was dead, the murderer dropped the body into the aisle beside an occupied pen, removed the rope, then shifted portable fence panels so bulls would be crammed into a tight space with the body. In a pen where no pen previously existed.

"It was a clever idea. It almost succeeded in selling the death as an accident. It certainly confused us. It also dispensed with a lot of physical evidence.

"But not the rope. The rope was taken by the murderer, perhaps with a thought to not throw suspicion on the person who'd lassoed Landry in the first place." A number of glances shot Heather's direction, with a few skipping to Vicky. "I believe that rope is now hidden in plain sight, mixed in with all the other ropes around the rodeo grounds with the hope it will never be singled out. But the murderer's wrong about that. Forensics will find it."

Alvaro twitched, but I kept on. It wasn't like I'd committed the sheriff's department to the expense of such a search. I just wanted someone uncomfortable about the possibility.

"But to the murderer, the biggest threat was Watt. His memory of history that someone wanted forgotten, his mouth loosening with drink, and, possibly, his conscience pricking him were problems for the murderer. Especially when Watt was overheard calling me, saying he wanted to talk. The murderer couldn't let that happen. So we come back to where we started. Last night and the attempt on Evan Watt.

"Step one was to get Watt and his truck away from the rest. A promise of any kind of job would have done that. Then it was simple. Hit him on the head, rig up the hose, close the windows, turn on the truck, and close the door with the lock depressed. It'll be hard to get fingerprints because of all the people who swarmed around to help rescue Watt . . . except on that door lock button. Only one person had reason to press that button."

Another twitch from Alvaro. I didn't care that it wasn't likely. As long as the murderer wondered if a print could be lifted, I'd added another layer of pressure, as well as distracting from the fact that I wasn't saying what account Watt had of last night.

No reaction from the others. I kept my gaze moving.

"That left plenty of time for step two—keeping me away long enough to let the carbon monoxide work. The murderer went back to what helped before—bulls. You were all here—"

"We left—" Vicky started.

"That's—" Newton sputtered.

"Quiet!" And they were. "You all had opportunity to hit Watt on the head and set up the attempt on his life. Most of you were here on the rodeo grounds. The Uptons could have circled back. Grayson was the first on the scene."

Every face turned toward the figure at the back.

"I was," he said.

"How'd that happen?"

"I saw his pickup."

"It was very dark under those trees by the creek. How did you see the pickup?"

"I was looking for it."

"Why?"

"His pickup had been parked next to mine since we pulled in last week, one right after the other. He hadn't gone anywhere, scraping by, picking up work where he could. I gave him food—"

"Real generous," interrupted Newton. "I heard you refuse to give him money. That's why I tried him in concessions, but he was a disaster, complete disaster."

"He used money to buy booze from other guys." Interesting that a mild tone could sound so contemptuous. "When his pickup was gone last night, I was worried. Went looking."

"Why look on the rodeo grounds?" I asked. "Why not think he'd left Sherman far behind?"

"Because I knew the truck was almost out of gas."

"So you say," muttered Newton.

"So I say," confirmed Zane.

"But there's no dispute that Zane was there first last night. As I said earlier, Oren was there. Pauline, too. Stan and Cas were. I saw them, so did Mike Paycik and Tom Burrell. Vicky and Heather could have been there, staying out of sight. Roy and Ellie, too. How about you, Linda?"

"I was in the rodeo office. When I heard the commotion, I came out. By that time, he was out of the truck and being helped. I called to make sure an ambulance was on the way."

I gave a neutral nod. "There were a lot of people around Watt's truck, trying to help, to get to him, to figure out what happened. Now we know one end of a hose was in the truck's back window and the other end duct-taped into the exhaust pipe, but it wasn't obvious at the time, because the truck had run out of gas. The engine wasn't running. No one initially knew what was wrong, except that Watt appeared passed out in his locked truck.

"Yet you—" I looked at Oren Street. "—went immediately to the back of the truck, dropped down in front of the tailpipe, and started undoing the tape. Tape you identified to Cas Newton as duct tape even before there was light to see it."

"Shit," breathed Cas. "That's right. It was dark as hell—no way could you have seen . . ."

"You already knew it was duct tape, and you knew it had been used to keep the hose in place, and you knew where the tailpipe was because you had put it all together."

Street did a slow head shake. I kept going.

"A while ago I said you shouted at Pauline for help getting the hose out, but that's not true, is it? You yelled at her to *get out* because—"

"So he yelled at me to get out, so what?" Pauline interrupted. "All these people yell at me to get out all the time. None of them want me around. He's no different from the rest."

"Yes, he is different from the rest. Because he's your father. And he murdered Keith Landry."

✧ ✧ ✧ ✧

FROM THE JUMBLE of voices, including Roy's high-pitched "I told you I didn't do it," I heard Pauline Street say, "You can't prove he is. You don't know—"

"Of course I can prove he's your father. I have a copy of your driver's license from Oklahoma with your last name, photo, and date of birth. Your home address is the same as his. And your birth certificate lists your father." When I said *have* it was in the most generous sense of *can possibly get my hands on.*

Street didn't even bother shaking his head. No tension came from him, as if he weren't really very interested in the proceedings now.

"But you said he wasn't part of the fraud," protested Linda. "Why would he kill Landry?"

"I said the paper trail we've found so far doesn't implicate him. But as a partner in the company, he benefited from the scam. And he had to have known what Landry was doing. Because it affected the movement and use of the livestock he looks after so carefully.

"Landry kept stock uncommitted in anticipation of these last-minute gouge jobs—even for the Fourth of July. The way Street looks after those animals, he had to be aware the company was going to get the last-minute contracts and how many animals would be used." I flicked a look toward the still-silent Alvaro. "That will take some digging."

"My God, he killed Landry to protect the livestock?" Newton said.

"No, he did it to protect his daughter."

I let that be absorbed, then went on. "No one knew better than his partner that Landry was crumbling. And that he would not be stopped in his pursuit of his scam—financial or sexual. When Street learned that Landry had his sights set on Pauline, he came here immediately to put a stop to it."

"He wouldn't . . ." Pauline whispered. "He's never cared . . ."

Street reacted at last. He looked at her and said, "It's true. I did it for you, baby."

Richard handcuffed Oren Street and recited his rights. Everyone else remained silent and frozen.

Street suddenly seemed to relax.

"I understand I have the right to stay silent, but not much sense in that with Evan Watt telling you about last night," Street said mildly. "Staying silent's what Keith expected of me all the time. He screamed so much I hardly heard it any longer. Not the screaming, and not the other. He called me from here Wednesday and started saying things were so fu—sorry, ma'am," he said to me, "screwed up that he was setting up a backup plan with a second-string piece of—girl. Said she had a streak of blue in her hair. I hadn't seen Pauline in two years, not since she run off, but she stopped to see her mama last month, and she had a streak just like that. I thought it couldn't be, but there was the streak, and my girl doing protests and such, because she loves animals."

And because a rebellious girl thought it was a way to get the attention of her father.

"I had to know if it was my girl. I couldn't let Landry . . . I came right up here."

That was why Linda and Stan and Tom had all denied that anyone on the rodeo committee told Landry they wanted the stock here early. Because they hadn't. Nor had Landry demanded the stock be brought early. Oren had dropped that lie early on, and I'd swallowed it whole.

Until I started wondering about when a cover-up isn't a cover-up, and the answer had come: When there's nothing to cover up.

In Street's push to get to Sherman, the truck with the panels got left behind, with the result that the stock was overnighted in the pens near the arena. That meant Heather had to alter her route, which let her blouse get caught, which allowed Landry to spot her . . . and the sequence rolled on to murder.

"He was . . . he was . . . It was like he had a fever or something," Street was saying. "Sense couldn't break through to him. Not one bit. I tried talking to him, kept trying. I went to Pauline, tried to get her to leave." He ducked his head, as if in apology for such effrontery. "She wouldn't talk to me."

A small, sucked-in breath came from Pauline, but her expression showed nothing.

"That night, well, he called and said to get to the pens right quick, and if I asked why, he'd kill me. I got there quick. He was trussed up and mad as fire. He started up yelling at me to get him loose. Screaming and saying things . . . horrible things about that girl who's the rodeo queen." His brows dipped. "Or maybe it was her mama. He was screaming so much it was hard to tell.

"I started working the loop loose from around his arms and middle. But I stopped, because he'd started saying things about Pauline . . . Those same things. I told him it was my daughter, my baby, he was talking about. And he said I'd best stop thinking about her as my daughter, because her being my daughter wasn't going to stop him. And she was no baby. That he'd seen her . . ."

He dropped his head, slightly muffling his voice.

"The rope was there. Right there. And he was still yelling at me to get it off him and stop standing there like a fool. All the time he was saying that about my baby. All the time."

He appeared to examine the toe of his right boot.

"The rope was there. Hanging loose like. Right there by my side. He'd pulled the loop up as far as his neck. I just . . . I pulled it. The end, I mean. I pulled it hard. And didn't let go."

Chapter Thirty-Eight

AS RICHARD ALVARO began to lead him out, Oren Street said to his daughter, "Pauline, baby."

She faced the wall, turning her back to him.

He headed for the door, stopping as they came even with me.

"I wasn't aiming to kill you last night, ma'am. Hoped to slow you down."

Maybe. But, he'd meant to kill Evan Watt. Who talked too much, remembered too much. Loosing the bulls had been a distraction, a delaying tactic to let the carbon monoxide do its work. If the bulls had done more than delay me? If they'd trampled me or Tom or both of us? An unexpected bonus, I guess.

And if he'd succeeded, he'd probably have dropped off to sleep, just as he had the day Landry's body had been found. Yes, on the rodeo office porch when I saw him in the evening, but earlier, too. Much earlier, when Jenks had seen him. When the adrenaline of committing murder had ebbed, and he'd slept what Dex had called the sleep of the guilty.

That's what I'd called Jenks about. Because I'd remembered a comment he made about Street being lucky to be able to sleep any place, any time. It hadn't meant anything at the time, especially not followed up by Street himself saying he caught sleep whenever he could. But then I'd wondered if Jenks had meant something more than that nap on the porch.

So I asked my question. Bingo.

Saw him catching a few winks sitting on a bale of hay right after they re-

moved . . . well, you know.

I knew.

And that's when I *really* knew who had killed Keith Landry. It had still been iffy whether he'd admit it, but with his leaving Sherman at any moment, I'd had to take my shot.

With her father across the threshold and Richard following, Pauline Street spoke. "Where are you taking him?"

Richard looked over his shoulder. "To the jail. It's by the courthouse. If you'd like, we'll get you a ride, information about the process. But you won't be able to see him for a while."

"I don't want to . . ." The denial faded into a whispered, "Okay," and she followed them out.

"I always said somebody's daddy would kill that son of a bitch Landry," Vicky Upton said with satisfaction.

Cas started toward the door, which had just closed after Pauline.

"What do you think you're doing?" Stan grabbed onto his arm, stopping him.

"She's all alone."

"That's her problem."

Vicky pushed her daughter. "Say something."

The push caught Heather off balance enough that she had to step forward to keep from falling. Cas turned his head toward her.

They looked at each other for what seemed like an hour, but was probably thirty seconds.

"Go after her. She *is* all alone," Heather said. "And nobody should be blamed for who their father happens to be, not even you or me."

Cas got it immediately.

Her mother took a moment longer. She'd sucked in a breath at Heather's first words—probably in preparation for smoothing over the misstep on her path of ambition—now it came out in a quick half-cough that turned into a real cough.

That might have done the smoothing-over trick, except Stan got it, too. And his yelling not only wasn't hampered by a cough, but it carried over Vicky's ongoing hacking.

"I will not be talked to that way—"

Cas didn't try to talk over his father's bluster, but said in a low, calm voice that came through clearly, "Gotta go, Dad."

He easily pulled his arm out of his father's hold, demonstrating that his father's strength hadn't been holding him.

On his way past, he cupped a hand around Heather's shoulder. "I'll call you later."

She nodded, but didn't believe him. And on that I think she was wrong.

Not only would he call because he'd said he would, but I had a feeling he might call because he wanted to. Because I'd started to agree with his aunt that he was one of the good ones in training and because of whom Heather had proven herself to be. Or, at least, on her way to becoming.

"If you go—"

Cas cut off his father's threat. "I'll call if I'll be after midnight." And he was gone.

Stan turned on Heather. "You should have stopped him. If you have any dream of becoming a Caswell-Newton, you better learn how to behave. And how to handle my son."

She rolled her eyes. But she didn't do it until she had lowered her head in what might be taken by some as acceptance of chastisement.

✧   ✧   ✧   ✧

WE WORKED almost straight through on the package for Live at Five.

Diana had suggested Mike and I take a break, but I was afraid that if I started resting, I wouldn't stop any time soon.

We had the package queued up for final review when Richard Alvaro knocked on the editing booth door, came in, and closed the door behind him.

That's not as easy as it sounds.

The editing booths at KWMT-TV would be scoffed at as closets in Tokyo. I've seen larger booths at public high schools. Also more elaborate ones.

I have fond memories of an old-time editor when I arrived in

Washington who manipulated the keys like he was playing a cathedral's organ. Compared to that, this was a toddler's toy piano. With four of us in the booth, it felt as if we'd been stuffed in that toy piano and the lid closed.

Mike craned his neck to see around Diana and me to where the newcomer was plastered with his back against the door. "Richard, shouldn't you be back at the sheriff's department while they play 'Hail to the Conquering Hero'?"

"More like Barely out of the Sh—Dog House."

"No," Diana protested. "Aren't you getting the credit?"

"I got the arrest, but from now on it's the brass' baby." He grimaced. "I'm back to errand boy, and that's why I'm here."

"That sucks," Mike said. "And on your day off."

"I was sent to get statements from Ellie and Roy, but she and the camper are gone." His mouth twitched. "Though I did deliver Roy, since he was at their campsite cursing and raving when I arrived. Now, I've been sent to collect the copy of Pauline Street's driver's license and birth certificate from you. Which—I was informed by acting Sheriff Thomason—I should have secured at the time, though how I was supposed to do that with a murder suspect to bring in . . . anyway, I'd like the license and certificate."

"Sorry. Only license I have is creative license."

"Holy—" Diana started, but cut it off at Alvaro's grim expression.

His voice matched his expression. "You *guessed* that she's his daughter?"

"Not entirely. There's a resemblance if you look beneath her makeup. I did know Oren Street's home address was in Enid, Oklahoma. And I'd been told Pauline came from Oklahoma. Then there were a lot of little things. Mike got the impression from Pauline that her family was in the cattle business—couldn't that be rodeo, rather than ranching?

"She was in full-blown rebellion. Wouldn't she rebel against something directly connected to her family? The other protestors hit a variety of events, but Pauline only goes to rodeos—that seemed personal. Plus, Street mentioned he and Landry worked this rodeo for the second time nineteen years ago, missing his daughter's birth. Watt also mentioned Street's daughter being born then—and I suspect his old memories, as well as his knowledge of Landry's treatment of the women, persuaded Street that he was too dangerous to have around.

"Last night by the truck, Street told her to get out, trying to protect her from any association with what had happened. Did you notice her eyes flicker to Street when I said his name the first time? She knew who he was."

"Eye flicker," Diana murmured.

I hurried past that. "But back to Pauline's birth—Cas gave her flowers on Wednesday for her nineteenth birthday. Heather was suspicious, and that night she found the receipt in Cas' gear bag. That's when she took one of his ropes by accident."

"Now that is a love triangle," Mike said, clearly trying to lighten Alvaro's glower. "The father of the girl you're dating is murdered by the father of the girl you've been stepping out with on the first girl."

"That bluff about Watt being conscious—that was a gamble," Diana said.

"A calculated risk," I said. "Street didn't know he *wasn't* conscious. With that and the possibility of the rope being found and a fingerprint on Watt's truck door button, I hoped he'd give up."

"And he did." She gave it plenty of emphasis, sending Alvaro a look. "With Watt truly regaining consciousness now, that will fill in any gaps."

"So timing wasn't important to the crime, after all," Mike said.

"Sure it was," I said. "Just like the experts say, there was a trigger that made *now* the time for the murder. A two-part trigger. Landry told Cas he intended to have a fling with either Heather or Pauline. Then he found out Heather was his daughter.

"That left Pauline. And Oren knew Landry well enough to know he wouldn't let her being the daughter of his partner stand in his way."

Mike considered that. "Some Wyoming juries might consider that Oren Street performed a public service."

"If he'd been interested in public service, he wouldn't have tacitly abetted Landry for years.

"Which reminds me, Deputy Alvaro, we won't be sending you back empty-handed. Our research assistant has uncovered the paper trail of Landry's scheme to con rodeos that she'll share with you. It might be another lever to work on Street." I turned to Mike. "Remember what you said about my shoe that night at the rodeo after Landry was found?"

"That it smelled like horseshit?"

"After that—that I'd gotten used to the smell. I suspect it was like that for Oren with Landry. He'd gotten used to all the crap and stopped smelling it. Until—"

"Until it was going to touch his daughter."

"Right. I think he was telling the truth when he said he didn't know what he'd do in the business without Landry."

"Something he recognized only after killing his golden goose?"

"Maybe. Although I'd tend to think he knew it ahead of time, and the drive to protect his daughter overrode it."

Mike eyed the still-silent Alvaro. "Thank heavens it wasn't another upstanding citizen of Cottonwood County. The mayor and commissioners and all the rest would have had to retreat to the Gobi Desert for a year to figure out their campaign after that."

"On second thought . . ." Diana said.

"Good point. Having them in the Gobi Desert for a year would have been nice."

"They could have taken Thurston with them, too," she said.

"And the lieutenant," Alvaro said.

We all looked at him. I was the one who risked a response. "Not sure his wife would like that with a new baby and all."

He grinned, an honest-to-goodness grin, erasing all law enforcement sternness. "Oh, yes, she would. I heard her over the phone, yelling at him to go to work because that way at least she'd only have one baby to deal with."

✧ ✧ ✧ ✧

I INSISTED PAYCIK do the live intro for our package on the five o'clock news. It was, after all, a rodeo story, and thus sports.

Well, sports and religion in Wyoming.

Fine protested, but not with his usual vigor. The whisper around the newsroom was that even for Les Haeburn, the coverage during his absence had provided a surfeit of Thurston.

Jenks had called in with thanks after seeing how we'd credited his footage and excluded anything gag-worthy.

Needham Bender had called with congratulations and grumbling about the scoop. I told him what we knew about the county leaders' weekend retreat. Haeburn would never let us report it, and Needham would do the story right.

The lead-in was taped for the late news, Diana was long gone, and Mike and I were headed out the door of KWMT-TV and into heat that yet promised a cool breeze once the sun finished its slow slide behind the mountains.

"Where to? Want me to take you home?" Mike asked, since my car was still in my driveway where we'd left it last night. "Or . . .?"

✧   ✧   ✧   ✧

MIKE AND I stopped at the hovel only long enough to refill Shadow's water dish. He came around the corner of the garage, and this time it truly was a wag of his tail. And I don't think it only had to do with the bacon treats I tossed to him from the bag Jennifer had left.

We returned to the rodeo grounds as the evening's competitors began rolling in.

I wondered if the regular rodeo would fill in this weekend now that the big Fourth of July Rodeo appeared poised to be officially canceled at a committee meeting starting in half an hour.

The meeting would be held without Stan Newton. He still owned the rodeo grounds, but word of the bribes had gotten around, and he'd been booted off the committee. That public punishment might be worse than whatever the legal system would—or wouldn't—do to him for kickbacks that could be hard to prove. Somehow, I didn't think Cas would testify against his father. No doubt it was against some Code of the West.

Linda Caswell and Tom Burrell stood on the rodeo office's porch, in the same doorway where I'd seen them six days ago.

"Have you heard? Evan Watt's improved and cooperating with the sheriff's department," Mike said to them as we approached.

I needed to talk to him about giving away what we wanted people to watch the news to learn.

"Good to hear, Mike. Evening, Elizabeth," Tom said.

I returned the greetings before asking, "What happens next?"

"We're meeting shortly to decide that," Tom said. "I've been asked to rejoin the committee."

"Any options other than canceling?" Mike asked.

"There are avenues we hope to explore," Tom said.

"Like what?"

"Avenues," he said, doggedly.

But Linda shook her head. "I don't know how we can do it now, not without Landry or Street. The contract is clear. Legally, we can't use their livestock without one of them signing off on it."

Her eyes glistened. This woman had spoken openly of family trag-edies, her broken heart, humiliating treatment at the hands of Keith Landry with no hint of eye moisture. But here were tears—pooling now, slipping free of her lower lashes—over a rodeo.

"Street might sign a waiver from jail. Or we'll keep trying to get animals from wherever we can."

"Tom." She rested a hand on his arm. "What stock we could get wouldn't be the caliber needed to keep top competitors. Do you know how many cancellations we've had? And we can't blame them. They need to be on good stock. They've got their seasons to think of. Without top cowboys, we won't sell the tickets we need to, not to mention not presenting a rodeo worthy of our tradition."

Tom put an arm around her shoulder. "It's not over yet."

She pushed at a tear. "I know. We'll do everything we can, and what happens, happens. Will you look at me, bawling like this."

I did look. And realized Linda Caswell was one of those rare wom-en who looked good crying. Really good. The only woman I'd ever seen who looked this good crying was a young reporter who came on when I was in Dayton, Ohio. She'd made full use of her talent by lobbying for every tearjerker story. Less than three months after she arrived, she'd parlayed her skill into marrying a top doctor, inviting the entire newsroom. She cried through her entire wedding and reception, and looked spectacular.

Linda stopped short of spectacular, but she did look the best I'd ever seen her. I wasn't the only one noticing.

Grayson Zane, standing across the open area from the rodeo office, had his eyes zeroed in on her.

She made another sound, this one not disgusted, and I knew she'd spotted him, too. And was staring back.

Just when the look either had to break or start one of them moving—and considering Burrell still had that shoulder lock on Linda, Grayson was the likely candidate—a truck moving at a crawl through the open area intruded.

I'd been so enthralled with the Beauty Cry and the stare-down that I hadn't noticed the truck arriving. That was quite a feat, considering it was a livestock carrier about a block long, and *eau de bulls* announced its presence.

The truck paused, the engine running. A man on the passenger side appeared to lean over the driver to talk to Grayson. It wasn't a long conversation. The passenger got out, shut the door, gave the side a *thunk* with the flat of his hand like a cowboy swatting the flank of a horse to get it moving. Sure enough, the truck crawled on.

The passenger—I'd tell you he was wearing jeans, boots, and a black cowboy hat, but what else was new?—walked straight toward us. Tom dropped his arm, but stayed beside Linda.

"Ms. Linda Caswell?"

"Yes. May I help you?"

"Well, ma'am, I'm hoping I'll help you." His thin lips spread in a slow grin. "I'm Digger Belasque, and I'm here on behalf of our stock contractors' association. We're real sorry to hear a fellow contractor— not a member of our organization, mind you—caused you any bother."

Another True West moment. A murder, fraud, and a few other felonies boiled down to *any bother.*

"Thank you." She spoke with her usual calm. Plus confusion.

"I'm here to make it right on behalf of my fellow contractors."

"I . . . I don't understand, Mr. Belasque."

"Please, call me Digger. It's simple, ma'am. We heard how the Sherman Rodeo was left high and dry by that unscrupulous piece of dried up cow dung, and we don't like it. It's not right. It's not how we want the folks counting on another fine Sherman Fourth of July Rodeo to think of stock contractors. When we heard about this, we put our heads together."

At the second reference to hearing, her gaze flicked past him to Grayson, visible again as the truck cleared. But only temporarily, because a second truck crawled in behind the first. Just as long and just as stinky.

"You brought livestock," she said.

If I ever have the chance to say, "I won the Nobel Peace Prize," that's the precise intonation I'll use.

"Yes, ma'am, we did. First we thought we'd each send a few head, but that woulda meant an awfully long haul for 'em coming from the south. Instead, the furthest fellas will send a few head to the ones a bit closer. Second group will send that number plus a few on their own behalf on to another contractor closer still, and on, until it came to me, being the closest to Sherman, you see. I left a few of my stock, they'll be supplemented with head from those other contractors down near the Colorado border where my assistant will run 'em real well to fill our contract for that there rodeo, and brought the rest up here to give Sherman the rodeo it deserves."

The look she gave Belasque was one I would save for my acceptance speech for the Nobel Peace Prize.

It disappeared beneath a new sheen of tears and a slow head-shaking. "All the withdrawals—Our entries don't stack up—"

"Now don't you worry none about that, ma'am. You know how fickle these cowboys can be. From what I've been hearing, a good number of those cancellations got uncancelled. A plane's making it so roughstock boys can hit two rodeos a couple of the days."

"A plane, but who—" Her gaze flickered toward Grayson, once more masked from us by a truck. "I don't understand."

"Understanding's way above my pay grade, ma'am. Now, if you'll excuse me, I'll go see to getting these animals settled."

The truck cleared, and there stood Grayson Zane, looking our way. Looking her way.

She made a sound. Low in her throat. It might have been from laughter or tears. Either way it came from down deep.

Slowly, still looking, he tipped his hat, the brim's shadow reaching his mouth as another truck came past.

Linda colored. Fast and bright. "I, uh– I have to go see . . . I have to make sure all these animals are seen to and have everything they need. This is—It's a miracle, isn't it?"

She flashed a beaming smile in our general direction, jogged down the steps, and headed off in a path parallel to the trucks.

In a new gap, we saw Grayson turn to apparently follow the same route on the far side of the trucks.

I was aware of Mike beside me, of Tom looking at me, but I was watching Linda Caswell and Grayson Zane, wondering if I could watch them long enough to see their parallel paths converge.

Epilogue

THAT YEAR'S Sherman Fourth of July Rodeo, I am told by those who have been to many others, was special. Not necessarily better competition, but an appreciation for something that had almost been lost.

Word was that the rodeo made enough money for Stan Newton to avoid his personal fiscal cliff.

With Cas applauding heartily from the stands, Heather performed her queen's ride with, no matter what Tom says about the word, panache. Her mother's pride was as fierce as ever. Her roping tricks were as impressive as Needham Bender had promised. She did not rope anything over a beam.

For me, the highlight was watching Mrs. Parens, wearing a split skirt and a glittery cowboy hat, in the parade of past rodeo queens. Later, the fireworks added spatters of color to a sky already dazzling with stars. It didn't hurt that I watched all this on a breeze-cooled evening while being warmed by the presence of Michael Paycik sitting on one side of me and Thomas David Burrell on the other, with Tamantha in front, informing us that it would all be done just a little better when she was queen.

~ THE END ~

For news about upcoming "Caught Dead in Wyoming" books, as well as other titles, subscribe to Patricia McLinn's free newsletter.

Don't miss the rest of the books in the
Caught Dead In Wyoming series:

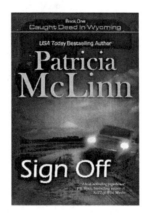

SIGN OFF

With her marriage over and her career derailed by her ex, top-flight reporter Elizabeth "E.M." Danniher lands in tiny Sherman. But the case of a missing deputy and a determined little girl drag her out of her fog.

Get SIGN OFF now!

LEFT HANGING

From the deadly tip of the rodeo queen's tiara to toxic "agricultural byproducts" ground into the arena dust, TV reporter Elizabeth "E.M." Danniher receives a murderous introduction to the world of rodeo.

Get LEFT HANGING now!

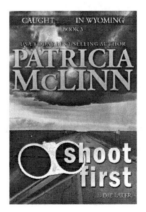

SHOOT FIRST

Death hits close to home for Elizabeth "E.M." Danniher – or, rather, close to Hovel, as she's dubbed her decrepit rental house in rustic Sherman, Wyoming.

Get SHOOT FIRST now!

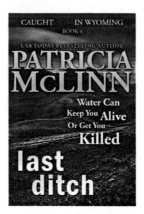

LAST DITCH

A man in a wheelchair goes missing in rough country in the Big Horn Basin of Wyoming. Elizabeth "E.M." Danniher and KWMT-TV colleague Mike Paycik immediately join the search. But soon they're on a search of a different kind – a search for the truth.

Get LAST DITCH now!

What readers are saying about the "Caught Dead in Wyoming" series:

"Great characters" ... "Twists and turns" ... "Just enough humor" ... "Truly a fine read" ... "Exciting and well-crafted murder mystery" ... "Characters and dialogue were so very believable" ... "Couldn't put it down" ... "That was fun!" ... "Smart and witty"

For excerpts and more on the "Caught Dead in Wyoming" series books, visit Patricia McLinn's website.

Dedication

To Cathy & Joe, who know how to treat houseguests—
with two legs or four.

Acknowledgements

Like the continuing characters who are vital to this story, some acknowledgements are ongoing. Thanks so much again to:

Bill White, whose answers would be worth a thousand times his going rate.

Bill Beagle, who enters into tales of TV news with welcome gusto.

Pat Van Wie, who doesn't falter in two challenging roles.

The author also gratefully acknowledges:

Robert Skiff, who taught a terrific class for writers on forensic evidence collection at Sirchie Labs as well as brainstorming scenarios. Also to Sirchie for holding the class and my fellow students for making it such fun.

The Cody Nite Rodeo in Cody, Wyo., which inspired the positive elements of the Sherman Fourth of July Rodeo and none of the negative ones.

Dan Morales of King's Saddlery/King Ropes in Sheridan, Wyo., who was so generous with his time and expertise, and Don King who welcomed a nosy writer.

About the author

USA Today bestselling author Patricia McLinn spent more than 20 years as an editor at the Washington Post after stints as a sports writer (Rockford, Ill.) and assistant sports editor (Charlotte, N.C.). She received BA and MSJ degrees from Northwestern University.

McLinn is the author of nearly 40 published novels, which are cited by readers and reviewers for wit and vivid characterization. Her books include mysteries, contemporary western romances, contemporary romances elsewhere in the world, historical romances, and women's fiction. They have topped bestseller lists and won numerous awards.

She has spoken about writing from Melbourne, Australia to Washington, D.C., including being a guest-speaker at the Smithsonian Institute.

She is now living in Northern Kentucky and writing full-time. Patricia loves to hear from readers through her website, Facebook and Twitter.

Dear Readers: If you encounter typos or errors in this book, please send them to me at: Patricia@PatriciaMcLinn.com. Even with many layers of editing, mistakes can slip through, alas. But, together, we can eradicate the nasty nuisances.
Thank you! – Patricia McLinn

I hope you've enjoyed LEFT HANGING, and that you'll consider sharing your experience with your fellow readers by leaving a review.

CPSIA information can be obtained
at www.ICGtesting.com
Printed in the USA
LVOW08s2315160417
531052LV00001B/173/P